British Women's Writing from Brontë to Bloomsbury, 1840–1940

Series Editors
Adrienne E. Gavin
Department of English and Language Studies
Canterbury Christ Church University
Canterbury, UK

Carolyn W. de la L. Oulton
Department of English and Language Studies
Canterbury Christ Church University
Canterbury, UK

This series, published in association with the International Centre for Victorian Women Writers (ICVWW), consists of five volumes of critical essays written by international experts in women's writing. Structured chronologically, with each volume examining a twenty year timespan, it explores the dynamic contiguities of literary realism, sensation, and the new as a frame for reassessing, decade by decade, how women's writing changed and developed in Britain from the 1840s to the 1930s. A transformative period in women's private, public, and literary lives, the century from 1840 to 1940 saw the rise and fall of the circulating library as an effectual censor of literary expression, the growth and achievements of the female suffrage movement, and a series of legislation that re-envisioned relations within marriage. Female higher education opened and expanded, employment opportunities for women substantially increased, and women's roles as single women, wives, mothers, and authors were recurrently debated.

More information about this series at
http://www.palgrave.com/gp/series/15858

Adrienne E. Gavin
Carolyn W. de la L. Oulton
Editors

British Women's Writing from Brontë to Bloomsbury, Volume 2

1860s and 1870s

Editors
Adrienne E. Gavin
Department of English and
Language Studies
Canterbury Christ Church University
Canterbury, UK

Carolyn W. de la L. Oulton
School of Humanities
Canterbury Christ Church University
Canterbury, UK

ISSN 2523-7160   ISSN 2523-7179 (electronic)
British Women's Writing from Brontë to Bloomsbury, 1840–1940
ISBN 978-3-030-38527-9   ISBN 978-3-030-38528-6 (eBook)
https://doi.org/10.1007/978-3-030-38528-6

© The Editor(s) (if applicable) and The Author(s) 2020
This work is subject to copyright. All rights are solely and exclusively licensed by the Publisher, whether the whole or part of the material is concerned, specifically the rights of translation, reprinting, reuse of illustrations, recitation, broadcasting, reproduction on microfilms or in any other physical way, and transmission or information storage and retrieval, electronic adaptation, computer software, or by similar or dissimilar methodology now known or hereafter developed.
The use of general descriptive names, registered names, trademarks, service marks, etc. in this publication does not imply, even in the absence of a specific statement, that such names are exempt from the relevant protective laws and regulations and therefore free for general use.
The publisher, the authors and the editors are safe to assume that the advice and information in this book are believed to be true and accurate at the date of publication. Neither the publisher nor the authors or the editors give a warranty, expressed or implied, with respect to the material contained herein or for any errors or omissions that may have been made. The publisher remains neutral with regard to jurisdictional claims in published maps and institutional affiliations.

Cover illustration: © ChrisGorgio

This Palgrave Macmillan imprint is published by the registered company Springer Nature Switzerland AG.
The registered company address is: Gewerbestrasse 11, 6330 Cham, Switzerland

'Mary Elizabeth Braddon with Horse.' (Image courtesy of the Mary Braddon Archive, International Centre for Victorian Women Writers (ICVWW), Canterbury Christ Church University)

To the conversation (and to making it new in the time of COVID-19)

Acknowledgements

This book is the second volume in the five-volume series *British Women's Writing from Brontë to Bloomsbury, 1840–1940*, which is itself a central part of the wider *From Brontë to Bloomsbury: Realism, Sensation and the New in Women's Writing from the 1840s to the 1930s* project directed by the International Centre for Victorian Women Writers (ICVWW), the aim of which is to recover, reassess, and reinterpret women's writing of the nineteenth century and beyond.

We wish here to acknowledge the support, assistance, and inspiring exchange of ideas we have had from an ever-growing international community of academics, independent researchers, and research students whose interest in and enthusiasm for the wider *From Brontë to Bloomsbury* project have stimulated our planning and thinking on this volume.

In particular, we would like to thank Canterbury Christ Church University for supporting our establishment of the ICVWW in 2012, and Michelle Crowther and Ian Simpson for curating and advising on the Mary Braddon Archive. Crucially we would like to thank Susanna Avery for allowing the ICVWW to house this important archive. We also wish to thank the ICVWW advisory board: Professor Christine Alexander, Professor Hilary Fraser, Professor Susan Hamilton, Professor Andrew King, Professor Graham Law, Professor Kate Newey, Professor Lyn Pykett, Professor Valerie Sanders, Professor Joanne Wilkes, and the late Professor Linda Peterson, for their support of our ventures.

ICVWW Research Associate Alyson Hunt has worked tirelessly and imaginatively, bringing verve and new ideas to the centre from its inception; thanks are also due to Susan Civale for her enthusiastic organization of and contribution to research events, and to Lizzie Sheppard for her innovative work launching and editing the ICVWW's newsletter.

Thank you to Palgrave Macmillan, especially editor Ben Doyle and Camille Davies for their enthusiasm for the project and support for making its publication a co-imprint with the ICVWW.

The *Brontë to Bloomsbury* project would not have been possible without the enthusiasm and generosity of the many scholars and students who have attended the ICVWW's series of international conferences, shared new perspectives on canonical women's writing, and introduced us to forgotten authors. May the conversation be ongoing!

We also wish to thank our families, Dewayne, Laura, Demia, and Riley, and Paul, Melissa, and Tom for always supporting us in our project and for welcoming decades of women writers into their homes.

Series Introduction

British Women's Writing from Brontë to Bloomsbury, 1840–1940 is a five-volume series comprising 80 original critical essays written by international experts on women's writing. A project of the International Centre for Victorian Women Writers (ICVWW), which the editors co-founded at Canterbury Christ Church University, UK, in 2012, it explores the dynamic contiguities of literary realism, sensation, and the new as a frame for reassessing, decade by decade, how women's writing changed and developed in Britain from 1840 to 1940. The series title acknowledges canonical authors and literary movements in its key terms 'Brontë' and 'Bloomsbury,' while significantly indicating the movement 'from' one to the other. This transition over a vital century of female authorship encompasses, but as the essay contributors show is not always neatly defined by, Victorian, *fin-de-siècle*, Edwardian, and modernist writing, and is shaped by numerous writers, reviewers, and literary consumers. Centrally re-examining the cultural and social contexts in which both canonical and lesser-known or 'forgotten' works by women were produced, the series is designed to be a substantial, consciously expansive, and inclusive project, which allows many critical voices and viewpoints to be heard. Accordingly, it includes discussions of proto-feminist authorship but avoids an exclusive focus on the 'advanced' woman author, whether she is depicted as representative of her time or, conversely, as sublimely indifferent to the opinions of a wider readership. Equally, in order to identify emerging trends and the impact of key debates on writers governed by the same laws and who had access to or cognizance of the same print culture, the series is confined to women authors who were British, living in Britain, or in other ways integrally part of a British tradition of writing. The series necessarily cannot survey all British women writers across the century, nor is it designed to do so; rather, the essays have been commissioned to focus on topics and writers that illustrate the aspects of women's writing that most reflect a decade-based periodicity. In this way the series constitutes a new intervention in the ongoing recovery and reinterpretation of British women writers.

The series is predicated on four central beliefs. First is that the continuing interest in Victorian and early twentieth-century women's writing needs to be contextualized through further attention both to social and cultural change and to the material context of publishing conditions and readerships. Second, the ongoing rediscovery of neglected women writers and texts (for example, through publication of scholarly editions) has created a demand for a supporting body of critical work. Third, the consideration of lesser-known alongside more familiar texts will be of benefit to scholars in establishing a wider frame of reference for further study. And fourth, a chronological, decade-based re-exploration of women's writing offers new critical insights and interpretations.

A transformative period in women's private, public, and literary lives, the century from 1840 to 1940 saw the rise and fall of the circulating library as an effectual censor of literary expression, the growth and achievements of the female suffrage movement, and a series of legislation that re-envisioned relations within marriage. Female higher education opened and expanded, employment opportunities for women substantially increased, and women's roles as spinsters, wives, mothers, and authors were recurrently debated.

As leisure increased across the century (at least for the middle class) as a result of new technologies and wealth, and as printing costs declined, a heightened demand for reading material was met by an array of literature adapted for perusal in a variety of contexts: expensively bound books for private houses, volumes for circulating libraries, serials for periodical publications, and cheap railway editions for commuters and tourists. Women both produced and encountered a vast range of literature during this period. Central to their reading and writing experience was fiction: the most dynamic, daring, and dominant genre across these ten decades. The popularity and length of the novel, in particular, enabled women writers' voices to be expressed and heard in both overt and covert ways. For such reasons this series primarily focuses on fiction in tracing the allusive works of writers who, in serial or volume form, responded to each other and to their predecessors as they engaged with and adapted different forms: negotiating the various demands of the three-decker in its early and mid-Victorian heyday, the new challenges posed by the one-volume and short story format of the late nineteenth century, and the experiments of Modernism (and counter-Modernism) that self-consciously destabilized the achievements of the previous century.

Central to the series' reassessment of women writers is close attention to the literary, cultural, and social contexts of the decades within which women wrote particular texts. Chronologically examining the ways in which women's writing changed and developed, adapted and innovated, each of the five volumes considers two decades of women's writing. In doing so, these volumes examine each decade discretely, offering an encapsulatory sense of its significance to female authorship, while also exploring the confluences and divergences each new decade brings. Considering women's writing chronologically is not of course new, but the specific attention to decades in this series aims to offer an enhanced precision to periodized discussion of writing. Compartmentalizing literature by decade is in some senses an artificial division as literary influences and interests naturally endure across decade (and century) demarcations. Nevertheless, decades, as they still do, had strong psychological resonance for readers, writers, and critics. The essays in these volumes certainly show clear identificatory characteristics evident in women's writing within each of the ten decades considered, providing an illuminating trajectory that allows new readings of female authorship.

The series builds on previous studies of women's writing across these periods by offering new connections and uncovering particular tensions. Recent work has questioned the preoccupation with a few canonical women writers that was a feature of critical discourse for much of the twentieth century, and which perpetuated a distorted view of the female-authored texts actually being written and read widely by an increasingly literate population. In addition to re-examining fiction by canonical authors such as Charlotte Brontë and Virginia Woolf, the series is significantly concerned with rediscovering and repositioning the work of neglected female authors, in order to explore the conflicted (and often conflicting) literary productions of women writers in their social and cultural context.

Critical attention to women's writing since the pioneering recovery projects of the 1970s and 1980s—such as Elaine Showalter's *A Literature of Their Own: British Women Novelists from Brontë to Lessing* (1978, 1999) and Sandra M. Gilbert and Susan Gubar's *The Madwoman in the Attic: The Women Writer and the Nineteenth-Century Literary Imagination* (1979, 2000)—has largely, and valuably, focused on charting a feminist tradition of subversive or politically engaged women's writing, but inevitably this has privileged the openly radical messages of Emily Brontë over the ambivalence of Mary Braddon or foregrounded the shock tactics of Sarah Grand over the class-inflected satire of Ellen Thorneycroft Fowler. Similarly, it has under-examined morally didactic works by writers such as Anna Sewell and Emma Worboise, as well as 'forgotten' bestsellers by authors including Caroline Clive and Mary Cholmondeley that clearly spoke to the period in which they were published. Bringing these authors together allows patterns to emerge across genres, revealing, for instance, the religious aesthetic of Thorneycroft Fowler and the sensational elements of Worboise's religious writing.

Developing on this earlier critical work, new interpretations of the cultural contexts of female authorship include Lyn Pykett's *The Improper Feminine: The Women's Sensation Novel and The New Woman Writing* (1992), Joanne Shattock's edited collection *Women and Literature in Britain 1800–1900* (2001), Talia Schaffer's *The Forgotten Female Aesthetes: Literary Culture in Late-Victorian England* (2009), and Jennie Batchelor and Cora Kaplan's more chronologically expansive ten-volume edited series of critical essays *The History of British Women's Writing* (2010–). Works such as *The Cambridge Companion to Victorian Women's Writing* (2015, ed. Linda H. Peterson) and *The Cambridge Companion to Modernist Women Writers* (2010, ed. Maren Tova Linett) have further consolidated scholarship on women authors. Interest in female writers' networking is also increasingly frequent in studies such as Susan David Bernstein's *Roomscape: Women Writers in the British Museum from George Eliot to Virginia Woolf* (2013). Studies such as Linda Peterson's *Becoming a Woman of Letters: Myths of Authorship and Facts of the Victorian Market* (2009) have begun to address the complexity of apparently conservative nineteenth-century women's writing such as religious biography and children's fiction, while others, including Valerie Sanders's *Eve's Renegades: Victorian Anti-Feminist Women Novelists* (1996) and Tamara Wagner's collection *Anti-Feminism in the Victorian Novel: Rereading Nineteenth-Century Women Writers* (2009), stress the need to allow space to the many voices raised in objection to women's emancipation. Focusing on the last decades of the nineteenth century, the nine-volume Pickering & Chatto series *New Woman Fiction 1881–1899* (2010–11) holds these opposing positions in tension while suggesting the difficulty of defining texts in the binary terms of 'pro' or 'anti' women's rights, however defined. Its contextualizing of a range of texts, for instance, positioning Ouida's antifeminist *The Massarenes* (1897) next to New Woman writing such as George Egerton's *The Wheel of God* (1898) and Mary Cholmondeley's *Red Pottage* (1899), alters the way each text is read by allowing the debate over women's 'value' and identity to ripple across very different novels which were written in isolation but likely to have been borrowed or purchased by the same readers. By placing such different texts in juxtaposition, it is possible to review the field of women's writing in new ways.

In a parallel strategy, this series on women's writing from 1840 to 1940 proposes interdependencies between the numerous texts discussed, different as their agendas, styles, and subgenres may be. Notably, while some apparently conservative female-authored texts may reveal a level of resistance to the social order by which the authors were bound—as recent critics of Elizabeth Gaskell's *Cranford* (1853) have increasingly argued—others clearly do not. Not all women writers were in rebellion against the political and social systems of their time, and crucially those who were in a state of more or less open revolt did not themselves write in a literary vacuum. Women writers were aware of, and in some cases subscribed to, the constraints imposed on female authorship. This in itself creates a productive tension, in the Victorian novel especially, between the exigencies of the plot and the moralizing role of the female narrator.

Where it is significant across this series, female authors are considered in relation to their male counterparts, but given the tensions inherent in women's entry into, and existence within, literary culture, its volumes are crucially preoccupied with the ways in which women writers defined themselves, whether as professional or amateur, politically engaged or emotionally intuitive. In placing diverse voices next to and sometimes against each other, the series affirms the importance of women's writing regardless of its terms of self-definition, and in doing so it seeks to create a more nuanced understanding of how Victorian and early twentieth-century female authors negotiated economic, social, and imaginative positions for themselves in and through their writing.

In its chronological coverage of a century of writing, and allowing for the potentially problematic convergence of the Victorian years and the first decades of the twentieth century, the series further seeks to question the emergence of modernism as the defining feature of 1920s and 1930s literature and literary culture. While many women authors consciously presented themselves as belonging to, or as distanced from, particular cultural and political standpoints, writers portraying the times in which they lived to their target readership did not necessarily expect themselves to be positioned through a clearly defined sense of 'period.' Towards the end of the nineteenth century, for example, writers such as Mona Caird stressed their sense of themselves as inhabiting a transitional zone, 'striding between two centuries' ('The Yellow Drawing Room' [1892] 30). As if to make just this point, the death of Queen Victoria one year in to a new century disrupts any completely tidy identification of 'Victorian' with 'mid- to late-nineteenth century.' In the same way, many writers in the first decades of the twentieth century were not modernist in style. Some of them, like Netta Syrett and Mary Braddon, had first made a name for themselves in the previous century and often continued writing in the manner to which they and their readers had become accustomed.

In order to understand the important changes in women's writing between the start of the Victorian period and the beginning of the Second World War then, an examination is needed with a scope that is broad enough to acknowledge a range of standpoints. Any such reassessment (incomplete and partial as it will inevitably be) must encompass both canonical and non-canonical texts, conservative ideology and radical protest, the forgotten late-career works of Victorian-born authors as well as the rise of the modernist aesthetic. Exploring connections and divergent approaches from 1840 to 1940, a period of vibrant literary and cultural change, this series therefore juxtaposes very different types of fiction by a range of authors. In the process it reminds us that the development of women's writing through these decades was often highly self-conscious, both in what it apparently rejected and in the sense of tradition it chose to reference.

Adrienne E. Gavin
Carolyn W. de la L. Oulton

WORKS CITED

Caird, Mona. 'The Yellow Drawing Room.' 1892. *Women Who Did: Stories by Men and Women, 1890–1914*. Ed. Angelique Richardson. London: Penguin Classics, 2005. 21–30.

Contents

1   Introduction   1
    Adrienne E. Gavin and Carolyn W. de la L. Oulton

Part I   Women's Writing of the 1860s   25

2   A Decade of Experiment: George Eliot in the 1860s   27
    Margaret Harris

3   'Duck him!': Private Feelings, Public Interests, and Ellen
    Wood's *East Lynne*   43
    Tara MacDonald

4   '[Tr]ain[s] of circumstantial evidence': Railway
    'Monomania' and Investigations of Gender in *Lady
    Audley's Secret*   57
    Andrew F. Humphries

5   'There is great need for forgiveness in this world':
    The Call for Reconciliation in Elizabeth Gaskell's *Sylvia's
    Lovers* and *A Dark Night's Work*   75
    Elizabeth Ludlow

6   'The plain duties which are set before me': Charity,
    Agency, and Women's Work in the 1860s   89
    Kristine Moruzi

7   '[S]mothered under rose-leaves': Violent Sensation and
    the Location of the Feminine in Eliza Lynn Linton's
    Sowing the Wind   105
    Carolyn W. de la L. Oulton

8   '[F]leshly inclinations': The Nature of Female Desire in
    Rhoda Broughton's Early Fiction   119
    Tamar Heller

9   Crumbs from the Table: Matilda Betham-Edwards's
    Comic Writing in *Punch*   135
    Clare Horrocks and Nickianne Moody

Part II   Women's Writing of the 1870s   149

10 Transcending Prudence: Charlotte Riddell's 'City Women'   151
    Silvana Colella

11 '[M]ute orations, mute rhapsodies, mute discussions':
    Silence in George Eliot's Last Decade   165
    Fionnuala Dillane

12 'His eyes *commanded* me to come to him': Desire and
    Mesmerism in Rhoda Broughton's 'The Man with the
    Nose'   183
    Melissa Purdue

13 '[E]mphatically un-literary and middle-class':
    Undressing Middle-Class Anxieties in Ellen Wood's
    Johnny Ludlow Stories   195
    Alyson Hunt

14 'Sinecures which could be held by girls': Margaret
    Oliphant and Women's Labour   213
    Danielle Charette

15 'More like a woman stuck into boy's clothes':
    Transcendent Femininity in Florence Marryat's *Her
    Father's Name*   229
    Catherine Pope

16 'I am writing the life of a horse': Anna Sewell's *Black
    Beauty* in the 1870s   245
    Adrienne E. Gavin

17 Forging a New Path: Fraud and White-Collar Crime in
    Mary Elizabeth Braddon's 1870s Fiction   265
    Janine Hatter

Index   279

Notes on Contributors

Danielle Charette is a PhD candidate with the University of Chicago's Committee on Social Thought, USA, where she focuses primarily on modern political theory and the rise of commercial society. She holds a BA in English Literature from Swarthmore College and in her work draws on literary examples whenever possible.

Silvana Colella is Professor of English at Macerata University and President of the European Consortium for Humanities Institutes and Centres. She is the author of *Charlotte Riddell's City Novels and Victorian Business: Narrating Capitalism* (2016), *Economia e letteratura* (1999), *Romanzo e disciplina: la narrativa di Charlotte Brontë* (1994), and *Il genere nel testo poetico: Elizabeth Barrett Browning e Christina Rossetti* (1992). Her publications in English include articles on Victorian print culture, Walter Scott, Fanny Burney, Anthony Trollope, Charles Dickens, and Dinah Mulock Craik.

Fionnuala Dillane is Associate Professor in Nineteenth-century British Literature at University College Dublin (UCD). Published works include essays on George Eliot, periodical print cultures, and memory studies; *Before George Eliot: Marian Evans and the Periodical Press*, joint winner of the Robert and Vineta Colby Prize for 2014; *The Body in Pain in Irish Literature and Culture*, co-edited with Naomi McAreavey and Emilie Pine (Palgrave Macmillan, 2016); and *Ireland, Slavery, Anti-Slavery, Empire*, co-edited with Maria Stuart and Fionnghuala Sweeney (2018). She is Associate Dean for Arts and Humanities at UCD.

Adrienne E. Gavin is Emeritus Professor of English Literature and Co-founder and Honorary Director of the International Centre for Victorian Women Writers (ICVWW), Canterbury Christ Church University, UK. She is also an Honorary Academic at The University of Auckland, New Zealand. Author of *Dark Horse: A Life of Anna Sewell* (2004), the proposal for which won the Biographer's Club Prize, she has produced critical editions of Caroline Clive's *Paul Ferroll* (2008), Henry de Vere Stacpoole's *The Blue Lagoon* (2010), C. L. Pirkis's *The Experiences of Loveday Brooke, Lady Detective* (2010), and Anna Sewell's *Black Beauty* (2012). She is editor of *The Child in British Literature* (2012) and *Robert Cormier* (2012) and co-editor with Christopher Routledge of *Mystery in Children's Literature* (2001), with Carolyn W. de la L. Oulton of *Writing Women of the Fin de Siècle* (2011), and with Andrew F. Humphries of both *Childhood in Edwardian Fiction* (2009; winner of the Children's Literature Association Edited Book Award), and *Transport in British Fiction: Technologies of Movement, 1840–1940* (2015).

Margaret Harris is Challis Professor of English Literature Emerita at The University of Sydney. Her publications on Victorian literature include *George Eliot in Context* (2013), *The Journals of George Eliot* (1998), with Judith Johnston, and an edition of *Middlemarch*, also with Judith Johnston, together with *The Notebooks of George Meredith* (1983), with Gillian Beer, and editions of several of Meredith's novels. She also publishes on Australian fiction of the nineteenth and twentieth centuries.

Janine Hatter's research interests centre on nineteenth-century literature, art, and culture, with particular emphasis on popular fiction. She has published on Mary Braddon, Bram Stoker, the theatre and identity, Victorian women's life writing, short stories as a genre, and nineteenth- to twenty-first-century Gothic. She is co-editor of *New Paths in Victorian Fiction and Culture* and *Key Popular Women Writers* for Edward Everett Root Publishers. She has co-edited a collection on *Fashion and Material Culture in Victorian Fiction and Periodicals*, as well as special issues for the *Wilkie Collins Journal*, *Revenant*, *Nineteenth-Century Gender Studies*, *Supernatural Studies*, and *Femspec*. She is conference co-organizer for the Victorian Popular Fiction Association and has co-founded the Mary Elizabeth Braddon Association.

Tamar Heller Associate Professor of English and Comparative Literature at University of Cincinnati, Heller is the author of *Dead Secrets: Wilkie*

Collins and the Female Gothic (1992) and has co-edited *Scenes of the Apple: Food and the Female Body in Nineteenth- and Twentieth-Century Women's Writing* (2003) and *Approaches to Teaching Gothic Fiction: The British and American Traditions* (2003). She has worked extensively on Rhoda Broughton and has edited both of Broughton's earliest novels, *Cometh Up as a Flower* (2004) and *Not Wisely, but Too Well* (2013). She is writing a study of Broughton's work entitled *A Plot of Her Own: Rhoda Broughton and English Fiction* and will also be co-authoring, with Graziella Stringos, a monograph on Broughton for the series *Key Popular Women Writers* (Edward Everett Root Publishers).

Clare Horrocks is Senior Lecturer in Media, Culture, and Communication at Liverpool John Moores University, UK, and is the Project Lead on a major collaborative project with Gale Cengage publishers working on transcribing and digitizing the *Punch Contributor Ledgers 1843 to 1919*. She is the author of *Reassessing the Social and Cultural Dynamics of Punch: A Methodological Approach for a Digital Age* (2017) and is working on an anthology of contributions from many of the unknown women contributors of the magazine for publisher Victorian Secrets.

Andrew F. Humphries holds a PhD in English from University of Kent and an MA from Cambridge University and is Senior Lecturer in English Education at Canterbury Christ Church University, UK, where he also lectures and supervises undergraduate and postgraduate students in English literature, specializing in twentieth-century literature and modernism. He has published a monograph *D. H. Lawrence, Transport and Cultural Transition: 'A Great Sense of Journeying'* (Palgrave 2017) and is co-editor with Adrienne E. Gavin of both the international award-winning *Childhood in Edwardian Fiction: Worlds Enough and Time* (Palgrave 2009) and *Transport in British Fiction: Technologies of Movement 1840–1940* (Palgrave 2015). His main research focus is modernist writers and themes and particularly the relationship between technology (transport especially) and literature. He is also interested in representations of the child and childhood in literature. He has taught and presented papers on British drama, Victorian literature, and children's literature. His doctoral study was on D. H. Lawrence and modernism, but he has also published on H. G. Wells, E. M. Forster, Katherine Mansfield, and Robert Cormier and has forthcoming chapters on Elizabeth Braddon and Dorothy Richardson.

Alyson Hunt has recently completed a PhD at Canterbury Christ Church University, researching the role of dress in Victorian short crime stories. A former Assistant Reviews Editor for *Nineteenth-Century Gender Studies*, she has guest-edited a special edition of *Victorians Journal* on Women of the Press in the 1890s (December 2017). She is also the Research Associate for the International Centre for Victorian Women Writers for which she has co-convened five international conferences, produced exhibitions, devised a digital adventure, and staged a mock trial. Her chapter 'Fashioning Modernity in *Fin-de-Siècle* Serialised Crime Fiction' is published in *Fashion and Material Culture in Victorian Fiction and Periodicals* (2019) ed. by Nickianne Moody and Janine Hatter (Edward Everett Root).

Elizabeth Ludlow is Senior Lecturer in English Literature at Anglia Ruskin University, Cambridge, UK. She is the author of *Christina Rossetti and the Bible: Waiting with the Saints* (2014) and has published articles in peer-reviewed journals including the *Gaskell Journal*, *Literature Compass*, *Victorian Review*, and *English Literature in Transition, 1880–1920*. Her research project considers prayer and the female body in Victorian women's writing.

Tara MacDonald is an assistant professor at University of Idaho, USA. She is the author of *The New Man, Masculinity, and Marriage in the Victorian Novel* (2015) and co-editor, with Anne-Marie Beller, of *Rediscovering Victorian Women Sensation Writers* (2014). She is reviews editor for the *Wilkie Collins Journal* and has published articles and book chapters on Victorian masculinity, sensation fiction, and neo-Victorian fiction.

Nickianne Moody was Principal Lecturer in Media and Cultural Studies at Liverpool John Moores University, UK, until her death in 2019. Her interests included early science fiction and fantasy writing, particularly by women writers, gothic and late twentieth-century feminist and cyberpunk utopias and dystopias. Her work tends to address the representation of animals and the environment, especially with regard to visual culture. Her latest research was based on the Liddell Hart Collection of Costume held at Liverpool John Moores University and co-ordinating public engagement with the Femorabilia Collection. Her publications include work on most popular genres, nineteenth- and twentieth-century fiction, popular culture, and more specifically cultures of reading. She was a vibrant presence and a respected scholar, as well as a good friend to many of the contributors to this series.

Kristine Moruzi is a senior lecturer in the School of Communication and Creative Arts at Deakin University, Australia. She published *Constructing Girlhood through the Periodical Press, 1850–1915* in 2012. Her second monograph is *From Colonial to Modern: Transnational Girlhood in Canadian, Australian, and New Zealand Children's Literature (1840–1940)* with Michelle J. Smith and Clare Bradford (2018). She has also co-edited *Affect, Emotion, and Children's Literature: Representation and Socialisation in Texts for Children and Young Adults* (2017), *Girls' School Stories, 1749–1929* (2014), and *Colonial Girlhood in Literature, Culture and History, 1840–1950* (2014).

Carolyn W. de la L. Oulton is Professor of Victorian Literature and Director of the International Centre for Victorian Women Writers at Canterbury Christ Church University, UK. She is the author of *Literature and Religion in Mid-Victorian England: From Dickens to Eliot* (Palgrave Macmillan 2003), *Romantic Friendship in Victorian Literature* (2007), *Let the Flowers Go: A Life of Mary Cholmondeley* (2009), *Below the Fairy City: A Life of Jerome K. Jerome* (2012), and *Dickens and the Myth of the Reader* (2016). She is the co-editor (with SueAnn Schatz) of *Mary Cholmondeley Reconsidered* (2009), and (with Adrienne E. Gavin) of *Writing Women of the Fin de Siècle* (Palgrave 2011). Her most recent poetry collection is *Accidental Fruit* (2016). She is researching the reading culture and literary representation of seaside resorts 1840s–1930s.

Catherine Pope was awarded her PhD in 2014 by University of Sussex for her thesis on feminism in the novels of Florence Marryat. She is now a publisher and freelance workshop facilitator. Her publications include an entry on Rhoda Broughton for Oxford Bibliographies, a critical edition, with Troy Bassett, of Helen C. Black's *Notable Women Authors of the Day* (2011), and a chapter on marital violence in *For Better, For Worse: Marriage in Victorian Novels by Women* (2018). She has recently finished writing a monograph on Florence Marryat for Edward Everett Root's Key Popular Women Writers series. She is the founder and managing director of Victorian Secrets, an independent publishing house dedicated to producing high-quality books from and about the nineteenth century.

Melissa Purdue is Associate Professor of English at Minnesota State University, Mankato, USA. She has published *New Woman Writers, Authority and the Body* with Stacey Floyd (2009) and a critical edition of

Rosa Praed's *Fugitive Anne: A Romance of the Unexplored Bush* (2011). Her most recent publications have been in *Domestic Fiction in Colonial Australia and New Zealand* (Ed. by Tamara Wagner, 2014) and *The Latchkey: Journal of New Woman Studies*. She is also a founding editor/co-editor-in-chief of *Nineteenth-Century Gender Studies*.

CHAPTER 1

Introduction

Adrienne E. Gavin and Carolyn W. de la L. Oulton

This volume is the second in the five-volume series *British Women's Writing from Brontë to Bloomsbury, 1840–1940*, which decade by decade critically reassesses women's fiction, examining the ways in which it propels and challenges discourses of realism, sensation, and the new across a century of dynamic social, cultural, and technological change. Analysing confluences and developments in women's writing across the 1860s and the 1870s, the 16 original chapters that follow critically reconsider fiction by canonical and lesser-known women writers, redefining the landscape of female authorship during these decades. By exploring women's fiction within the social and cultural contexts of the 1860s and 1870s, the collection distils in terms of women's writing how these decades discretely build on earlier

A. E. Gavin (✉)
Department of English and Language Studies, Canterbury Christ Church University, Canterbury, UK
e-mail: adrienne.gavin@cantab.net

C. W. de la L. Oulton
School of Humanities, Canterbury Christ Church University, Canterbury, UK
e-mail: carolyn.oulton@canterbury.ac.uk

© The Author(s) 2020
A. E. Gavin, C. W. de la L. Oulton (eds.), *British Women's Writing from Brontë to Bloomsbury, Volume 2*, British Women's Writing from Brontë to Bloomsbury, 1840–1940,
https://doi.org/10.1007/978-3-030-38528-6_1

work that is identifiably Victorian. In doing so, it reveals both points of departure and thematic and stylistic continuities.

The achievements and influence of the Brontës in the 1840s and 1850s, and of George Eliot from the 1850s, had already placed women's writing in the spotlight. That these writers published pseudonymously in itself drew attention to the ambiguous status of women authors, whose proliferation had been the subject of much agitated commentary in the 1850s. From the 1860s the stage was set for an intense, even obsessive, examination of gendered authorship—the question of who could write what, for whom, and in what context, is played out across both literary criticism and fiction from this point in the nineteenth century.

Defined historically by decade, with chapters ordered chronologically to suggest shifting emphases in fiction as each decade progresses, the volume considers a broad range of developments in female writing. It reveals that women's writing of the 1860s was able to incorporate melodramatic events into a realist mode, challenging readers to re-examine the type of novel they thought they were reading. In turn, female-authored fiction of the 1870s began to turn away from sensation to the serious, made women's relationship to money central, and voiced the unvoiced including in relation to physical sensation and female desire.

From the emotive articles in the popular press one might be forgiven for thinking that by the 1860s 'a book without a murder, a divorce, a seduction, or a bigamy, is not apparently considered worth either writing or reading; and a mystery and a secret are the chief qualifications of the modern novel' ('The Popular Novels' 262). As the chapters in this volume show, sensation fiction does not have a monopoly on provoking or depicting physical sensation and affect, nor on representations of empathetic grief and difficult emotion. Following the death of Prince Albert in 1861 Queen Victoria entered a period of public mourning that persisted until her death 40 years later. The need to balance private feeling with public restraint emerges as a serious concern in a number of female-authored novels from this time.

Time itself is examined in new ways, as it becomes increasingly unstable or at least multivalent in the context of scientific discovery and technological advance. Time was at one and the same time hugely expanded by evolutionary theory, most notably propounded in Darwin's *On the Origin of Species* in 1859, and—at the other end of the spectrum—collapsed through the sense of ever-increasing speed associated with the continued expansion of railway and transport networks throughout the 1860s and 1870s. As Elizabeth Ludlow argues in her chapter on Gaskell in this volume, that 'the secret of Dunster's murder (in *A Dark Night's Work* [1863]) is uncovered through the process of railway expansion is indicative of how, in a decade that saw a boom in train lines, technological progress transformed the spatial and temporal landscape of individual lives.' Indeed both Ludlow and Andrew F. Humphries here point to railway expansion as central to the discovery or solving of crimes, while 'Gaskell responds to the pressures of time with an emphasis on the urgent need for reconciliation' (Ludlow).

Greater mobility is also linked to the theme of disguise and the infiltration of the middle-class home by dissident adventurers in a number of sensation novels. The increasing difficulty of sustaining and policing social networks is set against the assurance that the criminal or interloper will finally be detected, as the rail network pits antagonists against each other in a race to discover or efface the past. The difficulty of recognizing figures from the past is also depicted in more nuanced ways across genres during these decades. Both Gaskell's *Sylvia's Lovers* (1860) and Ellen Wood's *East Lynne* (1861) feature disfigured parents returning in disguise to see their children; while in Anna Sewell's *Black Beauty* (1877) Black Beauty does not initially recognize 'an old worn-out chestnut, with an ill-kept coat and bones that showed plainly through it' as his once glorious friend Ginger (*Black Beauty* 131).

The volume is structured in two parts, each devoted to one decade so that specific trends can be identified. As Lucy Hartley observes, 'the possibilities for a writerly life for nineteenth-century women were various and the gendered division of literary work from home work was surmountable, though not, as ever, without struggles or steadfastness' (16). Both struggles and steadfastness are evidenced in women's lives and fiction of the 1860s and 1870s, with female authors not only driving and adhering to new trends but also reacting against and varying them.

The 1860s were acutely conscious of the sensational possibilities offered by a new generation of writers. Exploring, complicating, or simply contesting this new genre provided one means by which a woman writer could define her own position in the literary marketplace. In the 1870s women writers continued to draw on the creative opportunities that 1860s sensation writing had made available. Developing an increasingly serious focus, some novelists such as Eliot and Sewell produced works that were at once powerfully affective and concerned with moral questions on a level deeper than the 'moral' or 'improving' literature that had so often been the assumed literary lot of the Victorian woman author. Women's relationship to money also became a key 1870s concern.

Women's Writing of the 1860s

The 1860s saw new developments in technology as well as the early stages of what has been termed the 'Victorian crisis of faith' in the context of the Higher Criticism and Charles Darwin's *On the Origin of Species* (1859). At the same time, the press provided a new critical focus on women's writing and intense debate over the limits within which it should confine itself, as well as a renewed attention to its impact on female readers in particular, who supposedly needed to be policed for their own safety. While for the increasingly public female author literature in these years might be 'simply treated as an accessible profession' (Peterson 47), the visceral nature of reading is nowhere better exemplified than in the supposed dangers of sensation fiction, in which the bodies of heroines on the page assume a dangerous physiological function in channelling not only affective responses but also physical arousal in their unsuspecting female readers.

The desire to redefine social identities as well as to establish connections and form new and extended social groups manifested itself in other ways during this decade as cartomania, the collection of small photographs and *cartes de visite*, reached a peak alongside the explosion of female-authored railway reading associated with W. H. Smith and the ever increasing dominance of Mudie's circulating library. The debate over whether railway travel encourages the reading of more exciting, fast-paced fiction has never been wholly resolved. That it was widely believed to do so in the 1860s suggests that the publication of *Lady Audley's Secret* in 1862, the same year that London Victoria railway station first opened a direct line to a public keen to find quicker and more convenient routes to the seaside resorts in Kent, is coincidental but could hardly have been better planned.

The modern women's movement began in the 1860s, exemplified by the setting up of the feminist Victoria Press by Emily Faithfull in 1860, a parliamentary petition for female suffrage in 1866, John Stuart Mill's drafting of an amendment (which failed to pass) to the Second Reform Act in 1867 that would have given voting rights to female property owners, and both the inauguration (as the College for Women) of Girton College, Cambridge, and the publication of Mill's *On the Subjection of Women* in 1869. In 1869, too, the 'Edinburgh Seven,' led by Sophia Jex-Blake, became the first women to matriculate at a British university. Having won the right to study medicine at the University of Edinburgh, they were not allowed to take degrees or practise medicine (unless qualifying in Paris or elsewhere), but the opening of higher education to women had begun. In

1865 Elizabeth Garrett Anderson had become the first woman to be granted a licence to practise in medicine (through a loophole that was soon closed). The publication of Isabella Beeton's *Book of Household Management* in 1861 and Eliza Warren's bestseller *How I Managed My Household on £200 a Year* (1864) and *How I Managed My Children from Infancy to Marriage* (1865) stood as reminders of the ways in which female authors could become commercially successful without overtly breaking gender codes. A more extreme stance was adopted by the novelist Eliza Lynn Linton, whose own domestic irregularities did not prevent her from publishing a notorious series of antifeminist articles in *The Saturday Review*, beginning with 'The Girl of the Period' in 1868, in which she fulminated against the 'vitiated taste' of this immodest but characteristically modern young woman (340). These trends developed alongside and sometimes in opposition to less positive events, such as the death of Prince Albert in 1861, the major cholera outbreak that was particularly serious for large cities such as London in 1866, and the series of Contagious Diseases Acts (1864, 1866, and 1869) designed to regulate and compulsorily treat sexually diseased prostitutes (although not their clients) in English key ports such as Chatham. Class and gender debates also intersected in this decade, with the International Working Men's Association being founded in 1864 with Karl Marx giving the opening address.

By the 1860s women authors may have been under close scrutiny, but they were also able to position themselves in a new tradition by responding to recent literary models that were identifiably Victorian, as they successfully built on the achievements of 1850s genre fiction to shape and sometimes contest the emerging sensation fiction for which the 1860s remain famous. In the 1840s, at the start of the period covered by this series, the provincial fiction of the Brontës and others strongly suggests that gender roles were still in flux. This may have been especially true for communities that retained some degree of isolation across the country, as they started to construct new models of femininity under the first female monarch in more than 200 years. Coventry Patmore's 'The Angel in the House,' published in parts between 1854 and 1862, offered what is still perhaps the century's most famous model of conservative gender politics.

In the 1860s women authors continued to respond to the work of Charlotte Brontë, who had died in 1855, but who remained a much-contested prototype for the 'reclusive spinster novelist.' Julia Kavanagh also highlighted the importance of 'long dead' women writers of pre-Victorian generations 'to the formation of the modern novel' in her two-volume *English Women of Letters: Biographical Sketches* (1863) (Kavanagh, 'To the Reader' n.p.). Brontë's biographer Elizabeth Gaskell died in 1865, and at around the same time a new generation of women authors was starting to attract attention, as they variously responded to earlier traditions and found new modes of expression. Mary Braddon published *Three Times Dead (The Trail of the Serpent)* in 1860; Ellen Wood won a temperance competition with *Danesbury House* in the same year, and Rhoda Broughton challenged the boundaries of the sensation genre in a series of novels beginning with *Not Wisely, But Too Well* in 1867.

Women were, and could be seen to be, articulating a very public response to the demands and opportunities of modernity by the 1860s as symbolized on the one hand by the growing railway network and the increased leisure time of the middle and upwardly mobile classes, and on the other by the continuing debate over female employment. These responses included philanthropic and religious novels as well as aesthetically beautiful drawing-room volumes (a number of which were printed by Faithfull's Victoria Press) and a growing network of women writing journalism and serial fiction in the press. At the same time the 'newly combined and (to women) newly available role of author-editor was a position that could influence the ways in which fiction was shaped, produced, and consumed' (Palmer 3). Women's contributions to newspapers and periodicals meant, in effect, that they joined the debate about their own fitness to participate in public life, and gained a level of control over the terms on which women authors should be read. Drawing attention to Florence Wilford's novel *Nigel Bartram's Ideal* (1869), Elaine Showalter shows how women writers overtly engage in these debates. The eponymous character has written brutally about a pseudonymous female author, whom he unknowingly goes on to marry. Only his own illness makes him realize that 'just as it is no shame for a man to be weak, it is no disgrace for a woman to be strong,' enabling the couple to become 'literary partners' (Showalter 124).

The construction of a body of literature that could comment on and explain—perhaps if necessary even contain—this new sense of modernity necessarily came to include a high degree of self-consciousness about the positioning of the female author in particular, a critique that became increasingly polarized as the sensation craze took hold. The chapters in the current volume offer a reminder that not all women writers were tempted to climb onto this particular bandwagon. However, some of those who did so seem unlikely contenders, given the immoral associations of the genre, with its immediately recognizable tropes of bigamy, murder, and illegitimacy. More importantly sensation fiction raises new questions about the allocation of literary status when it is read in the wider context of the decade that brought it to the forefront of critical debate. Participation in social and often scandalous debates is not solely the province of maritally unorthodox figures such as Mary Braddon (indeed the equally compromised George Eliot largely eschews the sensational mode), and overtly religious authors demonstrated their sincerity and commitment through addressing difficult or even taboo subjects. Just as the unquestionably virtuous Josephine Butler scandalized her contemporaries by her willingness to enter publicly on subjects such as the Contagious Diseases Acts that respectable women were supposed to ignore, the sensation genre was both responding to and infiltrating texts that proclaim their own religious and social orthodoxy.

Reading women's fiction of the 1860s as the literature of a particular decade and not just in terms of its allocated genre allows a number of new connections to emerge. Indeed Alberto Manguel has provocatively claimed that in any age '[w]hatever classifications have been chosen, every library tyrannizes the act of reading, and forces the reader—the curious reader, the alert reader—to *rescue* the book from the category to which it has been condemned' (Manguel 199). This tension between categorization and the response of individual readers is particularly pertinent at a time when the imposition of a particular category could famously get an author banned from Mudie's Circulating Library stocklist.

While such classifications could be very difficult to determine (as the more strategic writers of the period realized) as well as being misleading in their attribution of supposed literary qualities, the impact on critical reputation could be far reaching. What emerges from a reading of sensation against realist fiction of the 1860s is that the boundaries between morally suspect and permissible literature are not as easily drawn as endemic critical opposition to the former might suggest. Both Society for Promoting Christian Knowledge (SPCK) authors such as Emma Worboise, and the notoriously antifeminist Eliza Lynn Linton (who is discussed in this volume) included recognizably sensational tropes such as burning houses (Worboise in the 1871 *Nobly Born* and Linton in *Sowing the Wind* in 1867), where romantic love can finally be declared or enacted by the respectable heroine as social conventions are suspended in the face of her imminent death. That this death is of course averted creates a high degree of tension in the subsequent narrative without contravening acceptable codes of representation; nonetheless there is no reason to doubt the sincerity of the religious content.

The religious passages of Ellen Wood's controversial *East Lynne* (1861) are often overlooked or dismissed by critics, but a number of her other novels use sensational plots to underpin a central Christian message—presumably this is the reason that when the Free Library in Folkestone overhauled its catalogue under the supervision of a deeply conservative local vicar in 1902, it either bought, or at least failed to remove, three additional copies of *East Lynne*. As Tara MacDonald here argues, *East Lynne* is not just a sensation novel with religious elements; it also uses affect to political ends that are communal and public and not simply focused on the ubiquitous Woman Question.

The chapters in the first section of this volume cover not just the contentious sensation fiction of the 1860s but also a wide range of women's fiction, from experimental realism to novels depicting marginalized mental states, and from expressions of spiritual or religious crisis to humorous *Punch* journalism. Several consider representations of intense feeling as a register of both individual expression and cultural cohesion or disruption, whether this appears in the context of affective responsiveness, forgiveness and philanthropy, or sensation and desire.

In 'A Decade of Experiment' Margaret Harris revisits George Eliot's writing of the 1860s to offer new perspectives on Eliot's experimentalism, ranging from historical fiction and classical mythology to nineteenth-century political debate. Arguing that she exceeds the sensation writers' challenge to social norms through a probing analysis of contemporary standards, Harris positions Eliot as an astute and sophisticated interpreter of contemporary moral values whose 1860s fiction reveals a writer of many moods and voices, mediated through multiple perspectives.

Discussing public feelings and private interests in Ellen Wood's *East Lynne* (1861), Tara MacDonald in '"Duck him!"' links the excessive feelings of Isabel Carlyle to the collective anger of the mob that belatedly exacts revenge on her seducer Sir Francis Levison, showing how affect leads in surprising ways to a renewed social cohesion at the end of the novel. Stimulating sympathetic feeling even as she investigates its appropriateness in different contexts, Wood uses intimate and gossipy narrative address to create a 'safe neighbourly space' in which readers can empathize with both the suffering of the fallen Isabel and the righteous anger of the working-class men who attack Levison and duck him in a pond. The transmission of sympathy in this reading not only resolves the plot through the punishment of the transgressive male figure as the working-class mob vicariously enacts the vengeance of the more restrained local gentry, but also enables the sensation genre to be reassessed as a moral form with the capacity to promote a political and social agenda.

Andrew F. Humphries considers the importance of linearity and railway time to the project of masculinity and social order in '"[Tr]ain[s]" of circumstantial evidence"' which explores 'Railway "Monomania" and Investigations of Gender' in *Lady Audley's Secret* (1862). A discussion of both the affective responses of railway travellers and the ways in which new technologies of travel served to regulate these responses suggests some of the ways in which railway modernity shifts from a subversive function in fostering the unconventional or disruptive behaviour of female characters to an agent of their confinement as the technology at the centre of the novel increasingly 'privileges the modernizing power and speed of legal surveillance.' As Humphries argues, Robert Audley in turn moves from a narrative of individual loss in the search for his friend's supposed murderer, to a heavily gendered crusade in which the railway plays an emblematic as well as an enabling role. Furthermore, through Braddon's mustering of 'civilization' and 'nation' as defining terms of masculinity, the monomania associated with Robert himself enacts and is legitimated by the wider agenda of Empire.

In contrast to Humphries, Elizabeth Ludlow explores the religious uses of time and eternity in the context of spiritual crisis and reconciliation, in '"There is great need for forgiveness in this world"' which examines Elizabeth Gaskell's *Sylvia's Lovers* (1863) and *A Dark Night's Work* (1863). Ludlow contends that in these texts (written at a time when religious orthodoxy was felt by many to be under attack both from within the Church and from arguments of rationalism and the Higher Criticism), the Unitarian Gaskell critiques Atonement doctrines of vicarious retribution, stressing instead the healing potential of confession and reconciliation between guilty characters. Importantly *A Dark Night's Work* critiques the terms of the sensation novel, while the revelation of secrets constitutes a moral turning point rather than merely reworking a familiar plot device. Gaskell's moral positioning in the contested space of the 1860s literary marketplace suggests that realist writers, notwithstanding their ambivalence, and in complex ways, participated in the sensational mode more often than critics tend to realize.

Kristine Moruzi's '"The plain duties which are set before me"' considers the ways in which the protagonists of three philanthropic novels,

Florence Wilford's *A Maiden of Our Own Day* (1862), Frances Carey Brock's *Charity Helstone* (1865), and Felicia Skene's *Hidden Depths* (1866), seek to resolve the tension between their familial roles and their commitment to the ideal of philanthropic work often recommended to women. Moruzi shows how these competing roles are inflected by the wider context of feminist calls for greater employment opportunities and women's rights. While the novels set out the limited range of options open to women, it is significant that two of the protagonists remain unmarried. These narratives can be seen as conservative, but they reflect the agency of 'independent girls and young women who make decisions based on their interests, their duties, and their moral responsibilities,' rather than conform to the traditional marriage plot.

In '"[S]mothered under rose-leaves"' Carolyn W. de la L.Oulton discusses violent sensation and the location of the feminine in Eliza Lynn Linton's *Sowing the Wind* (1867). Oulton argues that as one of the most conservative social critics of the 1860s Linton, like Gaskell, nonetheless adapts the sensational mode to her own ends, using it to ask insightful questions about the tension between feminine obedience and personal responsibility within the confines of an unhappy marriage. The increasingly complex portrayal of the heroine Isola Aylott, who is 'denied the free use of even thought' by her autocratic husband (*Sowing the Wind* 65), is explored partly through her relationship with her feminist cousin Jane Osborn, who herself succumbs to a slavish devotion to the unworthy man she seeks to marry. It is likely that Linton's sources for the obsessive husband included Caroline Clive's 1855 *Paul Ferroll* (discussed in volume 1 of this series), but her scathing treatment of the feminized St John Aylott implies that the husband rather than the wife forfeits respect when he 'descends' from his pedestal, in the process making a 'cancerous sore of home' (62). As the hero of the novel explains, '"self-sacrifice is not slavishness. To be of any value at all it is the voluntary gift of strength"' (149).

In '"[F]leshly inclinations"' Tamar Heller discusses the various manifestations of, and constraints on, female desire in *Not Wisely, but Too Well* (1867), *Cometh Up as a Flower* (1867), and *Red as a Rose Is She* (1870). While more than one of Broughton's heroines is rescued from what seems to be an inevitable sexual fall, Broughton is detailed and explicit in her portrayal of physical passion, offering an 'innovative representation of female desire that constitutes one of her distinctive contributions' to women's writing of the 1860s. Heller notes that while natural imagery is used to erotic ends in the novels, with a Romantic landscape counterbalancing the stifling domesticity endured by female characters, paradoxically one of Broughton's strategies for successfully representing desire is to align it with the disembodied voice of the consumptive heroine. At one level then Broughton reproduces the very anxieties her fiction seeks to investigate. Yet while her later fiction of the 1860s apparently supplies the traditional ending of the heroine's marriage, this message is undercut by an ambivalent irony.

Clare Horrocks and Nickianne Moody recover the female contribution to *Punch* in 'Crumbs from the Table' which examines Matilda Betham-Edwards's comic writing in *Punch*. Deconstructing the Victorian assumption that humour is essentially a male preserve, they showcase the contribution made by Betham-Edwards to *Punch*, a journal renowned for its satirical treatment of social tensions. Through her periodical contributions Betham-Edwards deviated from the modes more usually adopted by women writers keen to assert their professionalism and seriousness. In their analysis of this innovative strategy Horrocks and Moody highlight the difficulty of assessing humorous writing by writers of either sex, given that it does not constitute a recognized genre and has no established criteria by which it can be judged. In resisting expected patterns of feminine writing, Betham-Edwards therefore eludes easy definition. In her series 'Mrs Punch's Letters to Her Daughter' (1868) she both signals her place in a largely masculine comic tradition and finds new ways to reflect on the position of women in a changing world.

WOMEN'S WRITING OF THE 1870s

Perhaps because it lacks the new sense of Victorianness, hungriness, or Brontëan impact of 1840s and 1850s fiction; the transgressive verve of 1860s sensation novels; or the New-Woman politicization of 1880s and 1890s texts, Victorian women's writing of the 1870s has suffered from comparative critical neglect. It seems both paused and poised, as if reconsidering itself after the flamboyant excesses of 1860s sensation, yet it was anything but passive. Less interested in portraying 1860s-style extremes of scandal and criminality, many female authors of the 1870s instead drew attention to the normalized aberrations and difficult experiences of women's daily life and to issues, including money and career trajectories, that had been regarded as more typically masculine. Turning to interiority, some female authors of the 1870s produced deeply serious literature that focused on the bearing of painful yet quotidian individual experiences.

Strong, enduring female voices came through in this decade, in works not of popular moralism but with strong moral cores and depths of feeling. Quiet, secure landmarks in the history of women's literature appeared including George Eliot's *Middlemarch* (1871–1872)—which Virginia Woolf would later term 'one of the few English novels written for grown-up people' (Woolf, 'George Eliot')—Harriet Martineau's *Autobiography* (1877),[1] and Anna Sewell's *Black Beauty* (1877). Signalling a partial shift from arresting tropes and disruptive plotlines, such works focus in powerful ways on learning from experience, memory, and suffering.

Strands of Brontëan passion and sensation's extremes were of course still also evident in the decade, with some female authors in the 1870s being influenced by, or, like Mary Braddon, Florence Marryat, Dora Russell, and Rhoda Broughton, continuing to produce, sensation fiction. Sensation's influence is also seen, less overtly, in women writer's enhanced literary expression of both physical sensation and female desire. As Emma Liggins observes, however, even Queen of sensation Braddon was in the 1870s trying to write more serious fiction (Liggins).

There was a dip, too, in British women's production of crime fiction, which was at this time often associated with sensation writing. While the female tradition in crime writing was being furthered in America and Australia by writers such as the American 'Mother of Detective Fiction' Anna Katharine Green, who produced her influential detective novel *The Leavenworth Case* in 1878, in Britain, as Kate Watson comments, 'there is a dearth of women producing [crime fiction] in the 1870s and 80s' (64). As contributors such as Janine Hatter and Alyson Hunt here show, however, crime still had its place in women's 1870s fiction, although it was often depicted as financial in motive and nature.

Having entered the fictional field in the early 1860s writers like Braddon, Ellen Wood, and Ouida (Maria Louise Ramé/Marie Louise de la Ramée) were well established and continued to write across the 1870s. Braddon and Wood also published the work of other female (and male) authors. In 1866 Braddon had founded *Belgravia*, which she edited until 1876. From 1867 and throughout the 1870s (and until her death in 1887) Wood owned and edited *The Argosy*. In the 1870s, too, the highly prolific Margaret Oliphant was in the middle of her five decades as a writer; Eliza Lyn Linton published two of her best-known novels, *The True History of Joshua Davidson* (1872) and *Patricia Kemball* (1874), while other established writers like Charlotte Riddell, Charlotte Yonge, Rhoda Broughton, Florence Marryat, Frances Hodgson Burnett, and Anne

Thackeray Ritchie were regularly publishing. Writers in the later years of their careers included Dinah Maria Mulock Craik, who had been publishing since the late 1840s and George Eliot whose last work *Impressions of Theophrastus Such* was published in 1879.

Compared to the 1840s, 1850s, and 1860s, and possibly because of the profusion and productiveness of already established women writers, in the 1870s there seem to have been fewer new women writers emerging. Dora Russell entered the field, as did Helen Mather (Ellen Buckingham Mathews) with her bestseller *Comin' Thro' the Rye* (1875), and Anna Sewell, then in her fifties, wrote her only published work, *Black Beauty*, which would later become best known as a children's book.

In fact it was a strong decade for female-authored literature about or for children including *A Dog of Flanders* (1872) by Ouida, *The Little Lame Prince and His Travelling Cloak* (1875) by Dinah Maria Mulock Craik (writing as Miss Mulock), novels by Juliana Horatia Ewing including *A Flat Iron for a Farthing* (1873) and *Six to Sixteen: A Story for Girls* (1876), and works by Americans Louisa May Alcott with *Little Men* (1871) and Susan Coolidge with *What Katy Did* (1872). Strands of didactic literature about working-class children and homeless 'street Arabs' also continued under the impetus of such 1860s texts as *Patience Hart's First Experience in Service* (1862) by Sewell's mother Mary Sewell and *Jessica's First Prayer* (1866) by Hesba Stretton (Sarah Smith). It was in the 1870s that Brenda (Georgina Castle Smith), for example, started publishing philanthropy-urging works such as *Nothing to Nobody* (1873) and *Froggy's Little Brother* (1875).

Dominant in the decade's veer towards the more serious—and towards a late-Victorian sensibility, 'sensibleness,' and modernity—was a sustained fictional focus on the financial and on women's professional opportunities. Three months before Victoria ascended the throne in June 1837, Robert Southey had infamously advised Charlotte Brontë: "'[l]iterature is not the business of a woman's life, and it cannot be'" (Robert Southey to Charlotte Brontë, March 1837). By the 1870s not only had literature become well established as a business for women, but female authors were also increasingly writing about business itself in the commercial sense. As Silvana Colella here notes, a reviewer of *Austin Friars* (1870), one of Charlotte Riddell's novels of City life, termed the opening of the decade "'the day for female courage'" in women's writing ('Austin Friars' qtd. in Colella 748), with female authors braving new subjects and exploring new ways of presenting female experience. Foremost among these new emphases in the

1870s was women writing about money, not in the more traditional sense of depicting domestic economy, working-class struggle for survival, or women's quest for financial security through marriage, but through newer lenses which focused on finance in the public, commercial sense of making money, business, and its corollary white-collar crime. Financial concerns, debt, bankruptcy, fraud, women's career and income prospects, and their monetary position within marriage are sustained threads in women's writing of the 1870s.

'[E]verbody *does* want to make money in these days,' writes Yonge in the 'Money-Making' chapter of her 1876 work *Womankind*:

> Elder people can recollect when it would have been thought actually undignified to make any gain by any performance of a lady, and when, if her talents were too strong not to seek an opening, she would have shrunk from and put aside any payment as an insult .... The whole tone of mind was a curious contrast to the present, when everybody of every rank is only trying what is the market value of their accomplishments. (222)

The predominance of financial themes in women's 1870s fiction reflected this shift in attitudes to middle-class women's relationship to money. More generally it was influenced by the expansion of the credit economy in the mid-nineteenth century and the aftermath of the financial panic of 1866, which had been triggered by the collapse of London 'bankers' bank' Overend, Gurney and Company in the same year. As Tamara S. Wagner has discussed with regard to novels such as Margaret Oliphant's *At His Gates* (1872), too, 'sensational financial fiction' was a popular subgenre of Victorian fiction at this time (51).

More specific financial imperatives also motivated individual female writers who needed to earn to support spouses or dependants. City novelist Riddell, for instance, had to support her bankrupt husband, while the widowed Oliphant had to provide not only for her own children but those of her brother—Virginia Woolf half a century later decrying 'the fact that Mrs. Oliphant sold her brain, her very admirable brain, prostituted her culture and enslaved her intellectual liberty in order that she might earn her living and educate her children' ('Three Guineas' 166).

That money, and female access to it, became so significant in women's fiction of the 1870s was also undoubtedly propelled by a range of legal and professional changes and debates of the time concerning women's rights to learn, earn, and control their own finances. The decade opened with the passage of the Married Women's Property Act 1870 which legislated that wives now legally owned their own property. This in turn instigated increased practical attention to financial concerns for married women, among them women writers whose authorship was now producing income that was legally their own. As Colella discusses, Riddell was one of the first women writers to herself use its provisions in a law suit to try and maintain her financial rights to her future earnings as sole breadwinner in the face of her husband's bankruptcy, and to avoid his creditors taking them. As Colella shows, Riddell's 1870s novels centring on the financial City of London not only included men of business but also explored 'female economic agency' marked by 'the increasingly active role that women assume in the business sphere' and 'the growing cultural, social, and political relevance of questions pertaining to women's relations with money, property, and professional aspirations.'

As Hatter's chapter in this volume shows, in the 1870s Braddon, too, turned away from the early 1860s criminal subjects of bigamy and murder which had brought her fame as a sensation novelist towards stories of fraud, financial double-dealing, counterfeiting, embezzlement, forged documents, and false identities. Indeed Wagner has suggested that '[b]y the end of the "sensational sixties," financial crimes, even financial activity in general, had become standard features of villains. The connection between sensationalism and the popularization of financial themes became a cliché' (Wagner 63). Women writers of the 1870s expanded interest in women's position in relation to money even further. Passage of the Bankruptcy Act in 1869, too, inspired stories of bankruptcy by Riddell and other women writers. One such was Ellen Wood in her *Johnny Ludlow* story 'Bursting Up' (1871) which, as Hunt discusses, concerns 'male bankruptcy and fraud.'

Danielle Charette here explores women and finance in Margaret Oliphant's *Phoebe Junior: A Last Chronicle of Carlingford* (1876), which involves a forged cheque and considers 'sinecures which could be held by girls,' showing that the novel insists that 'the all-consuming power of English financial debates … are appropriate topics for young women to contemplate.' As Adrienne E. Gavin shows here, too, *Black Beauty* protests against the quest for money obscuring attention to humane treatment of the horses that were so central to producing Britain's wealth at the time.

Authors of the 1870s were also writing in the context of heightened concern with education, with the decade's bookending by the Elementary

Education Acts of 1870 and 1880 widening access to primary education, including for girls, and enabling women's election to school boards. Higher education and professional opportunities for women were also expanding in the 1870s. Cambridge's second college for women, Newnham College, was established in 1871, and Oxford's first women's colleges Lady Margaret Hall and Somerville College were founded in 1878 and 1879 respectively. In 1878 the University of London was the first university to admit women and men on equal terms (awarding the first degrees to women in Britain in 1880). Alice Vickery became the first qualified female pharmacist in Britain in 1873, and in 1874 Sophia Jex-Blake and Elizabeth Garrett Anderson established the London School of Medicine for Women to train female doctors. The Medical Act of 1876 permitted medical authorities to licence women doctors. As Sarah Bilston shows, too, a number of female novelists in the 1870s presented acting as a noble profession. Women's financial contributions were also publicly recognized with philanthropist Angela Burdett-Coutts becoming both a peer in 1871 and the first female Honorary Freeman of the City of London in 1872. In America Alcott's novel *Work, A Story of Experience* (1873) semi-autobiographically considered career possibilities for women, following the success of *Little Women* (1868, 1869—second volume as *Good Wives* in the UK) which made Jo March's independence and following of her authorial vocation inspirational to girl readers. Another American inspiration was Victoria Claflin Woodhull (later Woodhull Martin) and her sister Tennessee Claflin, who settled in Britain in 1877. Dubbed in the USA 'the Queens of Finance,' the sisters had founded both a radical newspaper (*Woodhull and Claflin's Weekly*) and the first female-run stockbroking agency on Wall Street in 1870. Woodhull in 1872 had been the first woman to run for the US presidency. A feminist and labour activist and an advocate of free love and women's rights to their own bodies, in Britain Woodhull wrote and gave public lectures on her views.

Women's civil and physical liberties were the concern, too, of rioters in Oxfordshire in 1873 who sought the release of the Ascott Martyrs, 16 women who were imprisoned with hard labour (and later pardoned by Queen Victoria) for attempting to dissuade strikebreaking agricultural workers and encourage them to join the National Union of Agricultural Workers. Similarly, campaigns continued throughout the 1870s for the repeal of the Contagious Diseases Acts (which were not repealed until 1886). In a public letter to *The Shield* in 1870 Josephine Butler, leader of

The Ladies National Association for the Repeal of the Contagious Diseases Acts, quoted the words of a prostitute regarding male control over women:

> It is *men, men, only men*, from the first to the last, that we have to do with! To please a man I did wrong at first, then I was flung about from man to man. Men police lay hands on us. By men we are examined, handled, doctored, and messed on with. In the hospital it is a man again who makes prayers and reads the Bible for us. We are had up before magistrates who are men, and we never get out of the hands of men till we die! (Letter III, Shield 9 May 1870, 79–80, qtd. in Jordan and Sharp 92)

From a more scientific stance, American Antoinette Brown Blackwell—the first female ordained minister of a mainstream protestant church in the USA—protested against male sexual dominance by publishing *The Sexes Throughout Nature* (1875) which critiqued the androcentricity of Charles Darwin's *The Descent of Man, and Selection in Relation to Sex* (1871).

For female authors of fiction, however, it was, female desire, or sexual engagement through choice, that garnered more attention, in works such as Broughton's 'The Man with the Nose' (1872) and Florence Marryat's *Her Father's Name* (1876) as Melissa Purdue and Catherine Pope here respectively discuss. Elaine Showalter suggests that female novelists 'of an older generation who survived into the 1860s reacted to the sensationalists with both genuine shock' and 'a degree of envy ... at the ease with which younger women were speaking their minds' (145), but it is clear, too, that some, like Oliphant, also introduced sensational tropes into their own work, particularly by the early 1870s. Showalter cites comments by the once 'daring' now 'guardian of the hearth' Geraldine Jewsbury, who was a reader for Bentley's throughout the 1870s, on Mrs Godfrey's *Dolly* in 1872: '"If I were a *man* reading this MS ... I shd [sic] enquire 'are the young women of England trying to qualify themselves for courtezans?'—the breaking down of all sense of shame & modesty opens the way to that bottomless pit"' (qtd. in Showalter 146). Although Jewsbury regularly attacked works by sensationalists like Broughton for their portrayal of female desire (an aspect of Broughton's work which both Heller and Purdue in this volume discuss), the interesting point about Jewsbury's comments on Godfrey is that she is *not* 'a *man*' reading the manuscript. Intentionally or not, a subtextual space is created for women's more positive reception of such work.

Fictional accounts also gave leeway to women's expression of the sexual and physical that the legal arbiters of non-fiction often did not allow. Woodhull, for example, had been imprisoned in America on obscenity charges in 1872 for publishing in her newspaper an account of an alleged affair. In Britain in 1877 social activists Annie Besant and Charles Bradlaugh were similarly prosecuted for their publication of American physician Charles Knowlton's 1832 birth-control manual *Fruits of Philosophy*. The doors to publication of such material were however opening and Besant followed this by publishing her own birth-control pamphlet *The Law of Population: Its Consequences, and Its Bearing upon Human Conduct and Morals* (1877).

In international terms, the 1870s were a decade of new Imperialism with Victoria being proclaimed Empress of India on 1 January 1877, the Franco-Prussian War being waged in 1870–1871, and the Anglo-Zulu War in 1879. Technological advances included the invention of the telephone by Alexander Graham Bell in 1876, the phonograph by Thomas Edison in America in 1877, and the light bulb by Edison in 1879. It was a period, too, when women were writing bestselling travel literature about their real-life adventures, including Isabella L Bird's *A Lady's Life in the Rocky Mountains* (1873) and Amelia B. Edwards's *A Thousand Miles Up the Nile* (1877). As the following chapters show, women's fiction of the 1870s is also marked by a sense of new departures and of moving forward, whether that is in terms of expressing moral strength, giving attention to women's finances and professions, or in speaking things that had often been unspoken, including female desire.

The opening chapter in part II, Silvana Colella's 'Transcending Prudence,' discusses Charlotte Riddell's 'City Women' in relation to female economic agency and entrepreneurship. While Riddell's City novels of the 1860s had explored 'the plights of individuals caught in the "vortex of business,"' her novels of the 1870s were reoriented 'towards the exploration of female economic agency,' and revealed the increasingly active roles of women in business. They also 'resonate with preoccupations about financial responsibilities, property ownership, insolvency, and the delicacy of the credit system, which had both personal and collective significance.' As Colella discusses, Riddell's husband was declared bankrupt in 1871, resulting in Riddell becoming the sole breadwinner. Leading up to the bankruptcy Riddell was involved in lawsuits that aimed to protect her future earnings from her husband's creditors under terms of the new Married Women's Property Act, 1870. Analysing Riddell's novels *Austin*

Friars (1870) and *Mortomley's Estate* (1874) against the backgrounds respectively of the Married Women's Property Act, 1870—which accorded married women separate property rights—and the Bankruptcy Act, 1869—the provisions of which Riddell attacks—Colella examines the ways in which both novels place 'heroines in extreme situations that elicit the exercise of their entrepreneurial spirit.'

In '"[M]ute orations, mute rhapsodies, mute discussions,"' Fionnuala Dillane explores silence in novels from George Eliot's last decade: *Middlemarch* (1871–1872) and *Daniel Deronda* (1876) and also touches on her final work *Impressions of Theophrastus Such* (1879). Discussing Eliot's 'sustained experiments with an aesthetics of silence,' Dillane considers how the decision to publish *Middlemarch* and *Daniel Deronda* in parts relates to Eliot's ongoing 'preoccupations with the relationship between form and affect.' Readers' 'interpretative mechanisms' are scrambled, Dillane suggests, by both the silent gaps between part publication of the novels and the unspoken interactions of characters. This forces readers to 'question acts of interpretation,' both their own and those of Eliot's characters and narrators. As structural and narrative acts, purposeful silences are Eliot's response to a dominant cultural and scientific push towards visibility and explanation. Dillane also discusses the ways in which Eliot draws attention 'to the felt but un-worded, to the feeling of reading, and to that always entangled relationship between the emotional and intellectual life that was increasingly important to her in her final decade.' Dillane concludes that Eliot's fascination with silence relates to her sense of mortality and increasing sense of her lack of control over her own literary legacy.

Melissa Purdue's '"His eyes *commanded* me to come to him"' discusses female desire and mesmerism in Rhoda Broughton's short story 'The Man with the Nose' (1872), which was also included in her *Twilight Stories* (1879). Known for shocking depictions of female passion in her sensation novels, Broughton in this supernatural story revealed female sexuality in even more boundary-breaking ways and 'without providing easy answers.' Narrated by an unnamed husband, the story recounts his honeymoon away with his young wife Elizabeth, who believes that they are being followed by a man with a prominent nose. This man reminds her of a past encounter, in which she had been mesmerized, and she experiences nightmares in which she claims that the man makes her act against her will. Regarding her fears as childish, the husband leaves her temporarily alone while he travels home to cultivate a bequest. When he returns he is told that she has left with the 'Man with the Nose,' and she is never seen again. Purdue shows that using the short story form and the fantastic/supernatural Broughton gives voice to unspoken female desire by 'revealing Elizabeth's true feelings through dreams and mesmeric states' and 'by undercutting the validity of the husband-narrator's observations.'

'[E]mphatically un-literary and middle-class' by Alyson Hunt discusses the ways in which the first series of Ellen Wood's *Johnny Ludlow* stories (collected in 1874) 'undress' the period's middle-class anxieties about gender and class using the medium of clothing and fashion. Initially published in Wood's magazine *The Argosy*, these middle-brow stories marked by detailed domestic realism moved away from 1860s sensation techniques and made prominent use of sartorial discourses. Analysing stories including 'Losing Lena,' its sequel 'Finding Both of Them,' 'Bursting-Up,' and 'Sophie Chalk,' Hunt shows that using 'Johnny Ludlow' as pseudonym and narrator allowed Wood 'to experiment with the short-story genre independently of her reputation for writing novels.' Wood did not declare the stories to be hers until 1879, although suspicion had been strong that, despite their 'androcentric narrative voice,' they were female-authored. Hunt argues that as well as revealing much about middle-class views of dress, class, and gender, the 'Johnny Ludlow stories deserve greater critical attention for what they reveal about [their] "unliterary and middle-class" readership.'

Discussing '"Sinecures which could be held by girls,"' Danielle Charette examines issues surrounding women's domestic labour in *Phoebe Junior* (1876), the last novel in Margaret Oliphant's *Carlingford* series (1863–1876). Rather than recycling the ecclesiastical concerns expressed by Trollope in his Barsetshire novels (1855–1867), Oliphant introduces a feminist twist to her treatment of class conflict and Carlingford's corrupt college sinecure by highlighting the 'inverted sinecure' of women's household labour. The novel asks 'what would it mean for a sinecure to exist for girls?' In doing so, Charette shows, it 'explicitly associates the inherent unfairness of unearned state income with gender inequality.' Demonstrating that women can 'judiciously comment on ecclesiastical controversy,' Oliphant also 'holds the very definition of a sinecure up to gendered scrutiny.' By bringing this public controversy over church compensation into the 'domestic realm of a young woman's daydreams,' Oliphant depicts the 'all-consuming power of English financial debates' and insists that it is appropriate for young women to consider such issues. As Charette reveals, the topic of the sinecure 'opens up a conceptual space for theorizing about women and work' which in turn enables Oliphant's young women to discover they have been toiling under an inverted sinecure.

In '"More like a woman stuck into boy's clothes,"' Catherine Pope discusses 'transcendent femininity' in Florence Marryat's *Her Father's Name* (1876), a novel which appeared when lesbian characters were becoming more conspicuous in fiction and which 'is distinctive in presenting a deliberate and sympathetic portrayal of lesbian desire.' Challenging 'the implication that Victorian lesbians are accidental and anachronistic,' Pope shows that Marryat uses sensation tropes such as murder, forgery, and disguise as 'a vehicle for exploring radical ideas around female sexuality.' Both looking back to the sensation fiction of the 1860s and anticipating the progressive ideas of New Woman fiction, Marryat's novel centres on cross-dressing heroine Leona Lacoste who inspires lust in both sexes and finds herself attracted to other women. Leona's 'protean nature,' and the fact that she is 'not limited by a particular identity,' nor 'defined by her behaviour,' enables Marryat 'to explore radical ideas in what is—at least on the surface—a pantomimic text.' For Marryat, as Pope shows, 'lesbian desire was a form of transcendent femininity' which permitted women to 'overcome the limits of their gender' and was therefore 'an empowering act, rather than one that ought to be ignored or suppressed.'

Adrienne E. Gavin's '"I am writing the life of a horse"' discusses Anna Sewell's *Black Beauty* (1877) in the context of the 1870s. Gavin shows that in writing her only novel Sewell expressed the experiences and beliefs of her life, particularly regarding the duty to intervene actively and prevent cruelty of all forms whether to humans or animals. In producing a book that focused on working horses, she also broke literary gender expectations about the subjects upon which women authors should write. Sewell's focus on horses was, too, acutely topical in the 1870s given that Britain's demand for horsepower was at its height and various forms of cruelty were pervasive. Sewell also drew on the sensual techniques of the sensation fiction that prevailed in the 1860s, but 'to starkly realist and didactic ends,' in creating the powerful empathetic bond readers have with her equine protagonist. In doing so, Sewell wrote more than 'the life of a horse' in the sense of equine autobiography, she also powerfully reminded readers that horses *had* lives and were not machines; they were living beings worthy of kindness and care.

'Forging a New Path' by Janine Hatter explores fraud and white-collar crime in Mary Elizabeth Braddon's 1870s fiction. Focusing on her novels *Taken at the Flood* (1874) and *The Cloven Foot* (1879) and her short stories

'Mr and Mrs de Fontenoy' (1870) and 'Dr Carrick' (1878), Hatter shows that Braddon's 1870s fiction reflected contemporary fears of financial fraud by portraying non-violent financially motivated crimes including counterfeiting money, identity fraud, embezzlement, forged wills, and postnuptial fraud. It coincided, too, with Braddon's attempts to expand her reputation beyond her fame as 'the author of *Lady Audley's Secret*,' that is, as a writer of sensational murder and bigamy plots, and with her move into publishing her work through a northern publishing syndicate. Passage of the Married Women's Property Act 1870 at the same time as the rise of fraud and white-collar crime, Hatter shows, also increased women's awareness of and susceptibility to fraudulent activity, making it a topic of public and fictional interest which Braddon cultivated. Hatter also notes that Braddon's lower-class fraudsters receive legal punishment, while her middle-class white-collar criminals escape it.

Across the 1860s and 1870s women writers can be seen responding to, and sometimes instigating, new debates in which the 'separate spheres' of public and private life were increasingly difficult to determine. The 1860s sensation fiction was best known for its dramatic revelations and guilty secrets within the home itself. By positioning such disruptive events in a realist mode, authors made their sensational storylines increasingly difficult to cordon off as somehow separate from the everyday. By the 1870s new developments in mobility, technology, and the law were making the potential for widespread social change ever more visible. Female authors not only responded with expressions of desire and ambition but also contributed their own accounts of bankruptcy, animal cruelty, and marital breakdown, as the normalized conditions of a woman's life. As critics, they sometimes contributed to the gendering of authorship in precisely these contexts. The public availability of these novels to a wide range of readers, however, meant that the secret of women's knowledge was well and truly 'out.'

Note

1. Although written in 1855, her *Autobiography* was, at Martineau's direction, posthumously published in 1877.

WORKS CITED

Bilston, Sarah. 'Authentic Performance in Theatrical Women's Fiction of the 1870s.' *Women's Writing* 11:1 (2004): 39–54.

Jordan, Jane and Ingrid Sharp, ed. *Josephine Butler and the Prostitution Campaigns: Diseases of the Body Politic.* Vol 2. *The Ladies' Appeal and Protest.* Ed Jane Jordan. London: Routledge, 2003.

Kavanagh, Julia. *English Women of Letters: Biographical Sketches.* London: Hurst and Blackett, 1863.

Liggins, Emma. 'Her Mercenary Spirit: Women, Money and Marriage in Mary Elizabeth Braddon's 1870s Fiction.' *Women's Writing* 11.1 (1 March 2004): 73–88.

[Linton, Eliza Lynn]. 'The Girl of the Period.' *Saturday Review* 25 (14 March 1868): 339–40.

———. *Sowing the Wind.* 1867. Ed. Deborah T. Meem and Kate Holterhoff. Brighton: Victorian Secrets, 2015.

Manguel, Alberto. *A History of Reading.* London: Flamingo, 1997.

Palmer, Beth. *Women's Authorship and Editorship in Victorian Culture: Sensational Strategies.* Oxford: Oxford University Press, 2011.

'The Popular Novels of the Year.' *Fraser's Magazine* (Aug 1863): 253–69.

Peterson, Linda. *Becoming a Woman of Letters: Myths of Authorship and Facts of the Victorian Marketplace.* Princeton: University of Princeton Press, 2009.

Sewell, Anna. *Black Beauty.* 1877. Ed. Adrienne E. Gavin. Oxford World's Classics. Oxford: Oxford University Press, 2012.

Showalter, Elaine. *A Literature of Their Own: British Women Writers, From Charlotte Brontë to Doris Lessing.* 1978. Rev and expanded edition. London: Virago, 2009.

Southey, Robert. Letter to Charlotte Brontë. 12 March 1837. Romantics and Victorians Collection. British Library. https://www.bl.uk/collection-items/letter-from-robert-southey-to-charlotte-bronte-12-march-1837. Accessed 11 February 2019.

Wagner, Tamara S. '"Very Saleable Articles, Indeed": Margaret Oliphant's Repackaging of Sensational Finance.' *Modern Language Quarterly* 71:1 (March 2010): 51–74.

Watson, Kate. *Women Writing Crime Fiction, 1860–1880: Fourteen American, British and Australian Authors.* London: McFarland & Company, 2012.

[Woolf, Virginia.] 'George Eliot.' *Times Literary Supplement.* 20 November 1919, 657–658.

———. 'Three Guineas.' 1938. *A Room of One's Own and Three Guineas.* Ed. Anna Snaith. Oxford: Oxford University Press, 2015.

PART I

Women's Writing of the 1860s

Engraving of women wearing hooped skirts in the 1860s. (Image courtesy of Getty Images, duncan1890, 646877216)

CHAPTER 2

A Decade of Experiment: George Eliot in the 1860s

Margaret Harris

The 1860s was a decade of significant experiment by George Eliot. After the critical success of her first works of fiction, *Scenes of Clerical Life* (1858) and *Adam Bede* (1859), she published *The Mill on the Floss* (1860), another novel in a similar pastoral vein. Still pastoral, with a fairy-tale inflexion, *Silas Marner* (1861) followed. *Romola* (1863), a historical novel set in fifteenth-century Florence, was a deliberate shift in place and time before she returned to a nineteenth-century English provincial setting in *Felix Holt, the Radical* (1866). By the decade's end, Eliot was well embarked on the work that became her acknowledged masterpiece, *Middlemarch* (1872). In addition to these various novels, she ventured into poetry, including the verse drama *The Spanish Gypsy* (1868), and published a short story 'Brother Jacob' (1864), and a number of essays.

The decade was a period of testing and exploration for Eliot, most evidently of her own range as a writer, but also of the literary milieu within which she was operating, and of many of her personal concerns, whether

M. Harris (✉)
Department of English A20, The University of Sydney, Sydney, NSW, Australia
e-mail: margaret.harris@sydney.edu.au

© The Author(s) 2020
A. E. Gavin, C. W. de la L. Oulton (eds.), *British Women's Writing from Brontë to Bloomsbury, Volume 2,* British Women's Writing from Brontë to Bloomsbury, 1840–1940,
https://doi.org/10.1007/978-3-030-38528-6_2

familial or political. For half a century, critical orthodoxy was represented by Miriam Allott's 1961 essay, 'George Eliot in the 1860's,' which fleshed out opinions dating back to some of Eliot's contemporaries, including her husband and biographer John Cross, and reaffirmed by Lord David Cecil in the 1930s and F. R. Leavis in the 1940s. Thus, 'She was a woman of ponderous and impressive intellectual gifts who also possessed a highly nervous, at times even unstable, emotional temperament. Although without these qualities she would probably not have become an artist at all, each in its own way helps to weaken even her finest writing' (Allott 94).

Shifts in the rules of critical engagement have opened dimensions in Eliot's writing that illuminate the 1860s in quite other ways. Janice Carlisle points out that the 1860s is 'the decade that marks the height of high Victorian culture even as it saw profound transformations in commerce, politics, and technology,' proposing that it brought 'the fruition of developments begun in earlier decades (e.g., franchise reform) or provided the conditions for future developments (e.g., corporate capitalism)' (Carlisle 1, 15). While Eliot's most popular works remain *Adam Bede* and *The Mill on the Floss*, together with *Middlemarch*, it is now apparent that in the prolific years of the 1860s she was engaging with contemporary cultural transitions like those Carlisle points out in ways that profoundly inform her fiction. The sheer intellectual reach of her work sets it apart in its time and since, not least because it is of an order not normally allowed to women.

THE MILL ON THE FLOSS

Eliot's first novel of the 1860s consolidated the image established by the hugely successful *Adam Bede*, a story 'full of the breath of cows and the scent of hay' (Eliot to John Blackwood, 17 October 1857, *Letters* 2, 387). Alexander Welsh uses the term 'pastoral' of Eliot's early fictions, 'not because of the setting in itself, but because of the contrast between sophisticated and simple points of view that is built into the narrative' (133). This discrimination is highly relevant to *The Mill on the Floss*, her most evidently autobiographical novel, which like *Scenes of Clerical Life* and *Adam Bede* draws at once from memory and family experience, concurrently invoking 'sophisticated' perspectives.

The contemporary reviews of *The Mill on the Floss* laid down the lines to which discussion of the novel adhered well into the twentieth century. Mostly it is read as the story of Maggie Tulliver, centring on the fortunes of the heroine who from her precocious childhood learns and grows through the tribulations of her family, especially her father's financial ruin and death. Maggie, always at odds with the gender and class expectations current in the town of St. Ogg's in the early nineteenth century, exceeds her earlier transgressions by her escapade with Stephen Guest, son of a major business owner and favoured suitor of her cousin Lucy. Thanks to a flood that has threatened rhetorically from the beginning of the novel, she is reconciled in death with her brother Tom, who has worked doggedly to repay his father's creditors. Reviewers were generally dissatisfied with this rushed conclusion, though Dinah Mulock (author of *John Halifax, Gentleman* [1856]) in *Macmillan's Magazine* admired the writing in the final volume while swelling the chorus of those expressing their indignation about the novel's perceived immorality (in Carroll 154–6).

Rather than opinions on particular aspects of the novel, however, the most striking feature of the reviews collectively is the status accorded to the author. '"George Eliot" is as great as ever,' declared E. S. Dallas in *The Times* (in Carroll 131). The *Dublin University Magazine* review was hostile but nevertheless made a serious attempt to accommodate Eliot (identified as female) in emergent traditions of the novel, employing a wide range of comparisons with (mainly male) writers, among them Oliver Goldsmith, Henry Fielding, Maria Edgeworth, Jane Austen, William Thackeray, and Charles Dickens (in Carroll 145–53).

The *Saturday Review*, maintaining that *Adam Bede* had been thought too good for a woman, judged Eliot to be 'in the first rank of our female novelists' with 'Miss Austen' (for 'minuteness of painting and a certain archness of style') and 'Currer Bell' (for 'strong and wayward feelings') (in Carroll 114). Eliot opens up new territory for the novel, the review claimed: 'the family life of the English farmer, and the class to which he belongs' (115). The reviewer's comment that the plot traces the lack of spirituality in the Tullivers and Dodsons and the ways this affects 'a lively, imaginative, impulsive girl' (117) is fair but limited. Not so the subsequent censorious decree that neither spiritual torment nor sexual passion is really a suitable topic for fiction, so that '[t]he third volume seems to belong to quite a new story' (119).

The diverse strands of *The Mill on the Floss* are indicated in titles Eliot considered then rejected: *Sister Maggie* (emphasizing the relationship of Maggie with her brother Tom), *St. Ogg's on the Floss* (focusing on the community and its environment), *The House of Tulliver, or Life on the Floss* (combining the sense of human dynasty with an anthropological perspective). Curiously, the impropriety that was such a cause of offence in 1860 became almost a cause for celebration a century later, when the novel became the go-to text for feminist critics of the 1970s and 1980s who in their respective ways argued for the flood as a symbol of irresistible psychological and sociological forces that deny a future to Maggie. It was not until the material turn of the 1990s that Jules Law made the case for reading legal matters, especially litigation over water rights, as central to interpretation of the novel. His analysis of how the novel develops issues of steam power, agricultural technology, and water rights augments previous discussions of the tension in St. Ogg's between the rural community and the values of the emerging mercantile class represented by Uncle Deane. More recently, Dermot Coleman has historicized the financial processes and assumptions at work around the ethical considerations of personal honour in respect of debt that rack the Tullivers, reflecting the mid-nineteenth-century move to a credit economy (Coleman 37–40). Such insights condition the 'sophisticated' perspectives noted by Welsh.

George Eliot in the Literary Marketplace

At the beginning of the 1860s, the secret of the identity of the author of *Scenes of Clerical Life* and *Adam Bede* was known in London literary circles. Adoption of the pseudonym 'George Eliot' had been due to more than female modesty, for Marian Evans had been living with the married critic and journalist George Henry Lewes since 1854. In the course of 1859, an ugly situation developed when Joseph Liggins, the son of a baker in the vicinity of Nuneaton, claimed authorship of *Adam Bede*. The ensuing controversy occasioned the revelation, initially to close friends, that Marian Lewes, as she demanded to be addressed, was 'George Eliot' (see Bodenheimer Chap. 5).

This secret in George Eliot's life is paralleled by the secrets that constitute plot hinges in much of her fiction. Entering the 1860s, Eliot had already established a nexus of recurrent concerns in her work, many of them involving secrecy in some way and frequently having sexual dimensions, whether potential or realized: so Maggie Tulliver conducts her friendship with the crippled Philip Wakem in secret, Godfrey Cass conceals his marriage to the addicted mother of his unacknowledged child in *Silas Marner*, and both Tito Melema's affair with Tessa in *Romola* and that of Arabella Transome and Matthew Jermyn in *Felix Holt* are hidden at least initially. Particular patterns of family relationships recur, featuring absent mothers, foster parents, and fraternal bonds, always involving questions about how individual lives determine and are determined by broader social contexts.

It must be borne in mind that Eliot came to writing fiction already familiar with the literary marketplace. The achievements of her unpaid and unsung editorship of the *Westminster Review* from 1851 to 1854 have been compellingly demonstrated by Fionnuala Dillane. They range from the polemic of the prospectus for the relaunched journal to reorganization and redesign of the content. After her active involvement in the management of the *Westminster Review* ended, Eliot continued her association by writing for the journal. She produced eight long articles, including 'Silly Novels by Lady Novelists' (1856)—which praises Harriet Martineau, Charlotte Brontë, and Elizabeth Gaskell, interestingly the authors most frequently invoked in reviewers' comparisons with Eliot herself. 'Silly Novels' is an assured and still amusing exercise that pillories the excesses of 'the frothy, the prosy, the pious, or the pedantic' fiction of contemporary lady novelists ('Silly Novels' 301). Both this essay and 'The Natural History of German Life' (1856) are frequently quoted to demonstrate that the opinions of Eliot as reviewer were enacted when she began to write fiction, privileging realism marked by 'truthful delineation of manners' and 'philosophic breadth' ('Silly Novels' 301). Dicta like 'Art is the nearest thing to life; it is a mode of amplifying experience and extending our contact with our fellow-men beyond the bounds of our personal lot' ('Natural History' 271) are paralleled in the novels in passages such as *The Mill on the Floss*, Book 4, Chap. 1, with its Wordsworthian—and Darwinian—reflections on the life of the common people.

Eliot's attitudes to particular women writers, and theirs to her, were mixed in the 1860s; for the most part the resentment apparent in the memoirs of Eliza Lynn Linton and Margaret Oliphant did not find expression until later (Showalter 107–8). Essentially she stood apart from other women writers: of those with whom she was compared, all the Brontës were dead by 1856, Martineau was writing mostly political economy, and Gaskell died in 1865.

Eliot had significant exposure to popular fiction while writing 'Belles Lettres' for the *Westminster Review* and was well aware of a wide spectrum of contemporary publication. She and Lewes read women novelists along with much else, including sensation fiction when it came to the forefront of the literary scene in the early 1860s. She did not aspire to the popular success of the sensation novelists, although writing to her publisher John

Blackwood about the slow sales of *Felix Holt*, she lamented that her books 'are not so attractive to the majority as "The Trail of the Serpent"' (Mary Elizabeth Braddon's first novel, *The Trail of the Serpent; or, the Secret of the Heath* [1861]) (11 September 1866, *Letters* 4, 309–10). The fashion for sensation fiction, epitomized by Braddon's *Lady Audley's Secret* (1862), was at its height in 1862–1863. It operated in a register of violated domesticity, reworking the female Gothic of the late-eighteenth and early-nineteenth centuries, and running counter to the domestic realism that was a norm of mid-Victorian fiction.

Nicholas Daly stresses the psychological aspect of sensation fiction's effect on readers. He sees 'sensation as the cultural dominant of the 1860s,' applying beyond fiction and appealing to the crowd, 'providing a series of shocks and frissons rather than any more elevating aesthetic experience' (4). The moral complexity of Eliot's novels clearly distinguishes them from the stereotype of the sensation novel: plot-driven 'fast' or 'newspaper' novels depending on bigamy, adultery, murder, blackmail, and forged wills (see Pykett, 'Sensation and New Woman Fiction'). Yet she uses some tropes generally attributed to the popular form: consider female anger in Maggie, or the melodrama surrounding Tito's various betrayals in *Romola*. Or, most striking of all, Arabella Transome in *Felix Holt*: the portrayal of this ageing woman's realization that the power that once she wielded in estate management is now lost is an extraordinary psychological study. Further, guilt about her adultery and pride in her family line contribute to the novel's intricate depiction of shifts in social structures in the era of parliamentary reform. The achievement of classic sensation novels like *Lady Audley's Secret* or Ellen Wood's *East Lynne* (1861) in challenging social norms, especially sexual ones, is not strictly comparable with Eliot's searching analysis of mid-nineteenth-century mores.

'Brother Jacob'

Following *The Mill on the Floss*, Eliot's work took a new turn, as she entertained various possibilities for what to do next. The journey to Italy on which she and Lewes embarked in March 1860 as *The Mill on the Floss* came out marked a watershed in several important ways. Her reputation was well established, and the concomitant material rewards enjoyed. They moved to central London, largely for the sake of Lewes's eldest son who had returned from school in Switzerland with them. There is reason to see Eliot's heightened concern in her fiction from this point with the respective responsibilities of children and parents as deriving from her personal situation. The relocation gave Eliot easier access to friends and cultural activities like attendance at theatre and concerts, although she was still cautious about going into society on account of her irregular marital status.

The first work she completed after *The Mill on the Floss* was the short story 'Brother Jacob,' written in the summer of 1860 although not published until July 1864, anonymously, in the *Cornhill Magazine* as a gift to George Smith to compensate for the relative failure of *Romola*. The idea of *Romola*, a novel set in the time of Girolamo Savonarola, had been mooted by Lewes during the 1860 Italian journey, but it was not begun in earnest until New Year's Day 1862. Where *Romola* has been accorded much attention, being both praised and pilloried, 'Brother Jacob' is relatively neglected. Indeed it was not acknowledged as Eliot's until the Cabinet edition in 1878, when, together with her other short fiction the gothic 'The Lifted Veil' (1859), it was packaged in one volume with *Silas Marner*. In both stories, Eliot experiments with narrative modes different from her accustomed realism. 'Brother Jacob' warrants attention precisely because it was written as she regrouped after her initial successes and considered ways in which she might branch out: it is by no means 'a wayward moment in the writer's career' (Fleishman 107). Eliot's insistence that her writings 'belong to successive mental phases' is pertinent. (To John Blackwood, 24 February 1861, *Letters* 3, 383)

The plot of 'Brother Jacob' centres on David Faux and his 'idiot' brother Jacob, who sees David stealing twenty guineas from his mother to fund his migration to America to seek his fortune. Jacob has no sense of monetary value, and David distracts him with yellow sweets in exchange for the gold coins. After a period in the West Indies, David Faux (false, fox) returns as Edward Freely, purporting to be the nephew of a Jamaican plantation owner, and becomes a successful confectioner. He turns sugar into elaborate creations, making large profits, and persuading Grimworth matrons to buy his confections rather than to bake themselves. Ultimately he is recognized by Jacob and disgraced.

Literary allusions proliferate in this satiric story, particularly to La Fontaine's animal fables as Eliot cleverly connects the equation of animal and human in fable with Lewes's studies of animal and human psychology. Sally Shuttleworth points out that 'Jacob, in the language of nineteenth-century evolutionary theory, is a throwback, or survival, an exemplum of a more primitive mindset' (xxxviii). But David is no more capable of learning or changing than his brother. His interpretation of the story of Inkle and Yarico, which goes back to Richard Steele's 1711 *Spectator* essay, grotesquely manifests colonial exploitation. His Grimworth business takes over labour previously performed by women in their homes, presenting a debased version of Jeremy Bentham's principle of utility and critiquing models of social progress based on individual self-interest. Eliot is working through implications of her ideas about the emerging capitalist economy broached in *The Mill on the Floss*, and deploying motifs that she reworks in *Silas Marner*.

Silas Marner: The Weaver of Raveloe

Eliot's next publication was the short novel *Silas Marner*, 'which came *across* my other plans by a sudden inspiration' (To John Blackwood, 12 January 1861, *Letters* 3, 371). Blackwood found the early sections 'sombre' and Eliot wrote reassuringly that rather than being a 'sad story ... it sets ... in a strong light the remedial influences of pure, natural human relations,' claiming that she conceived it 'as a sort of legendary tale, suggested by my recollection of having once, in early childhood, seen a linen-weaver with a bag on his back' (24 February 1861, *Letters* 3, 382). The story is a moral fable, drawing on elements of medieval romance (for instance, in the perceived transmutation of Silas's gold into the hair of a living child). The provincial setting in the late eighteenth century would have been familiar to Eliot's first readers, the impact of changes over the years intervening down to publication indicated without the historical specificity of *The Mill on the Floss*.

Silas Marner, an outcast from Lantern Yard—a Dissenting congregation in an industrial town—is a settler in the village of Raveloe. He has been falsely accused of the theft of church funds by his closest friend, the real thief. After years as a recluse in the village, his earnings are stolen by Dunstan Cass, the dissolute second son of Squire Cass. Providentially, the unacknowledged wife of Godfrey Cass, the elder son, dies in the snow outside Silas's cottage. Her two-year-old child finds her way in to the warm hearth where Silas is in a cataleptic trance as he had been during the theft in Lantern Yard. He insists on keeping the child, seeing her golden curls as a replacement for his lost gold, and is gradually drawn into the life of Raveloe with the help particularly of kind Dolly Winthrop, the wheelwright's wife. The culmination of this Wordsworthian integration into the community through love of the child comes after sixteen years, when

Dunstan's body and the gold are discovered, and Godfrey admits his paternity. Eppie resists the invitation of Godfrey and his wife to take her place as his daughter and live with them. Rather, she stays with Silas and marries Aaron Winthrop, all three living together in Silas's cottage surrounded by the Edenic garden Aaron has made. The dynamics of the rural community, in such scenes in those in the Rainbow Tavern and the New Year party at the Red House, are contrasted with the narrowness of the Dissenting community of Lantern Yard which Silas cannot find when he revisits the manufacturing town (it has been replaced by a factory).

Further to Eliot's experiment with genre in *Silas Marner*, she extends the conversation among her works. Like 'Brother Jacob,' the novel is concerned with the desire to escape a past life, and with the operations of memory. Fetishization of gold is once again central, as are the parallels between brothers. Eppie's rejection of social standing when her parentage is known prefigures Esther Lyon's decision in *Felix Holt*, where discovery of parentage is crucial also to Harold Transome. The reconstituted household over which Romola presides is another version of the ending of *Silas Marner*. Silas as good father contrasts with careless Squire Cass, and there is a critical element in the depiction of the Cass's failures in paternalism that echoes earlier works and prefigures both *Romola* and *Felix Holt*.

Romola

Romola is in important respects Eliot's most experimental work. Her decision to write a historical novel was itself significant, both as a move from her home ground and as an engagement with the genre of Victorian historical fiction. Eliot's debt to Sir Walter Scott, recognized as the progenitor of the genre, is well established, their affinity residing in demonstration of ways that characters are shaped by both natural and social environments. Like Scott, Eliot reflects on historical processes as she depicts historical personages along with imagined characters. No contemporary novelist, male or female, approached Eliot's obsessive immersion in the period she chose to write about, although there were other women writers like Elizabeth and Agnes Strickland (authors of *The Lives of the Queens of England* [1840–1848] and in Agnes's case several historical novels) who had some standing as historians.

Eliot's decision to set her novel in Florence in the late fifteenth century was variously motivated. At the most basic level, she saw scope for more ambitious exploration of her recurring theme of the individual in relation to community. Italian unification was topical in 1860, the year also of publication of Jacob Burckhardt's *The Civilization of the Renaissance in Italy*. The notion of rebirth involved Enlightenment identification of 'its own favoured predecessor, and signified the overthrow of the medieval, Christian order' (Hamnett 192, and 191–202 passim). Eliot counterpoises secular and spiritual, seizing on Fra Girolamo Savonarola to epitomize the excesses of medieval religion, and to anchor the plot in the history of Florence from 1492 and the death of Lorenzo de' Medici, through conflicts among Florentine political parties, to the submission of Florence to Charles VIII of France. Her imagined character, Tito Melema, is the new man, amoral and self-seeking, while the titular heroine embodies the altruistic possibilities of secular humanism.

In addition to its setting, *Romola* was innovatory in the arrangements made for its publication as a monthly serial in the *Cornhill Magazine*. Although *Scenes of Clerical Life* had come out initially in instalments, serialization of a full-scale novel was new to Eliot as she turned away from her first publisher, Blackwood, and yielded to 'the most magnificent offer ever yet made for a novel' by the entrepreneurial George Smith of Smith, Elder & Co. (George Henry Lewes Journal, 27 February 1862, *Letters* 4, 17–18). Blackwood's chagrin was explicable, having already borne with much of Eliot's painful process of composition, frequent bouts of ill health, and accompanying crises of confidence—though his courteous restraint was rewarded when she returned to his firm with *Felix Holt* and remained loyal to the end of her career.

Negotiations over *Romola* concluded by her accepting £7000 for twelve (ultimately fourteen) episodes of thirty-two pages, with exclusive rights for six years—less than the original offer of £10,000 including the entire copyright, but still momentous. The novel appeared monthly in the *Cornhill* from July 1862 to August 1863, with twenty-four illustrations by Frederic Leighton, and in three volumes from Smith, Elder in July 1863. Her payment for *Romola* was roughly twice what she had then earned from *The Mill on the Floss*, and compared very favourably with the £1000 Trollope received for the *Cornhill*'s rights to serialization of *Framley Parsonage* (1861). The terms on which *Romola* was published are significant not only because they underline Eliot's established eminence but because of what is revealed about her attitude to her work in the marketplace. There was a tension between her awareness of market forces and concern for her publishers: she consistently preferred to incur risk by retaining copyright rather than opting for a higher royalty (Coleman 65–8).

Eliot directed assiduous study to the physical and intellectual setting of *Romola*, visiting Florence in 1860 and 1861. Very few details do not evidently derive from her extensive preparatory reading, at times closely following or quoting her source (Brown xxv). She found serial publication demanding, having difficulty in producing copy in a timely manner. Her formal experiments have been discussed by Linda K. Hughes and Michael Lund in a detailed study of the serial version of *Romola* in comparison to other serials (specifically of historical novels). They demonstrate the novelty of Eliot's method: for example, in general, time does not pass between but within numbers as she made each instalment a discrete unit of plot, advancing 'all matters of the plot through a complete phase of action,' rather than ending with a cliff-hanger (Hughes and Lund 80–81). The experience shaped her later innovation of publishing *Middlemarch* and *Daniel Deronda* (1876) in half-volume parts, a more congenial scale that afforded definite material advantages.

Eliot intensifies her experiment with fable in *Silas Marner* in the episode where Romola flees the city and is seen as a Madonna figure in the plague-stricken village, an image reinforced by Frederic Leighton's illustration. The experience of liaising with an illustrator was new to her. In correspondence with Leighton she discussed both subjects for illustration, and his execution, as she came to appreciate their complementary roles.

The range of allusion in *Romola* is extraordinary, drawing for instance on classical mythology, Dante, and Christian imagery. Its extent is underlined by recent work which brings out in sharp detail previously unremarked aspects of the political situation in the novel, including gender politics (see Henry, 'The *Romola* Code'). Once again the narrative develops intricate parallels, for instance, in Tito's behaviour to his two 'wives,' Tessa and Romola, and to his two 'fathers,' Baldassarre Calvo and Bardo de' Bardi. For all the vividness of Tito's characterization, Romola is unquestionably central to the structure of the novel in her struggle to fulfil what she sees as her duty to her father, her uncle Bernardo de Nero, her brother Dino—a disciple of Savonarola, who is for a time her mentor—and her husband Tito.

Anthony Trollope wrote admiringly to Eliot in July 1862 after reading the first number, singling out for praise the descriptions ('little bits of Florence down to a door nail') and the characterization of Romola herself ('the perfection of pen painting;—and you have been nobly aided by your artist'). But he goes on to strike a note of caution: 'Do not fire too much over the heads of your readers. You have to write to tens of thousands, and not to single thousands' (28 June 1862, *Letters* 8, 303–4). Trollope's reaction foreshadowed subsequent opinions: although overburdened by Eliot's erudition, the ambition of *Romola* compels admiration.

For all that *Romola* is an intimidating novel, it is reassuring to be reminded of Eliot's capacity for levity: nearing the end, she exulted 'Finished Part XIII. Killed Tito in great excitement!' (16 May 1863, *Journals* 117). Her humour is in evidence also in 'Brother Jacob' and the four light-hearted essays using a female persona (Saccharissa) for George Smith's *Pall Mall Gazette* in 1865. These, and her other essay-length productions of the decade, were all written to oblige publishers: she wrote two essays in 1865 for the new *Fortnightly Review*, signed in accordance with policy, at the behest of Lewes as editor; and subsequently at Blackwood's urging she produced a conservative manifesto, 'Address to Working Men, by Felix Holt,' for *Blackwood's Edinburgh Magazine* (1868) (Dillane 238).

FELIX HOLT, THE *RADICAL*

Felix Holt of all Eliot's novels most closely responds to the political atmosphere of the time of writing. Published just before the passage of the 1867 Reform Bill, it is set around the time of the 1832 Reform Bill in the town of Treby Magna, loosely based on the Nuneaton of Eliot's early years. Treby is in transition from agrarian to industrial society. Eliot's memories were supplemented by considerable research, which this time did not retard her writing: the novel was completed in a little over a year from early 1865. Her return to familiar territory was far from a regression. There is a closer focus on the doings of the town than in *The Mill on the Floss*, ranging across a wider social spectrum, so that *Felix Holt* is often taken to be a sketch for the larger canvas of *Middlemarch*. While this is certainly the case, *Felix Holt* has distinctive strengths. An epigrammatic utterance of the narrator distils the theme—'there is no private life which has not been determined by a wider public life' (*Felix Holt* 45)—a proposition interrogated in detail through the novel, turning often on tensions between will and destiny, and generating an unusual number of plot coincidences. While the mismatch between the double plot of the story of the titular hero in his political candidature, and the inheritance story revolving around the Transomes and Esther Lyon, remains a difficulty, the impact of Eliot's paradoxical radicalism is powerful.

Felix Holt has frequently been read as a 'Condition of England' industrial novel, with an emphasis on Eliot's essentially conservative position as presented through the arrogant radicalism of the titular hero. Coleman argues persuasively for the novel as deriving from Eliot's awareness of debates about political economy and Utilitarianism in the mid-1860s, maintaining that 'the novel is all about money,' and tracing numerous instances in which Eliot's language is that of economic self-interest (80).

The action centres on the return to Treby of two sons: Harold Transome, rich from trading in the East and now the heir to the impoverished Transome estates, and Felix Holt, ostentatiously turning his back on financial security with his plan to make a living as a watchmaker while endeavouring to educate the working people. A reviewer's description of him as 'a grand *stump* of a character in an impressive but fixed attitude' is apt (in Carroll 258). Both men stand as Radicals in an election, to the consternation particularly of the Tory Transomes and Lingons. The parallels between them intensify when both become suitors to Esther Lyon, foster daughter of the Dissenting preacher Rufus Lyon, and as it turns out, the rightful heir to the Transome estates. She is pivotal to the extremely complicated legal plot, for which Eliot had much advice from the barrister Frederic Harrison. In addition, her testimony secures Felix a reduced sentence when he is tried for murder following a riot during the election in which a constable is killed, but not by him.

The women characters animate the novel, Esther in her emergence from absorption in fashionable things to moral stature, and Arabella Transome in her suffering at the hands of her former lover, the lawyer Matthew Jermyn, who is revealed to be Harold's father. Arguably Mrs Transome is the most radical person in the novel, her poignant story well outstripping the titillation of sensation fiction and carrying much of the weight of the novel's exposure of the complacency of the ruling classes. Harold has inherited Jermyn's energy and brashness and, despite the obscurity of his relationship with the mother of his son, is more honourable. Jermyn like Tito is an incomer, a new man bent on casting aside old ways without respect for the established values represented by the Transome estates. He exemplifies the social mobility that is one of the particular concerns of this novel, along with the physical mobility dramatized by the coach journey of the famous 'Introduction' that lays out the destabilization of established forms of social organization along with the reconfiguration of the landscape that accompanies the spread of industry. This set piece introduction alludes to classical Greek tragedy and to Dante, resonances developed as the action unfolds, often in the chapter epigraphs—a formal innovation continued by Eliot in later works that contributes to the establishment of multiple perspectives in the narrative.

In the latter part of the 1860s Eliot's attention shifted to poetry, taking on issues of race, heredity, duty, and destiny in *The Spanish Gypsy*. Her self-imposed tasks for 1869 included 'A Novel called Middlemarch' (1 January 1869, *Journals* 134). By 2 December 1870, it was taking shape: 'I am experimenting in a story, which I began without any very serious intention of carrying it out lengthily. It is a subject which has been recorded among my possible themes ever since I began to write fiction, but will probably take new shapes in the development' (*Journals* 141). Her experimentation of the 1860s continued into her crowning works of the 1870s. The formative achievements of the 1860s show her to be a writer of many moods and voices, deeply engaged with both intellectual culture and the practicalities of the literary world, relentlessly dedicated to analysis of the social fabric of Britain and to the moral possibilities of her art.

WORKS CITED

Allott, Miriam. 'George Eliot in the 1860's.' *Victorian Studies* 5 (1961): 93–108.
Bodenheimer, Rosemarie. *The Real Life of Mary Ann Evans: George Eliot, Her Letters and Fiction*. Ithaca and London: Cornell University Press, 1994.
Brown, Andrew. Introduction. *Romola*. By George Eliot. 1863. Clarendon Edition. Oxford: Oxford University Press, 1993. xi–lxxii.
Carlisle, Janice. 'The Scent of Class: British Novels of the 1860s.' *Victorian Literature and Culture* 29.1 (2001), 1–19.
Carroll, David. *George Eliot: The Critical Heritage*. London: Routledge and Kegan Paul, 1971.
Coleman, Dermot. *George Eliot and Money: Economics, Ethics and Literature*. Cambridge: Cambridge University Press, 2014.
Daly, Nicholas. *Sensation and Modernity in the 1860s*. Cambridge: Cambridge University Press, 2013.
Dillane, Fionnuala. *Before George Eliot: Marian Evans and the Periodical Press*. Cambridge: Cambridge University Press, 2013.
Eliot, George. *Essays of George Eliot*. Ed. Thomas Pinney. London: Routledge and Kegan Paul, 1963.
———. *Felix Holt, the Radical*. 1866. Clarendon Edition. Ed. Fred C. Thomson. Oxford: Oxford University Press, 1980.
———. *The George Eliot Letters*. Ed. Gordon S. Haight. 9 vols. New Haven CT: Yale University Press, 1954–1978.

———. *The Journals of George Eliot*. Ed. Margaret Harris and Judith Johnston. Cambridge: Cambridge University Press, 1998.

———. *The Lifted Veil and Brother Jacob*. 1859, 1864. Penguin Classics. Ed. Sally Shuttleworth. Penguin: London, 2000.

———. *The Mill on the Floss*. 1860. Oxford World's Classics. Ed. Gordon S. Haight, with Introduction and Notes by Juliette Atkinson. Oxford: Oxford University Press, 2015.

———. 'The Natural History of German Life.' 1856a. *Essays of George Eliot*. Ed. Thomas Pinney. London: Routledge and Kegan Paul, 1963. 266–99.

———. *Romola*. 1863. Clarendon Edition. Ed. Andrew Brown. Oxford: Oxford University Press, 1993.

———. *Silas Marner: The Weaver of Raveloe*. 1861. Oxford World's Classics. Ed. Juliette Atkinson. Oxford: Oxford University Press, 2017.

———. 'Silly Novels by Lady Novelists.' 1856b. *Essays of George Eliot*. Ed. Thomas Pinney. London: Routledge and Kegan Paul, 1963. 300–24.

Fleishman, Avrom. *George Eliot's Intellectual Life*. Cambridge: Cambridge University Press, 2010.

Hamnett, Brian. *The Historical Novel in Nineteenth-Century Europe: Representations of Reality in History and Fiction*. Oxford: Oxford University Press, 2011.

Henry, Nancy. *The Life of George Eliot: A Critical Biography*. Chichester: Wiley-Blackwell, 2012.

———. 'The *Romola* Code: "Men of Appetites" in George Eliot's Historical Novel.' *Victorian Literature and Culture* 39 (2011): 327–48.

Hughes, Linda K. and Michael Lund. *The Victorian Serial*. Charlottesville and London: University Press of Virginia, 1991.

Law, Jules. 'Water Rights and the "crossing o' breeds": Chiastic Exchange in *The Mill on the Floss*.' In *Rewriting the Victorians: Theory, History, and the Politics of Gender*. Ed. Linda M. Shires. London: Routledge, 1992. 52–69.

Peterson, Linda H., ed. *The Cambridge Companion to Victorian Women's Writing*. Cambridge: Cambridge University Press, 2015.

Pykett, Lyn. 'Sensation and New Woman Fiction.' In *The Cambridge Companion to Victorian Women's Writing*. Ed. Linda H. Peterson. Cambridge: Cambridge University Press, 2015. 133–44.

Showalter, Elaine. *A Literature of Their Own: British Women Novelists from Brontë to Lessing*. Princeton, N.J.: Princeton University Press, 1977.

Shuttleworth, Sally. Introduction. *The Lifted Veil and Brother Jacob*. 1859, 1864. Penguin Classics. Penguin: London, 2000. xi–l.

Welsh, Alexander. *George Eliot and Blackmail*. Cambridge MA and London: Harvard University Press, 1985.

CHAPTER 3

'Duck him!': Private Feelings, Public Interests, and Ellen Wood's *East Lynne*

Tara MacDonald

Ellen Wood's sensation novel *East Lynne* (1861) has been discussed by many critics in terms of its emotional effects on readers and the related suffering of its (anti-)heroine Isabel Carlyle. In an influential reading of the novel, Ann Cvetkovich emphasizes Isabel's excessive suffering and questions the social function of the 'maternal melodrama' that structures the end of the novel. She argues that *East Lynne* 'transforms a narrative of female transgression into a lavish story about female suffering, a suffering that seems to exceed any moral or didactic requirement that the heroine be punished for her sins' (99). While the maternal melodrama of the novel's third volume does seem to overwhelm the narrative, Wood's engagement with the cultural politics of emotion extends beyond the private suffering of its main character. Part of the drama of the final volume focuses not on the suffering Isabel but on her disgraced lover, Sir Francis Levison. Levison makes the ill-advised decision to return to the town of West Lynne and stand for parliament. He is hesitant to do so initially,

T. MacDonald (✉)
University of Idaho, Moscow, ID, USA
e-mail: tmacdonald@unidaho.edu

© The Author(s) 2020
A. E. Gavin, C. W. de la L. Oulton (eds.), *British Women's Writing from Brontë to Bloomsbury, Volume 2*, British Women's Writing from Brontë to Bloomsbury, 1840–1940,
https://doi.org/10.1007/978-3-030-38528-6_3

anticipating that he will still be shunned by the townspeople for his past behaviour, namely his running away with the wife of the well-respected Archibald Carlyle, who also happens to be his political opponent. Yet Levison's party whip, Mr Meredith, insists, '"Private feelings must give way to public interests"' (*East Lynne* 455). However, private feelings in the town are *not* separable from public interests. Rather than calmly receive Levison, an angry mob descends on him and humiliates him by ducking him in a local pond. How does this scene of 'group feeling' relate to the excessive feeling exhibited by Isabel and possibly the text's readers themselves?

The central claim of this chapter is that *East Lynne*, through its treatment of both emotional women and a rowdy mob, explores differing ways of *feeling along with* others or, put simply, empathy. While sympathy means the process of feeling *for* someone, empathy is an arguably more intense and possibly physiological reaction. In *Empathy and the Novel* (2007), Suzanne Keen defines empathy as 'a vicarious, spontaneous sharing of affect, [which] can be provoked by witnessing another's emotional state, by hearing about another's condition, or even by reading' (4). Empathy thus disrupts the very notion that private feelings can be detached from 'public interests' or from the feelings of others. Keen distinguishes between empathy and sympathy in this way:

Empathy:
I feel what you feel.

I feel your pain.

Sympathy:
I feel a supportive emotion about your feelings.

I feel pity for your pain. (5)

While the term empathy did not exist in the English language until 1909, this kind of collective feeling certainly existed in the Victorian period. As explained below, the ability to feel what you perceive others to be feeling was clearly of great interest to Wood and other female sensation writers of the 1860s.

Historically, terms like sympathy and fellow feeling had the same meaning as our contemporary understanding of empathy. Keen points out that eighteenth-century philosophers like David Hume and Adam Smith frequently used sympathy to mean taking on the pain or happiness of others, often through physical mimicry. This usage continued into the nineteenth century in the writing of Alexander Bain, Charles Darwin, and others. In *The Emotions and the Will* (1859), for instance, Bain explains that 'Sympathy and Imitation both mean the tendency of one individual to fall in with the emotional or active states of others' (172). The first step to reaching sympathy with another human being is the 'tendency to *assume a bodily state, attitude, or movement, that we see enacted by another person*' (italics in original; 174). In *East Lynne* Archibald Carlyle articulates what we now call empathy when he witnesses Isabel mourning her father and states, "'I feel for you all that you are feeling'" (87). While his response is compassionate, feeling what others (fictional or otherwise) are feeling is not always positive. Empathy can result in a shared understanding of human pain and suffering, but it can also involve the sensation of feeling another's anger or frustration. In this context, empathy, a 'spontaneous sharing of affect,' could even lead to mass hysteria, which is arguably the case with Levison's ducking.

The sensation novel is of special concern here as its potential to spread affects was a topical issue in the 1860s. As the name implied, the novels were thought to encourage physical sensations in the bodies of susceptible readers. For instance, Margaret Oliphant, reviewing Wilkie Collins' *The Woman in White* (1859–1860), claims that her 'nerves are affected' like those of the characters (572). As Janice Allan explains, this embodied aspect of the novels was a cause for alarm: 'Unlike "legitimate" art that attempts to elevate or ennoble through, for example, instruction or appeals to the sympathetic faculties, the sensational was condemned because it aimed only to shock and excite to produce a literal sensation upon the body' (87). Such excitement was particularly suspect when it came to women writers, who were of course held to a different standard; novelists like Mary Elizabeth Braddon, Rhoda Broughton, and Wood were often charged with promoting inappropriate feelings in their supposedly naïve, female readers through their depictions of reckless women. More to the point regarding *East Lynne* is that one of the notorious concerns related to this novel was the manner in which Wood's narrator bestowed pity on her flawed female character and encouraged readers to feel empathy for her, anticipating that they, for example, might cry along with Isabel. Oliphant's review highlights the dangers of Wood's approach:

> We have just laid down a clever novel, called 'East Lynne,' which some inscrutable breath of popular liking has blown into momentary celebrity. It is occupied with the story of a woman who permitted herself, in passion and folly, to be seduced from her husband. From first to last it is she alone in whom the reader feels any interest. Her virtuous rival we should like to bundle to the door and be rid of, anyhow. The Magdalen herself, who is only moderately interesting while she is good, becomes, as soon as

she is a Magdalen, doubly a heroine. It is evident that nohow, except by her wickedness and sufferings, could she have gained so strong a hold upon our sympathies. This is dangerous and foolish work, as well as false, both to Art and Nature. (567)

Oliphant's insistence that the novel is false to 'Nature' can be countered by Keen's observation that our empathetic responses to fictional characters are provoked more easily by negative feelings such as suffering, rather than by positive feelings of joy or pleasure (72). Keen further notes: 'Occasionally a [Victorian] writer earns a rebuke for inviting sympathy for a character judged unworthy by a reviewer' (53). *East Lynne* is such a case: one in which a reader like Oliphant could experience a confusing mix of moral critique with positive readerly emotion. That is, she recognizes Isabel's 'wickedness' but nonetheless feels with her, empathy working to flatten the distance between reader and character or between private and public feeling.

This chapter takes up these concerns about the limits of private and public feeling in the novel by discussing two differing representations of empathy as they relate to gender: (1) empathy as a positive outcome of 'womanly' feeling and (2) empathy as an unthinking, working-class, 'manly,' and group response. The first shows how women's supposed ability to feel empathy more easily than men makes them compassionate, caring individuals in the world of Wood's novel, while the latter shows how empathy transformed into masculine group anger results in the scapegoating of the adulterous Levison. While these two responses differ dramatically, Wood consistently demonstrates the positive outcomes of such empathy, that is, of taking on or sharing another's emotional state. The sharing of affect, in both cases, leads to social cohesion: although admittedly this cohesion comes about through the work demanded of female and working-class bodies. Wood's depiction of the transmission of affect as socially beneficial also permits a reassessment of the sensation novel itself as a potentially moral and edifying form.

Characters, Readers, and 'Womanly' Feeling

Debates over appropriate feeling are central to *East Lynne* and have been the focus of much of the criticism on the novel. Early in the text, Isabel confronts two debt collectors who insist that she has '"no feelings of a lady, if she don't come and speak to us,"' a judgement with both gendered and class implications (91). Feeling is of course evaluated along gendered lines in the novel, and this is perhaps most visible when characters' feelings do not match their gendered identity, as in the case of Archibald Carlyle's sister, Cornelia, and Barbara Hare's brother, Richard. Of Cornelia, the narrator notes, 'It was said in the town that she was as good a lawyer as her father had been: she undoubtedly possessed sound judgment in legal matters and quick penetration' (48). Yet in addition to being clever, Cornelia is consistently represented as hard and unfeeling. For instance, she cannot understand why Isabel might need a change of air for her sickness, attributing her illness to emotional weakness: 'If Lady Isabel would make an effort, she'd get strong fast enough at home' (199). In this way, Cornelia is much like Justice Hare, a stern man who cannot relate to his emotional wife. He insists to Mrs Hare, '"My belief is, that you just *give way* to this notion of feeling ill, Anne. ... It's half fancy, I know"' (229). While Isabel and Mrs Hare may revel in their suffering, each woman's capacity for strong feeling is nonetheless in line with appropriate models of womanly and maternal identity. The narrator contrasts Cornelia with 'poor Isabel,' who 'with her refined manners and her timid and sensitive temperament, stood no chance against the strong-minded woman' (167). While Justice Hare is cruel, Cornelia, whose harsh behaviour arguably drives Isabel out of the house, is not only cruel but unwomanly.

Just as Cornelia's gruff demeanour challenges her femininity, Richard Hare's soft disposition puts his masculinity in question. The way in which the novel marks his gentleness and meekness as completely incompatible with his identity as a man lays bare the relationship between gendered identity and the expression of feeling in the novel and in Victorian society more broadly. Wood makes Victorian gendered expectations explicit by comparing Richard to Mrs Hare, explaining that he is 'quite as yielding and gentle as his mother. In her, his mild yieldingness of disposition was rather a graceful quality; in Richard it was regarded as a contemptible misfortune' (50). It is not only a misfortune: his meekness and sensitivity arguably lead him to be accused of a murder he did not commit. As he himself realizes, '"They had better have made a woman of me, and brought me up in petticoats"' (53).

While Barbara and her mother present slightly different models of womanly feeling—Barbara's sympathy for her brother and love for Carlyle are arguably dwarfed by her mother's all-encompassing love and anxiety for her son—their capacity for feeling is nonetheless depicted as a sign of their ability to care for and empathize with others. Put simply, their sensitivity makes them good women in the world of the novel. Isabel, by contrast, represents a more ambiguous representation of womanly feeling. Many critics have been uncertain about whether the novel renders her strong feeling as a positive attribute. Cvetkovich, for instance, suggests that *East Lynne* 'wavers between depicting Isabel's susceptibility to feeling as the general condition of women and depicting it as a condition particular to her own situation' (108). Lyn Pykett similarly describes Isabel as 'all feeling' (120), explaining that she is 'a woman, and in particular a mother, who loves too much. Her maternal feelings, like other aspects of her emotional life, are characterised by excess' (129). Indeed, Isabel's 'maternal feelings' seem questionable when contrasted with the more reasonable model of motherhood later offered by Barbara. Yet Pykett also notes that the reader is encouraged to interpret Isabel's maternal pain in the third volume as 'natural' (130). Like Richard, Isabel's excessive feeling does perhaps contribute to her crimes: her jealousy, neediness, and attraction to Levison certainly all are factors in her leaving her husband. Yet the novel also sets up Isabel and Carlyle as mismatched lovers as his tendency to misunderstand or even ignore her feelings challenges an understanding of her character as one that 'loves too much' (129). Put another way, Wood shows how Isabel and Carlyle simply love differently. In contrast to Carlyle's lack of emotional intelligence, Isabel's emotionality, as Talia Schaffer suggests, actually 'makes her likeable as a woman and becomes the agency of her reformation; her despair and repentance are just as extravagant as her earlier feelings, carrying the reader along with her' (240).

A key example of Isabel's own likeability and capacity for feeling comes early in the novel, while her father is still alive. The organist from the local church, Mr Kane, comes to tune her piano, and her kindness leads him to request that she and her father, Lord Mount Severn, patronize and attend a concert that he will give the following week. Kane confesses that he and his seven children risk being turned out of his home without the funds that a well-attended concert would provide. Isabel has all of 'her sympathies awakened' in response to his plea (69). When she approaches her father, urging him to support the poor man, Lord Mount Severn responds honestly, '"I am poor myself"' (69). Not disputing this fact, Isabel explains how Kane's affective account has impacted her: '"I was so sorry for him when he was speaking. He kept turning red and white, and catching up his breath in agitation: it was painful to him to tell of his embarrassments. I am sure he is a gentleman"' (69). What Isabel describes is an empathetic response, one that moves quickly from empathy to altruism: she interprets

Kane's 'scarlet blush' as a sign of his shame, feels his pain herself, and translates this into compassionate behaviour (69). The language of empathy becomes even more explicit when she tells Kane that she will attend the concert: 'The tears rushed into Mr Kane's eyes: Isabel was not sure but they were in her own' (70). Yet her compassion comes with a judgement (as it arguably always does). Her insistence that he must be a gentleman is an assessment of both his class and 'innate' morality and assumes that he is deserving of her concern. Isabel furthermore recognizes that her social position demands the performance of her altruism: she cannot simply fund Mr Kane, she must make a show of attending the concert. While there is a crowd inside, there are also 'people going in to attend the concert, and the mob watching them' (78). Each aristocratic arrival serves to 'gratify the mob' outside (79). Private feelings and public interests collide, in this instance motivated by the empathy of a kind woman.

As Cvetkovich claims, Wood seems to locate this emotional and physical susceptibility to others as a quality linked to all women yet also specific to Isabel. For instance, as Isabel considers the possibility of Cornelia living with her, the narrator records, 'Isabel's heart sank within her ... but, refined and sensitive, *almost painfully considerate of the feelings of others*, she raised no word of objection' (emphasis added; 148). Schaffer points out that previous critics, such as Deborah Wynne and Andrew Mangham, have argued that the novel appears to 'reward the middle-class self-control of Carlyle and Barbara, while destroying the wayward, emotional aristocrats Levison and Isabel' (240). E. Ann Kaplan similarly insists that *East Lynne* 'shows that the only class capable of the correct balance between desire and its release is the middle class' (47). Certainly, the plot rewards Carlyle and Barbara, rather than the impulsive Levison and Isabel. Yet, in considering the novel's valuation of emotion, we must examine not just the plot but also the fact that much of the narrative is focalized through Isabel, allowing readers to develop an emotional investment in her character. For instance, the narrator often transcribes her heroine's private thoughts through free indirect speech, a manner of presenting the utterances of a fictional character as if from that character's point of view: 'The facts of her hideous case stood before her, naked and bare. ... What was she? A poor outcast; one of those whom men pity, and whom women shrink from' (296).

Readers are also carried along with Isabel through the narrator's direct addresses, which implore us to pity this woman. The narrator often uses second-person address when she defends her heroine's behaviour: when

Cornelia is unkind, she notes, 'you need not wonder that Isabel was not altogether happy' (171), and when Isabel walks alone with Levison, she writes, 'You may say that she should have remained in-doors ... But remaining in-doors would not have brought her health' (208). This technique is cannily employed by Wood but was certainly also used by other sensational and sentimental female writers in the 1860s. Yet in Wood's case, 'you' is most often directed at a woman reader. For instance, the narrator notoriously calls out to a 'Lady—wife—mother!' who might be tempted to 'abandon [her] home,' and urges her to learn by Isabel's sad example instead (283). Understanding—and feeling—Isabel's pain is an exercise in caution for the wayward reader. Thus, just as the narrator praises 'womanly feeling' in her characters, she demands it of her readers as well.

The Mob: Working-Class, 'Manly,' and Group Feeling

Wood's decision to describe the townspeople gathered outside Mr Kane's concert as a 'mob' is striking. They are not represented as particularly threatening, in contrast to the typical understanding of the crowd or mob in the period. Susan Schuyler, for instance, argues that Victorians found the crowd threatening because it 'embodied chaos; its character was subject to change at any moment' (169). Unlike Wood's depiction, Dickens's *Barnaby Rudge* (1841), set during the Gordon Riots of 1780, portrays a frightening vision of the mob: 'The great mass never reasoned or thought at all, but were stimulated by their own headlong passions, by poverty, by ignorance, by the love of mischief, and the hope of plunder' (484–5). Like Isabel herself, the 'great mass' was most often represented as all feeling or all body. Mark Willis describes the common representation of the Victorian crowd, and in particular the Dickensian crowd, in this way:

> The crowd is most commonly rendered as a murderous, unchained mob, however pacific its initial formation or the reasonableness of the fictive heroes who get caught up in it. It is the old Babylonian, primitive force, unleashed in the midst of civilization, the fault of a lawless residuum, and initiated by the poor conditions of an uncaring society, which the novelist seeks to reform. (88–9)

The fear of the mob (a fear not unique to the Victorian period of course) is that the mass of bodies and feelings will turn violent. Seen in terms of

Keen's definition of empathy as 'a vicarious, spontaneous sharing of affect, [which] can be provoked by witnessing another's emotional state' (4), the mob thus represents the dark side of empathy.

When Levison returns to town in the third volume of *East Lynne*, the mob becomes violent. As with Wood's depiction of Isabel, the mass of feeling exhibited by the mob itself is represented with a degree of ambivalence but is ultimately shown to be necessary and cathartic, leading to social cohesion rather than challenging it. The crowd gathers around Levison in response to an exchange between him and Cornelia. He makes the bold and mistaken move of raising his hat to her: 'Whether it was done in courtesy, in confused unconsciousness, or in mockery, cannot be told. Miss Carlyle assumed it to have been the latter' (465). A heated exchange follows, which is overheard by the farm labourers of the local Squire. Cornelia asks, '"do you think you can outrage me with impunity as you, by your presence in it, are outraging West Lynne? Out upon you for a bold, bad man!"' (465). Her outburst culminates in the following:

> Now Miss Corny, in so speaking, had certainly no thought of present and immediate punishment for the gentleman; but it appeared that the mob around had. The motion was commenced by those stout-shouldered labourers. Whether excited thereto by the words of Miss Carlyle—who, whatever may have been her faults of manner, held the respect of the neighborhood, and was looked up to only in a less degree than her brother; whether Squire Pinner, their master, had let drop, in their hearing, a word of the ducking he had hinted at, when at East Lynne, or whether their own feelings alone spurred them on, was best known to the men themselves. Certain it is, that the ominous sound of 'Duck him,' was breathed forth by a voice, and it was caught up and echoed around:
>
> 'Duck him! Duck him! The pond be close at hand. Let's give him a taste of his deservings! What do he the scum, turn himself up at West Lynne for, bearding Mr Carlyle? What have he done with Lady Isabel? *Him* put up for others at West Lynne! West Lynne's respectable, it don't want him; it have got a better man; it won't have a villain.' (465)

The narrator professes not to know the motivations of the 'stout-shouldered labourers' who swarm Levison. They may be spurred on by Cornelia's language, by a sense of loyalty towards her or her brother, by their master, or simply by 'their own feelings' (465).

What is clear by their language, specifically their mention of Mr Carlyle, Lady Isabel, and the town's respectability, is that they view Levison as a threat to social stability and morality in West Lynne. Presumably they also empathize with Cornelia's disgust. The bodies of the sturdy men descend upon the aristocratic Levison in what might be read as a fantasy of class revenge: 'They set upon him, twenty pairs of hands at least, strong, rough, determined hands' (466). By the time they arrive at the pond his 'coat-tails were gone ... One pulled him, another pushed him, a third shook him by the collar, half a dozen buffeted him, and all abused him' (466). Once his aristocratic clothing is mangled by the hands of the labourers, he is dunked and a 'hoarse, derisive laugh, and a hip, hip, hurrah! broke from the actors' (466).

While Cornelia arguably initiates this group feeling, it is notable that this is an entirely male, working-class mob. Yet rather than read this scene simply as a form of working-class revenge, the men can be understood to be acting out the desires and righting the wrongs of the upper-class characters. They chastise Levison's impudence in running against Carlyle and ask, '"What have he done with Lady Isabel?"' (465). While Carlyle insists that he must subdue his anger towards Levison (even after he discovers that his rival is a murderer), the mob appears to act out his suppressed rage. When Levison is dunked, the narrator notes that Cornelia 'stood her ground majestically' (466), and when Squire Pinner learns that his labourers were responsible for the dunking, he says, '"This is glorious news. My labourers? I'll give 'em a crown a piece for drink to-night"' (468). The labourers are ostensibly paid, then, for what is understood not as an act of rebellion but one of service to the upper- and middle-class residents of West Lynne.

This helps to explain why, in this specific context and in this specific novel, the mob is a positive example of empathy. This mob is not all that different from the mob gathered outside the recital to gawk at the concert-goers: these are not anonymous city dwellers, of the kind that Schuyler and Willis describe. Instead, in West Lynne, the familiar crowd allows for a kind of safe empathy, similar to the kind also offered by the experience of novel reading. As Keen suggests, 'readers' perception of a text's fictionality plays a role in subsequent empathetic response, by releasing readers from the obligations of self-protection through skepticism and suspicion. Thus they may respond with greater empathy to an unreal situation and characters because of the protective fictionality' (xiii–xvi). This explains why, for instance, readers may cry at the trials of a fictional character, but experience a less emotional response to the same scenario in real life.

While 'protective fictionality' may be an element of all novels, Wood's fictional worlds encourage a further sense of protection: readers ideally feel that they are placed within a safe neighbourly space. Wood encourages this not only through her narrator's use of second-person address, but also through her gossipy tone and references to her characters from other novels. In *St. Martin's Eve* (1866), for instance, Wood refers to her previous novel, *Mildred Arkell* (1865), noting, 'You have heard of these Carrs before, in a recent work' (198). As I have argued elsewhere, Wood's narrator thus serves as a 'confidential' informant to her readers, who themselves become part of this fictional world (MacDonald 191). *East Lynne* contains numerous addresses to 'you' or 'reader,' but again what is worth noting is that most of these moments relate to the narrator's demand that readers empathize with or pity Isabel, as in, 'Oh, reader! Never doubt the principles of poor Lady Isabel' (218).

Pykett points out that in addressing the reader directly, Wood 'assumes a shared experience and a community of values with her readers' (119). Yet she also works to build that community. For instance, the narrator has an imagined conversation with a reader whom she anticipates will be a 'moralist': this reader complains that Isabel should never have returned home disguised as Madame Vine. The narrator challenges the reader, insisting, 'You must sit down and abuse her, and so cool your anger. I agree with you that she ought never to have come back; that it was an act little short of madness: but are you quite sure that you would not have done the same, under the facility and the temptation?' (591). Wood anticipates her readers' judgements here, suggesting that they in fact might have acted similarly. This radical move implies that the real 'moralist' is one who refrains from blame and instead feels with and for this flawed character.

Wood here plays with the notion of what Blakey Vermeule describes as fictional characters being 'the greatest practical-reasoning schemes ever invented. We use them to sort out basic moral problems or to practice new emotional situations' (Vermeule xii). While having a reader's emotions and sensations merge with a character's was seen as frightening by many opponents of sensation fiction, Wood's novels deem such empathy an important and even ethical exercise that can lead to greater understanding and compassion. Even within the novel itself, as Carolyn Oulton shows, 'Wood aligns her characters with female readers, as she shows them discussing the Hallijohn murder, and later, Isabel's elopement, in cosy domestic settings' (Oulton). The empathy exhibited by characters such as Isabel, Barbara, and Mrs Hare, by the mob, and, ideally, by the implicitly female reader herself is ultimately rendered a positive social act.

Late in the novel, when Richard Hare is exonerated, the 'mob' once again gathers, this time in celebration:

> An English mob, gentle or simple, never gets up its excitement by halves. Whether its demonstration be of a laudatory or a condemnatory nature, the steam is sure to be put on to bursting point. With one universal shout, with one bound, they rallied round Richard; they congratulated him; they overwhelmed him with good wishes; they expressed with shame their repentance; they said the future would atone for the past. Had he possessed a hundred hands, they would have been shaken off. And when Richard extracted himself, and turned, in his pleasant, forgiving, loving nature, to his father, the stern old justice, forgetting his pride and pomposity, burst into tears and sobbed like a child, as he murmured something about his also needing forgiveness. (575)

The overwhelming emotion of the public mob finally prompts the tears of stern Justice Hare. Perhaps ironically, the middle-class character is educated into compassion by the mob. His remorse is so intense that he suffers a stroke of paralysis, a physical punishment, perhaps, for his lack of empathy earlier in the novel.

While Wood lauds her female characters' emotional susceptibility, what her model husband or father might look like is not entirely made clear in *East Lynne*. Justice Hare and Carlyle's lack of empathy and understanding bring great harm upon their families, but the novel does not map an ideal vision of manly feeling. Justice Hare's tears, however, do seem symbolic of a shift. If the mob earlier permits a cathartic release of Carlyle's anger, allowing him to maintain his stoicism, by the end of the novel even Justice Hare is not immune to the contagious affects of the crowd. Just as Oulton reads the gossipy female characters as readers, the crowd, too, might be read as a mass of readers, delighted by voyeuristic glances into the life of the aristocracy, angered at Levison's cruelty, and ultimately comforted by Richard's release. Schaffer argues that 'sensation fiction can make a case for an alternative set of values—a warmly spontaneous, personal, intensely affective mode. Readers loved the extravagantly emotional Lady Isabel, not her chillingly perfect husband—just as they chose melodramatic sensation fiction like *East Lynne* over rational, "improving" books' (59–60).

Indeed, in contrast to the kind of moral and intellectual lessons proffered by competing realistic novels such as George Eliot's *Mill on the Floss* (1860), Wood's novels suggest optimistically that empathy can itself be an ethical response, although one that does not exist outside of pre-existing social and moral codes.

WORKS CITED

Allan, Janice. 'The Contemporary Response to Sensation Fiction.' *The Cambridge Companion to Sensation Fiction*. Ed. Andrew Mangham. Cambridge: Cambridge University Press, 2013. 85–98.

Bain, Alexander. *The Emotions and the Will*. 1859. 2nd Ed. London: Longmans, Green, and Co., 1865.

Cvetkovich, Ann. *Mixed Feelings: Feminism, Mass Culture, and Victorian Sensationalism*. New Brunswick: Rutgers University Press, 1992.

Dickens, Charles. *Barnaby Rudge*. 1841. Ed. Gordon Spence. Harmondsworth: Penguin, 1973.

Kaplan, E. Ann. 'The Political Unconscious in the Maternal Melodrama: Ellen Wood's *East Lynne* (1861).' *Gender, Genre and Narrative Pleasure*. Ed. Derek Longhurst. London: Routledge, 1989. 31–50.

Keen, Suzanne. *Empathy and the Novel*. Oxford: Oxford University Press, 2007.

MacDonald, Tara. '"She'd give her two ears to know": The Gossip Economy in Ellen Wood's *St. Martin's Eve*.' *Economic Women: Essays on Desire and Dispossession in Nineteenth-Century British Culture*. Ed. Lana Dalley and Jill Rappoport. Ohio State University Press, 2013. 179–92.

Mangham, Andrew. *Violent Women and Sensation Fiction: Crime, Medicine and Victorian Popular Culture*. Basingstoke: Palgrave Macmillan, 2007.

'Novels Past and Present.' *Saturday Review* (14 April 1866): 438–9.

[Oliphant, Margaret.] 'Sensation Novels.' *Blackwood's Edinburgh Magazine* 91 (May 1862): 564–80.

Oulton, Carolyn. '"he'd let me turn the house into a theatre": Rewriting the Domestic in the Sensational World of *East Lynne*.' *Wilkie Collins Journal* 13 (2016). Accessed 26 May 2020. http://wilkiecollinssociety.org/hed-let-me-turn-the-house-into-a-theatre-rewriting-the-domestic-in-the-sensational-world-of-east-lynne/.

Pykett, Lyn. *The 'Improper' Feminine: The Women's Sensation Novel and the New Woman Writing*. New York: Routledge, 1992.

Schuyler, Susan. 'Crowds, Fenianism and the Victorian Stage.' *Journal of Victorian Culture* 16.2 (2011): 169–86.
Schaffer, Talia. 'The Sensational Story of West Lynne: The Problem with Professionalism.' *Women's Writing* 23:2 (2016): 227–44.
Willis, Mark. 'Charles Dickens and Fictions of the Crowd.' *Dickens Quarterly* 23.2 (2006): 85–107.
Wood, Ellen. *East Lynne*. 1861. Ed. Elisabeth Jay. Oxford: Oxford University Press, 2008.
———. *St. Martin's Eve*. 1866. Ed. Lyn Pykett. Vol 3 of *Varieties of Women's Sensation Fiction, 1855–1890*. 6 vols. Series ed. Andrew Maunder. London: Pickering & Chatto, 2004.
Vermeule, Blakey. *Why Do We Care About Literary Characters?* Baltimore: Johns Hopkins University Press, 2011.
Wynne, Deborah. *The Sensation Novel and the Victorian Family Magazine*. Basingstoke: Palgrave, 2001.

CHAPTER 4

'[Tr]ain[s] of circumstantial evidence': Railway 'Monomania' and Investigations of Gender in *Lady Audley's Secret*

Andrew F. Humphries

'My lady gone to London! … Then I'll follow her by the next train.'
Mary Braddon, *Lady Audley's Secret* (1862)

In the *Quarterly Review* of April 1863, the Reverend Henry Longueville Mansel attacked the new 'sensation' novel for the ways it contrived to 'carry the whole nervous system by steam' (Mansel 485). Linking narrative impacts upon the body to the physical and psychological assaults of modern railway culture, Mansel identifies in one fictional linear structure the presence of another to suggest that the experience of reading such novels inspired forms of mania or disturbance akin to the passenger's experience of modern transportation. Mary Elizabeth Braddon was one novelist who in her fiction at this time explored the impact of railway modernity on human behaviour. Her narrator in *Aurora Floyd* (1863), for

---

A. F. Humphries (✉)
Canterbury Christ Church University, Dover, UK
e-mail: andrew.humphries@canterbury.ac.uk

© The Author(s) 2020
A. E. Gavin, C. W. de la L. Oulton (eds.), *British Women's Writing from Brontë to Bloomsbury, Volume 2,* British Women's Writing from Brontë to Bloomsbury, 1840–1940,
https://doi.org/10.1007/978-3-030-38528-6_4

example, links the shifty and dangerous restlessness of the handsome rogue James Conyers to 'an unquiet fever, generated amidst the fibres of the brain, and finding its way by that physiological telegraph, the spinal marrow, to the remotest stations on the human railway' (245). By the 1860s the railway was becoming a convenient metaphor for human character, behaviour, and motivation. Nicholas Daly in his discussion of sensation fiction, including Braddon's novels, asserts that 'in the 1860s the sensation novel trained its readers to live within the temporality of the railway age' (50) and that 'clock time, location, and motion' were not 'incidental to the suspense' of these plots but a 'precondition' of them (49). Contemporary readers of sensation fiction in this way saw 'mobility become even more pronounced, and closely bound to the expanding railway network' (48). The Victorian 'fateful intersection between railways and fiction writing' Simon Bradley identifies (129) is notably evident in Braddon's 1862 sensation novel of crime and detection, *Lady Audley's Secret*, as interaction between railway structures, timetables, and human psychology become determiners of destiny and relationship.

This chapter explores Braddon's representation of the railway in *Lady Audley's Secret* as an engine of 'monomania' (*Lady Audley's Secret* 245). It foregrounds the tensions between emerging technological modernity and conventional mid-Victorian notions of gender to consider how a railway modernity, at first destabilizing in its fostering of female unconventional behaviour, shifts during Braddon's novel to privilege masculine linearity at the expense of female 'deviations' in mobility and identity. The railway modernity that in the novel first liberates protagonist Lucy Audley from hopeless domesticity becomes by stages the reactionary technology that returns her to confinement as a reaffirmation of the patriarchal order. Set in the 1850s, a period which expanded women's opportunities to travel great distances at speed, the novel pictures Lucy using the new mobility of growing train networks to evade geographical fixity and static identity in favour of social mobility. The train makes possible her audacious rise as subversively as it aids her eventual destruction. The novel's privileging of the detective quest of Robert Audley, which takes him up and down the country by train searching for clues to the whereabouts of his missing friend George Talboys, unravels the extraordinary history of Lucy's own female mobility. Transport has become integral to her freedom of identity, and her determined refusal to be constrained by the gender conventions of her time operates as a counter-theme to her criminal exposure by Robert Audley.

This exploration of the relationship between railway modernity and female liberty in *Lady Audley's Secret* also considers how Victorian society in the 1860s had begun to conform to what Wolfgang Schivelbusch describes as a 'new consciousness of time and space based on train schedules' (160). The Victorians' adventure with the railway began in 1830 and exploded through the Railway Mania of the 1840s with the rapid expansion of nearly 6000 miles of track across Britain to the point that by the end of the 1850s, as Saverio Tomaiuolo states, 'trains conditioned everyday life and the idea of movement through space in time' (48). The increasing dominance of the train in the mid-Victorian imagination coincided with both the emergence of the 'sensation' novel and the 'rise of railway bookstalls selling cheap paperback novels to divert commuters ... on their train journeys' (Pykett xxiv). The 'Yellowback' editions, as these cheaper novels were called, were 'produced for the commuter market' from the 1840s onwards as trains became celebrated 'as symbols of modernity, progress and freedom' but were also 'a locus for contemporary fears,' being 'depicted ambivalently as offering opportunities for crime or potential physical damage through accidents' (Gavin and Humphries 4–5). The sensation novels of the 1860s reflected the train's 'consequent unsettling of social conventions caused by the intermingling of classes and genders' (Gavin and Humphries 5). Lady Audley's posturing above her class and Robert Audley's association of her social mobility with danger and moral error reflect such unease. Braddon celebrates Lucy's audacity in her use of the new railways to progress and evade classification, but the writer's interest in transport detail is also exemplified through the male protagonist, Robert. His chronology of detection attempts to reduce the woman's freedom while his own life becomes more and more dependent upon train timetable as the story progresses. In exploring the rival appropriation of railway space by the novel's two main characters, this chapter examines through a gendered lens issues of women's mobility and the psychology of mechanized passenger experience at a time of growing railway, industrial, and imperial expansion.

When the eponymous anti-heroine of *Lady Audley's Secret* calls Robert Audley a '"monomaniac"' she likens his behaviour as her detective persecutor to that of someone suffering from an obsessive and dangerous psychological state (*Lady Audley's Secret* 244). Monomania as a psychiatric term is defined as 'a form of mental illness characterized by a single pattern of repetitive and intrusive thoughts or actions' and, in its wider application, as 'an exaggerated or fanatical enthusiasm for or devotion to one subject; an obsession, a craze' ('Monomania' *OED*). Robert's single-track madness in pursuit of his uncle's wife seems inspired by the agency that drives it: the railway. In identifying (as she tells Sir Michael) Robert's '"perpetual reflection upon one subject"' as a dangerous obsessive linearity where the '"thinking power of the brain resolves itself into a monotone"' (*Lady Audley's Secret* 244–5), Lucy unites her persecutor's psychology with the nature and structure of the dominant technology of the age. Robert's 'monomania,' however, goes further than the pursuit of evidence against his young aunt: railway technology becomes ultimately engaged in the reactionary services of misogyny. Disallegiance to gender roles becomes fictionally corrected, via Lucy's punishment, along established Victorian lines.

At the time this novel was written, railways were expanding rapidly across Britain to speed up commercial and industrial connections, often at the expense of contour and community. Braddon herself remarks in her 1864 novel *The Doctor's Wife* of a picturesque rural London walk from Temple to Camberwell in 1852 of the novel's setting: 'I dare say the railways have cut the neighbourhood all to pieces by this time' (16–17). The railway as brutal patriarchal symbol of the age's dominant technology has significance for sensation novels that were read in the 1860s by many train passengers. As Christian Wolmar states, during the Railway Mania of the 1840s and 1850s 'the deliberate ignoring of topography was particularly noticeable for putting forward "direct" railways, as if simply giving a railway that appellation automatically shortened the route' (95). Train passengers of the period had bought into the progressive virtues of directness and linearity. Yet Braddon ensures in *Lady Audley* that a railway-like linearity of plot governed by a patriarchal surveillance morality is in tension with a dissenting female mobility.

A young lawyer himself, Robert carries out an obsessive agenda of male railway detection that promotes as legal the repression of women. By the novel's end, women are relegated to a state of stasis and dependence which laws under challenge during the 1860s still supported. Robert Audley's masculine line of enquiry seeks to realign the female deviance he identifies in Lucy's evasive and tactical use of trains. Although the novel largely follows Robert's journeying, this nevertheless provides him with frequent evidence of Lucy's prior engagement with the railway network. In tracking her routes to locate her past, Robert maps her journeys by his own. He finds, for example, when visiting Lucy's former teaching colleagues Mrs Vincent and Miss Tonks at Acacia Cottage, the 'scraps of railway labels and addresses' pasted on the travel box left behind by Lucy when she moved on to a new life and identity at Audley Court. The box has been 'battered on a great many different lines of railway, and had evidently travelled considerably' (*Lady* 203). Lucy has been covering her tracks. Robert notices she has 'torn off' many labels or 'only fragments ... remained' (203). The discovery exemplifies her illegal duplicity. Robert discovers Lucy's change of identities from a label that is—as if characterizing its owner—hidden beneath another label (203-4).

Arriving as the new 'Lady' at Audley Court, Lucy has already travelled through several identities like station points—Helen Maldon, Helen Talboys, Lucy Graham—to arrive at the desired destination of the 'advantageous match' with Sir Michael (11). Trains have enabled her to escape her past and reinvent her life. The speed with which Lucy manipulates the railway and telegraph connection is evidence of how the modern transport system has become integrated into her strategic instincts. Even before George's disappearance Lucy has already shown her slickness of operation. Hearing from Sir Michael of his nephew Robert's sudden unexpected visit with George Talboys, she manoeuvres a quick escape to avoid being exposed as a bigamist when both her living husbands meet. She sends her servant, Phoebe Marks to '"London by the first train tomorrow morning"' to collect a dress for a ball (55). This lie to deceive Sir Michael masks Phoebe's real instructions which are to send '"a telegraphic message"' back to Lucy from London so she can persuade Sir Michael to leave immediately for the capital before Robert and her ex-husband arrive at Audley Court (55). The speed of Lucy's decisiveness matches the train and telegraph's directness. Her plan for Phoebe is 'so simple that it was told in five minutes' (55)—the specificity of time an indication of a clock precision she has become accustomed to and which gives her the initial edge in her plotting. The telegraph tells the lie that her former head teacher and colleague Mrs Vincent is 'dangerously ill,' imploring Lucy to visit her immediately. The message, as intended, galvanizes her husband, who commands her, '"Put on your bonnet, Lucy; we shall be in time to catch the express"' (56). Lucy confidently interacts modern technology with people to serve her interests.

After George's mysterious disappearance, Lucy knows she must immediately distract Robert from seeking him because she knows—or thinks she does—that George is lying dead within the grounds of Audley Court. He has fallen down a disused well while quarrelling with her during a secret meeting the evening before he was due to return to London with

Robert. Soon afterwards a further fabricated telegraph is sent by Lucy to her father Captain Maldon on the Isle of Wight where she knows Robert is to travel first to find the missing George. The telegraph, designed to be found half burnt in the fire grate with the address of the sender conveniently destroyed, is to send Robert off on a false errand '"to Liverpool to-night"' to '"make inquiries there"' about George's intended embarkation for a return to Australia (86).

Again, Lucy's calculation of the speed of reaction that the railway dictates is vindicated as Robert decides to go without delay. He is seduced from this point onwards into a wearying dependence on the railway and the railway begins to change him. The Robert Audley of the start of the novel, a 'handsome, lazy, care-for-nothing fellow, of about seven and thirty' (32) becomes galvanized by the railway into a model of mid-Victorian assertive masculinity. Gradually this dependency on railway travel grows into a monomania—a linear obsession—that nurtures in him a male desire to correct female deviance. Robert's language increasingly implies a wider mistrust of evasive female motion. He tells Lucy, as he prepares to reveal her crimes, that he will not '"be put off by feminine prevarication—by womanly trickery"' because '"link by link I have put together the chain of evidence, which wants but a link here and there to be complete in its terrible strength"' (229). Robert's recurrent use of 'chain' in the novel describes a train-like method of detection that traps his victim not by one sudden revelation but by stages like the progress of the railway. We see this in action when Robert visits the landlady Mrs Barkamb at the cottages in Wildernsea, Yorkshire, where Helen Talboys, alias Lucy, lived with her father and baby son after George had abandoned them to seek his fortune in Australia. Mrs Barkamb shows Helen's note, left, by the '"poor little woman"' to her father as she '"abruptly"' abandoned Wildernsea and her '"little boy, who was out at nurse in the neighbourhood"' (212). Stating that she was '"weary of my life here,"' Helen left home and child with her rent unpaid to become Lucy Graham and embark on a life 'disserved from every link which binds me to the hateful past' (213). Helen, like Robert later, characterizes life by 'link[s]': but as a woman she connects links less with opportunity than with an imprisonment she must escape. Reading Helen's note, Robert attempts to reconstruct the missing links of Lucy's story in terms of chronology, almost as if he were reading a timetable:

He wearied his brain in endeavouring to find a clue to the signification of those two sentences. He could remember nothing, nor could he imagine anything that would throw a light upon their meaning. The date of Helen's departure, according to Mr Maldon's letter, was the 16th of August, 1854. Miss Tonks had declared that Lucy Graham entered the school at Crescent Villas upon the 17th or 18th of August in the same year. Between the departure of Helen Talboys from the Yorkshire watering-place, and the arrival of Lucy Graham at the Brompton school, not more than eight-and-forty hours could have elapsed. This made a very small link in the chain of circumstantial evidence, perhaps. But it was a link, nevertheless, and it fitted neatly into its place. (214)

Robert's growing obsession with fitting everything logically 'into its place' gives a masculine detachment to a story that might otherwise be read (as Mrs Barkamb herself suggests with '"poor little woman"') more empathically. What Robert's discovery reveals, and Mrs Barkamb confirms about Helen Talboys, is a series of desperate attempts by an intelligent but impoverished woman to achieve escape from conventions that confine and immobilize her. When the cornered Lucy claims near the end of the novel that Robert in his madness '"chooses me for the victim of his monomania"' (235) she confirms what Robert has already admitted about the impact of his investigation: '"Am I never to get nearer the truth; but am I to be tormented ... till I become a monomaniac?"' (127).

For the mid-Victorians, as Daly states, a key 'aspect of modernization' involved 'the mechanization of everyday life' (3). For Robert to find George and expose what he terms the 'beautiful fiend' and 'demonic incarnation of an evil principle' Lady Audley (*Lady Audley's Secret* 294), he must master train maps and connect to the modern mobile world that Lucy commands and which has brought her from abandoned motherhood and impoverished domesticity to become mistress of Audley Court. The modernity of the train has served Lucy's social mobility.

Train timetables generate an urgency hitherto absent from the 'lymphatic' young lawyer (81). He becomes metaphorically identified with train mechanisms in that if 'resolve[d] upon any course of action' he would show 'a certain dogged, iron-like obstinacy that pushed him on to the fulfilment of his purpose' (81). The more he uses trains between Audley Court, London, Portsmouth, Southampton, Dorset, Liverpool, and

Yorkshire in search of clues, the more 'iron-like' and bound to the conventions of the train he appears. The 'iron' rails mechanize and systematize his quest. Just before visiting George's father Harcourt Talboys in Dorset, for example, he complains that his investigation is 'coming to a standstill' (155). As his investigation of Lucy's history and geography interlinks, his theorizing becomes concretized by railway allusion. This is clear when he taunts her with his '"theory of circumstantial evidence"' (107) in which '"a thousand circumstances so slight as to be forgotten by the criminal"' become '"links of steel in the wonderful chain forged by the science of the detective officer"' (107). The steel tracks laid rapidly across the nation during the Railway Mania become metaphorically connected with the linear logic of a well-wrought investigation. The comparison implies a certainty of outcome because of the way it links Robert's amateur sleuthing to the notion of a 'permanent way': Victorian terminology for the steel track rails invented in 1857 that led during the 1860s to the creation of 'rails rolled from steel' that when laid would last 'four times longer' than previous tracks (Bradley 5, 258). The 'permanent way' carried what Bradley calls 'a historical charge of its own' in that '[l]andscapes ... were suddenly scarred by gigantic embankments, or punctured by tunnels' while 'tens of thousands of bridges and viaducts carried the new routes across roads, rivers and streams, flood plains and estuaries' (5). Robert's confidence in the permanence and connectedness of evidence to track and entrap the elusive female resembles the railway's steely coercion of the contours of landscape in pursuit of its 'permanent way.'

So railway alignment, first symbolic of feminine liberty in the novel, shifts to become assertively masculine. Pykett's claim that 'in the sensation novel a detective quest becomes the hero's route to a properly masculine social identity' (xxii) is supported in the sense that Robert's maturation is achieved at the expense of the emergent modern notions of female mobility exemplified in Lucy. Defining this female mobility pejoratively as 'feminine prevarication' (*Lady Audley's Secret* 229), Robert the lawyer conveniently links notions of errant travel to judgements of errant morality. The link between morality and train travel was a concern of the period which the novel echoes in the duel emerging between the key male and female protagonists. Bradley's discussion, for example, of the railway of the 1850s and 1860s supports the picture of women's independent train travel as precarious. As he observes, despite the introduction from the mid-1840s of ladies-only compartments by some companies, this provision was optional and not a legal requirement. In addition to the threat of physical danger, women rail travellers faced a moral dilemma because even 'the most distant and formal conversation with a stranger risked placing her own respectability under a cloud' (Bradley 183). In these terms, the railway journey of the 1860s that coincided with the rise of the sensation novel might be 'a patriarchal nightmare, its public realm an oppressively masculine territory through which unaccompanied women ventured at risk of harassment or worse' (Bradley 183). Bradley argues that 'the arrival of the railways came to women, hardly less than to men, as a liberation,' but for women that 'liberation' could be precarious and restricting as 'the very act of gazing freely was a male prerogative, so that a woman who dared to match a male stare risked committing an ambiguous transgression' (183). The speed and access of railways that modernized and mobilized travel for women in the 1850s and 1860s still threatened to confine them or expose them to unequal scrutiny. This challenge of a female 'gaze' or 'stare' in a train compartment can be related in a broader sense to the 'transgression' of the female protagonist in *Lady Audley's Secret*. The liberty for women that trains made possible, and which Lucy's story might celebrate, becomes suppressed in Braddon's novel beneath the weight of the masculine moral imperative driving the Robert Audley narrative against her.

Discussing the ambivalence in Victorian women's writing over women's mobility, Wendy Parkins states that such mobility was 'not always depicted in positive or desirable terms' and 'may be coerced or involuntary or simply the last resort' (12). In examining 'how novelistic representations of mobility metaphorise women's agency,' Parkins argues that women writers showed female 'agency'—woman's ability to move and act freely while conscious of the social constraints upon them—contending with a patriarchal culture of mistrust of such 'agency' (12). For Parkins, 'mobility as a metaphor for sexual fallenness' was a dominant Victorian trope that 'reinforced assumptions about rational masculine agency' and 'posited a link between freedom of movement and female sexuality' in which 'the association between a potentially uncontrollable sexual agency and an always-already determined narrative of downward mobility' made the 'link between social and physical mobility … a particularly fraught one for women' (14). Lucy Audley, a woman whose agency is criminally nuanced but who, in fact, is tracked and exposed for having been an over-mobile woman, does appear to be sacrificed to such a 'rational masculine agency.' Though rightly criminalized in the novel for the acts she has committed, she also exemplifies elements of such heroines battling the patriarchal world for agency. Positioned after her confession and imprisonment within the 'fallen woman' trope, however, Lucy Audley serves, instead, less as an advertisement for female agency and more as a moral warning against 'dangerous' deviance in any Victorian woman.

The railway becomes a marker for fixing where characters are in relation to where they should be. Trains are ready to be caught and timetables are discussed over dinner as the railway becomes a central symbol of the novel's increasing subterfuge. Lucy demonstrates her well-tuned instinct for evasion in a pivotal railway episode early in the investigation, when she outmanoeuvres Robert by train to steal back incriminating letters from her past (written as Helen Maldon) which are stored at a lawyer's London lodgings. Gleaning this information from a conversation with Robert while he is staying at Mount Stanning near Audley, Lucy is quick to act. Robert's quizzing of the coachman who was to drive Lucy back to Audley Court from Mount Stanning after their meeting indicates the speed and precision of her deception and the challenge it sets for the novice detective:

> 'Have you taken Lady Audley back to the Court?' he said to the coachman, who had stopped to call for a mug of hot spiced ale.
> 'No, Sir; I've just come from the Brentwood station. My lady started for London by the 12.40 train.'
> 'For town?'
> 'Yes, Sir.'
> 'My lady gone to London!' said Robert, as he returned to the little sitting-room. 'Then I'll follow her by the next train; and if I'm not very much mistaken, I know where to find her.' (*Lady* 125)

Robert's later arrival at Shoreditch station in London is described in a passage rich in Braddon's keen observation of railway setting and behaviour. Robert 'hear[s] a bell ring and, looking at the clock ... remember[s] that the down-train for Colchester started at this time' (126). Crossing to the opposite platform he meets Lucy when she 'almost r[u]n[s] against [him] in her haste and excitement' (127). The cat and mouse game between them shows to her advantage. She evidently enjoys the chase. Lucy's request for Robert to play the gentleman, and '"open the carriage door for me: the train will start in two minutes,"' allows her to evade awkward conversation about her secretive journey but also conforms Robert suddenly to the custom and timing of the train itself (127). By the time he has helped Lucy into her seat and made her comfortable for the journey the train is about to leave. Lucy's assertive demeanour on the platform catches Robert off guard. Only hours earlier at Mount Stanning Lucy had appeared to Robert pitiful and diminished in response to his suspicions against her: now she appears supremely confident. Increasingly making the issue one of gender, Robert suspects Lucy has achieved 'some piece of womanly jugglery' (127). Further hints of what Robert terms Lucy's feminine deception lie in the symbolism of 'the huge velvet mantel in which her slender little figure was almost hidden' that Robert covers her with after helping her into her compartment seat. The 'mantel' ambivalently suggests the assumption of manly protectiveness in Robert that she now successfully exploits to cloak her deception, but which may also embody a final train ride of the novel towards her permanent incarceration that Robert will engineer (127). As her voice trails off with the departing train, however, her triumph over masculine coercion seems, for now, confirmed as 'the last Robert Audley saw of her was that bright defiant smile' (127).

Lucy's strategic awareness of railway timetable and convention is impeccable and directly aids her speedy action to steal the letters and erase the evidence against her. The Bradshaw pocket train timetable for British services first issued in 1839 (the term 'timetable,' Bradley reminds us, was 'another railway coinage' [15]) became a dominant feature in Victorian social culture and was reflected in fiction by the increasing precision of time references to mark significant moments of narrative development. Bradley states that 'the railways with their strict timetables also sharpened the sense of how time could be subdivided and refined, so that a minute or less could make a world of difference one way or the other' (21). The urgency and anxiety of detection in *Lady Audley's Secret* is fuelled by the detective precision of timetable chronology. Finding Lucy's letters gone on arrival at Fig Tree Court following their platform encounter, Robert is despondent. His search for George has become a compulsion that affects him psychologically as if he were '"tied to a wheel, and must ... go with its every revolution"' (*Lady Audley's Secret* 135). Railway metaphors haunt Robert's investigative journey which becomes industrially punctuated by '"links"' he must either '"drop at this point"' or '"go on adding ... to that fatal chain until the last rivet drops into its place and the circle is complete"' (135).

On his next journey, the express to Southampton, the commodification and dehumanization of Robert by railway is further suggested as he is wrapped like a 'perambulating mass of woollen goods' (138). Charlotte Mathieson argues that 'the travelling body ... features in literary depictions as a site through which concerns over the dangers of rail travel are articulated, but also functions as a site for the alleviation of fears through these assertions of protection from the physical, social, and psychological impacts of railway journeys' (49). She not only discusses how Robert's use of the rug integrates him into the train fabric itself but also indicates how such wrappings provided a protection from dangerous or compromising gender proximity that such carriages might present as an invitation to scandal and exposure (49). Railway travel characterized as a 'fever' or disruption of the human system continues in the picture here of Robert 'wrapped ... in the vast folds of his railway rug with a peevish shiver' as he feels 'inclined to quarrel with the destiny which compelled him to travel by an early train upon a pitiless winter's day' (*Lady Audley's Secret* 138). Railway and Fate combine as Robert suspects 'a stronger hand than [his] own ... pointing the way to [his] lost friend's unknown grave' (144).

Added to the compulsion of technology is the firm directive of love. On his visit to Dorset to speak with George's stern father Harcourt Talboys (who has disinherited his son for marrying Helen Maldon, '"the daughter of a drunken pauper"' [164]), Robert meets George's sister Clara. At first unimpressed by her quiet, taciturn mood, Robert is surprised when she rushes out of the house to delay him with a spirited command. With an early 'New Woman' assertiveness, Clara charges him to avenge the brother she assumes to be dead and declares she will '"do it myself!"' if Robert is incapable of acting (171). Her urgency raises the stakes. Speed of discovery becomes not simply a desire but a command. Robert finds himself now caught between two strong-minded women: women separated by distance but connected henceforth by the railway lines of investigation between Dorset and Essex. Emboldened by Clara to reinvigorate his flagging search, this encounter, nevertheless, unravels a paradoxical response to female agency in the bachelor lawyer. Pressured by the female imperative, he pauses to muse about the simpler love of an imagined 'girl on the kerbstone,' that his 'chariot shall have passed' (175). This pastoral archaism seems a wistful momentary escape from the hectic modern transportation that hurries him too quickly on in his own life. A passive figure by the roadside, this imagined woman he 'shall have passed' contrasts with the mobile real women, Clara and Lucy, with whom he must contend. He develops this negatively into a masculine diatribe against modern woman's increasing 'dominion' over masculine time and space (176). Women, Robert decides, are '*never lazy*. They don't know what it is to be quiet'

(177). Behind this recognition of female active mobility there appears a corresponding fear that such mobility is emasculating. His love for Clara is a burden that also fuels his developing mania as 'she forces me onward upon the loathsome path—the crooked byway of watchfulness and suspicion' (175). Robert associates this compulsion with a sense of dehumanization. He must become mechanized and commit to the 'unflinching regularity in the smaller wheels and meaner mechanism of the human machine, which knows no stoppage or cessation' (175). His fear of woman's power and mobility, therefore, requires that he demonize that power and 'hat[e]' woman's tendency to 'drive' a man 'full butt at the dear lazy machinery of government' where she 'knocks and buffets him about the wheels, and cranks, and screws, and pulleys' until he is moulded into something uncharacteristically dynamic (177). The language of mechanism linked to woman's impact is apt. Robert continues to be mechanically activated by Clara's scrutiny—she sends him periodic telegraphs with clues. Later she travels to Essex and surprises Robert to further prompt his detective progress.

Robert's narrative syntax also begins to internalize the railway's temporal precision. When he hears from his cousin Alicia Audley that Sir Michael is very ill, for example, his suspicion about his aunt's complicity spurs him into quick sharp movements towards the train:

> One course was clear before him; and the first step of that course, a rapid journey to Audley Court. He packed his portmanteau; jumped into a cab; and reached the railway station within an hour of his receipt of Alicia's letter which had come in the afternoon post. (182)

While Robert becomes nervously energized towards the end of the novel, Lucy becomes nervously static. Her responsibility as *Lady* Audley—the epitome of her rise and status—paradoxically reduces her opportunities for manoeuvre as she watches Robert come and go more freely from Audley Court. Robert, sensing imminent victory, is amused and encouraged by Lucy's discomfort as he realizes that '"my lady is anxious to know my movements"' (215). The final chapters' steady deliberation towards the caging of the offending woman seems pointedly symbolic. Elizabeth Langland argues that Braddon 'took the lead in foregrounding [a] dialectic between freedom and enclosure, privilege and confinement' (3), noting also Braddon's articulation of 'subtle connections between country house and madhouse ... disclosing how the class and gender position of the upper-middle-class lady might simplify her private transfer from one sphere to the other' (13). Trapped and facing exposure, Lucy becomes desperate. Her attempt soon afterwards to kill Robert in the arson attack on the Castle Inn is her worst crime of the novel in a list that includes her silence over George's whereabouts and 'death,' her bigamy, and other fraudulent evasions.

It is the success of Lucy's social mobility that finally immobilizes her. As Lady Audley her movements are scrutinized and her absences from Audley Court noticed. Her desperate murder attempt at the Inn has become, therefore, dangerously close to home. Her circle of movement has been reduced to a station point where earlier in the novel she was able to use railway time more freely and creatively to outrun her nephew's search. Rather as Jonathan Grossman suggests that train consciousness in the Victorian period impacted the settings it connected to so that 'the railway's speed [was] systematizing time into one for the people outside at the stations and in all the towns it network[ed]' (101), Braddon uses railway symbolism in the setting of Audley Court to make the final connection between Lucy's earlier audacious mobility and her final capture. In the hours following her arson attempt, Lucy feels trapped as she watches the archway from the house and awaits a messenger with news of Robert's death by fire. The natural surroundings of Audley appear to mimic railway features to symbolize the network that was once the agent of escape but which now brings her crimes to her doorstep. Systematized time holds her in its grip. Lucy is tortured by the 'steady ticking of the clock' (*Lady Audley's Secret* 287) as if the 'progress of time had actually stopped' (289). As the day draws on she paces the quadrangle and watches through the archway to the avenue, long and straight, that leads to the gardens and to the well where George's dead body, she thinks, still lies undetected. The natural setting resembles a Victorian train station with its avenue like a deep and dark railway cutting, its 'old arch and a clock tower' (7). William Powell Frith's painting *The Railway Station* (1862), for example, shows the railway arches' design where the linear track meets the station platform.[1] A reproduction of Chester station from 1860 also shows rows of arches and a clock tower, typical of the period design and evoked by Braddon's representation of Audley Court at this moment of Lucy's defeat.[2] The description of the evening mists rising around her and the 'flat meadows ... filled with a grey vapour' while 'under the archway the shadows of fast-coming night lurked darkly; like traitors waiting for an opportunity to glide stealthily into the quadrangle' give a sense of a railway station and steaming engine almost Gothically mapped onto the natural surroundings (*Lady Audley's Secret* 290). The 'fast-coming' fate brought by Robert's footsteps contrasts with Lucy's passivity. She is immobilized by fear—'her heart stopped beating' (291)—when Robert walks alive through the archway, as if he were alighting from a train onto the platform. Fate has outrun her. Her collapse against the archway—'crushed against the angle of the wall; as if she would have made a tomb for herself in the shadow of that sheltering brickwork' (291)—evokes the architecture of the contemporary station that was once her gateway to liberty but now signals the end of the line. The prostrate Lucy's association of this setting with a tomb is timely and prophetic. The train will soon entomb her in the asylum that repeats her mother's fate—'"the secret of my life"' she finally confesses to Sir Michael to explain her behaviour—the fate of hereditary madness and incarceration that has haunted and provoked her mobility from the start (294).

There should be some empathy for such a woman at this point, but the swift economy of Lucy's removal following her confession is brutal, systematic, and exclusively masculine. Designed to preserve from scandal the reputation and patriarchal heritage of the ancient Audley name, her banishment is devoid of female contact, as three men and a train condemn her for being a woman who has assumed too much liberty. Sir Michael cuts short her story and dismisses her from his life, packing his things immediately to catch the 'last up-train' to London (305). The mechanism for diagnosing and incarcerating a Victorian woman for madness required only the signatures of two doctors and her husband to activate. Robert completes this legalized violence against Lucy fittingly and rapidly by train-delivered telegram, exemplifying the fact that 'the telegraph network that accompanied the railways allowed swift transmission of news and information' (Bradley 93). He summons immediately from London 'a physician experienced in cases of mania,' Dr Alwyn Mosgrave, to certify what the doctor terms a '"dangerous"' woman (323). Like Robert, Dr Mosgrave is a product of the railway culture and a servant of its patriarchal systems as is characterized on his arrival by an obsession with time and urgency that befits his profession. He looks at his 'fifty guinea Benson-made chronometer' (319)—a watch that symbolizes masculine material power and announces '"I need not remind you that my time is precious"' (319). He comes to exile Lucy to a place where her control over time and mobility will cease (319). Modernity hurries Lucy to punishment as the doctor announces during Lucy's diagnosis that his '"time was up ten minutes ago; it is as much as I shall do to catch the train"' (324).

A final train journey spirits Lucy quickly and secretly abroad to an asylum where she is locked into a final false identity as Madame Taylor. Victorian punishment of madness in women was to treat aberration—that departure from the 'normal' and conventional—as a deviance that must be corrected rather as the Railway Mania corrected the errant topography of the landscape. Lucy's prison is cut off even from the reach of railways and the modern world she craves. As Dr Mosgrave chillingly admits: '"her life, so far as life is made up of action and variety, will be finished"' (324). Robert Audley confirms her isolation by checking in 'a volume of Bradshaw' (the continental version of the railway guide was first published in 1847), that the Belgian asylum in Villebrumeuse 'lay out of the track of all railway traffic and was only approachable by diligence from Brussels' (325). The train connections, however, make possible the swiftness and secrecy of her removal from British civilization. '"You have brought me to my grave, Mr Audley … to a living grave"' she tells her captor (333). She dies eventually of '*maladie de langueur*' (379), a wasting illness that in a final irony deprives her of energy and movement.

Lucy is not the only woman in the novel reduced symbolically as the railway expands. The conventionality of the novel's ending can be read as paradoxically modern and reactionary. Clara Talboys, by mid-Victorian standards 'masculine' and assertive in her guiding and surveillance of Robert's investigation during the novel, becomes finally, as his wife-to-be, a static and imprisoned female symbol just as Lucy is. Shifted back from the 'New Woman' towards the 'Angel in the House' model of Victorian womanhood, Clara's identity is changed by marriage as Lucy's is by exile and incarceration. Both must adopt new names and identities that restrict female freedom. Clara's new role as Robert's wife is to be secure and stationary while he is mobile: she is to rescue him from a 'flaneur' existence 'upon the smooth pathways that have no particular goal' by keeping home for him (272). It is her 'little hand' that accepts his proposal of marriage and a life in a 'dream of a fairy cottage' near Teddington Lock (375, 378), a mock-rural setting that attempts to regain the timelessness of Audley before Lucy Graham arrived to disrupt it. Robert becomes again a boyish young lawyer, the monomania that hounded Lucy, she claimed, '"basely and cruelly,"' now apparently forgotten as patriarchy is harmoniously revisualized.

As C. J. Lever observed in *Tales of the Trains* (1845): 'The steam-engine is not merely a power to turn the wheels of mechanism—it beats and throbs with the heart of a nation, and is felt in every fibre, and recognised in every sinew of civilized man' (Lever). What emerges through Braddon's ultimate synchronization of the railway to male detection is a modernizing definition of 'civilized' and 'nation' that is paradoxically also gender reactionary: the masculine monomania that pursues and neutralizes the 'dangerous' woman is not simply the illness or aberration of one man's obsession in a single work of sensation fiction: it is by 1862 a monomania at the core of the Victorian nation—the patriarchal monomania of Empire with its ruthless agenda to further standardize gender and time.

Notes

1. See this painting on the website *The Victorian Web* http://www.victorianweb.org/painting/frith/paintings/5.html.
2. A copy of this reproduction can be found on the website *Railway Wonders of the World* http://www.railwaywondersoftheworld.com/gwr.html.

Works Cited

Braddon, Mary Elizabeth. *Aurora Floyd*. 1863. Ed. P.D. Edwards. Oxford: Oxford University Press, 2008a.
———. *The Doctor's Wife*. 1864. Ed. Lyn Pykett. Oxford: Oxford University Press, 2008b.
———. *Lady Audley's Secret*. 1862. Ed. Lyn Pykett. Oxford: Oxford University Press, 2012.
Bradley, Simon. *The Railways: Nation, Network and People*. London: Profile, 2015.
Daly, Nicholas. *Literature, Technology, and Modernity, 1860–2000*. Cambridge: Cambridge University Press, 2004.
Gavin, Adrienne E., and Andrew F. Humphries. 'The Transports of Fiction 1840–1940': *Transport in British Fiction: Technologies of Movement, 1840–1940*. Ed. Adrienne E. Gavin and Andrew F. Humphries. Basingstoke: Palgrave, 2015. 1–28.
Grossman, Jonathan. H. *Charles Dickens's Networks: Public Transport and the Novel*. Oxford: Oxford University Press, 2012.
Lever, C. J. *Tales of the Trains*. 1845. Boston: Little Brown and Company, 1907. http://www.gutenberg.org/files/34884/34884-h/34884-h.htm. Accessed 17 February 2018.

Mansel, Henry Longueville. 'Sensation Novels.' *Quarterly Review* 113 (1863): 481–514.
Mathieson, Charlotte. '"A Perambulating Mass of Woollen Goods": Travelling Bodies in the Mid-Nineteenth-Century Railway Journey.' *Transport in British Fiction: Technologies of Movement, 1840–1940*. Eds. Adrienne E. Gavin and Andrew F. Humphries. Basingstoke: Palgrave Macmillan, 2015. 44–56.
'Monomania' *Oxford English Dictionary*. http://www.oed.com/view/Entry/121474?redirectedFrom=monomania#eid. Accessed 6 March 2018.
Parkins, Wendy. *Mobility and Modernity in Women's Novels, 1850s–1930s. Women Moving Dangerously*. London: Palgrave Macmillan, 2008.
Pykett, Lyn. Introduction. *Lady Audley's Secret* by Mary Elizabeth Braddon. 1862. Ed. Lyn Pykett. Oxford: Oxford University Press, 2012. vii–xxix.
Schivelbusch, Wolfgang. *The Railway Journey: The Industrialisation of Time and Space in the 19th Century*. Berkeley, California: California University Press, 1986.
Tomaiuolo, Saverio. *In Lady Audley's Shadow: Mary Elizabeth Braddon and Victorian Literary Genres*. Edinburgh: Edinburgh University Press, 2010.
Wolmar, Christian. *Fire and Steam: A New History of the Railways in Britain*. London: Atlantic, 2007.

CHAPTER 5

'There is great need for forgiveness in this world': The Call for Reconciliation in Elizabeth Gaskell's *Sylvia's Lovers* and *A Dark Night's Work*

Elizabeth Ludlow

> *'You must forgive him—there is great need for forgiveness in this world.'*
> (Elizabeth Gaskell, A Dark Night's Work, 175)

The last five years of Elizabeth Gaskell's life (1860–1865) were characterised by activity. She travelled in Germany, Switzerland, France, and Italy and was involved in relief work for the Lancashire Cotton Famine. She also wrote two full-length novels, a number of short stories, and several non-fiction pieces. Josie Billington comments on 'the sheer pressure of time' Gaskell was under when she was writing *Wives and Daughters*

E. Ludlow (✉)
Anglia Ruskin University, Cambridge, UK
e-mail: elizabeth.ludlow@anglia.ac.uk

© The Author(s) 2020
A. E. Gavin, C. W. de la L. Oulton (eds.), *British Women's Writing from Brontë to Bloomsbury, Volume 2*, British Women's Writing from Brontë to Bloomsbury, 1840–1940,
https://doi.org/10.1007/978-3-030-38528-6_5

(1864–1866): 'the result at once of an inordinately busy life and of the need to meet serial deadlines' (225). This chapter argues that in her novel *Sylvia's Lovers* (1863) and her novella *A Dark Night's Work* (1863) Gaskell responds to the 'pressure of time' with an emphasis on the urgent need for reconciliation. It also suggests that she negotiates the causal relationships between past and present by highlighting how the rifts of trauma might be transformed by a renewed understanding of oneself and one's community.

In *Sylvia's Lovers*, it is not until Sylvia Robson comes face to face with her estranged husband Philip Hepburn on his deathbed that she recognises the limits of her perception. While Sylvia puts aside her earlier desire for vengeance, Philip replaces his idolisation of her with a knowledge of heavenly comfort. Sylvia's broken words, '"Oh wicked me! Forgive me—me—Philip!"' (500), articulate the shift that both experience: from prioritising their own emotions to surrendering themselves and recognising their need for mercy. The final pages of *Sylvia's Lovers* reveal that Sylvia's story enters tradition in a distorted way as she becomes known as the wife who 'lived in hard-hearted plenty' while her husband died of starvation 'not two good stone-throws away' (502). These concluding remarks are indicative of what Deirdre D'Albertis describes as Gaskell's increasing anxiety about the ability of 'novelistic solutions' to 'represent (and if possible, heal), social discord' (81). More than this, they reveal Gaskell's growing scepticism about the idea of progress. Developing Marion Shaw's claim that 'the great lesson of *Sylvia's Lovers* is the painful truth of history that there is not necessarily a purposeful, progressive narrative of human life' (88), the following discussion reads Gaskell's late fiction in the context of the mid-nineteenth-century shift from a preoccupation with Atonement narratives of original sin and divine punishment towards a focus on an Incarnation-inflected teleology where the concern was with Jesus as a *man*. Boyd Hilton details how this shift involved a move from retributive attitudes towards a celebration of gentleness and compassion. He comments that, by 1870, 'it was commonplace for Anglicans to assert that a theological transformation had recently taken place, whereby a worldly Christian compassion, inspired by the life of Jesus, had alleviated such stark evangelical doctrines as those of eternal and vicarious punishment' (5). When Gaskell's late fiction is considered in terms of the shift Hilton details—a shift that was gaining momentum through the 1860s—its engagement with the intellectual context of Incarnational thought comes to the fore.

In October 1859 Gaskell's 'Lois the Witch' appeared in three instalments in Charles Dickens's *All the Year Round*. The story responds to the journal's preoccupations with historical re-imaginings with a scepticism about the reconciliation of past and present and about the place and significance of acts of Atonement. Serialised alongside Dickens's *A Tale of Two Cities* (1859)—which presents the execution of Sydney Carton as an act of heroic self-sacrifice—'Lois the Witch' has Ralph Lucy remark that, despite his joining in with the prayers of the repentant judge who condemned his beloved Lois to death, nothing can ever bring '"[her] to life again, or give me back the hope of my youth"' (225). Ralph's regret over the needless death of Lois points to a critique of the Atonement doctrines and a celebration of Incarnational compassion and co-operation that finds later expression in *Sylvia's Lovers* and *A Dark Night's Work*.

In a letter to her daughter Marianne Gaskell in 1854, the Unitarian Gaskell balances an expression of the comfort she finds in the communal prayers of the Anglican Church service with her conviction that 'Jesus Christ was not equal to His father.' It is important, she tells Marianne, to 'define ... to ourselves' the difference between Anglican and Unitarian doctrine on this matter in order that 'the nature of God, and tender Saviour' be understood and love be directed appropriately (May–June 1854: *Letters* no. 198a). As Timothy Larsen explains, Unitarians believed that

> Christ came to declare something that was equally true before his death: namely, that God is merciful. In this scheme, one simply repented and determined to live a future life in which one did not engage in sinful practices and then a merciful God allowed one to go forward in the expectation that this resolve would prove good. (149)

Both Gaskell's letters and her husband William Gaskell's sermons demonstrate a commitment to the role of human partnership with God in relieving the suffering of a broken world. In a lecture published in 1860, William Gaskell reasons that if Christ is to be regarded as 'one who could be "touched with the feeling of all our infirmities"' and as 'our brother ... there is a strong encouragement for us, and a power to quicken us in the pursuit of holiness, which we feel we should lose were we to adopt the ordinary [Trinitarian] belief' (23). The example of Christ is, he argues, 'his doctrine embodied and living before us, animating, strengthening, consoling and exalting one made in all things like unto ourselves' (24).

Gaskell's late fiction extends these ideas by enacting an Incarnation-inflected dynamic whereby the work of grace is enabled when characters forego self-interest and instead perceive of themselves as part of a larger community.

Although, as a Unitarian, Gaskell never subscribed to the doctrine of the Atonement, her fiction of the early 1860s corresponds with contemporaneous 'vogue' for historical reconstructions of the life of Jesus that prioritised a developmental, rather than revelatory, vision of God's interactions in the world (Hilton 299). While her earliest work considers the implications both of what it means for one man to die vicariously in the place of another and of revelatory transformation, the focus of her later fiction is on the continuous interpersonal relationships that have the potential to bring reconciliation. For example, while both the eponymous protagonist of 'The Heart of John Middleton' (1850) and Mr. Bradshaw in *Ruth* (1853) experience sudden revelations that move them from a Calvin-inflected focus on the Atonement to a more nuanced understanding of what it means to experience and express grace, the characters in Gaskell's later writings enact a more gradual and Incarnation-inflected development towards Christ-like compassion.

In her discussion of Gaskell's engagement with modernity, Linda K. Hughes describes how *Cousin Phillis* (1864) and *Wives and Daughters* (1865–1866) express a 'diminished reliance on structural dyads (worker and owner, north and south)' and reveal Gaskell's 'increasingly sophisticated ability to create a world embedded in an intricate matrix of ongoing social and historical change' ('*Cousin Phillis*' 106–7). Although Hughes offers a convincing argument for locating 'the turning point for this new development ... in the composition of *The Life of Charlotte Brontë* (1857),' which demanded the subject be placed 'in a fully imagined world within which multiple interactive influences ... shaped Brontë's complex life and works' (107), the wider context of the move from the 'Age of Atonement' to an age of Incarnation provides the backdrop through which this shift in emphasis can be more fully appreciated.

The Fragility of Human Connection in *Sylvia's Lovers*

Andrew Sanders comments that Gaskell's idea for *Sylvia's Lovers* had, almost certainly, 'grown both out of [her] long-fostered fascination with the sea and out of [her] new and extended acquaintance with Yorkshire as a result of the researches involved in the composition of *The Life of Charlotte Brontë* between 1855 and 1857' (vii). In acknowledging the tensions between the time of 'our forefathers,' who lived in the whaling-port of Monkshaven in Yorkshire during the French Revolutionary Wars, and the 'present time' (68), when Monkshaven had become a 'rising bathing place' (502), Gaskell's penultimate novel attends to how the passage of years brings changes for good and bad. The uneven gestation of *Sylvia's Lovers* and its expression of how the legalised 'tyranny' of impressment had far-reaching effects, transforming behaviour and expectations in family and romantic relationships, contribute to the text's changes in tone and pace (6). Biographer Jenny Uglow describes

> the vital, energetic realism of the first volume, written rapidly in the spring of 1860; the intensity of the second, full of death and loss, composed slowly during 1861; the spiritual allegory of the third, a desperate search for belief in a better world, written amid the shadows of the cotton famine. (504)

Amid the busyness of her life at this time, Gaskell remained a voracious reader as is seen in the allusions to contemporary fiction, poetry, and theology that permeate *Sylvia's Lovers*. She had, for example, begun writing *Sylvia's Lovers* after writing to George Eliot to express her admiration for *Adam Bede* (1859) on 3 June (*Letters* no. 431) and 10 November 1859 (*Letters* no. 449). Responding to the second letter, Eliot explains to Gaskell how she read the early chapters of *Mary Barton* while writing *Adam Bede* and acknowledges that she shared Gaskell's 'feeling of Life and Art' (11 November 1859, *George Eliot Letters* 3, 198–9). In *Adam Bede* and *Sylvia's Lovers*, a shared approach to writing historical fiction is evidenced through the similarities in the narrative voice; both novels consist of the reflections of an older narrator who, after the pattern of Walter Scott's *Waverley* (1814), reflects on events 'Sixty Years Since' (Shaw 77). In common with *Adam Bede*, too, *Sylvia's Lovers* emphasises the significance of confession, especially the disclosure of wrongdoing to another, over and above the giving and receiving of forgiveness.

In *Forgiveness and the Victorian Novel* (2015), Richard Hughes Gibson suggests how the practices of forgiveness that Eliot represents contribute to debates surrounding 'psychological and communal healing' (103). To illustrate this, he considers her rationale for replacing, in the prison cell exchange between Hetty Sorrel and Dinah Morris in *Adam Bede*, the more traditional conversion scene used by earlier novelists with a confession scene and argues that Eliot uses it to make a case for public confession in the sense of a confession that is performed and not something that takes place inside the mind. To underline the significance of performed confession, he suggests that it reinforces the truth of Mr. Irwine's earlier insistence to Adam Bede that human lives are 'as thoroughly blended with each other as the air they breathe: evil spreads as necessarily as disease' (qtd. in Gibson 108). Ultimately, evil is stemmed as, through speaking out, the confessor is brought to a humility that dismantles any façade, and a recognition of the 'blendedness' between confessor and hearer restores the interpersonal community of the novel's fictional world. The trial and confession scenes that Gaskell includes in both *Sylvia's Lovers* and *A Dark Night's Work* carry something of the germ of *Adam Bede* in that they enable the exposure of weakness and underline the interdependence that exists between the characters.

When Sylvia's father Daniel Robson is imprisoned in Monkshaven for his role as ring-leader in the rescue of men who had been taken by the press-gang, Philip welcomes the chance to bring his cousin Sylvia—whom he hopes to persuade into matrimony—and her mother to his home. From there, he tells them, they might have the opportunity to see Daniel before he is sent to York Minster for the assizes. On the night of their arrival, Philip lets slip the possibility that Daniel might hang. Following his clumsy declaration, '"There's not a thing I'll not do; there's not a penny I've got,—I'll give up my life for his,"' Sylvia is convinced of the probable fate of her father (301). She does not attend to Philip's offer to 'give up [his] life for [Daniel's]' because an atoning substitution is never really an option in this case. Nonetheless, Philip's desire to become a hero and to give up his life for another, thereby proving his worth, haunts the remainder of the novel. Under the burden of his treacherous secret—that he watched as Sylvia's lover Charley Kinraid was taken by the press-gang—Philip's expressed wish to *be* an atoning sacrifice is indicative of the 'religious feelings' with which he attempts to 'disguise' his dangerous passion for Sylvia from himself (358). While his ensuing recklessness and willingness to die makes him a fearless soldier, his misplaced search for heroism associates him with legality rather than compassion and the 'Age of Atonement' rather than the age of Incarnation. While, at the Siege of Acre, Philip acts heroically when he risks his own life to save his rival, his words—'"I niver thought you'd ha' kept true to her"'—are indicative of his continuing self-interest (431).

On his return to Monkshaven as a burnt and disfigured pauper, Philip acts heroically when he saves his daughter from drowning in the sea. Significantly though, it is not this act that calls for the reader's judgment to be mitigated. Instead, it is his subsequent humility; a humility that enables him to see Sylvia as she is for the first time. On his death-bed, Philip asks Sylvia for forgiveness: '"Little lassie, forgive me now! I cannot live to see the morn!"' (495). His sense of urgency, brought on by his awareness of approaching death, reinforces a sense of the pressure of time. As Gaskell's coda explains, the results of the act of repentance and forgiveness do not necessarily carry consequences for individual or societal progression: both Philip and Sylvia die young and their story is misremembered. Instead, it is implied that the consequences reach beyond the world and towards the eternal. Philip's final words, 'In heaven,' and his subsequent 'bright smile' indicate a perspective that transcends the earthly (500).

Philip had foreseen his death-bed reconciliation when, recuperating from battle, he had read himself into the story of Sir Guy, Earl of Warwick who, after seven years of fighting, returned home as a 'poor travel-worn hermit' and was reconciled with his wife Phillis on his death-bed (465). Philip's recognition that 'Guy and Phillis might have been as real flesh and blood, long, long ago, as he and Sylvia had even been' (466) testifies to Gaskell's increasing insistence that the trajectory of an individual is shaped by ongoing immersion in the narratives of others' lives. It also testifies to her prioritisation of ideas of adaptation, development, and conservation over the Atonement-inflected ideas of sudden conversion.

Forgetting the selfish reasons he had for keeping Kinraid's secret and for 'having acted as he had done' (465), Philip's dying confession offers a challenge to the reader: to repent of the facades and lies that stand in the way of true communion with God and with one another. The narrative of his transformation follows a similar trajectory to that of Philip Edmonstone in Charlotte Yonge's *The Heir of Redclyffe* (1853). In a letter to French publisher Louis Hachette recommending several novels for translation, Gaskell criticises *The Heir of Redclyffe* for its lack of 'event or story' but appreciates its representation of the 'progress of character' (?22 March 1855: *Further Letters* 131). Her use of the names Philip and Guy indicates that she had *The Heir of Redclyffe* in mind when writing *Sylvia's Lovers*. Discussing *The Heir of Redclyffe* as a 'parable of actual life,' which uses 'realism to bring Christian "higher truth" home ... to the massive novel-reading public of the mid-nineteenth century,' Susan Colòn details Yonge's representation of character progression (42). She describes how

Yonge 'reconfigures the types from the parable of the Pharisee and the publican from Luke 18' in order that a parabolic 'message of moral confrontation' might be delivered to readers (42). While *The Heir of Redclyffe* initially introduces Philip as the Pharisee and Guy Morville as the publican, it later re-introduces Philip as an 'analogue' to the apostle Paul (57). Despite the 'radical redirection' of Philip's life, Colón comments that 'many if not most readers have resisted the shift of sympathy' that the novel asks for in regard to him (58). One reason for this, she suggests, is that the novel uncomfortably 'exposes the reader's own likeness to Philip' (59). Similarly, Gaskell's representation of Philip Hepburn's painful self-recognition indicates her shared commitment to challenging readers and to enacting the message that 'the path to being a saint lies through the painful recognition of oneself in the Pharisee' (Colón 61). However, while *The Heir of Redclyffe* exemplifies the virtue of continual repentance through the characterisation of Guy, *Sylvia's Lovers* is very much of its time in that it draws on the wider intellectual context of Incarnation-inflected social thought in order to represent the 'great need' for reconciliation to mend broken connections and to enable a radical re-conception of oneself.

Sylvia's illiteracy means that, unlike Philip, she comes to the scene of confession unprepared. As Hilary Schor comments, Sylvia cannot have her resolution within history 'without a different alphabet, a different language' (170). Without a literary precedent, her knowledge of herself is very much one that is rooted in her body and emotions. In response to Philip's request that she forgive Simpson (the dying man who had given the evidence that led to Daniel's execution), she utters the words that come to haunt him: '"it's not in me to forgive … it's not in me to forget"' (332). Upon being pressed, her resolve hardens with the declaration, '"my flesh and blood wasn't made for forgiving"' (333). Although 'her heart gr[ows] sad and soft,' in comparison with what it had been when Philip's Pharisaic demand that she forgive had 'called out all her angry opposition,' the timing of Simpson's death means that her capacity to relent remains hidden from Philip (334). It is only at Philip's death-bed, where Sylvia has the opportunity for a public confession, that reconciliation is enabled. '"Will [God] iver forgive me, think you?"' she asks Philip. The realisation that she almost had him turned out to starve drives her to imagine herself '"among them as gnash their teeth for iver, while yo' are where all tears are wiped away"' (496). Following his own painful self-recognition, Philip is able to reassure Sylvia that God '"is more forgiving than either you to me, or me to you"' (496). Sylvia's reconciliation with Philip indicates her newfound humility: 'it was Sylvia who held his hand tight in her warm, living grasp; it was his wife whose arm was thrown around him, whose sobbing sighs shook his numbed frame from time to time' (499). This reconciliation testifies to the spiritual significance of human connections expressed through flesh and blood. Although the human connections might be forgotten or misunderstood through gossip, the novel's coda suggests that, with the emigration of Sylvia's daughter to America, their blueprint carries far-reaching effects. These effects are, however, wider than realist fiction can express and the silences that characterise the ending, point to the belief that practices of forgiveness and self-abasement find their appropriate conclusion in heaven.

THE BONDS OF CONFESSION IN *A DARK NIGHT'S WORK*

Gaskell's challenge to her readers in *Sylvia's Lovers*—to reconceive of themselves and their relationships—is indicitive of her awareness of the influence and reach of her fiction. In her discussion of 'Gaskell the Worker,' Linda K. Hughes explains that, between 1859 and her death in 1865, Gaskell was 'not only at the height of her powers but was also being brought before more readers than ever before as a result of contributing to the *Cornhill Magazine* and *All the Year Round*' (29–30). To emphasise the wide reach of Gaskell's later work, Hughes comments that whereas *Household Words* had averaged sales of only 36,000–40,000 issues per week, '*All the Year Round* initially sold around 100,000 copies per issue— and as many as 300,000 issues of its Extra Christmas Numbers' ('Gaskell the Worker' 29–30). In *A Dark Night's Work*, which appeared in nine instalments in *All the Year Round* between January and March 1863 and was issued as a one-volume novella in April that same year, Gaskell responds to her ever-widening readership by demonstrating an awareness of the changing tastes of the literary marketplace. According to *Fraser's Magazine* in 1863, 'a book without a murder, a divorce, a seduction or a bigamy, is not apparently considered worth either writing or reading; and a mystery and a secret are the chief qualifications of the modern novel' (qtd. in W. Hughes 4–5). As what follows will demonstrate, *A Dark Night's Work* not only responds to this definition of the 1860s bestseller but also critiques the new vogue for sensational material. This discussion adds to Graham Handley's recognition that the story subverts the sensation genre by offering not a 'whodunnit' plot 'but the continuum of differently shared knowledge after the doing' (66). Through its emphasis on shared knowledge, co-operation, and community, the narrative subverts contemporary expectations through its exploration of the continuities, discontinuities, and ruptures that are involved in the lived experience of personal, technological, and teleological time.

A Dark Night's Work is set in a provincial town 'about forty years ago' (1). On the 'night' to which the title alludes, Ellinor Wilkins, along with faithful servant Dixon, helps bury the body of Dunster, her father's business partner, whom he had murdered in a moment of rage. Recoiling from the horror of the night's work, Ellinor succumbs to a brain fever: a predictable malady for the sensation heroine. As she begins to regain her strength, she muses on how things might have been different had she, her father, and Dixon been open with one another in acknowledging the horror of the murder and burial:

> She began to see that if in the mad impulses of that mad nightmare of horror, they had all strengthened each other, and dared to be frank and open, confessing a great fault, a greater disaster, a greater woe—which in the first instance was hardly a crime—their future course, though sad and sorrowful, would have been a simple and straightforward one to tread. But it was not for her to undo what was done, and to reveal the error and shame of a father. (119)

As it is, the secret shame of complicity in the murder weighs heavily on Ellinor. It not only leads to the end of her engagement with Ralph Corbet, but, with its 'sudden shock,' the horror of the 'dark night's work' causes her to age prematurely and to experience time as a burden rather than as a gift (206).

As a reminder of the child she once was, Ellinor carries with her a locked writing case that holds the 'treasures of the dead': 'the morsel of dainty sewing' that her mother had left unfinished and 'a little sister's golden curl' (280). When her father dies, she adds to these treasures the half-finished letter he wrote on his death-bed requesting that Ralph stand by his daughter as a friend if the deeds of the dark night become known. Emerging at each turning point of the plot, the writing case stands as a reminder of an inheritance that is emotional. From the start of the story, the emphasis on inheritance is maintained. Although it failed to earn him the respect he desired, Edward Wilkins's concern in establishing his claim to the 'De Winton Wilkinses' arms' is described as fitting for a time when 'everyone was up in genealogy and heraldry' (30). In what follows, any claim to aristocratic ancestors is rendered worthless in the face of tragedy and it is the fragile and incomplete remembrances that Ellinor carries in her writing case that hold significant meaning.

The engagement between Ellinor and Ralph comes to an abrupt end after Edward Wilkins responds to Ralph's questions about the marriage deeds with an alcohol-fuelled outburst of anger and accusation. Following his expulsion from the house, Ralph writes to Ellinor to release her from the engagement, giving the mysterious 'secret affairs' as the reason (174). With ambitions for a 'high reputation' in law, he acknowledges his dread of an obstacle that could bring disgrace and end his career (173). Ellinor responds to his letter by taking on the role of proxy and mediator:

> I suppose I must never write to you again: but I shall always pray for you. Papa was very sorry last night for having spoken angrily to you. You must forgive him—there is great need for forgiveness in this world. (175)

As a participant in the 'dark night's work,' Ellinor sees it as her filial duty to intercede for her father, recognising the 'great need' that the world has for relationships to be mended. Her promise to pray for Ralph is indicative of her reliance on God's grace as the enabler of reconciliation. After the murder, it is only through prayer that she is able to draw strength. '"There is none other help but Thee!"' she prays in her illness (115). When, after her father's death, she moves to East Chester, she finds that the 'sense of worship' at the daily cathedral services 'calmed and soothed her aching weary heart' (195).

That Ellinor and Dixon can only find true and lasting peace once the awful secret is brought to light stands as the ethical turning-point of the novella. When Ellinor visits Dixon in prison, he recounts how he had, like her, sought to find relief in prayer as '"God knew what was in my heart better than I could tell Him"' (277). He confesses, however, that it would only be after breaking the long-held silence on the subject that he might rest. Thus, his prayers of repentance were quickly followed by prayers that Ellinor might come to him in prison (277). In her request that Dixon forgive her, Ellinor expresses her belief that performed confession brings comfort and relief:

> 'Forgive me all the shame and misery, Dixon. ...'
> 'It's not for me to forgive you, as never did harm to no one—'
> 'But say you do—it will ease my heart.'

'I forgive thee!' said he. And then he raised himself to his feet with effort, and, standing up above her, he blessed her solemnly. (296–7)

In common with Eliot, who had demonstrated in *Adam Bede* the healing power of public confession, Gaskell focuses on the dynamics of the relationships that restore life in moments of crisis. The fact that the secret of Dunster's murder is uncovered through the process of railway expansion anticipates the way in which Gaskell's *Cousin Phillis* (1864) and Eliot's *Middlemarch* (1871–1872) describe how railway expansion transforms the spatial and temporal landscape and calls for what Hughes describes as 'a new way of seeing that ignores traditions and local, even national boundaries' (Hughes, '*Cousin Phillis*' 96). Indeed, it is precisely in '*this* world' of technological progress and renewed vision that Gaskell uncovers the 'great need for forgiveness,' a power that can re-build broken connections between past and present. The end of *A Dark Night's Work* sees Dixon integrated or, to use Eliot's term, 'blended' into the family that Ellinor and Canon Livingstone start. His closeness to their 'two little fairy children' illuminates the generational and class bonds that confession brings (298).

While Gaskell concludes *A Dark Night's Work* as she had *Sylvia's Lovers*, by pulling the reader back into conversations of the present day, she does the opposite in many of her contemporaneous non-fiction pieces. In these, she begins with an anecdote of the present day before launching into a historical account of the manners or customs of a particular region or group. Published in three instalments in *Fraser's Magazine* in April, May, and June 1864, 'French Life' typifies this approach in its movement from descriptions of contemporary life in various French regions to an account of the murder of a seventeenth-century lady, Mme de Gange. Gaskell recounts that Mme de Gange, after a life full of tragedy, was brutally murdered by the brothers of her second husband. While she displays quick-witted responses to their attempts at murder by poison and sword that are worthy of any Gothic heroine, it is not her ingenuity that makes her story extraordinary. Instead, it is her willingness to forgive. As she lies dying, she forgives her husband and his brothers for their atrocities and, 'fearing that her little son might at some future time think it his duty to avenge her death … tried to make him understand the Christian duty of forgiveness' ('French Life' 749). As the above discussion of *Sylvia's Lovers* and *A Dark Night's Work* has suggested, such models of forgiveness and reconciliation, which Gaskell offers in her writing of the 1860s, challenge the perceptions of heroism and extraordinary individualism that characterise the 'Age of Atonement.' It is the struggle to be a compassionate parent, spouse, child, and neighbour rather than a hero that characterises her protagonists. Resonating with the dying plea of Mme de Gange, the struggles of Sylvia and Philip in *Sylvia's Lovers* and of Ellinor in *A Dark Night's Work* reinforce the 'great need for forgiveness in this world' and point to the repercussions of public confession in the next (*A Dark Night's Work* 175).

WORKS CITED

Billington, Josie. 'Watching a Writer Write: Manuscript Revisions in Mrs Gaskell's *Wives and Daughters* and Why They Matter.' *Real Voices on Reading*. Ed. Philip Davis. Basingstoke: Macmillan, 1997. 224–35.

Colòn, Susan E. *Victorian Parables*. London; New York: Continuum, 2012.

D'Albertis, Deirdre. *Dissembling Fictions: Elizabeth Gaskell and the Victorian Social Text*. London: Macmillan, 1997.

Eliot, George. *The George Eliot Letters*, vol 3 (1859–1861). Ed. Gordon S. Haight. London: Oxford University Press; New Haven: Yale University Press, 1954.

Gaskell, Elizabeth. *A Dark Night's Work*. London: Smith, Elder. 1863. Online. *Internet Archive*. Accessed 19 Feb 2018.

———. 'French Life' [iii]. *Fraser's Magazine* 69 (June 1864): 739–52. Online. *ProQuest*. Accessed 19 Feb 2018.

———. *Further Letters of Mrs Gaskell*. Ed. J.A.V Chapple and Arthur Pollard. Manchester: Manchester, 2003.

———. *The Letters of Mrs. Gaskell*. Ed. J.A.V. Chapple and Arthur Pollard. Manchester: Manchester University Press, 1996.

———. 'Lois the Witch.' 1859. *Elizabeth Gaskell: Gothic Tales*. Ed. Laura Kranzler. London: Penguin, 2000. 139–226.

———. *Sylvia's Lovers*. 1863. Ed. Andrew Sanders. Oxford: Oxford University Press, 1999.

Gaskell, William. *The Person of Christ: A Lecture*. London: H Brace. 1860.

Gibson, Richard Hughes. *Forgiveness in Victorian Literature: Grammar, Narrative, and Community*. London: Bloomsbury Academic, 2015.

Handley, Graham. '"A Dark Night's Work" Reconsidered.' *The Gaskell Journal* 21 (2007): 65–72.

Hilton, Boyd. *The Age of Atonement: The Influence of Evangelicalism on Social and Economic Thought, 1785–1865*. Oxford: Clarendon Press, 1988.

Hughes, Linda K. '*Cousin Phillis*, *Wives and Daughters*, and Modernity.' *The Cambridge Companion to Elizabeth Gaskell*. Ed. Jill L. Matus. Cambridge: Cambridge University Press, 2007. 90–107.

———. 'Gaskell the Worker.' *The Gaskell Society Journal* 20 (2006): 28–46.

Hughes, Winifred. *The Maniac in the Cellar: Sensation Novels of the 1860s*. Princeton: Princeton University Press, 1981.
Larsen, Timothy. *A People of One Book: The Bible and the Victorians*. Oxford: Oxford University Press, 2011.
Sanders, Andrew. Introduction. *Sylvia's Lovers*. By Elizabeth Gaskell. 1863. Oxford: Oxford University Press, 1999. vii–xvi.
Schor, Hilary M. *Scheherazade in the Marketplace: Elizabeth Gaskell and the Victorian Novel*. Oxford: Oxford University Press, 1992.
Shaw, Marion. 'Sylvia's Lovers and Other Historical Fiction.' In Matus, ed. *The Cambridge Companion to Elizabeth Gaskell*. 75–89.
Uglow, Jennifer. *Elizabeth Gaskell: A Habit of Stories*. London: Faber and Faber, 1993.

CHAPTER 6

'The plain duties which are set before me': Charity, Agency, and Women's Work in the 1860s

Kristine Moruzi

Although paid employment was out of reach for most middle-class British women in the 1850s and 1860s, the emergence of the philanthropic movement in these decades was viewed as a natural extension of middle-class women's domestic role, as 'charity work and almsgiving had traditionally been considered part of women's domestic duty' (Vallone 16). Moreover, charitable work aimed at assisting the poor, the sick, and the distressed became urgent by mid-century as demand for relief continued to increase. The Christian ethic of charity became central to constructions of femininity during this period, even as questions were raised about how and why women were engaged in charitable work. This chapter examines three novels from the 1860s to show how charity and

K. Moruzi (✉)
School of Communication and Creative Arts, Deakin University, Burwood, VIC, Australia
e-mail: kristine.moruzi@deakin.edu.au

philanthropy were mechanisms by which ideals of girlhood and young womanhood were defined and articulated. In Florence Wilford's *A Maiden of Our Own Day* (1862), Frances Carey Brock's *Charity Helstone* (1865), and Felicia Skene's *Hidden Depths* (1866), young female protagonists try to determine how their roles as sisters and daughters, and eventually as wives and mothers, could be incorporated with their responsibilities to others beyond the family circle. These relatively youthful protagonists, ranging in age from 16 to 25, must make key decisions about philanthropy and marriage that will affect the rest of their lives.

The feminine ideal of the 1860s is defined by Christian duty and feminine responsibility, but is also characterised by a lack of clarity about what girls would do in the future. The tragic heroine embodied in St John Rivers's ideal of Jane Eyre in 1848 had been supplanted by figures like Ethel May in Charlotte Yonge's *The Daisy Chain; or, Aspirations: A Family Chronicle* (1856) and Mrs Jellyby in Charles Dickens's *Bleak House* (1853) in which philanthropic women are critiqued for focusing on those in need outside the home at the expense of their families. In the novels of the 1860s discussed in this chapter, didactic depictions of female philanthropists are replaced by girls and young women who are sincere in their efforts to determine how they can fulfil their home duties and also respond to calls for charity in appropriate and productive ways. This tension between two competing demands on girls and young women in the mid-century reflects similar concerns in nineteenth-century American benevolence literature, in which 'the entire concept of the nineteenth-century American individual becomes a complex negotiation between the responsibilities toward oneself and toward others' (Bernardi and Bergman 1). The girls in these novels understand that they should help their families, but also believe they are capable of more than merely their domestic duties.

Education and work beyond the home had the potential to divert girls from their domestic duties. Sarah Bilston explains that the education of girls and women became 'an increasingly significant issue' because standards were uneven and girls were often educated at home (62). As a consequence, the question of women's duties in both the private and public spheres 'became a matter for debate, a subject open to question' throughout the decade (Bilston 62–3). This question is explored in *Papers for Thoughtful Girls*, an advice manual published in 1863 and reprinted in multiple editions until 1890, in which Sarah Tytler writes to girls whom she describes as 'very weak, very unstable, very erring, very imperfect … but who are in earnest about Christianity and their duty' (2).[1] What girls should do after completing their schooling is, Tytler explains, 'a problem of the present day' (3), the solution to which lies in 'thinking not of her herself, ... doing what is nearest and simplest to her hand, [and] living as much as possible in the well-being of others' (5). Tytler is not defining a new feminine ideal for the 1860s, but is instead engaged with the question of girls' futures and responding to concerns appearing in fiction and elsewhere in the periodical press. She articulates an ideal of feminine conduct that is based on a 'union' of 'domesticity, alms-deeds, and independence, woven into a Christian crown' (Tytler 4). The inclusion of 'independence' is important here because Tytler asks whether a girl shall 'discover her bent like a boy, pursue her profession fearlessly and innocently, [and] achieve independence' (3). This possibility of economic independence is presented to girl readers within a model of Christian femininity in which girls are nonetheless reminded that they must submit to fathers, brothers, and husbands. This tension lies at the heart of 1860s philanthropic fiction featuring female protagonists.

This feminine ideal was subject to further interrogation as women's rights activists such as Bessie Rayner Parkes, Emily Davies, and Josephine Butler agitated for employment, education, and social reform. While most middle-class girls were encouraged to adopt the ideals articulated by Tytler and appearing in the fiction of the day, these activists demonstrated that other options were possible. Yet generally the reality for a middle-class girl was to remain under her father's jurisdiction until her marriage, at which point she would move to her husband's home and under his control. The idea of charitable work provided an opportunity for women to extend their influence beyond the domestic sphere and a justification for their presence in what might otherwise be considered inappropriate spaces, encountering circumstances and people well 'beneath' them.

Although working-class women had traditionally worked outside the home, middle-class women's work in the 1860s was less common, in part because women were primarily occupied by domestic duties and child care. Nonetheless, women were increasingly occupied by paid and unpaid employment beyond the confines of domesticity. Barbara Onslow has demonstrated that women were engaged in a variety of paid work in the periodical press throughout the nineteenth century. In the 1860s women were increasingly writing for and editing children's periodicals such as *Aunt Judy's Magazine* (1866–1885), edited by Margaret Gatty and then subsequently by her daughters Juliana Ewing and Horatia Gatty. Some women made a living 'by contributing stories, poems or needlework patterns to the periodical press' while others 'worked as editors, sought employment in the printing rooms or opened newsagents' shops' (Van Remoortel 1). Activists including Frances Power Cobbe and Harriet Martineau promoted social reform through written contributions to a number of leading periodicals. Although, as Martha Vicinus explains, the 'ideal of domesticity masked the exclusion of middle-class women from political, economic, and social power' (2), women were engaged in a variety of different occupations that mobilised their feminine virtue.

Indeed, women leveraged their positioning as morally and spiritually superior to men to support their efforts to help others. They were, in fact, 'encouraged to utilize their influence to effect reform outside the home' (Kent 185). Christian morality and the responsibility to help those less fortunate prompted middle-class women to 'tackle social evils' (Perkin 205), such as poverty, inadequate housing and sanitation, and the dislocation caused by industrialisation. Women were heavily invested in the approximately 640 charitable institutions that flourished throughout England in 1862 (Thomson 28), providing much of the volunteer labour required to keep them running, either through direct charitable work like visits to the poor and the sick or through fundraising schemes such as bazaars, benefits, and subscriptions. As F. K. Prochaska observes, philanthropy emerged in the nineteenth century as a vocation for women and as an 'outlet for self-expression' through work that gave them agency and self-determination (5). Women applied their 'domestic experience and education, the concerns of family and relations, to the world outside the home' across a multitude of needy causes (Prochaska 7). Motivated by a desire to help those in need, and despite the fact that philanthropic organisations were often headed by men, women nonetheless had a fair degree of autonomy and authority in their charitable roles.

Philanthropic heroines in fiction of the 1860s reflect the complexities of girlhood and young womanhood, particularly in relation to their work outside the home, their potential as wives, and the suitability of their prospective suitors. The feminine charitable ideal in these novels is defined by the question of whether the female protagonist is able and willing to subordinate her philanthropic goals to her marital responsibilities and whether the potential husband is a good match. A woman's desire to contribute to the world through philanthropy was expected—and even applauded—and women were encouraged to make choices that were consistent with their philanthropic and religious goals, even if that meant they might forego marriage and motherhood. In her discussion of love, for example, Tytler reminds her readers that 'no good girl will consciously indulge and consummate by matrimony, a love for one whom she is forced to see is an utterly unworthy man' (199). The worthiness of the potential husband is of vital concern and an unsuitable prospect is to be rejected, consequently two of the three protagonists discussed in this chapter remain unmarried at the conclusion of their stories.

Given the increasing popularity of charitable work in English culture, fictional female protagonists involved in philanthropy became more commonplace. Novels about charitable work provided an opportunity to depict women's movement and action outside the home in a way that was not scandalous or disrespectable. Yet depictions of these characters and their charity work vary widely during this period since writers held considerably different opinions 'as to the scope and extent of charity advisable for their heroines' (Thomson 28). The novels discussed in this chapter demonstrate the range of options available to women, yet they also reflect how relatively narrow these options were. This model of sacrifice is part of a mid-Victorian ideal in which 'virtuous action could serve the collective benefit' (Blumberg 2). The religious imperative to help others explicitly frames this choice in which duty to God and the moral responsibility to help those less fortunate are privileged over romantic love. Only in *A Maiden of Our Own Day* do these objectives align because the suitor is sufficiently religious and moral. In the other two novels, *Charity Helstone* and *Hidden Depths*, the men are unsuitable as husbands because their exposure to the world means they lack adequate religious faith. Each protagonist balances her responsibilities to her family and her duties to others in different ways. Only one is able to fit her charity work within a strong family structure, while the others choose to forego marriage and motherhood to perform their charitable work when their romantic interests prove unsuitable. These women elect to pursue their philanthropic goals over the potentially disastrous consequences of marrying men who are incapable of the religious fortitude required of them. These choices regarding marriage and philanthropy reflect their agency as independent girls and young women who make decisions based on their interests, duties, and moral responsibilities.

The earliest of the novels discussed here, Florence Wilford's *A Maiden of Our Own Day* (1862), follows the traditional trajectory of mid-century Victorian domestic fiction in that the protagonist Gyneth Deshon learns—and eventually chooses—to sacrifice her own needs and desires in order to become a model of femininity who is rewarded with marriage to the man she loves. Girls were often discouraged from striving towards something that they felt was important: '[s]heer hard work, determination and ambitiousness—all the qualities which might be thought necessary to achieve *anything* of substance—were regarded as wholly unfeminine. Women's achievements, if they were to be acceptable to the Victorians, had to come about in an unrealistic, passive way' (Dyhouse 74). Gyneth's main preoccupation is with how she can participate in philanthropic activities. While her virtue and religious feeling are never in question, other aspects of her character must be improved, particularly her patience with respect to her charitable work. Concomitantly, she must also learn to sacrifice her own interests to fulfil her family's wishes.

Gyneth performs her charitable role under her grandmother's guidance from an early age. She lives a quiet life in which she 'read to grandmother, visited the poor, walked with [her friend] Rose, wrote stories, speculated, studied, and dreamed' (*A Maiden* 10). She spends five years in this 'healthful happy atmosphere' (*A Maiden* 10) until her family's return to England from an overseas military posting results in her moving to live with them. She is depicted as being an entirely normal young woman. Wilford 'pleaded no abnormalcy; no extenuating Evangelicism; no unhappy home circumstances. She would have us believe that Gyneth is (as indeed, the title indicates) a normal, contented, moderately high-church, Victorian young woman' (Thomson 31). Gyneth's reintroduction to her family produces a new set of expectations that revolve around the idea of work. She initially expects that she will be required to assist in household chores and with caring for her younger siblings, and

> expected to be obliged to give up much of her leisure, and had quite made up her mind to relinquish day-dreams, verse-making, and all pursuits which she could not share with her home-circle; she had had a vision of teaching the children, reading aloud to her mother, working for her father and brothers, writing notes and running messages for everybody, and though this ideal did not commend itself to her taste, it did to her sense of duty. (*A Maiden* 214)

Her expectations are based upon the needs of the family and a series of chores that must be completed. These duties do not eventuate because the family household has been running smoothly for some time without her. The increased prosperity of the middle classes meant that 'housewifery had been relegated to servants' and 'not only the marriageable girls in a house but also its mistress were casting helplessly around for something to do, something to occupy their vacant hours' (Thomson 14–15). While Gyneth's mother occupies her time with visiting and looking after her husband's garrison of soldiers, Gyneth, at 16, is too young to participate actively in these duties and she seeks other avenues to occupy her time.

Yet Gyneth's youth and inexperience impede her ability to choose what she should do. She explains to her older brother Lambert: '"I am so useless, not old enough to take a district, or anything like that, and needlework is a little stupid thing that anybody can do"' (*A Maiden* 89). The skills she does have, such as sewing and music, are deemed 'stupid,' presumably because Gyneth feels that all girls and women are accomplished in these areas, even though her skills are demonstrably superior to those of some other girls and young women. Even her education, which is sufficient to teach her younger siblings, has no use in the family because others—including a governess—have taken on that role.

Although the community struggles with poverty and the social ills that come from being a harbour town, issues that Gyneth could conceivably help to ameliorate, she is constrained by her obedience to her parents. The expectation that she abides by her parents' wishes means that she has very little latitude to engage in charity work in the community because nearby Harbourmouth is 'a terribly bad place ... where very little is done to counteract the evil' (*A Maiden* 85). Gyneth's father will not allow her to teach a boys' Sunday school class because the pupils are too rough and, unsurprisingly, also refuses to let her become a district visitor who visits the sick and the poor to provide material and moral support. His rationale is that she is '"too young"' and that parents often '"make a great mistake in allowing young people to take upon themselves responsibilities to which they are not equal, and which leave them no fresh youth, no happy time, in which they may be free and bright with no other care than to obey those set over them"' (*A Maiden* 253). He implicitly alludes to an ideal of childhood in which children—and girls especially—are to be innocent and protected from the cares of the world. While he is sympathetic to her 'desire to be useful' (*A Maiden* 253), she must be content with being useful in the home.

Home duties are the cornerstone of the feminine charitable ideal depicted in this novel. Although Gyneth genuinely desires to be '"on the side of goodness and mercy' against the battle against 'the evil and misery of the world"' (*A Maiden* 89), she eventually comes to understand her influence in the domestic sphere. Her brother's view is that by living quietly and 'performing the duties of a good daughter and good sister, [she] was thus doing her part on the side of right, and was shedding forth a pure influence which might reach further than she thought of' (*A Maiden* 90). Not until late in the novel does Gyneth come to this realisation for herself. She learns not to seek useful work beyond the home: 'All that she could attempt, and all that she could expect of interest, lay in her home: there, or not at all, must she seek to be useful; within its sphere she must find contentment or yield herself a prey to discontent' (*A Maiden* 258). By abandoning her ambition to help others beyond the home, her public work as a music teacher at a girls' school becomes possible. If she had refused to accept the importance of her role as daughter and sister, she might not have been given this opportunity.

The other female characters in the novel provide alternative perspectives on charitable femininity, with only one appearing as an appropriate model. Augusta Weatherhead provides a counterpoint to Gyneth. The motherless Augusta works tirelessly to look after her younger siblings as well as taking on responsibilities for public charitable work on behalf of her father, the Rector, including running fundraisers, district visiting, and teaching Sunday School classes. Overworked, she eventually falls ill and must learn to let others take on some of her work so that she can be a better daughter and sister. Importantly, she can fulfil this responsibility by being better informed and more thoughtful about Christianity. The slightly older Mrs Parry and her husband, by contrast, are described as 'charitable Guerillas … who prefer fighting ignorance and vice in their own independent fashion, instead of enrolling themselves in the regular army, with the rector for their head' (*A Maiden* 158–9). Charitable work for women was seen as appropriate when it fell within established institutions. The common view was that women should not be working independently or subverting the established channels of charity. Gyneth is explicitly told not to become one of these guerrillas who carries on the war against evil by acting independently. Instead, she must wait for opportunities to help the rector, which she finally does by caring for Augusta when she becomes ill. Gyneth's domestic skills and influence within her own family home are easily transferable to the Weatherhead household. The narrator describes Gyneth's 'true love and patience' as she cares for Augusta, 'the winsomeness with which she beguiled the young children into quiet, [and] the humility with which she tried to correct the occasional mistakes her want of experience made her commit' (*A Maiden* 420). This charitable work is appropriate for Gyneth because she is qualified to provide this—predominantly domestic—assistance, yet it does not expose her to the evils of the world. The Weatherheads are not quite equal in social status to the Deshon family, but they represent middle-class religious respectability and thus pose no threat to Gyneth's innocence.

Gyneth's willingness to help the family brings her to the attention of Miss Boyd, who is the most favourable model of charitable femininity in the novel. She works with the Rector rather than in opposition to him, running a girls' training school. She carefully explains that she does not 'meddle' with the boys' school run by Mr Weatherhead, instead focusing on the girls' school. Although she provides financial support to the boys' school, her charitable work falls within comfortable gender boundaries that do not expose her to the roughness of boys, while nonetheless performing an important service. Miss Boyd is so busy with this 'life-work' that she has little time for visiting (*A Maiden* 424), but she invites Gyneth to see her home and school. The rewards of this charitable work come from the orderly appearance and conduct of 'a row of girls in neat stiff dresses ... They all rose up, curtseyed, smiled, and resumed their work' (*A Maiden* 453). They are instructed in sewing, singing, and music as well as cooking, laundry, and housework. Miss Boyd also visits among the poor and has a district of her own, but wants to help anyone in need, including the wives of soldiers who have married without leave and lack adequate military support. In addition to her public philanthropy, Miss Boyd is also a loving daughter who cares for her elderly father and prioritises his wellbeing over her own interests.

With the assistance and inspiration of Miss Boyd, Gyneth becomes the model of feminine charity that is based on family duty and public good. She finally acknowledges that '"my business is not to find out how I could be most useful, but how I can fulfil most exactly and patiently the plain duties which are set before me"' (*A Maiden* 466). The reward for this patience and this willingness to do the work available to her is marriage to long-time friend Lewis Grantham, in whom she has hidden her interest when she thought he wished to marry her friend Rose. Although depictions of female philanthropists 'might implicitly endorse women's ambitious desires,' they also reflected societal anxieties about the implications of 'unleashing these desires' (Elliott 163). Thus, Gyneth's charitable ambitions are contained within heterosexual marriage only after she has been 'rightly educated' as to the proper scope for her work (Elliott 164). However, Gyneth's earlier decision to accept the relationship between Lewis and Rose is a choice that she makes because she feels it is her moral responsibility to forsake her own interests—romantic or otherwise—in favour of those she loves.

In *Charity Helstone* (1865), Charity makes a series of similar choices that demonstrate her agency as a philanthropic heroine. The most significant choice emerges with the shocking discovery that she is not related by blood to her Aunt Dorothy, who has raised her. This knowledge inspires Charity's development into a model of charitable Christian femininity. Her realisation that she is 'an unfortunate foundling, belonging to no one in particular, but born to poverty, shame, and sorrow' (*Charity Helstone* 106), prompts her renewed dedication to her studies so that she can earn her own living instead of receiving the 'bread of charity' (86). However, she realises she has a duty to return home to her aunt even though she sees this as yet another humiliating example of how she is the subject of further charity.

At the same time, this trial of being a foundling provides the motivation for her to develop true religious feeling and to genuinely embody the meaning of her name. The Rector's sermon in favour of the local foundling hospital opens her eyes to her value in the eyes of God. She chooses to become the embodiment of 1 Corinthians 13 in which 'charity suffereth long, and *is kind*' (*Charity Helstone* 149, emphasis in original). She never returns to school, instead choosing to devote herself to her aunt. The depth of her feeling changes as a result of her new-found religious belief. Her affection for her Aunt 'had acquired all the intensity and consciousness of matured years' (204). This daughterly devotion supplants any inclination to strike out on her own, and she busies herself helping her aunt and her community.

This decision to stay at home and support her aunt is not overtly discussed. Instead Charity's religious feeling and devotion to her aunt reinforce her youthful innocence. Although Charity had 'grown almost into womanhood,' she is still seen as a child: 'indeed, her aunt often told her that she grew younger in mind as she grew older in years, for as time added inches to her height it seemed also to add brightness to her cheek, light to her eye, and simplicity to her manner' (*Charity Helstone* 205). This innocence means that Charity is unwilling to accept Lord Huntley's proposal for she does not love him. This innocence is explicitly positioned as sexual since Charity is unaware that Lord Huntley is romantically interested in her. She simply rejects his proposal because she does not love him. Her love is dedicated to Edward Saville, a long-time family friend, but the example of her aunt's bigamous relationship with a man who is not sufficiently religious prompts her to reject his love as well. According to Elliott, the disciplining of Charity's behaviour is how she learns to 'curb her impulses, submitting her will and voice to the rule of Christian principle' (169). Yet her refusal of Edward is a decision that she does not make lightly or easily. Although inspired by her religious belief, she nonetheless consciously rejects marriage to an unsuitable man. As she explains to Edward, "'I dare not hinder my progress [towards a Godly life] by joining my steps with one who is not even attempting to walk in the same direction'" (292). She knows marriage to him is too great a risk to her soul. Like Jane Eyre when she refuses to live as Rochester's mistress, Charity resists the strong temptation to give in to the love she feels for him and chooses to remain unmarried.

Charity's decision to remain single enables her to follow her aunt's philanthropic impulses to help those in need through small acts of local kindness and support. The extent of Aunt Dorothy's benevolence only becomes known after her death when 'fresh stories of her bounty discovered themselves day by day' (*Charity Helstone* 335). After a substantial inheritance from her maternal grandfather, Charity is able to extend her charitable influence even further to include establishing a hospital, an almshouse, and a new church. Thus, her choices enable her to become a charitable figure who remains true to her beliefs and her moral responsibility to help others. She also enacts a maternal benevolence over her community as these charitable acts function as a substitute for the children she does not have.

The most radical model of charitable femininity is Ernestine Courtenay, protagonist of *Hidden Depths* (1866), whose religious belief inspires her to actively seek out 'degenerate' women who have fallen into sin through prostitution. Ernestine defines a charitable feminine ideal in which young women are able actively to fulfil their philanthropic duties in the public sphere. Presumably because of its provocative content, the novel was originally published anonymously and was only republished with Skene's name in 1886. Skene explains in her Preface that the book 'is not a work of fiction, in the ordinary acceptation of the term' (Preface 1.np),[2] but is instead based on her experiences prison-visiting in and around Oxford from the 1860s onwards (Sanders). Although the events of the novel 'did not occur precisely as here narrated, it is nevertheless actual truth which speaks in these records' (Skene, Preface 1.np). The 'hidden depths,' she states, are not suitable subjects for a work of fiction, for they ought not 'to be opened up to the light of day for purposes of mere amusement' (Preface 1.np).

Instead, the topic deserved serious attention, and Skene, who was preoccupied throughout her life with rescuing prostitutes, was in a position to write about these experiences. This novel was a call to action in which both men and women were to be held accountable for the double standard in Victorian society by which men seduced young women without any consequences, while those seduced women were abandoned to prostitution and starvation. As Judith Walkowitz explains, prostitution in the 1850s became enshrined as a 'great social evil,' and outreach programmes 'gained widespread popularity and momentum' (42). In *Hidden Depths*, Ernestine Courtenay is one of the few people willing to fight for these abandoned women and model charitable behaviour that transcends class and respectability. Yet, as for Charity Helstone, this charitable work must be performed alone if a partner of equivalent religious faith cannot be found.

Ernestine finds herself without useful work after her brother marries, but knows that she might do something: "'I do not know what else I can do at present ... I do so want to try and be of some use in the world'" (*Hidden Depths* 1.32). She feels that women can do more than 'spend their lives dressing and visiting, and working at their embroidery. It must be possible for them to be useful to others, without going beyond their own province' (1.32). Articulating a careful definition of useful work that remains within the scope of women's sphere of influence, she is not in danger of becoming 'a strong-minded female' who agitates for women's rights (*Hidden Depths* 1.32). Ernestine is looking forward to her upcoming marriage to Hugh Lingard but anticipates that it will be at least two or three years until he is financially able to marry her. In the meantime, she must wait, but this is, as she tells her brother George Courtenay, "'too long a time to waste in amusements which weary me beyond expression; and I am sure of one thing,—there must be in this great suffering world some work even for me, weak and ignorant as I am'" (1.33). At 25, Ernestine is older than both Gyneth and Charity, more aware of the evil of the world, and in a position to do something about it. Her perspective differs from the domestically inclined philanthropy embodied by Gwyneth and Charity, although both models are based on similar definitions of femininity, in which young women must consider how they can help others.

The charitable work that Ernestine takes on emerges from and is produced by her family circle. George has seduced and abandoned Lois Brook, who is pregnant with his child. Ernestine struggles to believe in the 'wickedness' of her brother and knows that if she acknowledges that he has 'fallen into the ashes of the worst corruption' (*Hidden Depths* 1.47), she will never be able to look at him with affection and love again. The sanctity and sanctuary of the domestic sphere, which is the source of Gyneth's duty, also prompts Ernestine's charitable impulses. Her 'whole soul burned with compassion for the utter misery which her woman's heart could understand so well' (1.47–8). The fact that Ernestine is a woman provides her with an emotional connection to this woman scorned and motivates her to seek the truth.

The heart of this novel is predicated on definitions of feminine purity in which sexual experience is defined by choice. A woman who has sexual experience outside the bonds of marriage was depicted in fiction and the periodical press as either a 'seduced woman' who is the 'helpless victim of a superior male' or a 'fallen woman' who is 'capable of sin and therefore responsible for her own destiny' (Mitchell x). In both cases, these women were meant to be ignored, although the seduced woman was perceived with some sympathy and was occasionally understood to be redeemable, like the eponymous protagonist of Elizabeth Gaskell's *Ruth* (1853). Lois is a seduced woman, as is her sister Annie, and consequently they both 'deserve' to be saved. The perceived risk to Ernestine is that her reputation will be sullied by her attempts to save these young women. Unlike the charitable work performed by Gyneth and Charity, which is relatively protected from unsavoury dealings, Ernestine ventures into geographical and emotional spaces that are destined to compromise her innocence. Although she is motivated by family feeling while Gyneth and Charity are engaged in more public charity, her actions are more difficult to justify. She takes action knowing that she will be criticised, but feeling that she has a duty to her brother's victim. She must sacrifice her innocence in her quest for the truth: 'Ernestine did not deceive herself; she knew that for a young lady of her rank in life to go out alone into the haunts of sin to seek one of the fallen and degraded of her own sex, would be considered a very reprehensible departure from the usages of the society in which she had always lived' (*Hidden Depths* 1.109–10). She meets criticism along the way, including from her male servant, who is 'disgusted' when his mistress 'thus demeaned herself (in his estimation) by asking questions about a person whose existence he conceived she ought to ignore' (1.51). The impure woman is meant to be ignored by people of every class, not only because of her sexual experience but also because her choice—has she been seduced, or has she fallen?—is unclear.

Ernestine's refusal to ignore Lois, and her demand that these women be seen and cared for, place the unequal treatment of women at the centre of her philanthropic life work. The fact that she is able to pursue this work is testament to her role as a 'brave true-hearted messenger' of God (*Hidden Depths* 1.109), who is dedicated to helping those in need. Her religious conviction enables her to perform this work without becoming tarnished. This work foreshadows Josephine Butler's attempts, beginning in 1869, to repeal the Contagious Diseases Acts, which authorised police to detain and examine women suspected of being prostitutes to determine if they had a sexually transmitted disease.

Ernestine models the charitable feminine ideal in her resolve to 'remedy [the] startling evils' in the lower classes (*Hidden Depths* 1.80), yet her range of influence is limited to what she can do as an individual. Once she becomes aware of the fraud being perpetrated on young women, who are swept up by upper-class men, wooed with romance and wealth, and then abandoned, she is determined that 'at least in the narrow circle of her individual existence, not only before her marriage, but always, so far as other claims permitted, she would work out this problem with all the energy, power, and devotion of which her life was capable' (*Hidden Depths* 1.81). Ernestine takes on this responsibility knowing that it will continue after she is married. The duty to care for these suffering women is a life-long concern that she expects her fiancé to support, both financially and emotionally. Although the book explicitly critiques men's actions and the inadequate system for handling prostitutes, Ernestine's duty is to provide individual respite to these women. She does not engage in political action or attempt to change the system. Instead, she uses her individual fortune to prepare a suitable house for women who seek to escape from a life of prostitution, providing these 'poor outcasts' with 'a simple shelter from evil, unencumbered by needless rules and constraints' and striving to show them 'the goodness of their Father in heaven reflected in the love and compassion of His creatures' (*Hidden Depths* 2.219). Ernestine's determination to help these unfortunate women is based on her own religious belief and a desire to save them from further sin.

Ernestine's dedication to—and experience arising from—this work means that her anticipated future husband is held to a high religious and moral standard that he fails to meet. She discovers that her fiancé Hugh Lingard was the man who seduced and abandoned Lois's sister Annie. Although she continues to love him, 'the natural happiness to which a woman looks in the ties of wife and mother could never now be hers'

(*Hidden Depths* 2.210). Her only consolation is that 'by the wreck of her own mortal happiness, she had secured eternal peace' for Annie, whose dying wish was to forgive her enemy in person (2.209). The charitable feminine ideal, as with Charity, is based on an unwillingness to compromise her religious and charitable ideals to obtain love and marriage. Charity and Ernestine give their hearts to men who are unworthy of the gift. They consequently reject their suitors, choosing charitable work over marriage, when the men fail to live up to their religious, moral, and ethical standards. Only Gyneth has a suitable suitor who is capable of the same faith and charity. For the other young women, the most appropriate decision is to reject men who will ultimately fail to live up to this standard.

Readings of these novels tend to emphasise the undoubtedly conservative nature of their conclusions, where opportunities to be both a philanthropic heroine and a wife and mother are rare. However, within the context of the 1860s in England, these novels are significant for the agency they bestow on their protagonists. In all three cases, these young women make choices about charitable work and romantic partnerships that enable them to remain true to their religious and moral beliefs. The ability to work outside the home is central to each protagonist, even if the boundaries of that work are somewhat circumscribed by expectations based on tradition, gender, and class. Where their romantic partners fail to live up to a single moral and religious standard, they are summarily rejected so that the charitable work will not be compromised. When the romantic partner is adequate, he proves his suitability by continuing to support his wife's philanthropic work, thus promoting a mid-Victorian ideal for both women and men that is based on religion and duty.

Notes

1. Henrietta Keddie wrote extensively under the pseudonym of 'Sarah Tytler,' publishing novels and contributing articles and fiction to a variety of periodicals.
2. *Hidden Depths* was published in two volumes. The citations in this chapter include volume number and page.

Works Cited

Bernardi, Debra and Jill Bergman. 'Introduction: Benevolence Literature by American Women.' *Our Sisters' Keepers: Nineteenth-Century Benevolence Literature by American Women*. Ed. Jill Bergman and Debra Bernardi. Tuscaloosa: University of Alabama Press, 2005.

Bilston, Sarah. *The Awkward Age in Women's Popular Fiction, 1850–1900*. Oxford: Oxford University Press, 2004.

Blumberg, Ilana M. *Victorian Sacrifice: Ethics and Economics in Mid-Century Novels*. Columbus: Ohio State University Press, 2013.

Brock, Frances Carey. *Charity Helstone: A Tale*. London: Seeley, Jackson, and Halliday, 1865.

Dyhouse, Carol. *Girls Growing Up in Late Victorian and Edwardian England*. London: Routledge, 1981.

Elliott, Dorice Williams. *The Angel out of the House: Philanthropy and Gender in Nineteenth-Century England*. Charlottesville: University Press of Virginia, 2002.

Kent, Susan Kingsley. *Gender and Power in Britain, 1640–1990*. London: Routledge, 1999.

Mitchell, Sally. *The Fallen Angel: Chastity, Class and Women's Reading, 1835–1880*. Bowling Green: Bowling Green University Press, 1981.

Onslow, Barbara. *Women of the Press in Nineteenth-Century Britain*. Houndmills: Palgrave, 2000.

Perkin, Joan. *Victorian Women*. London: John Murray, 1993.

Prochaska, F. K. *Women and Philanthropy in Nineteenth-Century England*. Oxford: Clarendon Press, 1980.

Sanders, Andrew. 'Skene, Felicia Mary Frances (1821–1899),' *Oxford Dictionary of National Biography*, Oxford University Press, 2004, online edn, Oct 2009, www.oxforddnb.com/view/article/25666, accessed 20 Feb 2018.

Skene, Felicia. *Hidden Depths*. 2 vols. Edinburgh: Edmonston and Douglas, 1866a.

———. Preface. *Hidden Depths*. 2 vols. Edinburgh: Edmonston and Douglas, 1866b. Vol 1 n.p.

Thomson, Patricia. *The Victorian Heroine: A Changing Ideal, 1837–1873*. 1956. Westport: Greenwood Press, 1978.

Tytler, Sarah. *Papers for Thoughtful Girls*. Boston: Crosby and Ainsworth, 1865.

Vallone, Lynne. *Disciplines of Virtue: Girls' Culture in the Eighteenth and Nineteenth Centuries*. New Haven, CT: Yale University Press, 1995.

Van Remoortel, Marianne. *Women, Work and the Victorian Periodical: Living by the Press*. Houndmills: Palgrave, 2015.

Vicinus, Martha. *Independent Women: Work and Community for Single Women, 1850–1920*. London: Virago, 1985.

Walkowitz, Judith R. *Prostitution and Victorian Society: Women, Class and the State*. Cambridge: Cambridge University Press, 1980.

Wilford, Florence. *A Maiden of Our Own Day*. London: Joseph Masters, 1862.

CHAPTER 7

'[S]mothered under rose-leaves': Violent Sensation and the Location of the Feminine in Eliza Lynn Linton's *Sowing the Wind*

Carolyn W. de la L. Oulton

Fiction of the 1860s is often associated with the series of shocks administered in more than homoeopathic doses by such writers as Mary Braddon and Wilkie Collins. However, this chapter considers Eliza Lynn Linton as a test case for the ways in which antifeminism finds ways to complicate literary boundaries during this decade. In the case of Linton herself it is possible to locate elements of feminist protest embedded in the framework of an otherwise conservative narrative stance. In the year before the publication of her infamous antifeminist essay 'The Girl of the Period' in 1868 she constructed a novel in which her antifeminist stance is not negated but subtly mediated through an ostentatiously sensational plot, that is in turn dependent for its effects on the traditional womanliness of the central protagonist.

C. W. de la L. Oulton (✉)
School of Humanities, Canterbury Christ Church University, Canterbury, UK
e-mail: carolyn.oulton@canterbury.ac.uk

© The Author(s) 2020
A. E. Gavin, C. W. de la L. Oulton (Eds.), *British Women's Writing from Brontë to Bloomsbury, Volume 2*, British Women's Writing from Brontë to Bloomsbury, 1840–1940,
https://doi.org/10.1007/978-3-030-38528-6_7

It has been argued that with the 'Girl of the Period' article in the *Saturday Review* for which she is primarily remembered, Linton strategically courted controversy in order to increase her visibility as a writer, while at the same time justifying her anomalous position as a female journalist separated from her husband and living independently. Predictably, since the 1860s she has most often been discussed in the context of her indictment of progressive feminist principles and her presentation of a troubling but instantly recognisable persona that becomes doubly interesting given the anomaly of her own independent personal life.

In fact, as Valerie Sanders argues, Linton and other antifeminist writers of the 1860s were writing at a time when marriage was coming increasingly under scrutiny, 'as if the Matrimonial Causes Act of 1857, which recognized a more widespread need for divorce, gave novelists fresh license to query the state their writing traditionally celebrated as the desirable norm' ('Marriage' 24). Sanders also points out, however, that while antifeminist writers such as Linton might reasonably be expected to promote traditional views of marriage in their fiction, actually 'the marriages they portray involve half-hearted endings, bizarre alliances, and an underlying atmosphere of sexual distaste' ('Marriage' 25), while nonetheless becoming eclipsed in the literary popular canon by the high-profile experiments of the decade's more newsworthy and deliberately shocking sensation fiction.

However, Linton's *Sowing the Wind* (1867) is itself clearly identifiable as a sensation novel, showcasing a number of the key motifs associated with this controversial genre: rebellious women, a near-fatal fire, a mysterious will, illegitimacy, a lost inheritance, attempted murder, and ultimately madness. Yet despite these ostentatious indicators of its sensational status, the novel also partakes in a painstaking and sustained debate about the limits of female obedience, in distinction to the sensation novel's more familiar insistence on gender transgression. In publishing this novel only a year before her first 'Girl of the Period' article, Linton offers a notably more nuanced response to the question of women's rights than she attempts in her *Saturday Review* journalism, despite publishing in a genre often associated with flamboyant characters and shocking gender relations. Responding to Pamela Gilbert's comment that 'Victorian authors are complicated, self-contradictory, smart, resistant to ideology and complicit with it by turns or simultaneously' (23), this essay argues that *Sowing the Wind* constitutes a deliberate engagement with questions of genre as a means of exploring and recalibrating extremes of freedom and obedience.

In its risky rehabilitation of the domestic angel within the demands of the sensational mode, it offers its readers an innovative approach to negotiating gender roles within marriage.

The novel's plot hinges on the obsessive response of the snobbish St John Aylott to his morally submissive but physically splendid wife Isola and her increasing resistance to his arbitrary demands. She is encouraged to question her husband's stance by the independent spirit of her cousin Jane Osborn, who is like a 'bath of life' in her direct speech and moral independence 'to the woman stifled by conventionalities and denied the free use of even thought' (65). The echo of the more familiar phrase 'free use of her limbs' emphasises the further constraints put upon Isola, but also reminds readers of her superior physical attributes.

St John's decision to remove his wife from the supposed contamination of her aunt and cousin, the first acquaintances she has been able to make since her marriage five years previously, provides the catalyst for his own flirtation with the pretty and manipulative Marcy Tremouille. It also leads to Isola's adoption of his illegitimate nephew after his rejection of his dying sister becomes known, and the final revelation of his own insecure status as the illegitimate son of an artist's model and the grandson of his country neighbour's gardener. By the end of the novel St John has lost his fortune (which more properly belongs to his nephew, as his sister herself was born after their parents' marriage) in disastrous speculation, and dies in a madhouse. Like other novels of the late 1860s, *Sowing the Wind* consistently draws attention to its own deployment of sensational tropes, creating a narrative that is essentially self-referential.

One likely source for the novel is the still more dramatic 1855 novel *Paul Ferroll* by Caroline Clive. In the earlier story the eponymous upper-class character lives in almost total seclusion, one apparent reason for which is his jealous obsession with his wife (which even excludes their daughter), although strangely this reclusive behaviour is partially rehabilitated when it transpires that the main reason is actually Ferroll's guilty past as a murderer. Like *Sowing the Wind*, Clive's novel includes a dramatic house fire and explores the dilemma of the wife whose husband rules her absolutely and actively discourages her affection for their only child.

However, the interplay between Isola and Jane is also immediately suggestive of the relationship between Marian Halcombe and Laura Fairlie in Wilkie Collins's *The Woman in White* (1860), a novel which famously features an autocratic upper-class husband who turns out to be illegitimate, financial ruin, madness, and an accidental fire. Adhering to the familiar conventions of the sensation novel showcased most prominently in *The Woman in White*, Linton makes doubling and splitting key to the positioning of the reader. Rather than simply replicating Collins's technique, however, she reworks this convention in innovative ways, to challenge readers' perceptions of the characters and to reconsider the choices open to them at different points. Crucially, the novel draws on readers' awareness of such literary precursors as Collins and Braddon in its sustained interplay between diverse characters and conflicting moral values. It does so partly in order to refute the simplistic binaries that may be read into sensational texts.

Isola's ambivalent response to St John's demands, for example, offers an initial clue to the subtle intelligence of her character. In the early stages of the novel she apparently accepts her husband's behaviour, although the metaphorical stunting of her own will signals a repressed 'struggle' rather than passive acceptance:

> Her husband ruled her life, without a question of divided authority ever rising between them; he tricked her out with jewels, loaded her with rich dresses and costly trinkets, till she scarcely knew what to do with the finery which no one but himself ever saw ... leaving on her a certain cramped and stifled feeling, as of one struggling in silken fetters, and smothered under rose-leaves. (30)

The image of smothering will be horrifyingly repeated towards the end of the novel, reinforcing the sense of obsessive selfishness that underpins St John's decking out and objectification of his wife.

Isola is beautiful and tractable, as Laura Fairlie initially appears to be—readers somewhat unfairly tend to overlook Laura's determined resistance to her husband's bullying later in Collins's novel, not least when she agrees to sign a paper only if her husband 'will treat me like a responsible being' (*The Woman in White* 250). However, Isola also shares some of the characteristics of the more 'masculine' Marian. She has large hands—a key attribute which will prove significant towards the end of the novel—and again like Marian 'a fit of weeping was as rare to her as to a man' (*Sowing the Wind?* 45). It is St John who shares the small feet as well as the slightly effeminate bearing of Frederick Fairlie, as well as the illegitimate birth and implied infertility of Sir Percival Glyde; Collins's mentally impaired Anne Catherick is replaced by the largely uneducated but conniving Marcy, who copies Lady Audley's tactics in staging a submissive ignorance in order to further her own ends, and it is St John himself rather than the Anne/ Laura or Lucy figure who is finally sent to an asylum for the insane.

In its use of doubling and other sensational motifs to negotiate extreme positions, *Sowing the Wind* also directs attention to the quotidian, in a subtle revision of gendered questions Linton discusses more stridently in her 'Girl of the Period' articles, including the attributes of maternity and female submission. When Jane insists that 'we are not our own but our generation's; and if we can do no good to that, we had better be done with and put away the soonest possible,' her mother challenges this position by a reminder that the weak have rights as part of this same generation. '"Then I hope that I shall never live to see that day," cried Mrs Osborn indignantly. "I am not very strong myself, and if all those who have weak hearts and poor foolish heads like mine are to be put to death, I am sure it will not be a very comfortable or Christian-like arrangement"' (67). In her vacuous prettiness Mrs Osborn is reminiscent of Charles Dickens's Dora Spenlow in *David Copperfield* (1849–1850), but like Dora she is allowed moments of perception, as in this conflation of 'weak hearts' with 'poor foolish heads,' that challenges both Jane and the reader to equate the marginalisation of the foolish with the execution of the physically unfit.

In her quest for independence even the determined Jane is exposed to the very real possibility that she will be rejected on the grounds of her gender, and she is forced into a subservient position with possible employers in her efforts to avoid being 'put away' as unfit for serious work. Valerie Sanders describes Jane's journalistic career as 'the most extensive fictional examination of women's role in journalism in the mid-nineteenth century,' one that both fictionalises Linton's own work on the *Morning Chronicle* and offers 'a brusque self-caricature' (*Eve's Renegades* 130).

In her speculative letter to *The Comet* newspaper, Jane anticipates the advice she is likely to be given, asking 'would he please not recommend her to be a governess? for she had a horror of children and hated teaching beyond everything else, and she would rather go out as a housemaid than as a governess' (35). Jane's fear of children, counterpoised as it is by her obvious aptitude for journalism, is presented as essentially comic, while Isola later becomes the ideal substitute mother to her husband's orphaned nephew Reginald Grant. A further and more unlikely doubling is suggested, too, in the pairing of Jane and her mother. It is Jane who is initially placed in charge of Aylott's nephew by his dying mother and who helps to look after him until he can be handed over to Isola. Notwithstanding her overtly feminine attributes and love of small children, the gentle and affectionate Mrs Osborn is less competent than Jane and has to be prevented from feeding Reginald unsuitable sweet food in his first few weeks of life:

> If Jane was rude and capable, she was gentle and feckless; if Jane was the one on whom to rely for presence of mind in moments of emergency, for thoughtful promptitude and for sturdy ability, her mother, who had not the courage of a mouse nor the quickness of mind of a child, would while away the easy hours by her unending flow of gentle babble, nursing the baby which Jane rarely touched or even looked at, but having to be narrowly watched all the same. (133)

Perhaps surprisingly, Jane's disavowal of the maternal instinct is repeatedly given fair play, as she declares, '"babies, and love, and the graces and prettinesses are all very fine, I dare say, but give me the real solid pleasure of work—a man's work—work that influences the world—work that is power!"' (248). As Barbara Onslow argues, '[t]he image of Jane Osborn, the newspaper woman, at the end of *Sowing the Wind* is a bleak one. Rejected by the man she loved and dedicated to her work, her physical appearance ... mirrors her emotional deprivation' (191). Yet it is surely significant that Jane's sense of deprivation is linked to a failed love affair and not necessarily to her innate failure as a woman and substitute mother. Rather than use Jane's difference from Isola to revivify the figure of the maternal woman, the narrator skilfully sets Jane's sense of responsibility despite her stated aversion to children against the contemptuous revulsion shown by the childless St John, who claims that 'mothers with their babies were only cows with a difference; and when it came to love for a child not her own, he said, a woman who could love and adopt a strange infant was just an animal and no more, without even the excuse of natural instinct' (170).

The narrator pointedly refuses the obvious contrast of the maternal woman and her supposedly 'unsexed' counterpart, choosing instead to emphasise the worth of maternity through making its recognition a litmus test for male characters. In his extreme reaction, St John reveals his own base instincts through a failure to value the higher moral qualities of his wife. As if to reinforce the point, Gilbert Holmes—the Walter Hartright figure of the novel whose masculine credentials are attested by a history of working the Californian gold mines—thinks Isola is never more beautiful than when she has the child in her arms.

Isola herself is physically active as well as maternal, demonstrating agility and stamina in clambering over rocks and hills, and escaping with Gilbert from a burning inn by climbing out of a high window and across the facing while her husband rushes into the street regardless of her safety:

> Clinging to the wall, holding that brave man's [Gilbert's] hand in hers— herself as brave and as unfaltering as he—her naked feet clasping the narrow band, and her golden hair streaming far and wide over her shoulders and about her marble throat, her white petticoat with its low body and short sleeves showing her neck and arms and marking out the undulating lines of her supple body as she pressed close against the wall, Isola looked like some angel-woman to the crowd watching below. (211)

This escape from the burning building invokes the scene in *The Woman in White* where Marian (confronted by equally hazardous rain) removes the encumbrance of her evening dress in order to listen to the conversation of Sir Percival and Count Fosco from the roof above. In this reworking, however, the adventurous woman who is 'herself as brave' as her rescuer is also the golden-haired angel whose body is eroticised through such phrases as 'naked feet,' 'low body,' and 'undulating lines': a reminder that '[e]ven in [Linton's] most virulently antifeminist novels ... there is an intriguing ambivalence' about gender construction (Anderson 120). St John characteristically rebukes his wife, when she reaches the ground, for appearing in public in her nightdress and in bare feet, an inappropriate reaction that effectively precludes the reader's own interpretation of such behaviour as being in any way transgressive.

It is not only in such dramatic scenes that an extreme insistence on feminine weakness and submission is undermined. Even in the most conventionally domestic scenes, the novel repeatedly deconstructs St John's failure to care and his obstruction of Isola's maternal instincts, in order to reconsider the limits of female obedience within marriage. Initially 'Isola did pity him; not loftily and from the cold height of superiority, but with the tender self-abasement of a woman striving to restore the man she loved to his due place, and to shut her eyes to the depth of his descent' (144). If St John's own insistence on 'wifely submission' is questioned through the portrayal of his own weak qualities as a husband, it is also increasingly qualified by the wider imperatives of independent judgement and religious conviction introduced by both the narrator and formidable characters such as Jane. Forbidden to invite her aunt to the marital home as etiquette requires, Isola is forced to confront what the narrator terms:

the cancerous sore of home, namely, the right of the woman to independent moral action in opposition to her husband's will—her duty to God as represented by her conscience, or her duty to the social law as represented by her wifely submission. And Isola was just beginning to be afloat between these two great tidal opinions. (62)

This question is contextualised through the domestic performances of a range of characters, several of whom discredit the literalised obedience St John fatuously claims as his right. These passages are more suggestive of the realist than the sensation novel, a reminder that the two modes borrow from each other or even coalesce at particular points. Working from the opposite side of the question, Tamara Wagner points out that 'domestic fiction's representation of self-sacrifice receives an additional impetus by the plot devices made available by the sensation craze' (139). It could be said with equal justice that sensation fiction is dependent for its effects on the expectations raised by readers' familiarity with domestic realism.

The conservative ideal is caricatured by Mr and Mrs Joyce, whose very happiness is derided by those around them, as their parodically inane behaviour is sharply defined against the sensational register of the main plot which they persistently fail to see or simply misrepresent. The conservative Mrs Joyce assumes that Isola rather than St John must be at fault because she 'could not tolerate anything like character in wives'; however the narrator is quick to point out that Mrs Joyce herself encounters no opposition from her adoring husband, and following her animadversions on Isola the couple 'expatiated on their mutual perfections till tea-time' (125). Tellingly in a serio-comic subplot Mrs Joyce's sister is unable to find a husband partly because she mimics this 'wifely' submission, making herself an object of pity through her inappropriately overt adoration of available men. Marcy meanwhile strategically caricatures feminine ignorance and submission in order to attract the dissatisfied St John. When Marcy deliberately exacerbates the tension between St John and Isola by claiming '"I am such a dreadful little creature I could not be my own mistress if I tried,"' the perceptive Isola points out that on the contrary, '"you are absolute in your own home"' and '"ten times more your own mistress than I am, or than anyone I know"' (174).

Comparing Jane's contempt for female submission with Mrs Joyce's uncritical view '"that we are born into the world only to be the slaves and shadows of men,"' Isola asks Gilbert '"how can we find out the truth between two such extremes?"' (149). His fairly conservative response is, "'[b]y avoiding each alike, and being neither a Griselda nor an Amazon. ... Is there no mean between defiance and slavishness?—no broad highway between barren crags and valleys of mud?'" (149). This philosophical rejoinder effects no practical compromise for Isola in her negotiation of either local politics or the misery of her life at home. St John's madness finally resolves the dilemma, but only by exaggerating his unfitness to 'rule' his household in the first place; his speculation leads to financial ruin, as he comes under the dangerous influence of the corrupt Harvey Wyndham and invests increasingly large sums in fraudulent mining schemes in an effort to assert his masculinity.

Like other sensation heroines, Isola actually derives a certain degree of independence from the loss of wealth, status, and husband. At this point in the novel the definition of feminine strength as forbearance and endurance is re-inscribed, and the narrator is forced to find new ways of presenting qualities that other narratives of the time (and several of the characters in her own novel) implicitly link to prescribed weakness. The Christian framework through which Isola's independent will was first enabled gives similar credibility to her moral triumph in adversity, as she successfully adapts to a circumscribed life in lodgings with the Osborns. In the overdetermined play on gender that is a key feature of the sensation genre and of Linton's writing in general, this focus on moral restraint and maternal love as strength, not weakness, must be counterbalanced by St John's parallel decline into feminised madness. This madness, as his class and gender identity is eroded, becomes the catalyst for St John's two attempts to murder his nephew when the family's removal to lodgings brings him into close proximity with the child for the first time. Initially he attempts poison but is prevented just in time by a suspicious Harvey Wyndham. On the second occasion Isola wakes to find him attempting to smother the child with a pillow. Isola, who herself began the novel being metaphorically 'smothered,' has been insistently characterised as having unusually large hands, and seeing what is happening she runs to her husband and physically restrains him.

This is the point at which action urgently replaces the combative language that Isola's commitment to the traditional model of marriage precludes her from using. Just in time to save the boy, she 'did not speak; she did not even utter a cry; but she seized [St John's] wrists and flung his hands from off the child, with almost the strength of a man' (308). In contrast to this accession of masculinised power, St John's failure of masculinity is metaphorically conveyed through his duplicitous attempts at infanticide, conceived as either poisoning or suffocation; significantly, he will also signally fail in his overtly 'masculine' attack on Gilbert.

However, in this scene, St John's madness also serves the secondary function of reconciling Isola's protectiveness of her adopted child with her perceived responsibility to her husband. Unable fully to forgive what he has done, she retreats into silence rather than articulate the unthinkable conflict between her marriage vows, her love for the child, and her moral responsibility to prevent any further attempt at murder. It is shortly after she has decided to send the child away that St John is consigned to a madhouse, making this final sacrifice unnecessary. The tension in this part of the novel, however, stands as a reminder that Isola's enactment of the perfect woman is itself provisional and impossible to sustain under the conditions in which she is placed. In this final dilemma she becomes a vehicle for a subtle exploration of the nature and function of sacrifice.

Sensation novels are often criticised for enabling the independent action or rebellion of a central female figure, who is then reinstated in a conventionally subordinate role by the end of the story. *Sowing the Wind* offers a more complex view, incorporating into its narrative structure a sustained debate on the very nature of sacrifice that lies at the heart of the feminine ideal, as constructed in this and other literature of the period. None of the commendable characters attempt to denigrate sacrifice as an ideal; rather they argue about its most appropriate form and motivation. Jane tells Isola that "'[t]o give up real good for the mere whims of another is no sacrifice righteously put, but a self-degradation—an immoral lying down to Juggernaut. Sacrifice yourself for a good cause if you like—for the progress of principles, for truth, freedom, humanity—but not to foolish whims and fancies like your husband's'" (67). Gilbert later argues on similar lines that "'self-sacrifice is not slavishness. To be of any value at all it is the voluntary gift of strength'" (149).

This view prepares the reader to accept Isola's apparent submission to her husband's abuse as a conscious deployment of latent strength, rather than a passive acceptance of the subservient role he dictates. When St John ultimately hits her:

> She might have been Joan of Arc when derided by the courtiers—Boadicea when her daughters were carried captive by the Romans—Constance when her son was slain—she looked so grand in her indignant grief! ... then came back the spirit of perhaps a truer dignity and a nobler womanliness—the

spirit of patience and forbearance—the patience of the healthy with the sick—the forbearance of the strong with the weak. (329)

This forbearance is explicitly registered as a choice made by a character whose moral force invokes female heroes rather than Griseldas, before becoming de-gendered altogether in the contrast of 'healthy' with 'sick' and 'strong' with 'weak.' This seemingly feminine acceptance of injustice notably links Isola to the similar forbearance shown by Gilbert, who conceals St John's knife attack upon him while St John himself shows an inherent failure of masculinity: '[a]fter a short time of exhaustion he fell into a violent fit of hysterics' (331).

Towards the end of the novel Isola's suicidal impulse is overcome by the needs of the child she has adopted, and the narrator takes the opportunity once again to point out to the reader the difference between unreflecting submission and the conscious act of sacrifice this involves, 'she took on herself a very different form of sacrifice from that which her husband had demanded. The one had been the annihilation of free will—the other was the free gift of love' (337). The final scene of the novel strongly suggests that Isola will marry Gilbert, but this union is shown to be more than a cheap narrative trick when it is ratified by none other than Jane Osborn, presumably because Isola has proved her credentials in convincing her cousin that she is in no obvious need of rescue.

Despite its use of plot devices that readers would be quick to identify with Collins and Braddon, *Sowing the Wind* is itself ambivalent about the sensational mode. The narrator writes that Isola 'was not a woman of trained intellect, and could not have taken up literature as a profession as Jane had done. I doubt if she could have written a novel, given bigamy, murder, and suicide as the triple basis' (254). It is the rather unsavoury Harvey Wyndham who makes the pre-emptive complaint familiar from Wilkie Collins that 'If we authors were to put into our novels half of what we know to be actual fact, we should have the critics down upon us for "unnatural incidents", "strained effects", and "want of truth to nature" generally' (56). His female counterpart Marcy Tremouille at one level embodies Jennifer Hedgecock's description of the mid-Victorian femme fatale, whose 'physical appearance works to construct an acceptable image of the mid-Victorian woman, easy to mistake as the domestic ideal, a woman suitable to bourgeois standards' (8), an appearance that belies her strategically devious behaviour. However, Marcy is also the victim of her own investment in this literary type, and her punishment is to be trapped into marriage after she accelerates St John's descent into madness by sending anonymous letters accusing Isola of infidelity. Significantly she sends these letters 'feeling much as she felt when she cut the leaves of an exciting novel and plunged into a new chapter' (326). Meanwhile she and her scheming companion Mrs McHugh 'both talked of St John Aylott's history as if it had been a new novel coming out in monthly numbers, and they were feverish with desire to see the next issue' (297).

The narrator offers a more chilling if less sensational account of events in which:

> Crime and horror do not go about with dishevelled hair and screaming voice. They may find themselves ultimately in a madhouse or on the scaffold, but in the meantime they tie their ribbons and brush their coats, and are careful of their teeth and nails, and break their daily bread like innocence and serenity, and no mere outsider can see the difference. (309)

The challenge for Isola is precisely that she does inhabit this social world of ribbon tying and convention, and does not see herself as a sensation heroine. As she is forced to realise, however, conventional existence in the novel is based on a false premise and is sustained by an unreflecting insistence on inane maxims as essential truths. Jane ends the novel luckless but defiant, and it is Isola who becomes the ideal heroine of Linton's imagination, because she triumphantly incorporates qualities presented by other sensation novels as subversive *within* feminine ideals of the maternal and angelic.

Works Cited

Anderson, Nancy Fix. 'Eliza Lynn Linton: *The Rebel of the Family* (1880) and Other Novels.' *Feminist Readings of Underread Victorian Novels*. Ed Barbara Leah Harman and Susan Meyer. New York and London: Garland Publishing 1996. 117–33.

Collins, Wilkie. *The Woman in White*. 1860. Ed. John Sutherland. Oxford World's Classics. Oxford: Oxford University Press, 1999.

Gilbert, Pamela K. 'Feminism and the Canon: Recovery and Reconsideration of Popular Novelists.' In Wagner, ed. *Antifeminism and the Victorian Novel*, 19–35.

Hedgecock, Jennifer. *The Femme Fatale in Victorian Literature: the Danger and the Sexual Threat*. New York: Cambria Press, 2008.

[Linton, Eliza Lynn]. 'The Girl of the Period.' *Saturday Review* 25 (14 March 1868): 339–40.

Linton, Eliza Lynn. *Sowing the Wind.* 1867. Ed. Deborah T. Meem and Kate Holterhoff. Brighton: Victorian Secrets, 2015.

Onslow, Barbara. *Women of the Press in Nineteenth-Century Britain.* Basingstoke: Macmillan 2000.

Sanders, Valerie. 'Marriage and the Antifeminist Woman Novelist.' In Nicola Diane Thompson, ed. *Victorian Women Writers and the Woman Question.* Cambridge: Cambridge University Press, 1999, 24–41.

———. *Eve's Renegades: Victorian Anti-Feminist Women Novelists.* Basingstoke: Palgrave Macmillan, 1996.

Wagner, Tamara S. 'Marriage Plots and "Matters of More Importance": Sensationalising Self-Sacrifice in Victorian Domestic Fiction.' In Tamara S. Wagner, ed. *Antifeminism and the Victorian Novel: Rereading Nineteenth-Century Women Writers.* New York: Cambria Press 2009. 137–67.

CHAPTER 8

'[F]leshly inclinations': The Nature of Female Desire in Rhoda Broughton's Early Fiction

Tamar Heller

In January 1870, Rhoda Broughton's publisher, George Bentley, dissuaded her from dedicating the forthcoming triple-decker version of her third novel, *Red as a Rose is She* (1870), 'TO MY ENEMIES, ALL AND SUNDRY.'[1] Although she grudgingly agreed not to fire this defiant salvo, the twenty-nine-year-old author had reason to feel embattled. Despite their popular success, her first two novels—*Not Wisely, but Too Well* and *Cometh Up as a Flower*, both published in 1867—had attracted critical hostility, even vituperation; Richard Romer, for example, concluded his *Athenaeum* review of *Not Wisely, but Too Well* by declaring he would no longer 'pollute' the journal's pages with the 'sickening blasphemy' of quotes from the book (569). Given the uproar over sensationalism in the 1860s, it did not help Broughton with reviewers that *Not Wisely, but Too Well* and *Cometh Up as a Flower*—stories featuring heroines who only

T. Heller (✉)
Department of English and Comparative Literature, University of Cincinnati, Cincinnati, OH, USA
e-mail: tamar.heller@uc.edu

© The Author(s) 2020
A. E. Gavin, C. W. de la L. Oulton (eds.), *British Women's Writing from Brontë to Bloomsbury, Volume 2*, British Women's Writing from Brontë to Bloomsbury, 1840–1940, https://doi.org/10.1007/978-3-030-38528-6_8

narrowly escape sexual fall—were associated with the genre. Indeed, in a prominent attack on sensation fiction in *Blackwood's Magazine* in September 1867, Margaret Oliphant singled out *Cometh Up as a Flower* as a prime example of the 'abomination in the midst of us,' as she described the 'unseemly' openness about 'forbidden knowledge' in the work of female sensationalists (268, 258). 'It is a shame to women so to write; and it is a shame to the women who read and accept as a true representation of themselves and their ways the equivocal talk and fleshly inclinations herein attributed to them' (Oliphant 275).

This chapter addresses the pioneering depiction of women's fleshly inclinations in *Not Wisely, but Too Well*; *Cometh Up as a Flower*; and *Red as a Rose Is She*. (*Red as a Rose Is She* is classified here as an 1860s, rather than an 1870s, text because its serial run in *Temple Bar* [May 1869–March 1870] was largely completed by the beginning of the new decade, and even its triple-decker incarnation was published only a few months into it). The first three of the twenty-four novels Broughton produced, along with a collection of ghost stories, over a fifty-three career, *Not Wisely, but Too Well*; *Cometh Up as a Flower*; and *Red as a Rose Is She* showcase the innovative representation of female desire that constitutes one of her distinctive contributions to Victorian women's literature. Although Oliphant complained that an 'intense appreciation of flesh and blood' characterized female sensation novels in general (259), Broughton's 'erotic sensationalism'[2] more explicitly portrays female sexuality than does the writing of other women associated with the sensation school. Whereas Mary Elizabeth Braddon's Lady Audley claims not even to care about '"the mad folly that the world calls love"' (362), the bodies of Broughton's protagonists, particularly those in her 1860s fiction, clearly register passion. In one passage in the version of *Not Wisely, but Too Well* serialized in *The Dublin University Magazine* (August 1865–June 1866), the heroine's sensations upon embracing the male lead even suggest orgasm: 'the strain that fulfilled the wild longing, the burning dreams of weeks, was quite painful' (397).

That Broughton deleted this passage from the novel's triple-decker incarnation, however, exemplifies the inhibiting effect of cultural taboos on her early work. The publication history of *Not Wisely, but Too Well*—the first novel Broughton wrote and serialized, but the second published in volume form—is an instructive example of the censorship pressures Victorian publishing houses exerted on authors of risqué fiction, especially women. Although the publisher Richard Bentley initially accepted *Not Wisely, but Too Well* on the recommendation of Broughton's uncle, J. S. Le

Fanu, who had serialized the novel in *The Dublin University Magazine*, the interference of Geraldine Jewsbury, Bentley's reader—surely one of the 'ENEMIES' Broughton had in mind in the discarded dedication of *Red as a Rose Is She*—derailed this agreement. After Jewsbury urged the publisher to void the contract, calling *Not Wisely, but Too Well* 'a bad style of book altogether & not fit to be published' (Geraldine Jewsbury to Richard Bentley, 2 July 1866, 379), Bentley and Le Fanu persuaded Broughton to substitute *Cometh Up as a Flower* as a (supposedly) more decorous choice. *Not Wisely, but Too Well* only appeared in triple-decker form after Broughton heavily revised it in order to 'expunge,' as she promised Bentley, the novel's 'coarseness and slanginess,' a process which necessitated rewriting 'those passages which c[ould] not be toned down' (381).[3]

Yet, even amidst this hostile climate for writing about sexuality, Broughton employed inventive strategies for depicting—and defending— female desire, strategies which the first section of this chapter will address in examining how *Not Wisely, but Too Well* and *Cometh Up as a Flower* employ images of nature to justify the heroines' erotic impulses. It is important to note, however, the degree to which this justification is complicated in these two books: in *Not Wisely, but Too Well*, by Broughton's evident ambivalence about female rebellion and, in *Cometh Up as a Flower*, by her paradoxical strategy of disembodying her heroine in order to present her adulterous yearnings sympathetically. Following the publication of her first two novels and her establishment as a popular novelist, moreover, Broughton distanced herself from sensationalism and its most scandalous representations of female sexuality. Not only is the sexual transgression of Esther Craven, the heroine of *Red as a Rose Is She*, milder than those of her predecessors, but, unlike these tragic heroines, Esther is allowed to marry the man she loves, a narrative and generic choice that established Broughton in the market niche she would thereafter fill, as a writer of romantic fiction aligned with the domestic, rather than the sensation, novel. In 1901, for example, E. A. Bennett referred to her as the '"typical novelist of our domesticity"' (qtd. in Wagner 204). Still, as the second part of this chapter will discuss, *Red as a Rose Is She* continues to address the topic of women's 'fleshly inclinations' so prominent in her first two novels, while also expanding their implicit critique of marriage. Replacing with a domineering and jealous fiancé the dashing male leads of her first two novels—figures for whose sakes the heroines are willing to engage in extra-marital sex—*Red as a Rose Is She* addresses the control of women's bodies at the heart of conventional domesticity.

Natural Bodies: Rhetorics of Female Desire in *Not Wisely, But Too Well* and *Cometh Up as a Flower*

In an unusually sympathetic contemporary response to these controversial fictions, a reviewer in *The Spectator* identified a pattern in *Not Wisely, but Too Well* and *Cometh Up as a Flower*:

> In each story the central figure is the same—a girl of a full and noble nature, round as to her lines mental and bodily, with full bust and an exuberant mental life, despising conventionality and contemning the usual cut-and-dried formulas for living, ensnared, but not stained, by a burning passion for a man who cannot, or does not, become her husband. (437)

Perceptively, the reviewer reads the heroines' bodies as apt signifiers for their unconventional energies: each girl is 'round as to her lines mental and bodily,' with a 'full bust' as well as a 'full and noble nature.' Unlike other, more scandalized reviewers, the *Spectator* critic absolves *Not Wisely, but Too Well*'s Kate Chester and *Cometh Up as a Flower*'s Nell Lestrange from the taint of fallenness, seeing them as 'ensnared' but not, finally, 'stained' by their 'burning passion' for men they cannot marry.

In this positive response to the 'round' and 'full' bodies of Broughton's heroines, the *Spectator* reviewer echoes the defence of female appetite implicit in the description of Kate's figure in *Not Wisely, but Too Well*:

> Many *women* affirmed it was too full, too developed for a girl of twenty. The Misses M'Scrag, whose admirers might have sat in comfort in the shade cast by their collar-bones, were particularly stiff on this point; but no *man* was ever yet heard to give in his adhesion to this feminine fiat. Anyhow, the light did seem to fall lovingly, as in the case of the 'Gardener's Daughter,' on 'the bounteous wave of such a breast as pencil never drew,' and on the waist—no marvel of waspish tenuity, but naturally healthily firm and shapely. (50)

Embodying her capacity for sensuality, Kate's lush figure defies the feminine ideal modelled by both the starved 'Misses M'Scrag' and her own conventional sister, Margaret. Sporting a fashionable '17-inch wasp waist' (55), Margaret not only exemplifies what Helena Michie has called 'ladylike anorexia' (12), but presumably also restricts her body in a corset to achieve the requisite 'wasp'-shaped figure associated with female beauty during the period. In contrast, Kate's apparently uncorseted, 'naturally healthily firm and shapely' waist is free from restriction. Linking the adjectives 'naturally' and 'healthily,' Broughton employs a rhetoric that associates her heroine's unconventional appetites with organic vitality.

The subversiveness of Broughton's representation of female embodiment is best measured when compared to Margaret Oliphant's attack on sensationalism in *Blackwood's*. Complaining that Broughton's *Cometh Up as a Flower* and other sensation fiction by women depict 'eagerness of physical sensation' as the '*natural* sentiment of English girls' (259; emphasis added), Oliphant implies that this representation is inaccurate and hence unnatural; no English girl not seduced into thinking otherwise would, presumably, feel the 'fleshly inclinations' that Oliphant scolds sensationalists for depicting. In the context of the Victorian Woman Question's debates about whether or not women had distinctive natures suiting them to domesticity, Oliphant's employment of the category of the 'natural' is ideologically charged, as is Broughton's: one woman writer proclaims how unnatural female desire is, while the other emphasizes the opposite. Each writer thus accuses the other of abetting false education, and of teaching female readers either to feel or not to feel, in certain ways that then become constructed as 'natural.' In order to authorize her construction of female desire as natural instinct, Broughton frequently positions her heroines' bodies against outdoor backdrops, a Romantic concept of untamed nature that opposes it to stifling culture. For instance, in *Not Wisely, but Too Well*, the 'naturally' and 'healthily' uncorseted Kate Chester—a heroine 'of a *nature* singularly susceptible ... to anything that spoke to the senses' (359; emphasis added)—meets with her married lover in such spaces as a woodland glade, a poppy-strewn meadow, and a moonlit beach.

At the same time, the representation of Kate's desire as positive and natural is complicated by Broughton's ambivalence about the type of female rebellion her heroine embodies. As Pamela Gilbert argues, Kate's 'uncontainable' passion, which crosses boundaries of genteel feminine behaviour, literally 'becomes a "bodying forth" of disease' (116) when she succumbs to brain fever following each of her two near-elopements, as well as when the pastor who unrequitedly loves her dies in an epidemic. To some extent, then, *Not Wisely, but Too Well* reproduces, rather than contests, anxieties about changing gender roles stoked by Eliza Lynn Linton's antifeminist essay 'The Girl of the Period,' an influential attack on changing gender roles published in 1868, the year after Broughton's first two novels. Like Kate, who sneaks out of her guardian's house for unchaperoned trysts with Dare Stamer, Linton's stereotypical modern young woman forswears traditional rules of modesty and obedience to authority; she is also, significantly, associated not with nature but with artifice: 'The Girl of the Period is a creature who dyes her hair and paints her face' (109). While Broughton's unconventional heroine is not associated with the same types of artifice—Kate has no interest in make-up and her sexual urges differentiate her from the young women Linton accuses of marrying solely for money—the images in *Not Wisely, but Too Well* which link female desire to health and nature are in tension with those which link it less positively with human manipulation of the natural world. For instance, the steamy scene which, in the serial form of the novel, described Kate's orgasmic response to Dare's embrace is set in a hothouse filled with tropical blooms 'with a depth and intensity of colour which our dear, pale-faced northern flowers never dreamed of putting on' (133). As Laurence Talairach-Vielmas says, this scene 'brings into play the radical possibilities of the greenhouse to expose the female character's passion,' and the conservatory with its imported blooms 'align[s] Kate with the eastern Other' by placing her in a harem-like space of artificially enhanced sensuality (103). Rather than invoking a Romantic defence of female desire, then, the hothouse recalls the reactionary late-Victorian ideologeme of 'going native.'

This anxiety about going native is reinforced when Dare's second attempt to seduce Kate takes place at the Crystal Palace, a glass-enclosed site reminiscent of a greenhouse which, by the late Victorian period, for many writers had come to symbolize imperial decline rather than (as was originally intended) British imperial hegemony (see Auerbach 207–09). Despite touching on these anxieties about imperial decline, however, Broughton continues elsewhere to invoke Romantic rhetorics of nature, as in the passage near the end of the triple-decker in which Kate hurries to the side of Dare, who has been mortally wounded in a carriage accident, in terms which valorize desire while condemning cultural repression:

> In moments of profound mastering emotion we shake ourselves free from the artificial constraints of society and education, as some strong runner, ere setting forth on a long hard race, casts away the heavy garments that would hinder his flight, and returns to the instinct and impulses of Nature. (367)

Cometh Up as a Flower is more consistent than *Not Wisely, but Too Well* in employing the trope of Romantic nature to defend female desire. Unlike Kate, who is an accomplished flirt (and hence adept at an artful and artificial manipulation of feminine charms), Nell Lestrange is, or at least presents herself as, naïve and artless; moreover, the circumstances of her romance are even more calculated to engage the reader's sympathy than Kate's. Whereas Kate (in an obvious revision of *Jane Eyre*[4]) is enamoured of a married aristocrat coded as a Byronic decadent, Nell falls in love with the impoverished, gallant soldier Dick M'Gregor, from whom she is separated by a particularly cruel stratagem. Nell's scheming, mercenary sister Dolly—as problematically artificial a version of femininity as one can imagine—forges a letter in her sister's hand to M'Gregor breaking off their correspondence; when the heartbroken Nell believes herself abandoned by her lover, Dolly is able to persuade her to marry a middle-aged aristocrat to please their dying, bankrupt father. Even Margaret Oliphant, who criticized Nell's 'free-spoken' allusions to sexuality, grudgingly conceded that it was 'not unnatural' for Nell, once she discovers her sister's duplicity, to implore M'Gregor to rescue her from her uncongenial marriage (268).

Nell's association with Romantic nature, as opposed to a culture obsessed with money and status, is repeatedly emphasized by her juxtaposition with the grounds and environs of her home, Lestrange Hall, a decaying country seat surrounded by pastoral spaces in which the tomboyish girl revels. Unsurprisingly, given the allusion in the novel's title to the biblical comparison of human life to a bloom that 'cometh up' and is then 'cut down' (Job 14:2), Nell is frequently positioned amidst flowers, including 'the pinks and the sweet peas and the larkspurs' which cluster around Lestrange Hall (97), roses which she trains to climb on the walls of the manor (96), and 'big primroses, shining in clusters in their starry paleness' in a meadow in which she meets M'Gregor (87). After refusing to sully her virtue by eloping with her, M'Gregor calls her 'my own little snowdrop' (424).

The 'snowdrop' metaphor, however, suggests an inherent paradox of Broughton's strategy of linking her heroine with what Kirby-Jane Hallum calls 'a Romantic preoccupation with nature' that 'calls upon the state of innocence associated with the natural world' (42, 43). Hallum insightfully claims that Broughton complicates this traditional association of nature with chaste femininity by having Nell 'alternat[e] between being a lily and a rose, or between being innocent and passionate' (43). Yet, in order to be a lily or 'snowdrop,' Nell must be represented as less desiring than Kate, whose sensuous body is flooded with '[f]rantic passion, utterly uncurbed' (90). In contrast to her frequent descriptions of Kate's sexual attraction to Dare, Broughton's descriptions of Nell's erotic feelings for M'Gregor are mainly limited to the girl feeling an 'odd shiver' in one of their early meetings (234). This paradoxical fusion of innocence and passion is captured by Nell's yearning, in an early part of the novel, that when she and M'Gregor meet in heaven they will not be 'sexless, passionless essences' (273). While this allusion to sex in paradise struck Oliphant as one of the disagreeably 'free-spoken' moments in the novel (268), it is nonetheless hard to imagine a deceased couple as fully embodied beings. Indeed, following M'Gregor's death of fever in India, Nell wastes away from consumption, an anorexic erosion of her desiring body that refines it for a heavenly reunion with her lover.[5]

In this sense, *Cometh Up as a Flower* reflects an increasingly complex— and evasive—strategy for representing sexuality on Broughton's part, a 'disembodied embodiment'[6] that acknowledges the existence of female desire while rendering it reassuringly etherealized. Although Broughton did not write *Cometh Up as a Flower* in response to Jewsbury's review of the 'thoroughly sensual' manuscript of *Not Wisely, but Too Well* (Appendix A, Letter 5, *Not Wisely* 378)—*Cometh Up as a Flower* already existed in serial form at the time (*Dublin University Magazine* July 1866–January 1867)—it is easy to see why Broughton's second novel seemed a reasonable choice when Bentley wanted a less racy substitute for her first. (Ironically, of course, even the relatively muted depiction of female sexuality in *Cometh Up as a Flower* failed to win Oliphant's approval.) Significantly, the most embodied depictions of sexuality in *Cometh Up as a Flower* are passages in which, echoing a Wollstonecraftian critique of marriage as 'legal prostitution' for women (148), Nell dreads consummating the marriage she contracts for economic reasons, as when she says of her middle-aged suitor: 'for so many pounds of prime white flesh, he has paid down a handsome price on the nail' (400). Like *Cometh Up as a Flower*, Broughton's third novel, *Red as a Rose Is She*, employs natural images to illustrate female sexuality, while also expanding on her second novel's references to the sexual objectification and control of women's bodies within marriage.

BUD OR BLOOM? THE AMBIGUOUS SEXUALITY OF ESTHER CRAVEN

Although Broughton's original dedication of *Red as a Rose Is She* to her 'ENEMIES' defied aspersions on the morality of her first two novels, she nonetheless begins her third by reassuring readers that it is not sensation fiction: 'those who enjoy the flavour of violent immorality will be disappointed if they look this way for the gratification of their peculiar idiosyncrasies' (3–4). Unlike Kate and Nell, who nearly enter into adulterous liaisons, Esther Craven, the heroine of *Red as a Rose Is She*, is merely guilty of concealing from one suitor the existence of a previous one. Having put off an importunate wooer, Robert Brandon, by promising to wait before definitively approving or rejecting his proposal, Esther—now considered Robert's fiancée by his family despite the ambiguity of the arrangement—falls in love with the aristocratic St. John Gerard on a visit to his house. When he returns her affection and proposes, Esther (whose last name 'Craven' conveys her timidity) procrastinates both about extricating herself from the awkward situation with Robert and informing St. John about it; fearing St. John's jealousy, in fact, she denies that she has any past romantic history. When St. John does find out about this history, he assumes that Esther, upon meeting a wealthier man, was planning to jilt Robert, and angrily breaks off his own engagement with her. Only after protracted suffering—rendered penniless by the sudden death of her brother, Esther toils in a dreary position as a paid companion and almost dies of fever—is she at length reunited with the mollified St. John.

Yet, while Esther's fibs about a quasi-engagement are scarcely the stuff of sensation fiction—the *Times* approvingly noted that her faults 'all fall within the pale of conventional respectability' (Review of *Red as a Rose* 4)—female sexuality is as central to Broughton's third novel as it was to her first two. Having the power to attract multiple men, Esther has the dark hair more commonly associated with the femme fatale than the modest maiden, and, as the narrator points out, '*beauté du diable*' rather than a 'Madonna face': hers is ... one of those little, sparkling, provoking, petulant faces ... that have been at the bottom of half the mischiefs the world has seen' (78). Significantly, Esther's sexuality is presented as a problem of interpretation: although the reader can see that Esther is not, as St. John thinks, a gold-digger, the question remains whether her '*beauté du diable*' is innocent or socially disruptive. In this sense, Broughton's ambiguous representation of Esther is self-reflexive, in that the conundrum of how to read her heroine's body is akin to the question posed by the critical controversies surrounding Broughton's own early novels, of whether they were harmless or corrupting texts for young female readers. As suspicious of Esther's virtue as Broughton's harsher critics were of the propriety of her fiction, the censorious St. John is also explicitly linked to the cultural backlash in the late 1860s against changing gender roles. Indeed, Broughton references what Elizabeth K. Helsinger, Robin Lauterbach

Sheets, and William Veeder call 'one of the great Victorian controversies' about gender (103) when St. John looks at Esther and is uneasily reminded of Eliza Lynn Linton's 'The Girl of the Period' (109), an essay mentioned earlier here, and a work whose publication in 1868, a year prior to that of *Red as a Rose is She*, provoked a heated debate over its author's claims that feminine modesty and submission were in decline.[7] That St. John's thinks not only of 'The Girl of the Period' but of 'Women's Rights' (109) when he looks at Esther suggests how the 'Girl of the Period' controversy intersected with cultural anxieties in the late 1860s about the increased visibility of Victorian feminism. The conclusion to which St. John will come about Esther—that she is only out to marry him for his money—in fact recalls one of Linton's rhetorical strategies for deauthorizing feminine rebellion. Although she herself was a former Wollstonecraftian feminist,[8] in 'The Girl of the Period' Linton chose to read young women's rejection of social convention as a sign, not of their resistance to female disenfranchisement, but of their embrace of the very thing Wollstonecraft decried, self-prostitution through marriage. According to Linton, 'The Girl of the Period' defines marriage solely as '[t]he legal barter of herself for so much money ... luxury and pleasure' (110).

As she had in *Not Wisely, but Too Well* and *Cometh Up as a Flower*, Broughton invokes Romantic images of nature to defend her heroine's sexuality (and, implicitly, her own fictional project in portraying sexual women), against St. John's Linton-esque suspicions that Esther is a 'coquette' (132) who uses art to ensnare men for monetary purposes. In contrast, Broughton emphasizes Esther's association with natural vitality: the title of the novel quotes Samuel Taylor Coleridge's allusion, in 'The Rime of the Ancient Mariner' (1798, 1817), to a blushing bride as being 'red as a rose' (l. 34). As she had in *Cometh Up as a Flower*, however, Broughton complicates traditional definitions of nature by associating her flower-like heroine not only with virginal innocence but mature female sexuality. At one point greeting St. John with the 'innocentest, freshest, shyest rosebud-face' (446), Esther blushes 'red as a rose in her burning prime' in another interaction with him (172). Such scenes illustrate what Ruth Yeazell calls the 'potential ambiguity' of the blush as a signifier in English courtship fiction: on one hand demonstrating an appropriate virginal modesty, on the other the blush evokes sexual desire (75, 74). For example, in another metaphoric association of blushing with a natural object, Esther's cheeks 'flushed with a deeper hue than the crimson lips of a foreign shell' (186)—a striking image of female arousal that prefigures the 'burning lips' with which she kisses St. John after accepting his proposal (185).

Still, while these images of 'burning' roses and 'crimson' shells convey Esther's capacity for passion—and as such are reminiscent of Kate Chester's orgasmic sensations upon embracing Dare in the serialized *Not Wisely, but Too Well*—Broughton tends to represent her third heroine less as desiring subject than as object of the male gaze. The narrator's ogling comments on Esther's '*beauté du diable*' are one example of a stereotypically male perspective, but a particularly vivid instance of male voyeurism is a scene in which St. John glimpses Esther lying down in her room:

> careless, restful on her couch, her two arms flung lazily upwards and backwards, to make a resting place for her head; the smooth elbows and shoulders glowing warm, cream-white ... and the up-looking face, childish in its roundness, and blooming down—but oh! most womanish—in the shafts of quick fire that greet him from the laughing, sleepy eyes. (107)

Even though the 'fire' in Esther's eyes suggests her own desire, the scene emphasizes St. John's perspective on Esther's charms, as does a scene near the novel's end in which Esther, alarmed at the possible presence of a male intruder, faints and is carried to her bedroom by St. John: 'He leans over her, gazing with passionate admiration at the heavy shut lids and upward curling lashes' (411). Avoiding the more explicit and self-aware representation of Kate Chester's attraction to Dare Stamer, the first of these scenes depicts Esther as only sleepily aware of her desire for St. John, while the second renders her unconscious that he is viewing her in a compromising position.

The predominance of the male gaze in *Red as a Rose Is She* thus enables Broughton to depict female sexuality without identifying her heroine's awareness of her own desire. At the same time, Broughton's representation of male voyeurism also allows her to address male power and control over women. In this sense, St. John recalls Dare Stamer of *Not Wisely, but Too Well*. Not only is Dare, like St. John, associated with a troublingly possessive version of the male gaze—in *Not Wisely, but Too Well* Dare ogles Kate 'like a Circassian slave at the market of Constantinople' (132)—but both men rail misogynistically against female perfidy[9] and are capable of violence. In the serialized *Not Wisely, but Too Well*, Dare murders Kate at a ball after she refuses to elope with him; castigating her for dancing with other men, he shoots first her, and then himself. While St. John does not attempt to kill Esther upon discovering her history with Brandon, his actions betray an underlying savagery: first kissing her 'with a violence he is himself hardly conscious of,' he then leaves 'crimson prints' on her arm when he grabs it after confronting her with his new-found knowledge (198, 199). Furthermore, even if this was not his intention, St. John's rejection of Esther nearly causes her death: after he breaks off their engagement, her labours in an ill-paid job cause her to waste away to a shadow of her former self, predisposing her to infection by the fever that nearly kills her. Tellingly, even after encountering the depressed and emaciated Esther at the house where she works as a companion, St. John continues to suspect her of using her sexuality to manipulate men, mentally labelling her a '"[d]amnable flirt"' because another male guest pays her attention (380).

Whereas Dare exemplifies male sexual possessiveness more generally, St. John—legitimate husband material in the way Dare is not—represents the specific threat to female autonomy posed by Victorian marriage. It is surely not coincidental that Broughton, an admirer of *Jane Eyre*, judging from her revision of its plot in *Not Wisely, but Too Well*, bestows on her male lead in *Red as a Rose Is She* the same first name as St. John Rivers, the puritanical clergyman in Charlotte Brontë's novel who attempts to tame Jane's passionate spirit by proposing she join him in a loveless marriage. Even though Broughton's St. John is not so hyperbolically repressed as Rivers, he nonetheless embodies disapproving male attitudes towards female sexuality; indeed, one reason that Esther does not tell St. John sooner about her arrangement with Brandon is her conviction that it would be easier to '"put my head into a lion's mouth"' than offend '"his fastidious, strict ideas of what a woman should be and do and look"' (151). One way in which St. John demonstrates his 'fastidious' ideas about female virtue is to police Esther's reading: shortly after meeting her, he urges her to stop reading a French novel she discovered in his family's library: '"Don't you know … this is a book no modest woman ought to read"' (137). Broughton uses this incident to comment on male anxieties about female sexuality—noticing the title of the novel, St. John is scandalized because 'men are always shocked that women should *read about* the things that *they do*' (136)—as well as to satirize male hypocrisy; when Esther returns the novel to the shelves, she notices several 'enticing Gallic titles' lying on the table where St. John has left them after reading them himself (139).[10]

St. John's attempts to control Esther's sexuality are troubling predictors of the type of husband he is likely to become. We hear, in fact, that St. John's father, Sir Thomas, delights in 'bullying' his wife, and before his first proposal to Esther, St. John warns her that, if they marry, he is likely to '"grow like Sir Thomas in time"' (183). When the couple are reunited at the novel's end, St. John admits that he will, in all probability, frequently be '"ill-tempered and jealous"' (427). Under the circumstances, the ending of *Red as a Rose Is She* may seem more ominous than joyous.

Red as a Rose Is She, then, is not only the first of Broughton's novels to end with the heroine's marriage, it is a forecast of the vexed relationship Broughton would have thereafter with traditional romantic finales. Not only, as Pamela Gilbert says, do even Broughton's 'most comic novels' frequently not provide 'a conventionally happy ending' (113),[11] but even those novels which do end this way, like *Red as a Rose Is She*, often ironically undercut the fairy-tale aura typically associated with marital closure. Other Broughton novels, both early and late, end with outright tragedy. For example, in the novel which followed *Red as a Rose Is She*, *Good-bye, Sweetheart* (1872)—a 'darker re-working,' according to Shirley Jones, of its immediate precursor (218)—the strong-willed heroine, rejected by her lover, dies of tuberculosis. In this narrative, whose plot strikingly resembles that of Germaine de Staël's feminist fiction, *Corinne* (1807), what dooms the heroine's romance is her lover's inability to stomach her brand of independence, as well as his inveterate jealousy.[12] As both this plot and that of *Red as a Rose Is She* evince, then, female sexuality continues to be a major topic in her fiction and is frequently linked to issues of marriage and female autonomy. In this regard, Broughton's 1860s fiction anticipates not only the pessimistic depiction of women's domestic experience in her own later works, but also that of women writers in the 1870s such as George Eliot in *Middlemarch* (1871) and *Daniel Deronda* (1876). At the same time, Broughton's 1860s fiction remains her most explicit and visceral portrayal of female desire.

NOTES

1. See her letter to George Bentley, 20 January 1870 (*Archives of Richard Bentley and Son*).
2. The term 'erotic sensationalism' is used to classify *Cometh Up as a Flower* in the series *Varieties of Women's Sensation Fiction*, Gen. ed. Andrew Maunder.

3. For an account of *Not Wisely, but Too Well*'s publication history and an appendix detailing changes between the serial and triple-decker, see Heller, Introduction to *Not Wisely, but Too Well* 5–6, 15–21, and 385–428.
4. For more on the *Jane Eyre* revision in *Not Wisely, but Too Well*, see Heller, '"That Muddy, Polluted Flood"' 92–96.
5. See Heller, Introduction to *Cometh Up as a Flower* xli–xlii and Hallum 50–52 for more on Nell's anorexia.
6. See Heller, Introduction to *Cometh Up as a Flower* xlii for more on the concept of 'disembodied embodiment.'
7. See Helsinger, Veeder, and Sheets chapter 6 (103–25) for a discussion of the 'magnitude' (113) of the cultural response to Linton's essay.
8. Deborah T. Meem discusses the evolution of Linton's stance on gender issues in her introduction to Linton's *The Rebel of the Family* 15–16.
9. See, for example, *Not Wisely, but Too Well* 423 and *Red as a Rose Is She* 154, 200, 202.
10. For another discussion of this scene, see Flint 288.
11. In chapter 5 of *A Plot of Her Own*, Heller discusses Broughton's innovations in varying the romance formula in the single-volume fiction she produced during the last decades of her career. Some of these late novels never clarify whether or not the heroine actually marries.
12. For more on *Good-bye, Sweetheart!*, see Heller, 'Rewriting *Corinne*.'

Works Cited

Auerbach, Jeffrey A. *The Great Exhibition of 1851: A Nation on Display*. New Haven: Yale University Press, 1999.

Braddon, Mary Elizabeth. *Lady Audley's Secret*. 1862. Ed. Natalie Houston. Peterborough, Ontario: Broadview Press, 2003.

———. *Cometh Up as a Flower*. 1867. Ed. Tamar Heller. Vol. 4B in *Varieties of Women's Sensation Fiction 1855–90*. Gen. ed. Andrew Maunder. London: Pickering and Chatto, 2004.

———. Correspondence with George Bentley. *The Archives of Richard Bentley and Son, 1829–1898*. Pt. 2, Reel 2. Cambridge: Chadwyck and Healey; Teaneck, NJ: Somerset House, 1979.

———. *Not Wisely, but Too Well*. 1867. Ed. Tamar Heller. Brighton: Victorian Secrets, 2013.

———. *Red as a Rose Is She*. 1870. London: Macmillan, 1899.

Coleridge, Samuel Taylor. 'The Rime of the Ancient Mariner.' 1817 (orig. 1798). *The Longman Anthology of British Literature*. Vol. 2A: *The Romantics and Their Contemporaries*. Ed. Susan Wolfson and Peter Manning. 3rd ed. Pearson-Longman, 2006. 580–95.

Flint, Kate. *The Woman Reader, 1837–1914.* Oxford: Oxford University Press, 1996.
Gilbert, Pamela. *Disease, Desire and the Body in Victorian Women's Popular Fiction.* Cambridge: Cambridge University Press, 1997.
Hallum, Kirby-Jane. *Aestheticism and the Marriage Market in Victorian Popular Fiction: The Art of Female Beauty.* London: Pickering & Chatto, 2015.
Heller, Tamar. *A Plot of Her Own: Rhoda Broughton and English Fiction.* Manuscript.
———. Introduction. *Cometh Up as a Flower.* 1867. By Rhoda Broughton. Ed. Tamar Heller. Vol. 4B in *Varieties of Women's Sensation Fiction 1855–90.* Gen. ed. Andrew Maunder. London: Pickering and Chatto, 2004. xxxiii-l.
———. Introduction. *Not Wisely, but Too Well.* 1867. Ed. Tamar Heller. Brighton: Victorian Secrets, 2013. 5–30.
———. 'Rewriting *Corinne*: Sensation and the Tragedy of the Exceptional Woman in Rhoda Broughton's *Good-bye, Sweetheart!*' *Critical Survey* 23.1 (2011): 58–74.
———. '"That Muddy, Polluted Flood of Earthly Love": Ambivalence about the Body in Rhoda Broughton's *Not Wisely but Too Well.*' *Victorian Sensations.* Ed. Kim Harrison and Richard Fantina. Columbus, OH: Ohio State University Press, 2006. 87–101.
Helsinger, Elizabeth K., Robin Lauterbach Sheets, and William Veeder. *The Woman Question: Society and Literature in Britain and America 1837–1883.* Vol. 1: *Defining Voices.* Chicago: University of Chicago Press, 1983.
Jewsbury, Geraldine. Letters to Richard Bentley. 2 and 3 July 1866. Appendix A. *Not Wisely, but Too Well.* 1867. By Rhoda Broughton. Ed. Tamar Heller. Brighton: Victorian Secrets, 2013. 378–79.
Jones, Shirley. '"LOVE": Rhoda Broughton, Writing and Re-writing Romance.' *Popular Victorian Women Writers.* Ed. Kay Boardman and Shirley Jones. Manchester: Manchester University Press, 2009. 208–36.
Linton, Eliza Lynn. 'The Girl of the Period.' 1868. *The Woman Question: Society and Literature in Britain and America, 1837–83.* By Elizabeth K. Helsinger, Robin Sheets, and William Veeder. Vol. 1: *Defining Voices.* Chicago: University of Chicago Press, 1983. 108–12.
Meem, Deborah T. Introduction. *The Rebel of the Family.* 1880. By Eliza Lynn Linton. Ed. Deborah T. Meem. Peterborough: Broadview Press, 2002. 9–16.
Michie, Helena. *The Flesh Made Word: Female Figures and Women's Bodies.* Oxford: Oxford University Press, 1990.
Oliphant, Margaret. 'Novels.' *Blackwood's Edinburgh Magazine* (September 1867): 257–80.
Review of *Red as a Rose Is She. The London Times* 7 March 1870: 4.
[Romer, Sir Richard.] Review of *Not Wisely, but Too Well. Not Wisely, but Too Well.* 1867. By Rhoda Broughton. Ed. Tamar Heller. Brighton: Victorian Secrets, 2013. 429–31.

Talairach-Vielmas, Laurence. *Moulding the Female Body in Victorian Fairy Tales and Sensation Fiction*. Aldershot: Ashgate, 2007.

Wagner, Tamara. '"The False Clues of Innocent Sensations": Aborting Adultery Plots in Rhoda Broughton's *Nancy*.' *Women's Writing* 20.2 (2013): 202–18.

Wollstonecraft, Mary. *A Vindication of the Rights of Woman*. 1792. Ed. Carol H. Poston. 2nd ed. New York: Norton, 1988.

Yeazell, Ruth Bernard. *Fictions of Modesty: Women and Courtship in the English Novel*. Chicago: University of Chicago Press, 1991.

CHAPTER 9

Crumbs from the Table: Matilda Betham-Edwards's Comic Writing in *Punch*

Clare Horrocks and Nickianne Moody

In memory of Nickianne Moody, expert in popular fictions, preserver of female culture, cat lover, humourist par excellence, and the originator of the ICVWW lemon torte joke.

As a matter of record, Marion Spielmann in 1895 reports that 'on the 25th July, 1868, a lady contributor made her debut in Punch's pages. This was Miss M. Betham-Edwards' (371). Spielmann introduces her as a well-known travel writer and explains that she came to be commissioned for a series in *Punch* on the strength of a 'clever skit' of hers that a friend had sent to the periodical's first editor Mark Lemon (Spielmann 372). By using the term 'skit' for Matilda Betham-Edwards's comic writing, referencing light satire, parody, or caricature, Spielmann suggests that it does not need to be contained, refined, or feminine. Although she was a keen social and personal observer, and continued to publish until her death in

---

C. Horrocks (✉) • N. Moody
Liverpool John Moores University, Liverpool, UK
e-mail: C.L.Horrocks@LJMU.ac.uk; N.A.Moody@LJMU.ac.uk

© The Author(s) 2020
A. E. Gavin, C. W. de la L. Oulton (Eds.), *British Women's Writing from Brontë to Bloomsbury, Volume 2*, British Women's Writing from Brontë to Bloomsbury, 1840–1940,
https://doi.org/10.1007/978-3-030-38528-6_9

1919, Betham-Edwards is not often comic in her later writing. During the late 1860s and early 1870s Betham-Edwards established herself as a commercially successful novelist. The popularity of her novels, travel writing, and accounts of European public figures is evident in a life-long writing career.

Contributors to *Punch*, as to many other periodicals in the Victorian period, were anonymous. While the creators of the journal's cartoons and illustrations have long since been identified, its writers can only be traced through the *Punch* Contributor Ledgers.[1] Betham-Edwards is the first 'Miss' to occur in these ledgers as a paid contributor. Other women writers such as Kay Kendall were recorded under the names of men who submitted their work, in Kendall's case Andrew Lang. It was only through later republication of pieces in collections of her work that they were attributed to Kendall. There may have been women writers prior to 1868 in the ledgers, whose names are shielded by family members or pseudonyms, but Betham-Edwards is the first clearly recorded female contributor to *Punch*.

The significance of this achievement lies not in its impact on her career: she did not become a journalist, she did not take advantage of the literary networks connected to *Punch*, and she did not pursue her talent as a comic writer. Instead, it is significant because it illuminates the difficulties faced by women who were writing for entertainment media in the nineteenth century and in how such female authors could negotiate topics for the respectable *Punch* reader that male authors had been unable to manage.

In 1868 Lemon needed to find someone who could respond to the cause célébre of the moment, Eliza Lynn Linton's 'The Girl of the Period' (1868), which had quickly provoked a public debate and become a comic meme across the periodical press. With its excessively conservative attitude to domestic life and exaggerations of female fashion and behaviour, it should have been a suitable subject for *Punch*, but the journal barely references it until later in the 1870s. The existing contributors could not find a way to deal with the modern woman outlined by Linton. This was in spite of spending a decade mocking her through the motif of the excesses of 'crinolineomania' in which *Punch* did lead the comic press pack and for which its images and puns are still remembered.

Betham-Edwards challenged Linton through the creation of a daughter of marriageable age who is travelling in Europe and whose mother writes her letters of advice that focus largely on the mother's own chaotic encounters with manners, morals, and politics. Using as a model Douglas Jerrold's 1842 *Punch* series 'Mr Punch's Letters to His Son,' which was sentimental and nostalgic, Betham-Edwards's 'Mrs. Punch's Letters to Her Daughter' series in 1868 (the first of which was actually published on 4 July) looked to the future, anticipating change and is indicative of how *Punch*'s longevity among Victorian humorous periodicals is based on its ability to recognize and deliver culturally resonant comic forms. To understand both its difficulty in responding to Linton's essay in the late 1860s and its willingness to publish women writers it is necessary briefly to consider how *Punch* established itself as a market contender during the 1840s and 1850s.

During the 1820s–1840s a viable commercial market emerged for commercially produced visual culture which used comedy to connect with new audience formations (Maidment 3). In the 1830s a variety of short-lived comic magazines were produced which tried to negotiate the shift away from the moral righteousness of Regency satire that employed 'extreme political partisanship, open obscenity, salacious scandal and gross personal attack' (Leary 10). *Punch*, founded in 1841, was able to establish a tone, which Patrick Leary terms 'good natured moralism,' that made it suitable for family reading (139). The moderated address to its audience allowed the publication to comment on political events, public figures, and scandal but eschewed subjects which threatened its respectability.

Jerrold's contributions to *Punch* in the 1840s, for example, retained the radicalism of his earlier career, using caricature to critique the new Poor Law and aspects of social life and governance which he felt were in need of reform. Simultaneously he created nostalgic domestic series, the most popular of which was 'Mrs. Caudle's Curtain Lectures' (1845). These successful and moderate contributions to *Punch* meant that it could move beyond the excesses of Regency satire while still reproving some aspects of social injustice and exposing hypocrisy and corruption in other sections of the publication. This explains why women of the mid-Victorian period were able to read *Punch* but not why they were excluded from writing for it.

In a publication of the 1860s a reader would expect all kinds of comic writing: jokes, verse riddles, parodies, caricatures, puns, illustrations, satire, and laughter-provoking trifles. Relying on the display of wit, education, and knowledge of current affairs, most of this writing was considered unfeminine. Betham-Edwards, however, was able to emulate and extrapolate Lemon's use of comic writing and illustration to hold politicians and other institutions to account and to find a common language to visualize and oppose social injustice. This was a risky undertaking as Regenia Gagnier examines in her exploration of how women's humour is problematic not only because it may threaten the male/patriarchal social order but through the mechanics of its production (137). Humour has the function of promoting group cohesion and women's writing may not do this for a male audience or editorial process. Humour allows the reader to sympathize with the breaker of rules, but a female character as an agent in this context was in the mid-Victorian period difficult to imagine, realize, and sustain. Comedy could be conciliatory and flexible but it had to be very carefully managed by the woman writer. Betham-Edwards's creation of Mrs Punch, although she is a figure of fun, demonstrates her ability to move beyond Jerrold's caricature of Mrs Caudle and the domestic grudges and arguments she lavishes on her long-suffering husband through the imaginative construct of a wife who is a likeable maverick.

The nature of *Punch*'s production and adherence to masculine cultural practice also firmly excluded women writers and illustrators. As is well documented, the suggestions for the main political cut for each issue and for potential series, jokes, and other inclusions took place during the weekly *Punch* dinners, held every Wednesday. Leary notes in *The Punch Brotherhood* (2010)—which draws on the diaries of *Punch*-staffer Henry Silver, who recorded the conversations around the dinner table—that 'it is important to emphasize ... the homosocial colloquial freedom offered by the intimate and exclusive setting of the weekly dinners' (29). This was distinctly male fellowship and provided those invited with the space to voice the 'personal invective and bawdy humour that had characterised much of the comic press at the time' and then exclude it from the publication (Leary 39). Nevertheless, *Punch* retained 'the culture of conversation in clubs, taverns, coffee houses, offices, theatres, galleries, dinner parties and more particularly the workplace' (Leary 2) to which Betham-Edwards had very limited access. Women writers were often therefore denied, not just by education, but also by homosocial editorial practices, the cultural capital to write commercially for the popular press.

In 1895, when Spielmann published his history of *Punch*, Betham-Edwards was a well-known popular writer. He notes that before the *Punch* series she had already published her first book of travel writing, *A Winter with Swallows* (1867), and her second, *Through Spain to the Sahara* (1868), was about to be published. By the 1890s, as well as being a commercially successful novelist, she had established a literary reputation as a non-fiction travel writer. The period in which she contributed to *Punch* (1868 to 1871) was significant to the development of her career and the intellectual networks in which she participated. However, the decision that she made at this time to pursue a socialist and anti-capitalist rather than feminist predilection is the most likely reason that she has been overlooked as a significant female author. In her preface to Betham-Edwards's final work,

Mid-Victorian Memories (1919), Sarah Grand considers the contradiction between Betham-Edwards's ambiguous position on women's suffrage and her life-long friendships with social reformer Rosamond Davenport-Hill, physician Elizabeth Blackwell, suffrage campaigner and educationalist Frances Power Cobbe, and women's rights campaigner and educationalist Barbara Bodichon.

Betham-Edwards was a younger, rurally raised cousin of the better-known writer Amelia Blandford Edwards.[2] Blandford Edwards's reputation has had far more longevity, and she is known for her journalism, travel writing—especially *A Thousand Miles up the Nile* (1877)—novels, and her promotion of the Egypt Exploration Society. Matilda Edwards was born in 1836; she added 'Betham' to her name from the surname of her aunt and godmother Mary Matilda Betham (1776–1852). Betham had been a writer who moved in the literary circles of Robert Southey, Samuel Taylor Coleridge, and Charles and Mary Lamb and had published *A Biographical Dictionary of Celebrated Women of Every Age and Country* (1804) (Rees 6). Betham-Edwards herself, after spending a brief time as a pupil-teacher, first published poems and short stories in the 1850s, including 'The Golden Bee' for *All the Year Round* in 1853. She published her first novel, *The White House by the Sea*, in 1857 when she was twenty. In her twenties she started her extensive European travels. Following the death of her father and sister in 1865 she set up home in London where she met Barbara Bodichon. Her autobiographical writing, *Anglo-French Reminiscences* (1900) and *Mid-Victorian Memories* (1919), shows that she was interested in people who chose unconventional paths in life, but in her own life she focused on her literary ambitions and did not become overtly involved in political causes. Her biographer Joan Rees, assessing what made her work successful, suggests that her novels were 'not drawing-room romances but at the centre of each there is, invariably, a challenging idea of immediate contemporary relevance which opens areas outside the round of ordinary domestic life' (2). In Rees's opinion Betham-Edwards's fiction was marred by being written too quickly so that she could earn a living. What is significant, however, is the observational style of writing that she maintained: currency and topicality also being central requirements of sketches submitted to *Punch*. It is this contemporaneity that makes Betham-Edwards so apposite a choice as the first female contributor to *Punch*.

In chapter eighteen of *Mid-Victorian Memories*, 'More London Souvenirs,' Betham-Edwards writes of her interest in socialist debate during 1867 and 1871. She recalls hearing Karl Marx speak at the International

Workingmen's Association meetings in High Holborn, John Stuart Mill speak at the London Society for Women's Suffrage, and meeting the exiled French utopian socialist Louis Blanc. She had signed the 1866 petition to parliament for female suffrage. Therefore by 1868 Betham-Edwards had joined a rich variety of social, cultural, and professional circles which may have brought her to Mark Lemon's attention. Between 1868 and 1871 while she lived in Kensington she also attended 'George Eliot's conversaziones, Madame Bodichon's cosmopolitan gatherings and Lord Houghton's celebrated breakfasts' (Rees 36). One of her most successful novels, *Kitty*, serialized in May 1868 in *Temple Bar: A London Magazine for Town and Country Readers* then published in volume form in 1869, explored the finances and morality of a North London bohemian community. Through her friendship with Bodichon Betham-Edwards was, too, brought into the social and professional world of John Maxwell, the businessman publisher and owner of *Belgravia* magazine who introduced her to other popular women writers, including Mary Elizabeth Braddon, Florence Marryat, and Rhoda Broughton. After the 1860s, Betham-Edwards continued to extend her social and professional networks by writing *The Sylvestres* (1871), which was serialized monthly in *Good Words* from January to December, then published by Tauchnitz to whom George Lewes had introduced her (Betham-Edwards 52). Further periodical contributions included the publication of a series of short stories for *All the Year Round* (21 March–2 May 1885), which were collected as *The Flower of Doom; or, the Conspirator and Other Stories* (1885). After this period she travelled extensively in France, motivated by her desire to be an intermediary for Anglo-French understanding. She was recognized for her efforts by the French government and awarded a medal at the Franco-British Exhibition in 1908.

Fionnuala Dillane's study of George Eliot, *Before George Eliot: Marian Evans and the Periodical Press* (2013) is a model for 'reconfiguring the writer in the context of debates about the professionalization of women's work more generally in the nineteenth century' (Dillane 7). It is clear from a study of Betham-Edwards's periodical contributions that, as with Marian Evans, writing for the periodical press was a key and formative part of her career as a professional writer. What is not so clear is why she chose to write for *Punch*. Through examining her deviation from the model of the professional women writer by writing humour, there is an opportunity to reflect on why that genre was her output of choice at this particular time in her career in the 1860s and what this tells us about myths surrounding women writers being unable successfully to manipulate comic forms. *Punch* was not a natural home for women with interests in reform and inequality.

Spielmann, for example, quotes May Kendall's recollection that '"it seemed very wonderful to be in *Punch* which I had venerated from my youth up"' (qtd. in Spielmann 394). However, the work that Kendall submitted to *Punch* (between 1884 and 1895 there are twenty articles acknowledged by the ledgers) does not address the issues of poverty and social inequality that she had most interest in during this time. Writing about Kendall's career and frustration during this mid-1890s period, Diana Maltz claims that Kendall became disillusioned with journalism, and then fiction, as a means of investigating social injustice. The poems and articles that she contributed to *Punch* form a series, but they focus on elderly upper-class men, the process of writing, and the vicissitudes of courtship: all suitable subjects for *Punch*, but a great contrast with her other contemporary writing which attempts to observe the poor for a middle-class audience.

Maltz argues that Kendall is not able to use humour to reposition the way that the late Victorian middle class viewed the poor or indeed newly educated middle-class women readers. Although Maltz is not discussing *Punch*, she examines how Kendall's worker poems attempted to combine pathos and light entertainment but left the reader unclear about how to respond, setting up 'a tension that was irresolvable, wherein the ideological content of the verse battles against itself and strains against its form' (Maltz 316). Therefore, Maltz argues, Kendall fails as a humourist because 'the butt of the joke is unclear' (322).

In part because it is in itself such a broad, non-specific, umbrella term, humour remains a neglected area of consideration in the field of women's writing, for there are no clear criteria against which to judge the use of the form. Deviating from Spielmann's use of the term humour, as a style of writing, we can start to see why Betham-Edwards was actually able to enjoy success at *Punch*. 'Humour infiltrates every area of social life and interaction, even rearing its head in situations where it is not normally regarded as appropriate … For this reason, humour is not synonymous with comedy; it extends beyond it and is not exhausted by its more formal stagings' (Lockyer and Pickering 6). By this definition we are looking for writers who are keen observers, which Betham-Edwards clearly was. Her tone of writing is ludic, a more playful form of engagement, not something written to make people laugh out loud. A further problem is that the few critical works examining women writers engaged in satirical, humorous writing have tended to focus on the genres of drama, poetry, and the novel. This presents a distorted view of the form if we are to consider the commercial imperatives of the female journalist and writer who chose to write specifically in this style.

'Mrs. Punch's Letters to Her Daughter' is clearly informed about the political debates and concerns about social reform which Betham-Edwards was party to following her move from Suffolk to Kensington in 1865. Although Spielmann disparages her humour as 'contributions of the worldly-wise order, cynical, satirical and shrewd' (271), Betham-Edwards brought a lively knowledge of current and social affairs to her writing for *Punch*. The skit that she had written and which interested Lemon might well have been an initial parody of Eliza Lynn Linton's 'The Girl of the Period' articles for the *Saturday Review*, the first of which was published on 14 March 1868. The letters in Betham-Edwards's series are sent by a self-deprecating Mrs Punch, who manages her husband and is up to date with topics of the day', to her daughter Judiana. Linton's 'The Girl of the Period' parody certainly provoked a response from the Punch Brotherhood, with Henry Silver recording a conversation at the *Punch* table between himself and Lemon less than two weeks after Linton's series began:

March 25 1868
    Pater and I talk of novels. Praise those of old. Miss Edgeworth. Scott and I hate such sensation stuff as 'Cometh up as a flower' which I read on Sunday at Croydon. Mixture of coarseness, scraps of scripture, snobbism and skit.
    Professor applauds the Saturday for pitching into 'The Girl of the Period' who dyes and paints and talks slang and only lives for pleasure and fine dresses. Mark and I agree with him in a measure. But do you know such girls? says Shirley. No not altogether but the taint soon spreads and Swellesses are copied. Miss Gascoigne dyes her hair and Annie R powders her face. Still they are both nice girls notwithstanding. But certainly a modest mien is rarer than it was. And I prefer delicacy and softness to a bold face and hard in another. ('Nights at the Table,' Henry Silver, MS 88937/2/13)

Given the interest in the topic of the Girl of the Period, it is significant that Punch's series about it is given to a 'lady' contributor, the first recorded as contributing to the magazine. Other comic papers were associating risqué versions of 'The Girl of the Period' with actresses and non-respectable women. Betham-Edwards, by contrast, reconstructs her 'Girl of the Period,' Judiana, as a daughter who is facing an uncharted womanhood but one which is much more calm and settled than the farcical attempts of her mother to mix with contemporary society and politics.

The topics of the eleven articles Betham-Edwards contributed to *Punch* cover a range of subjects which make fun of middle-class pretension, young men and women, and husbands but in a moderate and playful way which includes Mrs Punch as the butt of the jokes. More specifically across the series the letters address: the rights of men (Letter 1), dress (Letter 2), choosing a husband (Letter 3), the Continent (Letters 4, 5, and 6), travelling (Letters 4, 5, and 6), seaside literature (Letter 7), becoming the head of the female Liberal Party (Letter 8), the Social Science Congress in Birmingham (Letter 10), 'Reading for Instruction "The Girl of the Period"' (Letter 5), 'The Young Man of the Period' (who is an ass) (Letter 9), Christmas (Letter 11), and 'Children of the Period' (Letter 11). The manner in which Mrs Punch signs off her letters emphasizes how Betham-Edwards is able to capture the respectable tone of *Punch*; she is 'aspiring' (Letter 1), 'devoted and patriotic' (Letter 2), 'ambitious' (Letter 4), 'excited' (Letter 5), 'slightly depressed' (Letter 6), 'unpretending' (Letter 7), 'perplexed and would-be Un-political, Mother' (Letter 8), 'domestic but not benighted Mamma' (Letter 10), and finally, Judiana's 'affectionate Mother' (Letter 10). The letters read as one female generation handing off to the next.

The illustrated initial letter of the first letter in the series sets up the imaginative speculation of fifty years hence and the prophecy of changes made by 'your dear Papa, MR JOHN STUART MILL, and all reformers' ([Letter 1] 4 July 1868: 7). In response to this Mrs Punch exclaims 'that the very thought of being alive then, and of having daughters, makes my hair stand on end' (7). Betham-Edwards appropriates and plays with the pleasure of these changes for male and female readers. She may ridicule the fashion of others and the chignon in particular (in keeping with *Punch* for the year) but she does not pathologize women. Instead, Betham-Edwards takes the strategy of visualizing women assuming roles of greater authority as both absurd and anticipated. Mrs Punch writes only to advise Judiana and trusts to her daughter's good sense. Positioning Betham-Edwards within the debate stirred up by Eliza Lynn Linton regarding 'The Girl of the Period' returns us to the significance of commercial writing for women of the 1860s and 1870s. Betham-Edwards was able to bring together the concerns pursued by *Punch* and conform to the style which results in payment.

The Liddell Hart Collection of Costume, held by Liverpool John Moores University, has an interesting set of scrapbooks containing cuttings from periodicals between 1868 and 1872. The unknown compiler has selected cartoons and comic articles which parody 'The Girl of the Period,' particularly discussions of the chignon, the theatre, and the exaggerated dress which begins to make up a visual caricature. The cuttings are taken from a variety of sources: *Tomahawk, Punch, The Daily Telegraph*'s references to 'The Young Man of the Day' in articles and the letters page, *The Times, Quiz, Fun, The Saturday Review, Belgravia Magazine, Judy* (with the work of Adelaide Claxton and Marie Duval noted and emphasized), *Will o' the Wisp, The Razor, The Grasshopper, Chambers' Journal, The Graphic,* and *The Penny Melodist*. Included amongst these parodies is Betham-Edwards's seventh letter for *Punch*, published on 5 September 1868, in which Mrs Punch dwells on the behaviour of ladies at the seaside. The parodies, responses, and appropriations of Linton's article are regular, creative, polemic, and trade in reversals testifying to the cultural resonance of the original piece. In the Liddell Hart scrapbook the caricature of the changing social mores of the next generation of young women extends to 'A Bonnie Lassie of the Period,' 'A Ballet Girl of the Period,' 'A Flower Show of the Period,' 'The Girl of the Period in Court,' 'The Factory Girl of the Period,' 'The Waist of the Period,' 'Some Tourists of the Period,' until it becomes just 'The Period.'

Eliza Lynn Linton's anti-feminist stance in her articles for *The Saturday Review* raises a common paradox for popular women writers. While she herself enjoyed an independent lifestyle she appeared to advocate a more restricted one for other, often younger, women. In reviewing Linton's career, Andrea Broomfield examines how popular journalism develops in the 1860s and how women writers of the 1870s were able to profit from the new focus of writing. The transition in style and approach to entertainment which emerged in the late 1860s allowed Linton to perceive anti-feminism as a 'particularly salient theme which in [her] creative hands gave her the audience demand and editorial respect that she needed in order to remain a viable author,' rather than a subject for the expression of her own beliefs (Broomfield, 'Much More' 268). Broomfield argues that Linton deliberately chose to write about what would sell in the commercial market rather than produce unprofitable progressive novels as she had done in the 1850s ('Much More' 269). Her work needs therefore to be judged by the standards of professional journalism and her ability to identify a resonant theme, create a memorable caricature, understand her audience, and develop a commercial style trading in accessible extremes and excess.

In a later article Broomfield argues that the style Linton developed for *The Saturday Review* commodified the woman's rights debate in the press (Broomfield, 'Eliza Lyn Linton' 251). More importantly, Linton created a form of popular rhetoric which could be later appropriated by feminists, especially Sarah Grand and Ouida in their discussions of the New Woman in the 1890s (Broomfield, 'Eliza Lyn Linton' 253). Methodologically, journalists need to be understood as sharing 'allegiances to their profession, irrespective of their ideological differences, other motivations or interests' (Broomfield, 'Eliza Lyn Linton' 265). Linton's stylistic management rendered 'a threatening topic such as woman's rights and wrongs' an issue which 'could be profitable if periodicals exploited its incendiary or entertaining elements' (Broomfield, 'Eliza Lyn Linton' 257). *Punch* had already established this in its visual and verbal register in the 1840s when it challenged attitudes to urban reform and it was a style suited to the series that Betham-Edwards contributed in 1868.

The anonymous scrapbooks in the Liddell Hart Collection demonstrate the reach of Linton's imagery in contributing to the broader debate on women's rights, making it accessible to different writers, interested parties, audiences, publications, and popular forms. Margaret Beetham identifies 'The Girl of the Period' as a key example of a cultural reference point which was 'endlessly repudiated, joked about and imitated across a spectrum of periodicals,' making it possible for readers to enter into the circulation of ideas and images including Bodichon's bid to improve women's role in society (Beetham 235). The comic press continued to use 'The Girl of the Period' as a cultural reference point but by the mid-1870s the character had become associated with the transgressive identities of the actress rather than a respectable middle-class daughter who needs firm guidance from her parents. In the theatre and music hall the character was used to address male fears about independent women (Buszek 155) and, more significantly, proposed a model of self-aware female sexuality (Buszek 143). The scrapbooks very clearly equate 'The Girl of the Period' with different classes, social situations, and ages of women and a broader debate about everyday experience, women's life and work outside the home, and acceptance of change. Betham-Edwards was able to capitalize not only on her own ability for satire but also on the extrapolation of the growing public debate Eliza Lynn Linton had encapsulated.

At this early stage Betham-Edwards appears to have chosen a much safer path for her own writing. The greatest accolade she received was the republication of her novel *The Lord of the Harvest* (1899) in the Oxford World's Classics series. As many women writers found, particularly those who like Betham-Edwards were unmarried, in order to earn a living, a commercial author had to identify themes and issues which were meaningful to changing audiences across their lifetime. Betham-Edwards can therefore be grouped with writers who were interested in changing attitudes to religion and female autonomy and the social networks in Britain and France which allowed her to make assessments of the later nineteenth century and anticipations of the twentieth. The longevity of her books, many of which were still in print at the time of her death in 1919, and her prolific output make her an unrecovered example of a successful nineteenth-century women writer.

Sarah Bilston also includes Betham-Edwards in a set of novelists who contributed to a forgotten genre of women's writing that represented acting as a noble and ennobling tradition (40). During the 1870s this fiction reconceptualized theatrical life and invited readers to identify with self-directed and self-supporting heroines (Bilston 41). Betham-Edwards's heroines are more complex than they appear and she expresses ambivalent attitudes to marriage, motherhood, and women's participation in education and professional careers. As Bilston argues, in *Bridget* (1877):

> the desire for liberty and the sense of ambition are explicitly described as sexless—as something that both young men and young women will experience, but that only men have traditionally been able to articulate and satisfy. However Betham-Edwards subtly suggests that women are *particularly* qualified for artistic success. (Bilston 45)

Bilston suggests that in the way that she examines her heroines' self-determined acting, Betham-Edwards challenged Linton's anger that 'The Girl of the Period' would seek the ability to create and self-make. Betham-Edwards's wide-ranging interests and understanding of current affairs enabled her to write for *Punch* in a style that was acceptable to the editor and its largely masculine readership. She demonstrates that women were able to produce commercial comic writing. This series that she created for Mark Lemon is significant because it demonstrates her keen interest in the political concerns of her age which allowed her to write for the comic press. Moreover, it provides insight into her ability to access public debate without introductions from her family or a husband familiar with these networks. She did not exclude herself from comic writing because of fears of impropriety, and she was able to meet the terms of her commission. However, her contribution to *Punch* was not a turning point in her career but a generic dead end as she did not produce further humorous work until much later in her life, and *Punch* did not provide her with support for the development of her career, which she then took in new directions. Her *Punch* 'letters' nevertheless form a significant strand in the late 1860s widening of opportunities for women writers across a broad spectrum of emerging literary and commercial genres.

Notes

1. In 2014–2015 Clare Horrocks undertook the transcription and identification of the contributors from the records of commissions and added these to the Gale-Cengage *Punch* Historical Archive 1841–1992 so that they are now easily accessible.
2. In fact when 'Miss Edwards' appeared in the *Punch* ledgers the project team working on identifying *Punch* contributors (see note 1) initially confused her with her better known cousin Blandford Edwards.

Works Cited

Beetham, Margaret. 'Periodicals and the New Media: Woman and Imagined Communities.' *Women's Studies International Forum* 29:1 (2006): 231–40.

Betham-Edwards, Matilda. *Anglo-French Reminiscences*. London: Chapman and Hall, 1900.

———. *Mid-Victorian Memories*. 1919. London: John Murray, 2001.

[Betham-Edwards]. 'Mrs. Punch's Letters to her Daughter.' [Letter 1]. Punch 55 (4 July 1868): 7–8.

———. 'Mrs. Punch's Letters to her Daughter.' [Letter 2]. Punch 55 (11 July 1868): 12–13.

———. 'Mrs. Punch's Letters to her Daughter.' [Letter 3]. Punch 55 (25 July 1868): 44.

———. 'Mrs. Punch's Letters to her Daughter.' [Letter 4]. Punch 55 (1 Aug 1868): 46.

———. 'Mrs. Punch's Letters to her Daughter.' [Letter 5]. Punch 55 (15 Aug 1868): 65.

———. 'Mrs. Punch's Letters to her Daughter.' [Letter 6]. Punch 55 (29 Aug 1868): 95.

———. 'Mrs. Punch's Letters to her Daughter.' [Letter 7]. *Punch* 55 (5 Sept 1868): 99.

———. 'Mrs. Punch's Letters to her Daughter.' [Letter 8]. *Punch* 55 (3 Oct 1868): 143.

———.'Mrs. Punch's Letters to her Daughter.' [Letter 9]. *Punch* 55 (24 Oct 1868): 180.

———. 'Mrs. Punch's Letters to her Daughter.' [Letter 10]. *Punch* 55 (7 Nov 1868): 197.

———. 'Mrs. Punch's Letters to her Daughter.' [Letter 11]. *Punch* 55 (26 Dec 1868): 268.

Bilston, Sarah. 'Authentic Performance in Theatrical Women's Fiction of the 1870s.' *Women's Writing* 11:1 (2004): 39–54.

Broomfield, Andrea. 'Eliza Lynn Linton, Sarah Grand and the Spectacle of the Victorian Woman Question: Catch Phrase, Buzz Words and Sound Bites.' *English Literature in Transition* 47:3 (2004): 251–77.

———. 'Much More than an Anti-Feminist: Eliza Lynn Linton's Contribution to the Rise of Victorian Popular Journalism.' *Victorian Literature and Culture* 29:2 (2001): 267–83.

Buszek, Maria-Elena. '"Awarish": Burlesque, Feminist Transgression and the Nineteenth Century Pin Up.' *The Drama Review* 43:4 (1999): 141–62.

Dillane, Fionnuala. *Before George Eliot: Marian Evans and the Periodical Press.* Cambridge: Cambridge University Press, 2013.

Gagnier, Regenia. 'Between Women: a Cross-class Analysis of Status and Anarchic Humour. *Women's Studies: An Interdisciplinary Journal* 15:1–3 (Oct 1988). 135–48.

Leary, Patrick. *The Punch Brotherhood: Table Talk and Print Culture in Mid-Victorian London.* London: British Library, 2010.

[Linton, Eliza Lynn]. 'The Girl of the Period.' *Saturday Review* 25 (14 March 1868): 339–40. Lockyer, Sharon and Michael Pickering. *Beyond a Joke: The Limits of Humour.* London: Palgrave Macmillan, 2009.

Maidment, Brian. *Comedy, Caricature and the Social Order, 1820–50.* Manchester: Manchester University Press, 2013.

Maltz, Diana. 'Sympathy, Humour and the Abject Poor in the Work of May Kendall.' *English Literature in Transition* 50:3 (2007): 313–32.

Rees, Joan. *Matilda Betham-Edwards: Novelist, Travel Writer and Francophile.* Hastings: The Hastings Press, 2006.

Scrapbooks. Liddell Hart Collection of Costume. Liverpool John Moores University Special Collections and Archives. 391.009 HAR.

Silver, Henry. 'Nights at the Table.' *Punch* Archive. British Library. MS 88937/2/13.

Spielmann, M[arion]. H[arry]. *The History of Punch.* London: Cassell and Co., 1895.

PART II

Women's Writing of the 1870s

Women workers in a pen factory operating stamping presses to slit pen nibs, during a royal visit to Gillott's factory, Birmingham, in 1874." Image courtesy of Victorian Picture Library http://www.victorianpicturelibrary.com

CHAPTER 10

Transcending Prudence: Charlotte Riddell's 'City Women'

Silvana Colella

[T]here never was a story told since the creation but a woman figured in it somewhere.
—Charlotte Riddell, *A Life's Assize*, 1871

By the late 1860s, Charlotte [Mrs J. H.] Riddell (1832–1906), the celebrated author of *George Geith of Fen Court* (1864), had reached the apex of her literary career.[1] She was able to command high prices in the market for fiction (Tinsley I, 98); her novels captured the attention of both established journals and metropolitan and provincial newspapers; and the editorship of the *St. James's Magazine*, which she held for seven years (1867–1873), further contributed to consolidating her media identity. Riddell was a popular author, though her popularity did not prove long lasting.[2] Born in Carrickfergus (Northern Ireland), Charlotte Eliza Cowan

S. Colella (✉)
Humanities Department, University of Macerata, Macerata, Italy
e-mail: silvana.colella@unimc.it

© The Author(s) 2020
A. E. Gavin, C. W. de la L. Oulton (eds.), *British Women's Writing from Brontë to Bloomsbury, Volume 2*, British Women's Writing from Brontë to Bloomsbury, 1840–1940,
https://doi.org/10.1007/978-3-030-38528-6_10

(later Riddell) moved to London in 1855 in pursuit of a literary career. She made her mark in the crowded literary marketplace of mid-Victorian England by narrating stories that are mostly set in the City of London, the centre of commerce and finance, and revolve around the *homines novi* of commercial modernity: City men, accountants, manufacturers, clerks, merchants, traders, and businessmen. 'I was and still am heartily in love with the City,' she declared in an interview (Blathwayt 3). Although some publishers tried to dissuade her from pursuing such (for a female author) unconventional topics, Riddell persevered: 'All the pathos of the City, the pathos in the lives of struggling men entered into my soul,' she explained, 'and I felt I must write, strongly as my publisher objected to my choice of subject, which he said was one no woman could handle well' (Blathwayt 3).

The hallmark of her fiction is a unique and striking combination of financial and literary writing; her 'wonderful and fearful knowledge of matters financial,' as one reviewer described it (Noble 371), coexists with psychological realism and the exploration of affects related to the changing dynamics of both the business world and the domestic sphere. The City novels published in the 1860s—*Too Much Alone* (1860), *City and Suburb* (1861), *George Geith of Fen Court* (1864), and *The Race for Wealth* (1866)—explore the plights of individuals caught in the 'vortex of business' as Victorian commentators liked to describe the hectic world of entrepreneurial capitalism.[3] Her fiction zooms in on small capitalists, rather than larger-than-life figures of speculators, drawing inspiration from what historians have defined as British 'personal capitalism'—the capitalism of small family firms or partnerships which were the preferred form of enterprise throughout the nineteenth century.[4] More systematically than her fellow novelists, Riddell offered readers paradigmatic stories of self-help based on a model of economic individuality in which the acquisitive urge is neither moralistically condemned nor entirely condoned.

The main difference between her earlier novels and those she wrote in the 1870s is the increasingly active role that women assume in the business sphere. In the decade inaugurated by the Married Women's Property Act 1870, which changed the common law doctrine of coverture to include the wife's right to own, sell, and buy separate property,[5] Riddell reoriented her fiction towards the exploration of female economic agency, though still retaining a focus on City men. The type of stories she imagines for her 'City women' testify to the growing cultural, social, and political relevance of questions pertaining to women's relations with money, property, and professional aspirations. No advocate for women's rights, Riddell nonetheless contributed to redefining the imaginative contours of women's participation in the life of the market.

As Linda Hughes explains, in the 1870s 'mid-Victorian legacies [coexisted] with an underlying shift toward modernity' (35). A similar shift can be detected in Riddell's fiction especially as regards the enlargement of women's sphere of action in the imagined world of her novels. This may reflect the author's sensitivity to broader cultural and political issues, but it is also the result of specific biographical circumstances. On 26 September 1871, her husband, Joseph Hadley Riddell, declared bankruptcy.[6] This ruinous and traumatic event was to cast a long shadow on their existence: Joseph never resumed trading, and Riddell became the sole breadwinner, increasing her productivity, diversifying her output, and going on to write the ghost stories for which she is still best known today. Like the heroines she imagines in the novels here under scrutiny, *Austin Friars* (1870) and *Mortomley's Estate* (1873), Riddell herself had to cope with pressing financial responsibilities and with the consequences of her husband's disastrous business failure. In the months leading up to the bankruptcy, Riddell was also involved in a series of legal suits—which she brought against her husband and one of his creditors—upon which she embarked with the hope of protecting her future earnings from the demands of dissatisfied creditors by taking advantage of the newly passed Married Women's Property Act. The Bill of Complaint she filed in 1871 states that 'the plaintiff had expressly told the defendant that she was determined upon one thing, which was, that she would never work for any creditor again, and that, if he imagined she was going to work any more to pay her husband's debts, he was quite mistaken.'[7] As the defiant tone of this assertion reveals, the 1870 Act had empowered Riddell to fight for her separate property, though the circumstances under which she was asserting her newly granted rights were dire in the extreme. Riddell's novels of the 1870s resonate with preoccupations about financial responsibilities, property ownership, insolvency, and the delicacy of the credit system, which had both personal and collective significance. The remainder of this chapter will examine two novels, *Austin Friars* (1870) and *Mortomley's Estate* (1874), in which the role of women as participants in the 'race for wealth' comes to the fore. Although not radically disruptive of consolidated gender roles, these novels nonetheless test the limits of domestic femininity by placing heroines in extreme situations that elicit the exercise of their entrepreneurial spirit.

AUSTIN FRIARS: AN IMMORAL BOOK?

Austin Friars was declared an 'immoral book' and criticized by the *Saturday Review* and the *Athenaeum* for playing too loosely with the ethics of fiction ('Austin Friars' 748). What standards of respectability or propriety did Riddell's novel contravene? The first chapter seems designed to play havoc with readers' expectations. The novel opens with a scene of demure domesticity set in the heart of the City of London: a young, pensive woman waits for her husband to return from work, a basket of needlework at her side: 'they had never grown indifferent,' explains the narrator, 'never fallen into the state of conjugal rudeness which makes a woman less courteous to her husband than she would be to a guest' (6). This layer of modest domesticity, however, is soon lifted to reveal a more modern and improper arrangement: the heroine, Yorke Haddon, and her loved one, Austin Friars, are unmarried and have been living under the same roof for some years, protected by the tolerant or indifferent attitude of City neighbours. In the pre-history of the novel, a very young Yorke is given in marriage to a much older man. Unable to bear the situation, Yorke flees from home, finds employment as a companion, falls in love with Austin, and agrees to follow him to London. To crank up the tension, Riddell adds a commercial twist: Yorke and Austin are now partners in business; her money (a thousand pounds inherited from her former employer) is invested in the unspecified business venture the couple has been managing together. When, in Chap. 2, Austin decides to opt out and marry the daughter of a rich merchant, Yorke demands that the money she has invested be returned to her since she plans to continue trading with the help of an experienced City man. As the narrator explains somewhat redundantly halfway through the story, pictures of 'pure domestic felicity' tend to be less compelling than those 'where the passion of our humanity has transcended its prudence ... and the life has been lived fully, though madly' (177).

The 1860s vogue for sensationalism in fiction had already habituated readers and critics to improper forms of familial relationships (bigamy and adultery *in primis*). Yet Riddell's interpretation of sensationalism in this novel remains striking for the way in which it connects the intimate and the commercial: the jilted woman, or the 'woman who has sinned' (*AF* 224), Yorke, refuses to give in to victimhood and responds to her affective and social predicament with a vigorous assumption of liberal subjectivity.

In the urban setting of the City of London, where trade, money making, and business more broadly define the spirit of the place, even fallen women or adulteresses seem to have the chance of redeeming themselves by adopting a model of economic rationality usually associated with male characters. It takes Yorke very little time to devise a course of action intended to secure her economic independence and to disentangle herself from both affective and commercial ties with Austin: 'Pride, indignation, wounded affection, and a perfect horror of dependence, all stimulated her desire to strike out some course which she might at once follow' (27). What Yorke devises is more specifically a business plan: with Austin gone, she intends to carry on the business herself, with the help of Luke Ross, 'book-keeper in a third-rate City house' (7). The scene in which she communicates her intentions to Luke reads like a full-blown liberal fantasy in which the fallen figure is metamorphosed into a 'character,' a liberal subject defined by her rationality, self-interest, and self-sufficient moral consciousness. As John Stuart Mill famously put it, 'A person whose desires and impulses are his own ... is said to have a character' (60). Yorke comes closer to embodying this abstract notion when she assumes a business identity.[8] This metamorphosis entails a degree of gender crossing or the transition to a form of selfhood conventionally understood as masculine. As Yorke explains to her bewildered interlocutor: '"Do you think me a perfect idiot? Do you not know that the sort of education I have had for years has made me feel like a man, judge like a man? Do you imagine I am going to be ... satisfied with the thirty-five or forty pounds a year I should get from my thousand pounds if I invested it safely?"' (*AF* 45). Yorke's decided assumption of economic rationality is further emphasized when she lays out to Luke 'the full brilliancy of her plan' and appears 'vexed at his male stupidity'; appealing to his latent desire for upward mobility, Yorke offers him a better job than the one he holds and the prospect of higher returns:

> She proposed, she went on to explain, that a portion of the £1000 should be mentally devoted to salaries, rent and so forth. She enlarged upon the fact that, no matter how long he remained with Messrs Hurward & Gaskarth, or how hard he worked for them, he could only hope to better his position a little; whereas if this venture proved successful, he might ultimately make a large fortune. She grew eloquent in advocacy of her plan, for she had set her heart on carrying out the scheme. (45)

Considering both the impropriety of Yorke's adultery and her rapid veering towards a rational business solution, the scandalized reactions of Victorian reviewers are understandable. *Austin Friars*, however, does not narrate the story of a businesswoman empowered by the liberal dream of economic independence and self-determination. The premises for this story are sketched in the first ten chapters. Although a plot centred on Yorke's economic agency appears plausible, the narrative falls into more conventional grooves as the story unfolds. No sooner does Yorke try to implement her business plan, she realizes that 'it is impossible for any one to be man and woman too' (52). She is gradually removed from the City scene, while the novel focuses persistently on the vicissitudes of the one thousand pounds that Austin is reluctant or unable to return. *Austin Friars* is a 'eulogy to the commercial City,' as Ranald Michie has argued (71): it painstakingly details how the 'little bills' which represent Yorke's capital are exchanged, discounted, transferred, renewed, and even dishonoured. City men of various denominations—accountants, merchants, traders—mediate between Yorke and her money, striving to uphold the value of the bills issued by Austin just as vigorously as they defend Yorke's honour. In narrative terms, this defence entails a regressive movement towards conventional feminine virtues: Yorke returns to the countryside and to her ailing husband; she suffers tortured moments of repentance and self-doubt; and her domestic virtues are showcased when she devotes herself to nursing her sick husband, relinquishing agency in the business sphere. However, it is significant that Riddell ultimately rewards the adulteress with solid wealth, a new husband (Luke), and a good life after much suffering. As the *Saturday Review* remarked: 'It is rare that a lady novelist has the courage to give her heroine to three men in the course of her three volumes, but this is the day for female courage, and the authoress of *Austin Friars* has not been behind the rest of her sex' ('Austin Friars' 748).

Riddell mustered a good dose of 'female courage' not so much in devising a happy denouement for the narrative destinies of an adulteress with a talent for business, but in producing a novel that so relentlessly discusses and explains the workings of the credit economy, especially in times of severe credit squeeze. Each stage in the progress of 'those little bills' is accurately detailed, as if Riddell's intentions were to provide readers with the rudiments of a financial education, alerting them to the complex interconnectedness of the credit system which ensures the negotiability of paper promises. Most reviewers considered these particulars as 'almost too technically related' or 'unintelligible to the ordinary reader,' while simultaneously admiring Riddell's commercial expertise ('Austin Friars' 748). As the *Times* observed, *Austin Friars* is 'as full of the tricks and turns of City brokerage and speculation as though its plot had been hatched within the quiet and respectable precincts from which it took its name' (Rev. of 'A Life's Assize' 4).[9] Even for the capacious standard of nineteenth-century realism, such an intense focus on technical financial details appeared excessive. Unladylike and misaligned with aesthetic models of value, Riddell's knowledge of finance and business was an integral part of her personal experience: in the troubled months preceding her husband's bankruptcy, the question of insolvency and dishonoured bills must have loomed large in her domestic environment. It is not surprising that the volatility of credit became such a central topic in *Austin Friars*. In the tension between acknowledging and disclaiming the different stories that commercial and financial modernity could potentially license—a tension that is tangible in the way Yorke's narrative destinies are plotted—one can see a reverberation of the hopes and anxieties specific to the 1870s, a decade which was already looking forward to a new phase of modernization but was also still grappling with the legacy of mid-Victorian cultural formations.

Facing Ruin: *Mortomley's Estate*

One of the most controversial pieces of legislation passed during William Gladstone's first premiership, the 1869 Bankruptcy Act, is the 'hero' or rather the villain of Riddell's novel of bankruptcy, *Mortomley's Estate* (1873), in which she gives vent to a great deal of indignation against institutional systems of power: legal and financial. What follows is a specimen of the narrator's heated rhetoric:

> Whether the gentlemen, commercial and legal no doubt, who concocted the Bankruptcy Act of 1869, and the other gentlemen of the Upper and Lower Houses who made it law, ever contemplated that an utterly irresponsible person should be placed in a responsible position it is not for me to say, but I cannot think that any body of men out of Hanwell could have proposed to themselves that the whole future of a bankrupt's life should be made dependent on the choice of a trustee, since it is simple nonsense to suppose a committee selected virtually by him and the petitioning creditor have the slightest voice in the matter. And if any man in business whose affairs are going at all wrong should happen to read these lines ... let him

remember liquidation means no appeal, no chance of ever having justice done him, nor even remote contingency ... of setting himself right with the business world. (*Mortomley's Estate* 210)

Equated to 'Dante's Inferno,' going into liquidation (which Riddell's husband did in 1871) appears to be the irreversible first step down a precipitous slope culminating in utter ruin. In the intentions of the legislators, however, liquidation was meant to be a less hostile form of arbitration of a debtor's liabilities than going through the bankruptcy court. Riddell was not alone in criticizing liquidation for placing undue power in the hands of trustees and creditors: for the *Saturday Review* liquidation was a 'gigantic evil,' a nasty system 'fostering a tribe of harpies who fatten on bankruptcies' ('Bankruptcy' 4); for the *Examiner*, likewise, the uncontrolled power of trustees in liquidations was 'liable to the grossest possible abuses' ('Our Bankruptcy' 1227). By the early 1870s, as Markham Lester writes, 'disenchantment with the new Bankruptcy Act had become widespread' (171). The novel Riddell wrote in the wake of her husband's financial failure is an atypical novel of bankruptcy, more polemical and fastidiously technical than other Victorian novels which feature scenes of bankruptcy, and significantly different from the type of fiction Riddell had written up until then.[10] The template of the City novel, which she had honed throughout the 1860s, appears strangely skewed. First of all, the insolvent City hero, Archibald Mortomley, a colour manufacturer, is notable for his textual invisibility: ill, enfeebled, and confused, he disappears behind the scenes at 'the first mutterings of the storm' (75). Secondly, the difficult task of managing the crisis falls upon his wife, Dolly, whom we see dealing to the best of her abilities with vociferous creditors, inattentive lawyers, sleazy accountants, and a small crowd of zealous bailiffs. Finally, Riddell's fascination with the City acquires distinctly negative connotations as she traces the increasing power of corporate interests against which individual traders stand little chances of redress.

A bitter text, filled with invectives against the law and its practitioners, *Mortomley's Estate* is also a wishful story of resilience centred on the rather incongruous figure of a female protagonist who is, initially, blissfully ignorant of finance, business, and the law. The bankrupt's wife, Dolly, is repeatedly portrayed as a 'little heathen' with a marked 'tendency to flame up' (38), or a 'lazy little sinner' (42), with a 'biting tongue' (44) and a penchant for complicated hairdos and fashionable clothes. She hardly coincides with the ideal of what the sensible wife of a City man should be, as the narrator likes to point out. Riddell is playing with literary stereotypes: the name she gives to Mortomley's wife—Dolabella Gerace—is evocative of Minerva Press heroines whose adventures lack the kind of realism dear to the 'novelist of the City'; Dolly's interest in fashion and colourful clothes, even after the crisis, contravenes recognized standards of modesty demanded especially of a bankrupt's wife; and her fiery temper singles her out from other heroines in Riddell's canon, whose self-control remains unperturbed even in the direst of circumstances.

Riddell approaches the subject of bankruptcy from two extreme angles: on the one hand, the narrator parades an astonishing knowledge of legal and financial matters that was bound to jar on the fastidious ears of Victorian reviewers, who were mostly unimpressed by such an array of specific information so polemically conveyed; on the other hand, the story's focalization on Dolly's perceptions, steep learning curve, and management of the crisis brings to the fore the painful process of slowly coming to terms with what liquidation actually means, how it affects the victims, and how difficult it is to realize what is going on until it is too late. This process of gradually reckoning with 'ruin' is the emotional, affective centre of the novel, rendered more poignant by the choice of a heroine who does not know how to respond to the crisis but learns how to react—a position with which, one could argue, Riddell's female readers could have sympathized.

Bankruptcy was a widespread phenomenon in Victorian England and by the 1870s it had already acquired a literary and artistic profile, as Barbara Weiss observes. While authors such as Charles Dickens, William Thackeray, or George Eliot tended to place significance on one particularly distressing moment—the household clearance scene, usually narrated in one chapter—inviting readers to sympathize with the sense of bereavement consequent upon the sale of cherished objects imbued with sentimental value, Riddell opted for a different configuration. Sentimentalized heirlooms turned into mere commodities do not convey in her text the tragedy of loss; what brings home the point that 'death is bankruptcy' (3) is the very slow process, painfully traced over many chapters, whereby Dolly comes to understand the consequences of going into liquidation and to devise a plan of action that will later ensure her husband's return to trading. Nostalgia for the ideal of middle-class domestic serenity, reflected in the sentimental value attributed to objects about to be transformed into commodities, is less relevant for Riddell than the agonizing process of tracing with precision how a home is dismantled, how difficult it is to accept the inevitable, and how best to respond to a situation of crisis.

Mortomley's Estate is both a re-enactment of the trauma of ruin experienced by the author and a powerful fantasy of redress pivoting on the actions of the bankrupt's wife. Dolly's interventions ensure that the secret formula for the production of Mortomley's famous colours be saved from the clutches of creditors, thus granting her husband the possibility of resuming trading in the future. Not only does Dolly manage to procure her husband's discharge (the certificate allowing bankrupts to resume business), she also fends off possible competitors, writes to old customers inducing them to come back, and supervises the activities of the new colour manufactory, until Mortomley recovers from his illness. The novel is determined to offer the kind of 'justice' and 'humanity' that the law claims to protect but does not seem automatically to guarantee.[11] Taking the 'business bull by the horns' (364), Dolly proves a formidable problem-solver and a resourceful woman of business. Yet, in the last chapter, Riddell opts for a tragic ending, killing off her most intriguing and unclassifiable heroine—a narrative choice that suggests how reluctant Riddell was to imagine the full restoration of happiness after the trauma of ruin.

In *Austin Friars* and *Mortomley's Estate*, Riddell expands the limits of realism by insisting on the representation of technical 'facts,' legal discourses, and financial details that, in her experience, weighed heavily on the chances of both men and women achieving a measure of security in the world of scantly regulated nineteenth-century capitalism. The reconfiguration of her 1870s City novels, in which the economic agency of women becomes the main focus of attention, can be viewed as Riddell's own contribution to contemporaneous discourses about women's rights that were very much alive in the public mind. Speaking with growing confidence and authority, Riddell uses the form-giving power of fiction to address pressing questions—bankruptcy, insolvency, granting and obtaining credit, overdue bills and the chronic instability of financial markets—that (it is safe to assume) many of her readers would have recognized as crucial aspects of their everyday life. That Riddell was 'courageous' enough to push the boundaries of fiction in order to include the representation of these aspects is to her credit, even if some Victorian professional readers (and later critics) found such intrusions of the economic real in the world of fiction unpalatable or questionable. In the 1880s and the 1890s, when writers like George Gissing were developing their own brand of literary naturalism and economic determinism, Riddell went on to write City novels—*The Senior Partner* (1881) and *Mitre Court* (1885)—that project a gloomy vision of the failed promises of commercial modernity. But she also wrote a semi-autobiographical *Künstlerroman*, *A Struggle for Fame* (1883), centred on the vicissitudes of a woman writer in the competitive environment of the mid-nineteenth-century publishing market. The heroine's successful struggles are one further illustration of Riddell's enduring belief in the philosophy of self-help, effectively adapted to a story of female self-determination. By the end of the novel, the protagonist, Glenarva, neither dies nor is returned to domestic roles—the shrinking of opportunities that mars the trajectories of male characters in Riddell's 1880s novels does not affect the narrative destinies of this heroine. *A Struggle for Fame* is the only novel in Riddell's canon that has not slipped off the critical radar.[12] Unlike her male-centred City novels, this text can be more easily read and interpreted using the heuristic paradigms of feminist criticism. Yet, it is as a woman author writing about City men and City life that Riddell was well known at the time. Her stance on Victorian capitalism is well deserving of critical attention. It is also noteworthy that it was only in the 1870s that female economic agency and entrepreneurship come to the fore in Riddell's novels. Her 'City women' and their predicaments testify to the growing centrality, in this transitional decade, of issues pertaining to women's cultural, political, and economic emancipation.

NOTES

1. *George Geith of Fen Court* was Riddell's most famous novel. It went into several editions and was adapted for the stage in 1877 by Wyman Reeves. After the publication of this novel, Riddell dropped the male pseudonym F. G Trafford and became known as Mrs J. H. Riddell.
2. On Riddell's popularity, see Srebrnik, Kelleher, and Peterson.
3. See Anon, *Business Life* and Smith.
4. See Rose and Colli.
5. On the legislative reforms introduced over the course of the nineteenth century, see Holcombe, Shanley, and Wynne.

6. Joseph Hadley Riddell held various occupations in the City. Census data lists him as a 'civil engineer,' 'boiler manufacturer,' and 'agent to patent American stove merchant.' See Census 1851 (RG 9/495); 1861 (RG 9/795); 1871 (RG10/1340), The National Archives, London.
7. See *Riddell v. Riddell and Smith*. Riddell had offered as security (to her husband's creditor) the copyright to some of her novels; later she attempted to protect her future earnings by invoking the Married Women's Property Act 1870. Since half of this Chancery case is missing from the National Archives, it is difficult to establish the final outcome of this legal suit. Certainly, by suing her husband and his creditor, Riddell was trying to take advantage of the recently passed Married Women's Property Act.
8. On the centrality of the idea of character in 'Britain's liberal path to modern governance,' see Goodlad (24).
9. Austin Friars is a street located in the City, off Old Broad Street. In Riddell's novel this toponym is used as the protagonist's name.
10. In her cultural and literary history of bankruptcy in Victorian England, Barbara Weiss describes as 'novels of bankruptcy' texts such as Charles Dickens's *Dombey and Son* (1848), William Thackeray's *The Newcomes* (1855), George Eliot's *The Mill on the Floss* (1860), and Anthony Trollope's *The Way We Live Now* (1875). In these and other novels, scenes of bankruptcy, charged with emotional significance, are crucial turning points in the narrative.
11. In Blackstone's *Commentaries on the Laws of England* (1811), bankruptcy laws are said to be based on the principle that debtors, too, ought to be exempted 'from the rigor of the general law': 'the laws of bankruptcy are considered as laws calculated for the benefit of trade, and founded on the principle of humanity as well as justice; and to that end they confer some privileges, not only on the creditors, but also on the bankrupt or debtor himself' (II, 471). The liquidation clauses introduced in the 1869 Bankruptcy Act were meant to promote a potentially less severe attitude towards the debtor, who could avoid the public shame of going through the bankruptcy court and could continue trading—if the business was considered valuable—under some form of supervision.
12. See Peterson. An independent Irish publisher, Tramp Press, issued in 2014 a new edition of this novel.

Works Cited

Anon. *Business Life: Experiences of a London Tradesman with Practical Advice and Directions for Avoiding Many of the Evils Connected with our Present Commercial System and State of Society*. London: Houlston and Wright, 1861.
'Austin Friars.' *The Saturday Review* 29.762 (4 June 1879): 748.

'Bankruptcy.' *The Saturday Review* 27.712 (19 July 1879): 69.
Blackstone, William. *Commentaries on the Laws of England: A New Edition with the Last Corrections of the Authors.* London: William Reed, vol. 2. 1811.
[Blathwayt, Raymond]. 'Lady Novelists—A Chat with Mrs. J. H. Riddell.' *Pall Mall Gazette* (18 February 1890): 3.
Colli, Andrea. *The History of Family Business, 1750–2000.* Cambridge: Cambridge University Press, 2003.
[Collyer, Robert]. 'Novels of the Week' (Rev. of *Austin Friars*), *The Athenaeum* 2222 (28 May 1870): 707–08.
Goodlad, Lauren. *Victorian Literature and the Victorian State: Character and Governance in a Liberal Society.* Baltimore: Johns Hopkins University Press, 2003.
Holcombe, Lee. *Wives and Property: Reform of the Married Women's Property Law in Nineteenth-Century England.* Toronto: University of Toronto Press, 1983.
Hughes, Linda K. '1870.' In *A Companion to Victorian Literature and Culture.* Ed. Herbert F. Tucker, Oxford: Blackwell, 1999. 35–50.
Kelleher, Margaret. 'Charlotte Riddell's *A Struggle for Fame*: The Field of Women's Literary Production.' *Colby Quarterly* 36 (2000): 116–31.
Lester, Markham V. *Victorian Insolvency: Bankruptcy, Imprisonment for Debt, and Company Winding-Up in Nineteenth-Century England.* Oxford: Oxford University Press, 1995.
Mill, John Stuart. *On Liberty and Other Writings.* 1859. Ed. Stefen Collini. Cambridge: Cambridge University Press, 1989.
Michie, Ranald. *Guilty Money: The City of London in Victorian and Edwardian Culture, 1815–1914.* London: Pickering & Chatto, 2009.
[Noble, John Ashcroft]. 'New Novels.' *The Academy* 709 (5 December 1885): 71–2.
'Our Bankruptcy Law.' *The Examiner* 3687 (28 September 1878): 1227.
Peterson, Linda. *Becoming a Woman of Letters. Myths of Authorship and Facts of the Victorian Market.* Princeton: Princeton University Press, 2009.
Rev. of 'A Life's Assize.' *The Times.* 14 January 1871, 4.
Riddell, Charlotte. *Austin Friars.* 1870. London: Hutchinson & Co, n.d.-a
———. *A Life's Assize.* London: Tinsley Brothers, 1871.
———. *Mortomley's Estate.* 1873. London: Hutchinson & Co., n.d.-b
Riddell v. Riddell and Smith. R133 (1871). British National Archives C16/747.
Rose, Mary B. 'The Family Firm in British Business, 1780–1914.' In *Business Enterprise in Modern Britain from the Eighteenth to the Twentieth Century.* Ed. Maurice Kirby and Mary B. Rose. London: Routledge, 1994. 61–87.
Shanley, Mary Lyndon. *Feminism, Marriage, and the Law in Victorian England, 1850–1895.* Princeton: Princeton University Press, 1989.

Smith, Henry M. D. *High-Pressure Business Life, its Evils, Physical and Moral.* London: J. A. Brook and Co, 1876.
Srebrnik, Patricia. 'Mrs. Riddell and the Reviewers: A Case Study in Victorian Popular Fiction.' *Women's Studies* 23 (1994): 69–84.
Tinsley, William. *Random Recollections of an Old Publisher.* 2 vols. London: Simpkin, Marshall, Hamilton, Kent & Co., 1900.
Weiss, Barbara. *The Hell of the English: Bankruptcy and the Victorian Novel.* Lewisburg: Bucknell University Press, 1986.
Wynne, Deborah. *Women and Personal Property in the Victorian Novel.* Aldershot: Ashgate, 2010.

CHAPTER 11

'[M]ute orations, mute rhapsodies, mute discussions': Silence in George Eliot's Last Decade

Fionnuala Dillane

George Eliot made very particular strategic decisions about how her two novels of the 1870s, *Middlemarch* (1871–1872) and *Daniel Deronda* (1876), were to be published. These novels of reform, set respectively in the reforming periods of the 1830s and the 1860s, signal a departure from her previous work in a strikingly obvious way: against publication trends of the time, they appeared first in serial parts.[1] This pragmatic decision also constitutes reform of sorts—structural, economic, and aesthetic—that allowed Eliot to retune her relationship with her readers. She was resetting the temporal, affective and authoritative dynamics of her fiction in the last decade of her life as her sense of mortality and questions of legacy were ever more pressing.

The effects of her publication decision are as complex as the motivations: the economic advantages and consequences for the form and initial

F. Dillane (✉)
School of English, Drama and Film, University College Dublin, Dublin, Ireland
e-mail: fionnuala.dillane@ucd.ie

© The Author(s) 2020
A. E. Gavin, C. W. de la L. Oulton (Eds.), *British Women's Writing from Brontë to Bloomsbury, Volume 2*, British Women's Writing from Brontë to Bloomsbury, 1840–1940,
https://doi.org/10.1007/978-3-030-38528-6_11

reception of the two novels have been well parsed (Sutherland; Martin). This chapter will consider some aspects of how the decision to publish in parts relates to Eliot's ongoing preoccupations with the relationship between form and affect. These concerns take on new dimensions for the writer in the decade following, among other factors, the vertiginous success of sensation fiction with its structural and thematic emphasis on shock and suspense to arrest attention in the increasingly distracting environment of an industrializing century, to which the genre contributed and responded (Daly). Another crucial context was her deepening interest in new developments in the science of psychology, to which her life partner, George Henry Lewes, contributed throughout the 1870s. The still unresolved tension between inductive and deductive understandings of mind-body interactions was not unremoved from sensation fiction's core preoccupations. Eliot's evolving relationship from mid-century with nineteenth-century psychology has been analysed at length (e.g., Shuttleworth; Davis, *George Eliot* 2006). This chapter attends instead to George Eliot's response to the drive to explain, to fix, and to claim mastery over the mysteries of human interactions and behaviour, whether played out in the almost aggressively insistent return to domestic stability in the strong endings of mid-century fiction; the drive to explanation and the reassuring expulsion of transgressive agents in sensation fiction; or in the growing authority of deductive sciences of the mind. It argues that Eliot's work in the 1870s demonstrates sustained experiments with an aesthetics of silence that forces readers to question interpretative confidence, their own and that of her characters and narrators. Her final fictional works, moreover, convey an increasing insistence on the limitations of her cultural moment's drive to matters of fact. The push towards visibility, which Kate Flint, among others, diagnoses as a dominant structural and cultural paradigm from the mid-century ironically, is increasingly under pressure as knowledge systems expanded, diversified, and became more specialized (Flint).

Eliot takes on this paradigm to draw attention to the felt but unworded, to the feeling of reading, and to that always entangled relationship between the emotional and intellectual life that was increasingly important to her in her final decade. These ideas underscored Lewes's scientific writings of the late 1860s and 1870s, in both the *Physiology of Common Life* (1859) and *Problems of Life and Mind* (1874–1879), the last two volumes of which, *The Study of Psychology* and *Mind as a Function of Organism* were seen into print by Eliot, following his death in 1878. Her immersion in the increasingly specialized study of the biology of the 'mind,' including developing neurosciences, physiological psychology, and, especially compelling for Eliot, the complex interactions of consciousness and the somatic produced a structural and aesthetic refiguring of her fictional work in the 1870s.

In her late work, the power relations that pertain between articulated speech and disarticulated but aesthetically expressive feeling are rooted in an understanding of the mind/body relation that is social, cultural, and historical, as well as physiological. The play of silences in her work points to these contextual dynamics, and she implies, the relations cannot be disaggregated without compromising or limiting our reading of a situation, a person, or a text. The mutually sustaining affordances of the discourses of science and art, the mutual interactions of thinking and feeling, under threat from an increasingly modernizing, categorizing, industrializing century are everywhere present in her final works as she foregrounds the incommensurability of the somatic with over-determined drives towards the systematic.

In a letter to a troubled agnostic struggling to reconcile her intellectual acceptance of the material nature of our universe with humane values, Eliot writes of the need to balance the truth-claims and categorizing impulses of both experimental and deductive science with an acknowledgement of the specificities of the individual feeling life as an equally valid form of knowing:

> One might as well hope to dissect one's own body and be merry in doing it, as take molecular physics (in which you must banish from your field of view what is specifically human) to be your dominant guide, your determiner of motives, in what is solely human. That every study has its bearing on every other is true; but pain and relief, love and sorrow, have their peculiar history which make an experience and knowledge over and above the swing of atoms. (10 December 1874, *Letters* 6, 99)

Writing here in 1874, between the publication of *Middlemarch* and *Daniel Deronda*, Eliot is reaching towards the need to accommodate the 'peculiar' or unique histories that constitute a type of embodied knowledge, that which is felt in the body and communicated through the body. In her work, silence becomes both a multi-faceted concept and an aesthetic strategy to redress the swing towards atoms, to validate the authenticity of the somatic and other non-worded forms of understanding as equally compelling as the categorical.

The decision to publish her work in parts was one important dimension to Eliot's active engagement with the rhetorical function of silence. The silence between parts was a means of drawing attention to questions of interpretative authority in art, in science, as in life. At its most basic but effective level, she left her original readers waiting. They waited in the external, real-world pauses between the bi-monthly or monthly parts, filling the vacuum with their own version of what would happen next while the author remained silent. Readers also waited for the multiple plots to converge in the internal pauses between the distinct strands of the stories (*Middlemarch*'s 'Miss Brooke' and Middlemarch sections, and *Daniel Deronda*'s even more pronounced so-called English and Jewish halves). Eliot's foray into this particular type of multi-plot (and multi-part) fiction, as David Carroll observes 'foregrounds the question of interpretation in quite new ways,' (Carroll 234). Into the spaces between parts, into the spaces between plots, readers speculated.

Eliot, Lewes, and her publisher John Blackwood were keenly alert to the marketing advantage, the creation of a stir, and the sense of anticipation part publication generated. Blackwood reported to Lewes in December 1872 of *Middlemarch*: '[t]he public mind is about as full of the book as well could be' (21 December 1872, *Letters* 5, 348). Preparing for the publication of *Daniel Deronda* three years later, Blackwood confirmed 'I do not think we can do better than follow Middlemarch only making the publication monthly as the audience are more ready'; in other words, more attuned to experiment from this always challenging author (18 October 1875, *Letters* 6, 178). A review of the second book of *Daniel Deronda* in the *Examiner* in March 1876 picks up on these points about the potential of this serial format and notes, tellingly, that the format at once frees the reader and ties him or her even more firmly to the author's commanding authority; 'fragmentary' part publication gives:

> ample time ... for the study and free social discussion of the characters, for speculation as to their unrevealed past and their unreached future. ... Opinions during the last month have been much divided as to what she intends to make of her heroine; bets have been freely laid, and if the gifted authoress were open to secret [negotiations] she might add indefinitely to the profits, if not to the artistic unity, of her work, by consenting to accept suggestions from interested parties. (Qtd. in Martin 245)

The gaps signalled by publication mode invite a new type of transactional arrangement between writer and reader, an affective gamble, as readers invent around the 'unrevealed past' and 'unreached future' of characters to whom they have been introduced in as yet un-unified multiple plot strands. It is a gamble that no doubt consciously mirrors the famous first scene of *Daniel Deronda*, one fraught with possibility, anxiety, and uncertainty in equal measure: will the investment in this heroine, for instance, pay off? Even the sense of who will take the chief role is undecided. Readers of the first parts of *Middlemarch* thought Tertius Lydgate and Dorothea Brooke were the centre of romantic interest in the novel, and in line with the familiar patterns of much mid-century fiction, that they were destined to marry, thus bringing the two parts of the sprawling novel together with an affirming, definitive, predictable ending. The *Athenaeum* puzzled in its third review of the unfolding *Daniel Deronda* that the '"hero, who gives his name to the story, has not yet become the chief character"' (qtd. in Martin 222). Do we bet on him? The five unanswered questions with which *Daniel Deronda* begins reinforce this sense of speculation into striking silence:

> Was she beautiful or not beautiful? and what was the secret of form or expression which gave the dynamic quality to her glance? Was the good or the evil genius dominant in those beams? Probably the evil; else why was the effect that of unrest rather than of undisturbed charm? Why was the wish to look again felt as coercion and not as a longing in which the whole being consents? (*Daniel Deronda* 7)

This opening, as Alex Woloch observes, 'increases readerly self-consciousness and establishes ... a deeply experimental approach to consciousness and intersubjectivity, hinging on the unspoken interactions between Deronda and Gwendolen' (171). The extraordinary decision to publish her final novels in part format is a serial reinforcing of that experimental approach, buttressing the gaps that signal unspoken communication—'reinforcing' because that interest in pauses and silences is a persistent feature of her narrative aesthetic in the 1870s.

In her last novels Eliot repeatedly draws attention to the limitations of words, of naming, and of narrative foreclosure to emphasize instead both the more aleatoric and flexible communicative possibilities and interpretative impossibilities of silences. In *Daniel Deronda*, that affective gap is more pronounced, just as the two main storylines are more fissured.

Daniel Deronda, which was Eliot's last novel, ends with a tactical withdrawal that leaves characters and readers in a vacuum, spatially, emotionally, and socially. 'There will I know be disappointment at not hearing more of the failure of Gwendolen and the mysterious destiny of Deronda, but I am sure you are right to leave all grand and vague,' Blackwood wrote to Eliot of the novel's final part (12 July 1876, *Letters* 6, 272). In *Daniel Deronda* and *Middlemarch*, there is a shift from the recognizable pattern of strong endings rooted in temporal, domestic, and emotional stability, that dominant feature of mid-century fiction. With the notable exception of *The Mill on the Floss* (1860), which controversially featured a sacrificial death by drowning of her protagonist, Maggie Tulliver, Eliot's novels from *Adam Bede* (1859) to *Felix Holt, the Radical* (1866) situate her main characters in family structures that are embedded in a community and flourishing at novel's end with their reassuring normative promise of future generations, notwithstanding the unusal configuration of some of those domestic arrangements.

In contrast, *Middlemarch*'s bitter-sweet conclusions, summarized in the compact and devastating afterword, are everywhere underscored with a sense of how we are misremembered and forgotten: the withering of Lydgate's ambition and his premature death, frustrated and unknown; the melancholic reminder that perhaps Dorothea's choice of marriage and motherhood limited the recognizable scope of her potential for enduring good work; the misrecorded authorial legacies of Fred Vincy and Mary Garth. *Daniel Deronda*'s conclusions are even more opaque, as Blackwood noted, with both Deronda and Gwendolen Harleth on the precipice of potentially momentous change but their futures are purposefully not imagined for us by the narrator. Such attention to the problems of ending, signals intensifyies in George Eliot's work in the final decade of her career as she became ever more conscious of how her work would be remembered, how it would last, how it gestures beyond its moment to other futures 'on the other side of silence' (*Middlemarch* 180). If there were such futures for this questioning atheist, they would be in the afterlife of her creative works alone.

It must be acknowledged that this emphasis on silence over words in her 1870s work may seem counterfactual. *Middlemarch* and *Daniel Deronda*, after all, are George Eliot's longest novels, densely detailed, and capacious. They share with all of her writings an insistence on matter, but as has been amply demonstrated by her readers, then and now, these novels offer even more large-scale, engrossing, intelligent explorations of the living, feeling, thinking body in a concrete social world. Moreover, in all her later work her protagonists are anything but silent. Her poetry and fiction of the late 1860s and 1870s are notably full of passionate communicators and vocal advocates. These are tellingly, for the most part, singers or vocal and visionary reformers and include the protagonists of her longer poems, Armgart, Jubal, and the Spanish Gypsy, Fedalma; *Middlemarch*'s Dorothea, Lydgate, Nicholas Bulstrode, and Will Ladislaw; *Daniel Deronda*'s Alcharisi, Gwendolen Harleth, Mirah Lapidoth, Deronda, and Mordecai. Moreover, the defining (celebrated and criticized) feature of her writing style from her journalism and through two decades of fiction and poetry to her final collection of satirical essays, *Impressions of Theophrastus Such* (1879) is that penetrating, mediating, varyingly compassionate and bitingly satirical explanatory narrative voice. It is full, ever-present, interpreting and guiding and directing, both telling us the story and telling us what to think about the story, so much so that Philip Davis has recently claimed that it becomes the most important character in her fiction.

Davis roots that narrative creation in her biography: throughout her writing life, he argues, her driving motivation was to bring everything to the surface, she wants to tell us all: lonely, frustrated, unsure of her vocation or her future, the young Mary Ann Evans first used her correspondence 'to get whatever was within out—to *outer* all of it, if only she could. ... What she believed in was close and direct communication—as though, originally, thoughts were always *meant* to be spoken out loud' (Davis, *The Transferred Life*, 54), as if the word constituted the real. In her later life, Davis suggests then, George Eliot's expansive realist novels provide creative rendering of these pressing desires to communicate, to fill in and fill out. They seem to achieve the wishes expressed by the writer early in her career in the summer of 1856 as she contemplated trying her hand at fiction writing:

> I never before longed so much to know the names of things as during this visit to Ilfracombe. The desire is part of the tendency that is now constantly growing in me to escape from all vagueness and inaccuracy into the daylight of distinct, vivid ideas. The mere fact of naming an object tends to give definiteness to our conception of it—we have then a sign which at once calls up in our minds the distinctive qualities which mark out for us that particular object from all others. (22 July 1856, *Journals* 272)

This is the voice of the journalist and editor who spent years copy-editing other people's work for clarity and communicative purpose. It is the voice of the newly-practising amateur scientist, scrambling along the sea-shore of Tenby and Ilfracombe with Lewes, carefully registering rock types, gathering specimens of anemones into newly purchased clear glass jars all the better to prepare for Lewes's illuminating and entertaining 'Sea-Side Studies'. The 'Studies' were published in *Blackwood's Magazine* from August 1856, five months before the first of her 'Clerical' stories—welcomed for the ways in which they depicted the natural history of ordinary English men and women—appeared in the same periodical.

Such gathering, naming, and categorizing impulses are fit work for scientists and realist novelists, but this desire to harness signifier to signified, to differentiate, to fix, contrasts with the refusal to name that marks the charged interactions in *Middlemarch* for instance between Dorothea Brooke and the romantic dreamer, Will Ladislaw, the cousin of her husband, Edward Casaubon. Their mutual regard is expressed through the ease with which they openly communicate in Rome. Their encounters in England, however, are full of what is not said and what readers are not told. At the end of Book Six, for example, Will and Dorothea part for what they both think will be the last time. Will, with new understanding about the bitter codicil to Casaubon's will that precludes him from pursuing his relationship with the newly widowed young woman, has come to say goodbye and to communicate that he now knows what Dorothea and the rest of their acquaintances had kept secret from him: 'Will turned around quickly, and the next moment Dorothea was entering. As Mrs Kell closed the door behind her they met: each was looking at the other and consciousness was overflowed by something that suppressed utterance. It was not confusion that kept them silent for, they both felt that parting was near, and there is no shamefacedness in a sad parting' (*Middlemarch* 496). Catherine Bond Stockton has explained the unspoken tension of this scene as relating to the 'shame' both characters feel because of their strong mutual sexual attraction (233). But important, too, is the acknowledgement of the fact that George Eliot stresses that for Will and Dorothea there is no confusion about what they feel. We, the readers, are excluded however and interpret into the gap of 'suppressed utterance.'

This type of unspoken understanding that excludes the reader is to be distinguished from Eliot's practised and compelling use of free-indirect discourse or the acts of thinking reported to us that are either repressed or purposefully withheld in the story-world interactions of the novel's characters. These features are perhaps the more familiar dimensions of Eliot's use of silence. In that compressed meeting between Will and Dorothea, for example, Eliot returns again and again to non-speech, not just to their 'relation which neither of them could explicitly mention' (*Middlemarch* 497). There is Will's 'wretched silence' that words will never be enough to express the love he feels towards Dorothea (498): 'what could he say...? ... what could she say...?' (498). Dorothea's jealousy of Will's relationship with Rosamond Vincy is fuelled by the impossible pliability and opacity of language: because 'everything he said might refer to that other relation' and not to her hope for his love for her. Words are not doing the work of communication and so she 'stood silent with her eyes cast down dreamily' (499). Will, in silent response, 'was not surprised at her silence' but does not know how to proceed: 'he was feeling rather wildly that something must happen to hinder their parting—some miracle, clearly nothing in their own deliberate speech' (499).

It is telling that it is a miracle of sorts that intervenes to close the gap between what these characters feel and what they say: a chance encounter, a coincidence, that Dorothea turns up at Rosamond Vincy's house on a mission of mercy the very day that Will is back in town, when Rosamond's husband Lydgate is away, when the household's servant, Martha introduces Dorothea to the room unannounced just at the precise intimate moment when Will comforts a tearful Rosamond. The potential misreadings of this encounter are corrected in subsequent scenes in terms that force the revelation of love on both sides and bring Will and Dorothea together. Yet it is by chance, by first misreading, by much not-saying.

This potential for divergence in understanding, that which characterizes in practice the many failed marriages of Eliot's fiction, is one aspect of her later work that critics such as J. Hillis Miller and D. A. Miller have diagnosed with different sets of emphasis as the unravelling impulses of her more mature style. It is a movement into more troubled modernity marked by an increasing disaggregation of the individual from the social; a deepening interest in the critical distances between bodies that converge with developing interest in the psychological noted earlier. Some critics, such as K. M. Newton have argued, such stylistic features are a certain demonstration of Eliot's status as a modernist. More than deconstructive unravelling, however, Eliot's decision to communicate through gaps and silences in terms that stall or block interpretative closure is a striking withdrawal of omniscience and a new departure in codifications of silence that inform this later work.

It is unsurprising then that in her last work, *Impressions of Theophrastus Such* (1879), her omniscient narrator finally stages an exit to leave us in the hands of her opinionated and contradictory guide, Theophrastus, and his 'impressions.' Not since her 1859 story 'The Lifted Veil,' published in *Blackwood's Edinburgh Magazine*, had she used a first-person character-narrator. That narrator, Latimer, tormented by an ability to read others' minds, with his 'preternaturally heightened sense of hearing, making audible to one a roar of sound where others find perfect stillness' ('Lifted Veil' 18) is a perversion of the celebrated omniscient narrator figure that came to define realist fiction and an early signal of George Eliot's reflexive interrogation of that authoritative, parsing voice so celebrated in her own fiction. Latimer leaps into the blank silence of Bertha's mind, the object of his desire, to rationalize his actions. Her thoughts are obscured from him for some mysterious, never-explained reason in this puzzling tale, and it is a disastrous leap. It leads to one of the many incompatible marriages in Eliot's work that are structured to fail because of an inability to communicate, or to read affective gaps. Paradoxically, through these failures she helps us to understand the volatility of perspective is related to the instability of language as an expressive medium and points to the need to attend to the silences.

In her 1870s fiction Eliot continues to foreground the connection between failed marriages and silence but without the Gothic pyrotechnics and preternatural high jinks of 'The Lifted Veil' or the predominantly class-based incompatibilities of her early 1860s work. Throughout the late 1860s and the 1870s, as noted earlier, she was immersed in Lewes's explorations of the relationship between physiology and psychology that spoke to her own long-held interest in Baruch Spinoza's philosophical reading of the feeling mind. Through her Sunday salons she was increasingly in the company of physiological psychologists such as Alexander Bain (founder of the journal *Mind* in 1876) and James Sully, who shared her interest in the affective capacity of reading and whose collection of essays, *Sensation and Intuition: Studies in Psychology and Aesthetics* (1874) was owned and read by Eliot and Lewes (Brilmyer 43).

In Eliot's novels of the 1870s, an understanding that 'silence veils the most intense forms of martial cruelty' (Dowling 333) gains specific traction, in particular in the relationships between Dorothea and Casaubon, Rosamond and Lydgate, and, most viciously, Henleigh Grandcourt and Gwendolen. However, there is more than one-directional repression at play in these works. Dorothea's compulsion to read into Casaubon's silences, for instance, sees her amplifying his sparse words with ardent meaning because of her personal needs, her ardent desire for something to matter. She embodies the anticipating reader of the serial instalment to instructively heavy cost. 'Dorothea's faith' we are told, 'supplied all that Mr Casaubon's words seemed to leave unsaid' (*Middlemarch* 68). Like a keen Saint Teresa, she is determined to overwrite her pinched life with some full faith in anything outside herself. It is a fatal filling in. Casaubon's oppressive silences towards Dorothea in the aftermath of their disastrous honeymoon become the keynotes of their miserable marriage. They remain mutually 'blind' (and deaf) to each other's 'inward troubles' (*Middlemarch* 185).

Lydgate and Rosamond replicate this pattern of broken misreading and mishearing. Wrapped up in their own egotistical drives (Rosamond for social status and acknowledgement of her separateness from the prosaic life of her midlands mercantile town; Lydgate, for knowledge and recognition as a man of science), they fail to consider and to interpret each other in terms beyond their own narrow needs. Lydgate's sense of the irretrievable gap in their mutual sense of each other is figured in the growing spaces of silence in their interactions, which are extended in each encounter until 'the silence between them became intolerable to him; it was if they were both adrift on one piece of wreck and looked away from each other' (*Middlemarch* 584). That sense of isolation at sea, together and silent, takes on more chilling literal as well as metaphorical connotations in Eliot's final novel.

The relationship between Grandcourt and Gwendolen has exceptionally vicious dimensions. John Picker, in his wider discussion of what he describes as the 'sonic contexts and concerns of [Eliot's] later experimental writings' (84), pays particular attention to Grandcourt's dangerous, torturous manipulation of Gwendolen's mental and physical life through his persistent, studied non-communication (Picker 93–9). The damaging and painful misreadings of *Middlemarch* are ratcheted up in *Daniel Deronda* in terms of both the consequences (Gwendolen's mental collapse, Grandcourt's death) and the expanding codifications of silence's aesthetic possibilities. The crushing silences of *Middlemarch*'s marriages are transformed into more violent metaphors: Gwendolen repeatedly feels 'throttled into silence' (*Daniel Deronda* 669). That physical choking and aggressive suppression of selfhood has as its counterpart in her roar at the other side of silence both before and after her marriage to Grandcourt in the multiple instances of her collapse into sustained periods of shrieking.

The 'hysterical violence' of her screams 'again and again' punctuate the text (359). These scenes of non-worded communication protest not just the repression of her identity through her marriage, but communicate a wider realization of the blankness of her existence. She does not believe in God, in people, in her own desire or capacity to desire; she shrinks from physical contact with anyone but her mother. Every fact gestures towards an unprocessed traumatic experience that remains unspoken in the text, a strategic silence that Jill Matus unpacks in her analysis of Gwendolen as a traumatized subject (Matus 138–44), but tellingly, Eliot does not provide an account of a traumatic event to explain or rationalize Gwendolen's volatility. In marked contrast to the detailed 'natural histories' of Maggie Tulliver in *The Mill on the Floss*, whose carefully explicated childhood of gendered exclusion and repression provides clear basis for her adult actions, or the misunderstanding of Silas Marner's catalepsy as the understandable basis for his choice to live as a recluse, Gwendolen Harleth remains a silent, shrieking mystery.

It should be remembered also, however, that Gwendolen chooses her only way out of poverty and social erasure in choosing Grandcourt. It is a studied choice, made in full knowledge of his secrets and therefore of his character so this is not a mistaken marriage, not a sensational melodrama or the product of unspoken expectations that are sounded in the mind of one partner only as in the case of Dorothea and Casaubon in *Middlemarch*. Gwendolen knows all already and so do Eliot's readers. From their first encounter, she and Grandcourt embark on a dangerous power play that uses not silence but, most deliberately, the 'pause' as its weaponry. The pause is a space of no-sound that is more suggestive than silence in its multiple significations that turn around 'play': the sexual tension of courtship; the dramatic pause so central to effect in the staged play; the pregnant space between two notes the musician understands as integral to music making. That first meeting is an extraordinary experimental sequence that teases out the ontological, narratological, and temporal functions of the pause:

> 'I used to think archery was a great bore,' Grandcourt began. He spoke with a fine accent, but with a certain broken drawl, as of a distinguished personage with a distinguished cold on his chest.
> 'Are you converted to-day?' said Gwendolen.
> (Pause, during which she imagined various degrees and modes of opinion about herself that might be entertained by Grandcourt.)

'Yes, since I saw you shooting. In things of this sort one generally sees people missing and simpering.'
'I suppose you are a first-rate shot with a rifle.'
(Pause, during which Gwendolen, having taken a rapid observation of Grandcourt, made a brief graphic description of him to an indefinite hearer.)
'I have left off shooting.'
'Oh then you are a formidable person. People who have done things once and left them off make one feel very contemptible, as if one were using cast-off fashions. I hope you have not left off all follies, because I practise a great many.'
(Pause, during which Gwendolen made several interpretations of her own speech.) (*Daniel Deronda*, 112)

The calculated 'parenthetical dilations of conversational time transgress normal realist practices,' Nicholas Dames writes of this strategy, linking the method to that of a play script 'as if only stage directions could give sufficient weight to the not-said of this interaction' (Dames 159). In the metafictional leak, the author exposes the narrator's usual off-stage directorial action to explosive effect. In this use of silence and pauses Eliot moves to separate her fiction in the 1870s from her narrator's categorizing grasp.

Elizabeth Ermarth has drawn attention to the 'particular narrative quality' of *Middlemarch* that speaks to this undercutting of the presumed narrative control, that is the 'frustrating reversibility of almost every generalisation it sponsors' (Ermarth 109). *Daniel Deronda* takes this erosion a step further, it could be argued, as demonstrated in readings of Daniel as a 'George Eliot' narrator avatar, so hypersensitive and alert to the many-sidedness of all things, like some type of more fully drawn Latimer, he is paralysed into inactivity (Hertz 130–31). The more differentiated effects that the gaps produced between conflicts in interpretation, the enclosures of free indirect discourse, or the aggressions of personal and social claims outlined up to this point underscore Eliot's persistent questioning of the moral clarity of sympathetic identification. Such morality is at the root of social reorientation that is so often indexed to the rise of the bourgeois realist novel and the coercive reasonableness of its omniscient narrators.

The silence of repression (self-exercised or externally applied) is undoubtedly core to character representation in these novels; less overt, yet just as important, is the range of somatic, affective, and emotional silences that are not necessarily negative but always press towards the relation between the body and the unconscious mind. These operate outside of language in ways that mean they defy us; full meaning escapes us and leads us to speculation in ways that mirror both the inventive filling-in and the felt frustrations of Eliot's original serial readers. *Middlemarch* and *Daniel Deronda* use these states of silence on one level to draw fuller attention to the potential and limitations of sympathetic understanding as an intellectual activity or moral alignment.

Non-articulated communication of emotion that characterizes many of these interactions short circuits the mediating intelligence reports of Eliot's disembodied narrators and competes with those narrators for claims on readers' interpretation of events, thus disrupting the categorizing impulses of literary realism. I suggest that these late novels reinforce the view that it is a misreading of silence to think its only opposite is communication. In both *Middlemarch* and *Daniel Deronda* silence does not always comprise emptiness or blankness: rather it can present as non-sounded yet fully interactional communication that is gestural and emotional but without speech and interpretative parsing. In *Middlemarch* these scenes are strikingly emotional, transformative, and expressive of new realities that cannot yet be spoken because the exchanges they represent, though fully felt, are not yet fully embodied in real terms. Dorothea and Rosamond, misreading each other as failed wives, desperately trying to communicate their mixed emotions, can 'find no words' so Rosamond, 'involuntarily… put her lips to Dorothea's forehead which was very near her, and then for a minute the two women clasped each other as if they had been in a shipwreck' (612). Rosamond begins to explain her relationship with Will 'while she was still feeling Dorothea's arms around her— urged by a mysterious necessity to free herself from something that oppressed her as if it were blood guiltiness' (612). Felt connection as a positive catalyst in clarifying personal relations (and forwarding plot) drives this scene. Yet Eliot remains sceptical of the positive effects of articulation beyond the haptic moment described here: Rosamond's ability to communicate with Lydgate does not improve; the 'mysterious necessity' remains mysterious.

The disgraced banker Bulstrode's meeting with his wife Harriet across the new divide produced by reports of his criminal actions plays out another apparently intimate, revelatory scene, but its unworded interactions scramble our interpretative mechanisms:

> He raised his eyes with a little start and looked at her half amazed for a moment: her pale face, her changed, mourning dress, the trembling about her mouth, all said, 'I know;' and her hands and eyes rested gently on him. He burst out crying and they cried together, she sitting at his side. They could not yet speak to each other of the shame which she was bearing with him, or of the acts which had brought it down on them. His confession was silent, and her promise of faithfulness was silent. Open-minded as she was, she nevertheless shrank from the words which would have expressed their mutual consciousness, as she would have shrunk from flakes of fire. She could not say, 'How much is only slander and false suspicion?' and he did not say, 'I am innocent.' (*Middlemarch* 580)

Harriet Bulstrode's movement towards her husband that starts here in the gentleness of her eyes and the choice to sit beside him, has been celebrated for its apparent expression of dignified acceptance of personal commitment, of the renunciation of ego that Eliot supposedly champions as necessary for the formation of strong social relations, especially for her women characters. However, the decision to relate this apparent rapprochement in gestures and in the refusal of words ('She could not say'; 'he did not say') allows for a more complex affective encounter that is shot through with silent ambiguities that could potentially shriek fear and panic as readily as solidarity. Readers' final encounter with Harriet, who is crippled with grief, frightened by the collapse of her moral coordinates, living 'unconstrainedly with the sorrow that was every day streaking her hair with whiteness and making her eyelids languid' (630), shows, Nina Auerbach suggests, that 'no one is healed or redeemed,' and that her 'glorious gesture of fidelity leads only to a shared decay' (Auerbach 99), that is, I suggest, if it was a glorious gesture of fidelity in the first place. Eliot structures the exchange in terms that are replete with the potential to read otherwise. There is a purposeful abdication of intervention so that the interaction is amplified into meaning through the feeling body but in deliberately nonspecified ways that in the end are puzzlingly opaque, like the grand and vague ending of *Daniel Deronda* as Blackwood remarked.

In her final work, Eliot's narrator projects himself into a future where silence dominates. *Impressions of Theophrastus Such*, published in 1879, the year before her death, offers a vision of a future life that outstrips our Anthropocene era and ego-driven feeling, desiring, haptic bodies. Technology has acquired the capacity to self-reproduce, human consciousness has departed the scene, and a highly efficient, mechanistic, silent universe prevails:

> Thus this planet may be filled with beings who will be blind and deaf as the inmost rock, yet will execute changes as delicate and complicated as those of human language and all the intricate web of what we call its effects, without sensitive impression, without sensitive impulse: there may be, let us say, mute orations, mute rhapsodies, mute discussions, and no consciousness there even to enjoy the silence. (*Impressions* 142)

The repetition of 'mute' leaves us in little doubt about the eerie stillness and silence of this brave new world, which I and others have written about as chilling and utterly dystopian in its imagined projections (see, e.g., Henry xxxii; Dillane 191, 197). Recent criticism proposes other more persuasive readings. 'For the space of that elegant sentence,' Rosemarie Bodenheimer observes with specific reference to the quotation above, 'I fancy that George Eliot is enjoying the non-human silence quite a bit. Sensitivity is always a double-edged capacity in her work: recall *Middlemarch*'s 'other side of silence,' the tortured mind of hypersensitive Latimer in *The Lifted Veil*' (Bodenheimer 617). This chapter has been exploring not the refined attunement to environment figured as that 'roar' at the other side of silence but the places of silence in George Eliot's last fiction. The capacity for silence to communicate more than one thing in her writings, its multiple signifying potential, is exploited to dramatic effect in her final works, structurally, thematically, and emotionally. Silence signals a destructive and oppressive exercise of power, a terrifying realization and acknowledgement of our aloneness, a full and generous felt response to otherness, a vacuum or a plenitude, a something beyond the edge of words that is unconscious and inexpressible but decidedly felt. Ultimately, this chapter suggests that in these final works, Eliot's aesthetics of silence signifies the sometimes contradictory workings out of her ongoing interest in the tension between the known and the unknown, the knowable and unknowable, the limits and capacities of the mind and the body that pressed ever more insistently as she and Lewes approached their own deaths.

Note

1. *Middlemarch* appeared in eight half-volumes in bi-monthly parts between December 1871 and December 1872, the last book appearing a month after book seven; *Daniel Deronda* was published in eight monthly parts from February 1876 to September 1876. Eliot's first fiction, later republished as *Scenes of Clerical Life* (1858) was published as a series of stories in *Blackwood's Edinburgh Magazine* in 1857; George Smith published *Romola* in fourteen monthly parts between July 1862 and August 1863 in his *Cornhill Magazine*. The 1870s experiment, however, is distinctive because separate part publication had been on the wane since the early 1850s. On the history of this publication format and the correspondence between Blackwood, Lewes, and Eliot about this decision, see Martin; Sutherland.

Works Cited

Auerbach, Nina. 'Dorothea's Lost Dog.' In Karen Chase, ed. *Middlemarch in the 21st Century*. Oxford: Oxford University Press, 2006. 87–105.

Bodenheimer, Rosemarie. 'George Eliot's Last Stand: *Impressions of Theophrastus Such*.' *Victorian Literature and Culture* 44 (2016): 607–21.

Bond Stockton, Catherine. *God Between Their Lips: Desire between Women in Irigaray, Brontë and Eliot*. Stanford: Stanford University Press, 1994.

Brilmyer, S. Pearl. '"The Natural History of My Inward Self": Sensing Character in *Impressions of Theophrastus Such*.' PMLA 129.1 (2014): 35–51.

Carroll, David. *George Eliot and the Conflict of Interpretations: A Reading of the Novels*. Cambridge: Cambridge University Press, 1992.

Daly, Nicholas. *Sensation and Modernity in the 1860s*. Cambridge: Cambridge University Press, 2009.

Dames, Nicholas. *The Physiology of the Novel: Reading, Neural Science, and the Form of Victorian Fiction*. Oxford. Oxford University Press, 2007.

Davis, Michael. *George Eliot and Nineteenth-Century Psychology: Exploring the Unmapped Country*. Aldershot: Ashgate, 2006.

Davis, Philip. *The Transferred Life of George Eliot*. Oxford: Oxford University Press, 2017.

Dillane, Fionnuala. *Before George Eliot: Marian Evans and the Periodical Press*. Cambridge: Cambridge University Press, 2013.

Dowling, Andrew. '"The Other Side of Silence": Matrimonial Conflict and the Divorce Court in George Eliot's Fiction.' *Nineteenth-Century Literature* 50.3 (Dec. 1995): 322–36.

Eliot, George. *Daniel Deronda*. 1876. Edited by Terence Cave. Harmondsworth: Penguin, 1995.

———. *The George Eliot Letters*. Ed. Gordon S. Haight. 9 vols. New Haven and London: Yale University Press, 1954–1978.
———. *Impressions of Theophrastus Such*. 1879. Ed. Nancy Henry. Iowa City: University of Iowa Press, 1994.
———. *The Journals of George Eliot*. Eds. Margaret Harris and Judith Johnston. Cambridge: Cambridge University Press, 2000.
———. 'The Lifted Veil.' 1859. In *The Lifted Veil and Brother Jacob*. Edited by Helen Small. Oxford: Oxford University Press, 1999. 1–44.
———. *Middlemarch* (1871–72). Ed. Gregory Maertz. Peterborough: Ontario: Broadview, 2004.
Ermarth, Elizabeth. 'Negotiating *Middlemarch*.' *Middlemarch in the 21st Century*. Ed. Karen Chase. Oxford: Oxford University Press, 2006. 107–31.
Flint, Kate. *The Victorians and the Visual Imagination*. Cambridge: Cambridge University Press, 2000.
Henry, Nancy. 'Introduction.' *Impressions of Theophrastus Such*. By George Eliot. 1879. Ed. Nancy Henry. Iowa City: University of Iowa Press, 1994. vii–xxxvii.
Hertz, Neil. *George Eliot's Pulse*. Stanford: Stanford University Press, 2003.
Martin, Carol A. *George Eliot's Serial Fiction*. Columbus: Ohio State University Press, 1994.
Matus, Jill. *Shock, Memory and the Unconscious in Victorian Fiction*. Cambridge. Cambridge University Press, 2009.
Miller, D. A. *Narrative and Its Discontents: Problems of Closure in the Traditional Novel*. Princeton: Princeton University Press, 1981.
Miller, J. Hillis. 'Optic and Semiotic in Middlemarch.' *The Worlds of Victorian Fiction*. Ed. Jerome H. Buckley. Cambridge MA: Harvard University Press, 1975. 125–43.
Newton, K. M. *Modernizing George Eliot: The Writer as Artist, Intellectual, Proto-modernist, Cultural Critic*. London: Bloomsbury, 2011.
Picker, John M. *Victorian Soundscapes*. Oxford: Oxford University Press, 2003.
Shuttleworth, Sally. *George Eliot and Nineteenth-Century Science: The Make-Believe of a Beginning*. Cambridge: Cambridge University Press, 1984.
Sutherland, John. 'Lytton, John Blackwood and the Serialisation of *Middlemarch*.' *Biliotheck* 7 (1975): 98–104.
Woloch, Alex. '*Daniel Deronda*: Late Form, or After *Middlemarch*.' In Amanda Anderson and Harry E. Shaw (Eds.), *A Companion to George Eliot*. Sussex: Wiley-Blackwell, 2013. 166–77.

CHAPTER 12

'His eyes *commanded* me to come to him': Desire and Mesmerism in Rhoda Broughton's 'The Man with the Nose'

Melissa Purdue

Rhoda Broughton often created passionate heroines who pushed the boundaries of acceptable female behaviour. Although seldom given voice in Victorian realist fiction, female desire was often addressed in sensation fiction of the period, a genre in which Broughton frequently published. As the anonymous author of an 1884 biographical piece in the *Minneapolis Tribune* states, 'Broughton was a novelist who in her day has done more to shock the sacred routine of domestic existence than any other writer of the contemporary age' ('A Novelist at Home' 10). Broughton's first three books—*Not Wisely but Too Well* (1867), *Cometh Up as a Flower* (1867), and *Red as the Rose Is She* (1870)—'were considered to be particularly risqué in their descriptions of female passion and adultery' (Liggins i). Although it is not as frequently discussed, Broughton's supernatural short fiction also addresses female sexuality.

M. Purdue (✉)
Department of English, Minnesota State University, Mankato, MN, USA
e-mail: melissa.purdue@mnsu.edu

© The Author(s) 2020
A. E. Gavin, C. W. de la L. Oulton (Eds.), *British Women's Writing from Brontë to Bloomsbury, Volume 2*, British Women's Writing from Brontë to Bloomsbury, 1840–1940,
https://doi.org/10.1007/978-3-030-38528-6_12

Supernatural fiction of the 1870s was different from earlier short fiction, in content and in form. Florence Goyet in *The Classic Short Story, 1870–1925: Theory of a Genre* (2014), discusses the uniqueness of the late nineteenth-century story before the advent of modernist fiction. She argues that this short fiction can be divided into two categories: 'lengthy stories and fantastic tales' (187). Fantastic tales of the period, like Broughton's 'The Man with the Nose' (1872), which is the focus of the current chapter, are a missing link between pre-1870s 'classic' short fiction and 'modern' forms. These fantastic stories are often fragmented 'in order to portray an unexpected mental universe' (Goyet 188). Further, 'in the fantastic story, the reader can no longer be sure of anything, and is unable to occupy the unusual comfortable and clear position he was granted in the classic short story' (189). Broughton's 'The Man with the Nose,' with its concentration on mental states altered through mesmerism, certainly fits this categorization. Kate Krueger, in *British Women Writers and the Short Story, 1850–1930: Reclaiming Social Space* (2014), also discusses the uniqueness of literature of the 1870s. She argues that 'the supernatural qualities that made ghost stories hugely popular in periodicals such as *Belgravia* and *Temple Bar* in the 1860s and 1870s trafficked in deviance much more radically than sensation novels' (14). In particular, Krueger points out that authors like Mary Elizabeth Braddon and Rhoda Broughton 'insist upon the instability of the domestic household' in their short fiction (15). Part of what makes this fiction radical is a pushing back against societal expectations for women. While sensation novels share this trait, many also work to contain the dangerous behaviour threatening the domestic sphere by punishing or removing 'errant' women in their conclusions. The form of the short story, however, allowed authors to play with possibilities and break with convention in ways the novel did not. Supernatural fiction in particular freed women writers to address taboo subjects without providing easy answers.

Twilight Stories (1879),[1] Broughton's only collection of short fiction, includes ghostly tales about such subjects as death, murder, supernatural hauntings, and mesmerism. Many of the stories share similarities in theme and style. They are often narrated by middle-aged or older women; sceptical and dismissive husbands are common; and travel, letters, prophetic dreams, and a fear of foreigners all feature prominently. 'The Man with the Nose,' originally published in *Temple Bar* in 1872, is unique in the collection in its use of a male narrator, its focus on a young female heroine, and its inclusion of mesmerism. The story focuses on a newly married woman,

Elizabeth (no surname), who suffers from the supposed continued effects of mesmerism. It begins with Elizabeth and her fiancé (an unnamed man who also serves as the story's narrator) discussing possible honeymoon destinations. Elizabeth shudders at the suggestion of the Lake District and explains that it is because she once went to see a mesmerizer there and afterwards was very ill and confined to her bed. The couple proceed with their honeymoon elsewhere, and Elizabeth comes to believe that a man with a prominent nose, who reminds her eerily of the mesmerizer from her past, is following them. She suffers horrible nightmares in which she claims that the man makes her act against her will. Her husband, in typical Victorian fashion, dismisses her fears as childish and even leaves her alone for a time to take care of family business back home. When he returns, she is gone. Hotel employees tell him that she has departed with a foreign-sounding man with a prominent nose, and she is never seen from again. Although on the surface the story is a chilling tale about a frightened young woman whose husband fails to protect her, a close reading reveals that there is more to Elizabeth than we initially suspect. Most significantly, Broughton plays with and gives voice to unspoken female desire by revealing Elizabeth's true feelings through dreams and mesmeric states, by undercutting the validity of the husband-narrator's observations, by describing a revealing visit to Antoine Wiertz's studio, and by emphasizing the husband's own sexual timidity.

The story begins by introducing the reader to the paternalistic relationship between Elizabeth and her fiancé-turned-husband. While the husband demonstrates affection for Elizabeth, he clearly does not respect her in any real way. He finds her a silly, young girl prone to irrational worries. He continually infantilizes her, referring to her variously as 'my little beloved' (14), 'my little bride elect' (16), and 'my little one' (20). After purchasing a new hat for her, for example, he condescendingly describes her as 'a delicious picture of a child playing at being grown up, having practised a theft on its mother's wardrobe' (18). Throughout the story, the male narrator taps into stereotypes about Victorian femininity—namely women's supposed innocence, their fragility, and their propensity to suffer from hysteria. However, many of Elizabeth's actions call for us to read her character very differently as Broughton repeatedly subverts and undercuts the male narrative voice. As a woman author she is able simultaneously to 'reproduce a voice which trivializes her experiences, while at the same time maintaining an alternative subtextual authority—her own—with its insider's knowledge of the conditions of women's lives'

(Federico 344). The contrast between the narrator's condescending descriptions of his new bride and other moments in which her true character is revealed paints the *narrator* as naïve and Elizabeth as much more complicated than we are originally led to believe.

This alternate portrayal of Elizabeth begins to take shape in the description of her experience with the mesmerizer in the Lake District. She is at first hesitant to disclose what has occurred and, as Nick Freeman points out, her husband immediately reads her experience in sexual terms (196). In a 'jealous heat and hurry,' he demands to know what she is hiding (14). She 'timidly' kisses his hand and reveals:

> I do not remember anything; I believe I did all sorts of extraordinary things that he told me—sang and danced, and made a fool of myself—but when I came home I was very ill, very—I lay in bed for five whole weeks, and—and was off my head, and said odd and wicked things that you would not have expected me to say—that dreadful bed! (16)

The experience is initially harmless. She sings and dances and makes a fool of herself all in good fun. However, after her return home—her return to what is typically coded as feminine space with particular expectations for female behaviour—she falls ill. She is 'off her head' and says 'wicked things.' Further, there are hints that her inappropriate behaviour is of a sexual nature. She shudders thinking about the 'dreadful bed' in which her sickness occurs and describes the lasting impact. She tells the narrator that she tries not to think about it, 'but sometimes, in the dead black of the night, when God seems a long way off, and the devil near' it comes back to her strongly (16). She says, 'I feel, do not you know, as if he were *there*—somewhere in the room, and I must get up and follow him' (16). It is not only the effects of mesmerism that haunt her, but the mesmerizer himself. She recalls him in her bedroom at night and feels compelled to go to him. There are clear sexual undertones to Elizabeth's history that conflict with her husband's simplistic portrayal of her as a naïve girl. The narrator, however, refuses to acknowledge her experience. He simply laughs it off and changes the subject.

It is particularly significant that the dreams that haunt Elizabeth, and the strange encounters with the 'man with the nose,' occur on her honeymoon just as she is introduced to the expectations of marriage and wifehood. Emma Liggins argues that the dreams 'allow Broughton to voice her heroine's anxieties about the conjugal act' (vi). While the dreams certainly give voice to Elizabeth's sexual anxieties, rather than revealing, as Liggins argues, her fear of sexual contact with her husband, these dreams can be read as showing Elizabeth's desire to explore her sexuality in a way that her marriage will not allow. Her husband misreads her throughout the story, infantilizes her, and shies away from his own sexuality. Her dreams might be read as her subconscious rejection of this stifling relationship. Rather than expressing fear of the conjugal act or even of the mesmerizer, Elizabeth's dreams might instead reveal her anxiety about her new, confining role as wife. These dreams do occur, after all, as she is lying in bed next to her husband, as she herself points out when, awaking from a nightmare she does not believe was only a dream, she states: 'no—in a dream I should have been somewhere else, but I was here—*here*—on that bed' (20). She dreams of a man standing next to the bed looking at her and describes his nose in detail: 'it was very prominent ... sharply chiseled; the nostrils very much cut out' (20). The man's eyes '*commanded*' her to come to him, just as 'the eyes of the mesmerizer at Penrith did' (20). The concentration on the man's nose, which seems to be a clear phallic reference, verges on the comical, but it also reveals Elizabeth's unspoken desires.[2] Unsatisfied in her new marriage, her sexual desire is transferred to a strange man who *commands* that she leave her husband. 'I loathed it—abhorred it. I was ice-cold with fear and horror, but—I *felt* myself going to him,' she confesses (20). The dream allows her to engage in behaviour that is 'scandalous' for a proper, married woman—the abandonment of a husband for another man—without judgement. Thus the effects of mesmerism cause her to act inappropriately for a Victorian woman, but without repercussions. Her behaviour is simply a dream or hypnotic trance; she cannot be held responsible.

It is also interesting to note the frequency with which bedrooms figure as places of violence and distress throughout *Twilight Stories*. For example, in 'Behold, it was a Dream!' (originally published in *Temple Bar* in 1872) a middle-aged couple are brutally murdered in their bed. The horrific event is foretold in another woman's dream, but the husband refuses to take the warning seriously. Likewise, in 'The Truth, the Whole Truth, and Nothing but the Truth' (originally published in *Temple Bar* in 1868), the sighting of an apparition in a bedchamber causes a maid to go insane and a young man (a suitor to the young lady of the house) to die dramatically gasping, 'Oh, my God! I have seen it!' (12). The young woman he has been courting begs him not to enter the bedroom, her blushes fading to pale shock at the suggestion, but he persists on spending the evening there to prove that her fears are childish and unfounded. Broughton establishes a clear pattern of men foolishly ignoring the women in their lives and subsequently meeting dark ends. That these ends often occur in bedrooms seems to be an added indictment of marital arrangements which stifle women's voices and agency.

As in Broughton's other stories, Elizabeth's husband fails to take her dreams and her history with the mesmerizer seriously. He dismisses his wife as silly and emotional and does not hold her responsible for any actions committed in a hypnotic state. According to popular Victorian beliefs, in a mesmeric state she would not be in control of her own behaviour. As Hilary Grimes explains, '[a]lthough many theories circulated about how mesmerism worked ... it was widely understood as a process in which the mesmerist (usually male) had the power to influence the thoughts and actions of the subject (often, although not always, female), using his hands to make "passes" over her and sending her into a mesmeric trance' (62). In the 1760s, Franz Anton Mesmer claimed to have discovered a universal fluid which he believed could be harnessed by magnets and used for healing purposes. 'Using his hands or a magnetized wand, Mesmer would make passes over his subjects in order to restore the natural flow of the universal fluid' (Grimes 61). Although the subjects of mesmerism were often portrayed as passive puppets for the mesmerizer, others described the mesmerized as more active participants in the process. For example, in his handbook *Human Magnetism or How to Hypnotise: A Practical Handbook for Students of Mesmerism* published in 1897, James Coates clarifies that the mesmerist is powerless to do anything 'contrary to the [subject's] will' (209). This definition that posits hypnotized individuals are unable to act against their own desires complicates Elizabeth's description of her actions. Even if only subconsciously, the story suggests a complicity in her behaviour. Rather than telling a story of a powerless victim then, Broughton's story might alternately reveal Elizabeth's unspoken but very present desires for another man.

Elizabeth's reaction to a visit to Antoine Wiertz's studio on their honeymoon serves as further evidence that she is not the simple and naïve girl her husband believes her to be. There is a disturbing combination of violence, sexuality, and supernatural danger in Wiertz's work that aligns in interesting ways with Broughton's story. Wiertz, an early-nineteenth-century Belgian artist, was known for his horrific paintings. In an 1879 article about him in *Macmillan's Magazine*, Mary Meason describes his paintings as 'characterized to a painful degree by the same fantastic morbidness that marks the writings of Edgar Allan Poe—a morbidness hardly falling in with the healthy tastes of Englishmen' (349). And Ouida, the prolific nineteenth-century author best known for her novel *Under Two Flags* (1867), echoes Meason's sentiments in her 1872 sketch of Wiertz for *London Society*: 'he loved horror for its own sake, found pleasure in it, and took his sport in it' (30). Clearly, Wiertz's paintings *should* be shocking to a young, innocent woman like Elizabeth. However, she shows no signs of distress during their visit to his studio and instead even seems to enjoy it. The paintings displayed at Wiertz's studio did indeed tackle horrific themes. Violent, often enormous paintings like *The Guillotined Head* (1855), *The Suicide* (1854), and *The Last Thoughts and Visions of a Decapitated Head* (1853) (a triptych, no less) filled the museum's walls.[3] Depictions of death and violence would have surrounded Elizabeth. Consider Wiertz's *Hunger, Madness, and Crime* (1853), for example—a particularly disturbing painting of a mother who has murdered her child. The mother is shown laughing with a sick smile upon her face, holding a knife in one hand and her dishevelled hair with the other. Her child's foot can be seen sticking out of the cauldron next to her.

These violent paintings were hung side-by-side with others that featured young females, often nude or in provocative poses. In *The Confidence* (1864) one nude woman whispers into the ear of another; the attempted escape of a woman from her would-be ravisher is depicted in *The Outrage of a Belgian Woman* (1861); *The Beautiful Rosine* (1847) shows a young, nude woman gazing at a smiling skeleton; and *The Young Witch* (1857) depicts yet another young naked woman straddling a broomstick with numerous faces looking on.[4] *The Reader of Novels* (1853) is particularly interesting in its depiction of a young woman reading while lying nude on her bed. A mirror hangs directly to her left, reflecting her body for the viewer, and a sly hand belonging to a horned man sneaks up the bed to her right, seemingly placing another tempting novel on the bed. The idea that the woman might possess inappropriate knowledge—particularly knowledge of a sexual nature—mirrors Elizabeth's own character in 'The Man with the Nose,' particularly her previously described weeks spent in bed saying 'wicked things.'

Another Wiertz painting, the one described at length by the narrator in the story, is *The Premature Burial* (1854):

> We have been peering through the appointed peep-hole at the horrible cholera-picture—the man buried alive by mistake, pushing up the lid of his

coffin, and stretching a ghastly face and livid hands out of his winding-sheet toward you, while awful grey-blue coffins are piled around, and noisome toads and giant spiders crawl damply about. On first seeing it, I have reproached myself for bringing one of so nervous a temperament as Elizabeth to see so haunting and hideous a spectacle; but she is less impressed than I expected—[certainly] less impressed than myself. (17–18)

The narrator worries that gruesome portrayal of a cholera victim might cause Elizabeth's nightmares to get worse, and indeed one wonders at his honeymoon choice of such a violent exhibit, but she only jokes, 'When you bury me, dear, fasten me down very slightly, in case there may be some mistake' (18). Rather than turning away from these graphic paintings, Elizabeth makes a joke about being buried alive. Perhaps she is here considering her own 'premature burial' in a marriage to a man who repeatedly misreads and infantilizes her and is plotting her own escape.[5] Her behaviour again stands in stark contrast with her husband's image of her. Broughton clearly suggests by this visit that Elizabeth is stronger and savvier than her husband realizes.

The narrator's own uneasy reactions to bodies and sexually charged moments paint Elizabeth's husband as the one who is truly fearful of his sexuality. Consider the honeymoon scene in which Elizabeth and the narrator take a boat ride, for example. Rather than showing affection for one another, they sit and judge 'a rival bride and bridegroom under an umbrella, looking into each other's eyes instead of at the Rhine scenery' (22). The narrator finds the public affection displayed by the other couple distasteful and restricts his own behaviour in response. He is also particularly appalled by the lunch on the boat during which he sees people feeding themselves 'ravenously.' His mention of a handsome girl thrusting 'her knife halfway down her throat' is particularly telling (22). The way in which these strangers embrace their bodily desires—particularly the attractive girl 'thrusting' her eating utensil into her mouth—deeply disturbs him. Unsettled, he decides to forego lunch to escape from the scene. The boat ride continues with the narrator noting with distaste both a fleshy woman who accidentally shows 'two yards of thick, white cotton legs' as she leans over the side of the boat and the drunken behaviour of 'almost every lady' aboard (23). The narrator claims that Elizabeth was frightened by all of the commotions, but in the absence of her own voice his graphic descriptions, particularly of women acting 'inappropriately' and with desire, do more to reveal his *own* discomfort (23).

Further evidence of the narrator's repressed sexuality can be found in a later scene at Lucerne when he and Elizabeth are sitting hand in hand by a 'solemn monastery' with narrow windows 'calculated to hinder the holy fathers from promenading curious eyes on the world, the flesh, and the devil, tripping past them in blue gauze veils' (25). Next to this place where pleasures of the flesh are denied, they argue because he wants to leave her for a time. He believes he should return to an ailing uncle—an uncle who will secure their financial well-being with his inheritance—but she wishes him to stay. It is their honeymoon, after all. She lifts 'two pouted lips' to be kissed, but he avoids meeting them and responds 'with an air of worldly experience and superior wisdom,' calling her 'my dearest child' and pointing out that one cannot live upon kisses alone (26). In this scene Elizabeth reaches out to him desiring contact, showing no fear of marital affection. He is the one that repulses her advances, insisting yet again that she is simply a child.

The narrator's eyes then stray to the nearby mountains:

> Pilatus on the right, with his jagged peak and slender snow-chains about his harsh neck; hill after hill rising silent, eternal, like guardian spirits standing hand-in-hand around their child, the lake. As I look, suddenly they have all flushed, as at some noblest thought, and over all their sullen faces streams an ineffable, rosy joy—a solemn and wonderful effulgence. (26–27)

The description of the landscape, with its clear phallic and orgasmic imagery, fills him with emotion. He exclaims, 'Would God I could stay!' Elizabeth snaps back 'passionately' questioning why he calls out to God when it lies within himself to make the decision (27). She warns him that if he leaves she feels it 'would be the end of all things' (27). He, of course, disregards her wishes and returns home without her. The passage suggests Elizabeth's desire for affection, perhaps even the consummation of their marriage, in the face of her husband's hesitation.

When the narrator finally travels back to Lucerne to be with Elizabeth again, she is gone. A waiter tells him that she left with a man with a prominent nose who she seemed to recognize. The narrator tells us 'never have I seen my little Elizabeth again' (31). And of course he never would see her again if the story is about his wife's sexual awakening. He has demonstrated that he is blind to viewing her as a sexual being—an adult woman with desires of her own—and has repulsed her advances. This is reinforced by his final description of her as 'my little Elizabeth.' The pair is last sighted by peasants who claim to have seen a carriage with 'a dark gentleman with the peculiar physiognomy which has been so often described, and on the opposite seat a lady, lying apparently in a state of utter insensibility' (30–31). Here again Elizabeth's agency is questioned. Is she truly insensible and at the mercy of the mesmerizer or is she a willing participant in her escape? The narrator's own reaction to the news is telling: 'So this is it! With that pure child-face, with that divine ignorance—only three weeks married—this is the trick she has played on me!' (29) Clearly the narrator comes to believe that his wife is complicit in her disappearance. He begins to view her 'child-face' as a mask hiding her true identity. Further evidence for this alternate reading can be found in 'Under the Cloak' (originally published in *Temple Bar* in 1873), another story in Broughton's collection. In it a woman acts as if she has been drugged, pretending to sleep and snore, while a man on a train robs her. While in this situation the woman pretends to be insensible to avoid harm, the story raises the possibility that a woman might feign unconsciousness for her own purposes.

'The Man with the Nose' haunts the reader with unanswered questions about Elizabeth's whereabouts, but, as Kelly Hurley argues, 'when the fantastic text refuses closure ... it disrupts conventional meaning systems and makes room for new ones to emerge' (7). Using the genre of supernatural fiction, Broughton is able to question traditional expectations for Victorian women and open up the space for new possibilities. She gives voice to female desire through a layered narrative that plays with discourse surrounding mesmerism and discards the observations of an ineffectual male narrator. The story teases out the 'unsaid and the unseen of culture: that which has been silenced' and makes it visible (Jackson 4). Although on the surface a story about an innocent young woman in need of rescue and protection, Broughton's 'The Man with the Nose' certainly makes room for alternate readings that attempt to uncover what might be hiding behind Elizabeth's mask of a 'child-face.'

Notes

1. The collection was originally published in 1872 as *Tales for Christmas Eve*. It was republished by Richard Bentley & Son with the title *Twilight Stories* in 1879. The five stories in the collection were originally published between 1868 and 1873 in *Temple Bar*. The 1879 edition of 'The Man with the Nose' contains no differences from the original 1872 publication.

2. Emma Liggins points out in her introduction to the Victorian Secrets' edition of the collection that the repeated references to the mesmerizer's nose might also 'carry connotations of Jewishness' and thus anti-Semitic fear (vi).
3. Wiertz's *Greeks and Trojans* is more than eight metres long, for example.
4. *The Undressed Coquette* (1856) and *The Rosebud* (1864) are also examples of works that concentrate on the nude female form.
5. Adultery is hinted at elsewhere in the collection in 'Poor Pretty Bobby.' The story is persistently vague about the background and parentage of a young man welcomed into the home of the main characters. The female narrator's father treats Bobby as if he were his own son rather than simply a soldier in his command, and Bobby dies before the narrator's possibly incestuous desire for him can be realized and the father's secret exposed.

WORKS CITED

'A Novelist at Home.' *Minneapolis Tribune* 2 December 1884: 10.
Broughton, Rhoda. *Twilight Stories.* 1879. Brighton, UK: Victorian Secrets, 2009.
Coates, James. *Human Magnetism or How to Hypnotise: A Practical Handbook for Students of Mesmerism.* London: Nichols, 1907.
Federico, Annette R. 'The Other Case: Gender and Narration in Charlotte Bronte's *The Professor.*' *Papers on Language and Literature* 30 (1994): 323–45.
Freeman, Nick. 'Sensational Ghosts, Ghostly Sensations.' *Women's Writing* 20.2 (2013): 186–201.
Grimes, Hilary. *The Late Victorian Gothic: Mental Science, the Uncanny, and Scenes of Writing.* Burlington, VT: Ashgate, 2011.
Goyet, Florence. *The Classic Short Story, 1870-1925: Theory of a Genre.* Cambridge, UK: Open Book Publishers, 2014.
Hurley, Kelly. *The Gothic Body: Sexuality, Materialism, and Degeneration at the* Fin de Siécle. Cambridge: Cambridge University Press, 1996.
Jackson, Rosemary. *Fantasy: The Literature of Subversion.* London and New York: Methuen, 1981.
Krueger, Kate. *British Women Writers and the Short Story, 1850–1930: Reclaiming Social Space.* New York: Palgrave, 2014.
Liggins, Emma. Introduction. *Twilight Stories.* By Rhoda Broughton. Brighton, UK: Victorian Secrets, 2009. i–vii.
Meason, Mary Laing. 'Antoine Wiertz.' *Macmillan's Magazine* 40 (1879): 349–53.
Ouida. 'Antoine Wiertz: A Sketch.' *London Society* 22 (1872): 23–32.

CHAPTER 13

'[E]mphatically un-literary and middle-class': Undressing Middle-Class Anxieties in Ellen Wood's *Johnny Ludlow* Stories

Alyson Hunt

In 1868 Ellen [Mrs Henry] Wood began a series of stories which would go on to entertain the British reading public for more than twenty years in over 120 issues of the sixpence monthly magazine *The Argosy*, a publication which she edited from 1867 until her death in 1887.[1] Writing under the pseudonym Johnny Ludlow, Wood created a popular hero-narrator of the same name who recounts his experiences and exploits within a rich country family in rural Worcestershire, investigating crimes and mysteries, playing pranks, partaking in adventures, and even foraying into romance. The longevity of the series testifies to the stories' popularity and yet today the tales are largely forgotten and critically neglected, perhaps owing to their slow-paced action and middlebrow content. As early as 1897 the stories were subject to criticism: in *Women Novelists of Queen Victoria's Reign: A Book of Appreciations* (1897) Adeline Sergeant referred to the stories as 'emphatically un-literary and middle-class' (174), despite being

A. Hunt (✉)
Canterbury Christ Church University, Kent, UK
e-mail: ash16@canterbury.ac.uk

© The Author(s) 2020
A. E. Gavin, C. W. de la L. Oulton (eds.), *British Women's Writing from Brontë to Bloomsbury, Volume 2*, British Women's Writing from Brontë to Bloomsbury, 1840–1940,
https://doi.org/10.1007/978-3-030-38528-6_13

'emphatically on the side of purity, honesty, domestic life, and happiness' (188). Nevertheless, as realist short stories the tales are useful to scholars of Victorian fiction in that they reveal middle-class anxieties of the late 1860s and early 1870s, through their focus on everyday life. The most obvious anxiety they express is evidenced in Wood's use of a male pseudonym which suggests concerns about gender and the literary marketplace. Contemporary critics were quick to highlight that the unknown writer's work was conspicuously feminine, manifesting a tension between the (suspected) female author, the male pseudonym, and the male narrator. An anonymous reviewer in *Fun* in 1868, for example, postulated: 'if she were writing *incog.* [sic] how easy it would be to guess the work a woman's. The petticoat peeps out so—at all events the "gathers" would betray her' ('Our Fun-done Letter' 116). The reviewer's analogy draws attention to sartorial discourses, which feature prominently throughout the stories and which are inevitably loaded with expectations of class and gender: key anxieties of the period. Utilising the 1874 collected edition of the first series of *Johnny Ludlow* stories, published in three volumes by Richard Bentley and Son, this chapter explores how such anxieties are played out through dress and clothing. By considering how Johnny's descriptions of dress might be regarded as especially feminine and unpacking the symbolism of dress for Victorian readers, this chapter argues that the Johnny Ludlow stories deserve greater critical attention for what they reveal about this 'unliterary and middle-class' readership.

Although some of these stories were initially published in the late 1860s[2] the appearance of the collected edition in the 1870s is significant in the context of women's writing within that latter decade for several reasons. First, in the 1870s the short-story format was comparatively marginalised, with the three-volume novel still outselling any other genre thanks to the popularity of sensation fiction in the 1860s. Secondly and relatedly, Wood had gained her literary reputation in the previous decade with the publication of her best-selling sensation novel *East Lynne* (1861) and a further fifteen novels in the following seven years (Mitchell).[3] The use of the Johnny Ludlow pseudonym allowed Wood to experiment with the short-story genre independently of her reputation for writing novels, and her editorship of *The Argosy* gave her a platform on which to do so. The publication of the collected edition confirms sufficient popularity of the stories with the reading public for the publisher to justify the costs involved; thus the 1874 edition constitutes a mark of her success within the short-story format. For Wood, the success of the stories and her continued effort to keep writing them throughout the 1870s and beyond suggests that she found enjoyment in the character and an appreciative readership which encouraged her to continue writing although she was no longer driven by financial considerations as she had been at the start of her literary career.

Johnny Ludlow was not Wood's first male narrator. As Sally Mitchell notes in her entry on Wood in the *Oxford Dictionary of National Biography*, she 'had first used a male persona as early as 1854 in "Stray Letters from the East"' (Mitchell). Wood nevertheless successfully kept up her anonymity as author of the Johnny Ludlow stories until 1879 when, tired of numerous spurious claims of authorship, Wood publicly acknowledged the stories as her own creations. Without doubt, the androcentric narrative voice provided by the male narrator allowed Wood increased authority within the texts, and yet the self-repression of her own feminine voice also suggests an attempt to shake off constraints on female expression and subject matter, an attempt reiterated in her use of a male authorial pseudonym. As Beth Palmer notes, '[b]y cross-dressing as Johnny Ludlow, Wood created an alternative persona in the pages of her magazine—one that reinforced the "healthy" moral tone she wanted for *Argosy* and at the same time gave readers (particularly male ones) another figure to identify with' (101). Johnny not only narrates the Johnny Ludlow stories, but also features in every issue alongside his extended family and a number of peripheral characters: local farmers, tradesmen, and gentry who function as a 'cast' with sundry problems and concerns of their own which form the focus of the stories.[4] The domestic settings of the stories and the preoccupation with the minutiae of everyday life did not always present a masculine figure with which male readers might identify, however, with a reviewer in *The Pall Mall Gazette* in 1874 criticising the stories' reliance on deathbed scenes to create pathos and the narrator's repeated need to reassert his identity. The critic advises that '[h]e should not asseverate after every statement of a fact which he desires to emphasize, "I, Johnny Ludlow, saw this;" "These were the very words spoken to me, Johnny Ludlow;" "I declare upon my honour that this actually happened"' ('Johnny Ludlow' 11). The inference of this review is that the narrator tries too hard to convince the reader of his reliability and of the credibility of his narrative, a credibility which this chapter argues is weakened by the emphasis placed on dress.

Predominantly domestic, the stories frequently feature the very poor and their struggles to obtain employment, food, shelter, and clothing.

Often starvation, the workhouse, and death signify the reality of such poverty, with tattered garments and scanty or inappropriate clothing visually illustrating impoverished characters' plights. Wood places emphasis on poor characters' attempts to maintain moral integrity even in the depths of penury by using sartorial standards not just as a marker of poverty but as a measure of decency. In 'Dick Mitchel' (April 1870), for instance, a beleaguered mother of eight apologizes to the affluent Mrs Todhetley that her 'four young grubs in tattered garments' cannot be kept decent because she has 'not got no soap nor no clothes to do it with' (1.264; quotations from all stories are taken from the collected *Johnny Ludlow. First Series* [1874]; bracketed dates are dates of first publication in *The Argosy*). Schoolmistress Miss Timmens suggests the absence of clothing as an explanation for the falling number of children attending her school in 'Our Strike' (November 1871), lamenting that 'the strike has carried all the children's best things to the pawnshop, and they've nothing left to come abroad in that's decent' (3:125). 'Lease, the Pointsman' (January 1869) describes the bedraggled appearance of the poor children of the title character as they unexpectedly descend into extreme poverty. Reflecting symbolism not unusual in Victorian realist fiction and certainly familiar to a middle-class readership, dress functions as a device to mark social status, and its frequent mention signifies the importance to characters, regardless of their class or affluence, of appearing respectable in every situation. As K. Theodore Hoppen points out in *The Mid-Victorian Generation 1846–1886* (1998), 'few things more strikingly indicated one's place in society than appearance,' indeed 'almost the whole power-structure of an age might be reconstructed from its clothing' (347). The stories' descriptions of rustic dress provide necessary context and invoke sympathy but they also sharply juxtapose with the descriptive detail and feminine enthusiasm with which Johnny describes fashionable dress across many of the stories. Certainly, in this first series of the tales almost every story relies upon or contains strong references to clothing which pose a tension between, on the one hand, visual fascination and pleasure and, on the other hand, moral judgement.

In the first story of the series, 'Losing Lena' (February 1868),[5] dress is thematically a key indicator of both class and wealth, but the story also serves to establish Johnny's own class and social position. Raised by the rich Squire Todhetley after the death of his father, the orphan Johnny is bought up on equal terms with the Squire's son Joe (known as Tod throughout the stories) and Joe's half-siblings, Hugh and Lena Todhetley.[6]

The Squire's wealth, his position as landowner (he owns two considerable properties, Dyke Manor and Crabb Cot) and his role as magistrate elevate him to a raised status within the locale which supersedes that of Johnny's father, William. Although the two elders were great friends before William's death, the Ludlows are presented as slightly socially inferior, merely owning 'the Court' which was 'not a property of so much importance as the [Squire's] Manor' ('Losing Lena' 2). Johnny's assumed rather than innate position in the household and the differences of opinion he has with the Squire and Tod represent to some extent the struggle of the burgeoning middle-classes to establish themselves in a social system dominated by ancestral families and rich landowners like the Todhetleys. Johnny's position in the midst of a social scale which offers destitution and death at one end and grossly indulgent wealth at the other allows him to function as the everyman narrator and thus to pass comment on the situations which unfold.

'Losing Lena,' is a tale of child abduction in which Johnny's well-off younger stepsister, aged between four and five, is snatched and stripped of her expensive clothes. Lena's attire is described in detail by Johnny early on in the story: 'she had on a blue silk frock, and a white straw hat with daisies round it; open-worked stockings were on her pretty little legs. By which we saw she was about to be taken out for show' (1:6). Lena is the epitome of childhood innocence, symbolised by the daisies[7] and the white straw hat which suggest gentle summer leisure. Johnny's description of the stockings further invokes Lena's wealth: open-work indicating decorative gaps left in the fabric through which Lena's pretty legs, unspoiled by dirt or labour, can be displayed. Johnny is evidently familiar with the terminology of this ladies' garment and appreciates its aesthetic qualities. That Lena is to be taken out 'for show' demonstrates pride in the family name, their economic position, and in Lena's sartorial appearance, and displays to onlookers the family's refinement and social success.

Lena, however, does not get taken out for show as intended. In her childish innocence she runs after Tod who (to spite the children's nurse Hannah, who has earlier been curt with him) convinces her to hide. Unable to find Lena, Hannah seeks assistance from others at the house, who scour the grounds for the missing girl. Content that Hannah 'had had enough of a hunt for that day' (1:9) Tod goes to retrieve Lena from her hiding place only to discover that she is indeed missing. Both family members and staff fear the worst, with Mrs Todhetley assuming Lena has drowned in a pond and the cook insinuating that she has been stolen by a gypsy recently turned away from the door of the house. When Lena's disappearance is reported to the police, the lower-class officer, Jenkins, reads in Lena's sartorial description not childhood innocence but economic value and criminal motive. The monetary value of the clothes is crucial to Jenkins in order for him to establish a motive for the abduction. His questioning also confirms that the theft of dress is relatively common[8]:

> 'That's bad, that dress is,' said Jenkins, putting down the pen.
> 'Why is it bad?'
> 'Cause the things is tempting. Quite half the children that gets stole is stole for what they've got upon their backs. Tramps and that sort will run a risk for a blue silk, specially if it's clean and glistening, that they'd not run for a brown holland pinafore.' (1:15)

Jenkins's differentiation between silk and holland demonstrates a common level of material knowledge based upon monetary value which prizes costly garments. The desire for such items both compels their theft and sustains a resale market in which they can be sold on. Jenkins's sartorial knowledge is likely to be professional and based upon his experiences of the criminal trade rather than his own personal interest in dress, as his colloquial vernacular suggests that he is lower class and therefore does not have the means or need for such refined luxuries as silk. Lena's entitlement to dress in lavish clothes when all around her people are starving is not questioned in this story: fine dressing is implicitly perfectly acceptable if it fits one's class, even if it does leave one more at risk of robbery. Moreover, the sequel story 'Finding Both of Them' (March 1868) expresses a fear not that the child-abductor will strike again, but of the 'daily dread of seeing Lena's blue-silk frock and open-worked stockings hanging in a shop window' ('Finding Both of Them' 1:40). Her clothing serves as a reminder of the abduction and of Lena's brush with the criminal fraternity. The sense of dread also reflects the very personal and intimate nature of dress being put on public display for all to see, especially tailor-made clothes which are designed to fit a particular body, thus invading the privacy of the owner/wearer and, certainly in this story, of the wider family unit. In a brutal irony, the garments have the potential to be put on show just as Lena herself was put on show before the abduction, suggesting that Lena's sartorial identity can be traded as a commodity on the open market, an item to be bought and sold. This is reinforced by Tod and Johnny's initial assumption that Lena has been stolen by gypsies to be sold on, although they have no notion as to why this might be, avoiding any potentially scandalous references to child prostitution, a prominent social concern of the period.

Lena is eventually found by the 'gypsy' whom Tod had accused of abducting her. Tod's accusation is based on racial stereotypes of gypsies as child-stealers and unfounded assumptions which equate the poverty which is clearly visible in the gypsy family's appearance, with immorality. In fact, Lena's clothes have been stolen by an unknown woman who has left her tied to a tree, 'stripped to the skin ... save for a dirty old skirt that was tied around her' (Losing Lena 1:24). This reduction of circumstances aligns Lena sartorially with the child of the 'gypsies,' 'a little girl who was nearly as bad off for clothes as that [dirty skirt]' (1:29), who subsequently dies from a poverty-induced illness. The parallels between the two are made clear when Tod briefly thinks the dead child may be his sister, but Wood does not utilise this story to chastise Tod for the assumptions he makes about the lower-class gypsies (who in fact, are not gypsies at all). Although Johnny is sympathetic to the plight of the destitute family, Tod is more worried about getting into trouble for losing his sister, suggesting his primary anxiety lies within his own family unit rather than the wider social situation that Johnny perceives.[9] From this initial story alone, it is clear that dress is not just used as a means of constructing character but of interpreting it, too, a visual language which allows for, and is suggestive of, judgements of class, economics, social inclusivity, and even moral integrity.

The prevalence of dress is noteworthy in the Johnny Ludlow stories because short stories generally devote less time and space to describing characters than do novels, usually privileging plot over narrative. In *The Classic Short Story, 1870–1925* (2014) Florence Goyet claims that short stories are inclined towards 'paroxystic characterisation' (13), that is, overdetermined or excessive characterisation in which an individual's traits and disposition are made obvious. She further suggests that in 'the realist story, every feature is pushed to its extreme' (24) and marked by the use of superlatives which give the commonplace a greater sense of importance across the narrative. This certainly seems true of the Johnny Ludlow stories and yet, discussing the archetypal content of the classic short story, Goyet also states that 'the short story never simply tells how someone named Peter married a woman called Mary' (25), a banality to which Wood's stories often do succumb. Indeed, such ordinariness formed part of the attraction of the Johnny Ludlow stories to readers of the 1870s, a determined break from the 'sensation novel with its tawdriness of incident and language' ('Johnny Ludlow' *Saturday Review* 1874, 603) which characterised the 1860s. The Johnny Ludlow stories do not appear wholly to fit the conventional short story format that Goyet has in mind but rather incline towards middlebrow fiction which focuses on the ordinary over the extraordinary. It is perhaps because of the commonplace nature of the plots and the slow-paced action that the many references to dress and appearance stand out. Within the *Johnny Ludlow* stories dress is not necessarily the central narrative feature but the frequency of observations and the level of description given seems especially prominent. As narrator, Johnny is the middleman between the reader and the principal actors in the scene and his responses are calculated to impart all of the required information to the reader. However, some of the detail that Johnny provides does not seem necessary to the plot and although it may help build character or set the scene, it feels awkward given the brevity of the tales. The descriptions of women's fashionable dress are particularly noticeable because of the technical vocabulary and haptic emphasis Johnny places on certain items, which seems beyond the expected level of detail for a male observer, particularly given his age and rural upbringing. For example, in 'Bursting-Up' (June 1871) he declares, 'If I were able to describe their attire I would, it beat anything for gorgeousness I had ever seen' (3:172), demonstrating Goyet's notion of superlative excess but offering an ambiguous interpretation to the reader. Johnny implies that he lacks the words to describe the dress he sees but equally there is a suggestion that the dresses are so gorgeous as to be beyond words. Yet the statement also indicates that he has noted the magnificence of attire before and has experience of such sartorial excesses. Despite his protests to the contrary, he subsequently describes this attire admirably, describing 'glistening silk skirts under robes of beautiful lace; fans in their hands and gossamer veils in their hair' in sensually exorbitant scenes reminiscent of a fashion plate ('Bursting-Up' 3:172). Indeed, one contemporary commentator in the *Saturday Review* remarked that the level of description of clothing in these stories 'is almost equal to the descriptions of costumes that we find in the acting copies of a play' ('Johnny Ludlow,' 1880, 619).

The construction of class is a point of central importance in the *Johnny Ludlow* stories for which clothing is seen as a key visible marker. The manner in which individuals wear their clothes, as well as the actual physical garments themselves, are seen as indicators as to whether a person belongs to a particular social milieu. This is prominent in 'Bursting-Up,' a story which tells of a lavish summer-fair hosted by the Clement-Pells, a wealthy family who derive from more humble roots. The head of the family, Mr Clement-Pell, is a successful banker who supports philanthropic endeavours within the community but also freely indulges in 'upstart grandeur and [a] profusion' of material goods for himself and his family. Their lifestyle is criticised by Mr Brandon[10] who berates '"the lavish and absurd and sinful profusion"' of goods paraded by the Clement-Pells:

> Is it seemly, or right, or decent, the way they live in? ... The mother holding her head in the air as if she wore an iron collar: the daughters with their carriages and their harps and their German governesses, and their costly furbelows that are a scandal on common sense? ('Bursting-Up' 3:180)

The criticism of furbelows, showy ornaments or trimmings which adorn women's clothing, suggests that Mr Brandon's view is that ostentatious clothing should not be used as a means to flaunt wealth and that such excesses of dress and material goods are distasteful. The Clement-Pells epitomise the 1860s, a period which clothing historian C. Willett Cunnington refers to as an era marked by 'extravagance, luxury, and ennui among the "leisured class"' (*Fashion* 172) caused by the breaking-down of 'certain time-honoured restraints which defined social intercourse' (172). Mr Brandon's critique emphasises the breakdown of these time-honoured social systems and the Clement-Pells look absurd in his view because '"[t]hey were not born to this kind of thing; were not reared to it; have only plunged into it of recent years; and it does not sit well with them"' (3:181). For Mr Brandon, clothing is representative of an assumed falseness, a facade of class which cannot hide the truth as he sees it, and his anxiety stems from the usurping of traditional social hierarchies.

As Cunnington suggests, from the 1860s onwards 'the wardrobe of the average woman was ... increasing ... [and] there was a growing complaint of "feminine extravagance"' (*English* 207). Ostentatious accoutrements ceased to be the privilege of the upper classes and became an aspirational desire for the middle-classes who sought to compete not with the rich but with friends, neighbours, and their immediate public associates to demonstrate economic and social success by their dress. Within 1870s society fashion became more prominent than it had ever been before, particularly in urban areas and industrialised cities, as the increased prosperity of the wealthy middle-classes, rising social mobility, and the increase of leisure time made changing fashions and the culture of consumption the ideal catalyst for the beginnings of a retail revolution. Dress constituted a troubling medium from which to ascertain social class because of the constant changing of fashions, the increase of manufactured goods, the second-hand market, and the increased availability of sewing-machines and patterns which allowed the lower classes to emulate their social 'superiors.'[11] If class was an anxiety throughout the 1870s then it was even more of an issue when concerns of gender were added in. As Cunnington states '[i]n addition to sex-attraction the feminine Attitude [sic] is greatly influenced by the Herd Instinct, or the wish to imitate, in appearance and conduct, those in the same social group' (*Fashion* 2). Put more simply by Mary Eliza Haweis in her 1878 treatise *The Art of Beauty*: 'a woman's natural quality is to attract, and having attracted, to enchain' (3). This instinct is, according to Cunnington, 'much stronger in Women than in Men' as a result of primitive impulses with the result that '[t]o be "in the fashion" gives ... [a woman] a peculiar glow of sensuous satisfaction' (3, 3). Fashion, he suggests somewhat derogatorily, makes women happy because it both attracts men and aligns them with other women in the same position, a sisterhood of women trying to attract 'mates.' Fashionable excesses of dress had frequently been linked to immoral women in fiction through figures such as the fallen Esther in Elizabeth Gaskell's *Mary Barton* (1848), the adulteress protagonist of Gustave Flaubert's *Madame Bovary* (1856), and of course the 'brazen hussy' Afy Hallijohn in Wood's sensation novel *East Lynne* (1862) (*East Lynne* 351). These characters were all notable for their decadence of dress and their associated inclinations towards vanity, idleness, and social dissatisfaction which proved to be partly responsible for their ultimate moral decline. The *Johnny Ludlow* stories feature a number of tales in which women delight in fashionable dress as a means to attract male attention in relation to which the feminine style of narration becomes apparent. 'Sophie Chalk' (September 1869) charts the exploits of a fashionable city girl who seemingly always finds herself dressed inappropriately for the Squire's country manor. Sophie's background is unknown save that she lives in the capital, a city of sartorial temptation where 'London girls are [lauded as] something to look at' (2:110). The description of Sophie Chalk emphasises her attractiveness, framing her as an alluring pre-Raphaelite beauty: 'a very small, slight person, with pretty features white as ivory; and wide-open light blue eyes, that were too close together, and had a touch of boldness on their surface' (2:111). Sophie's 'stunning lot of hair' (2:112) attracts Johnny's attention: he describes it as 'brown but with a red tinge in it, and about double the quantity [of Anna Whitney's, and] nature or art was giving it a wonderful gloss in the light of the setting sun' (2:112). As Anne Hollander states in *Seeing Through Clothes* (1978), 'more than at any other time women's hair was important in the nineteenth century ... [and had] immediately erotic overtones. ... Thick and abundant female hair safely conveyed a vivid sexual message in an atmosphere of extreme prudery' (73). Again, Johnny's description is ambiguous here, the use of the superlatives 'stunning' and 'wonderful' denoting admiration, and the contrast with another woman, Anna Whitney, suggests he views Sophie's appearance with the traditional male gaze. Yet Johnny's questioning of whether art or nature colours her hair implies a suspicion that Sophie is not all that she seems, that she may be artfully enhancing her sexual allure, a view reinforced by the story's repeated references to fairies and sirens: dangerous hybrids of nature and artifice who are equally alluring and treacherous. It is her dress, however, which is most attentively described as Johnny undoubtedly takes pleasure in relating its intricate details whilst simultaneously claiming to shun her extravagances. At the outset of the story, Sophie is described alighting from the train as 'a little lady in feathers,' highlighting the absurd contrivance of city fashion in the sartorial backwaters of rural Worcestershire (2:111). This artifice is made all the more apparent in Johnny's ensuing description of her appearance: 'her dress was some bright purple stuff trimmed with white fur; [and] her hands, lying in repose on her lap, had yellow gauntlets on' (2112). The loud, clashing colours illustrate ostentatious display, typical of the later 1860s as Cunnington observes: '[such] dress was clearly designed to catch the eye—and the man—by its arresting contrasts of hue. Discordant clashing of colours imply [sic] a psychological disharmony [about women's place in society]' (*Fashion* 199). From a sartorial perspective, Sophie's dress illustrates women's increased confidence in their social position and, Cunnington notes, 'a [short-lived] revival of Exhibitionism' which contrasted with the 'excess of Gothic sentiment' of the preceding period (*Fashion* 182, 182). Sophie's description highlights this idea of unnatural display, the purple woven material and yellow gloves contrast with the naturalness of the white fur, itself unnatural in the context, and the use of the term gauntlets rather than gloves suggests a masculine form of provocation more readily associated with warfare than fashion. Johnny's focus on colour is significant since the use of aniline dyes had become commonplace by the 1870s, with the result that artificial hues were associated with the masses and came to be seen as common and vulgar. Vulgarity, in turn, was equated with immorality. Indeed as Rosy Aindow highlights in *Dress and Identity in British Literary Culture 1870–1914* (2010), 'the ultimate expression of the vulgarity of bright colours was in the clothing of the prostitute, brightness being a means of attracting attention to the body' (94). Johnny's description of Sophie and the emphasis he places on unnaturalness when describing her dress has the capacity to transform Sophie from intriguing stranger to a source of potential moral danger who threatens conventional respectability.

The inference of sexual promiscuity resounds in Johnny's ensuing descriptions, particularly during Sophie's entrance for dinner:

> She came like a gleaming fairy, her dress shining in the fire-light; for they had not been in to light the candles. It had a green-and-gold tinge, and was cut very low. Did she think we had a party?—or that dressing for dinner was the fashion in our plain country house—as it might have been at a duke's? Her shoulders and arms were white as snow; she wore a silver necklace, the like of which I never saw before, silver bracelets, and a thick cord of silver twisting in and out of the complications of her hair. (2:113)

The reader's perception of Sophie is strongly swayed by Johnny's rhetorical questions which claim that she is exposing too much flesh and that her gratuitous indulgence in fashion leaves her dressed unsuitably for the occasion. Whereas Johnny is entirely accepting of Lena being taken out for show in the earlier story, Sophie is lambasted for dressing in a showy fashion, a moral duality influenced by familial bias and his provincial assumptions about how women (as opposed to the child, Lena) should dress. The contrast of Sophie's snow-white arms against the artfully manipulated silver jewellery wrapped sensuously around her neck, wrists, and hair and the attention given to her décolletage implies a deliberate sexualisation to which Johnny is a critical voyeur; his comments seem more typical of a jealous woman vying for attention than a potential admirer. Once again, the superlative emphasis that he has never seen anything like this before lends an ambiguous interpretation to the scene: is the jewellery so unusual or indulgent that he has never seen better or has he simply had limited exposure to seeing women's jewellery at all? Perhaps, given the numerous repetitions of this claim across the stories, this is simply Wood's way of suggesting Johnny's gendered naivety. Johnny repeatedly refers to Sophie's dress in rather spiteful terms throughout the story as if to remind the reader exactly how she looks, which serves to denigrate her character but also suggests a certain pleasure in both looking at her and relaying her appearance to the reader.

As Adeline Sergeant affirms, 'Mrs Wood's essential love of detail, and of somewhat commonplace detail, asserts itself again and again' in the *Johnny Ludlow* stories (180), manifesting itself in an almost obsessive interest in dress, regardless of the subject matter of the narrative. Her sartorial accounts of the characters demonstrate a level of detail which contributes towards a sense of realism but also at times makes the characters appear static, almost like mannequins of fiction which Wood—and by extension her narrator Johnny Ludlow—luxuriates in dressing. Wood's representations of dress go beyond the necessary level of realist depiction because the same level of focus is not given to other everyday aspects such as food or travel. Johnny's repeated and detailed depiction of dress feels uncomfortable because he possesses knowledge beyond the expectations of his gender. This detracts from both the narrative realism and the didacticism of the stories. Johnny's knowledge of dress throughout the first series extends beyond the basic acknowledgement of type, colour, or fit which a reader might expect in order to differentiate between, or construct, characters within a short story. His familiarity includes an awareness of the sounds fabrics make: Mrs Parrifer's 'silk gowns rustl[e] as if lined with buckram' ('Major Parrifer' [September 1868] 1:94–95); an appreciation of a garment's trimmings, such as 'black silk, with the simple white net quilling round the neck' ('The Game Finished' [November 1869] 2:202); and the ability to identify a wide range of fabrics including nankeen, muslin, gauze, silk, and velveteen. Men were involved in aspects of the fashion industry throughout the Victorian period, working as designers in haute couture fashion houses such as Charles Worth, trading cloth, or running textile factories, but typically this was centred around urbanised areas and industrialised cities. As a middle-class orphan from the rural West Midlands Johnny has limited access to sartorial discourses save what he observes around him or what he may glean from reading material or conversations

Despite the excesses of dress and the implausibility of the narratives, the stories gained instant popularity owing to their diverse themes, range of characters, and ordinary language which provided something for every class, age, and type of reader. Their contradictory and ambiguous moral interpretations proved to be a testament to their novelty and a crucial part of their success, while their brevity and frequency allowed divisive elements to pass by relatively quickly, usurped by the next instalment in the magazine.

Wood's nom-de-plume was calculated to disguise the number of contributions she personally made to *The Argosy* but her distinctive manner undermined her alias from the outset. Despite her son Charles Wood's claims in *Memorials of Mrs Henry Wood* (1894) that 'no one knew or even guessed at the authorship' (248), the *Saturday Review*, amongst other publications, cast suspicion over the writer's gender, commending the stories 'of whatever sex the author may be' ('Johnny Ludlow,' 1880, 618). By 1894 Sergeant summarily declared that 'it now seems extraordinary that there should have been the slightest doubt as to the authorship of these stories, for Mrs Wood's peculiarities of style are observable on every page' (185). The foremost of these gendered peculiarities is the excessive use of detail, which as Jennifer Phegley suggests 'was cited by many critics as a sign of women's inability to do anything other than copy in minute detail what they saw around them'. ('Domestic' 187)

Despite this perceived feminine weakness, the stories were evidently well received by reviewers as an 1880 review in *The Athenaeum* illustrates:

Mrs Wood deserves to retain her laurels for having struck out such a thoroughly distinct and pleasant path in fiction. The best characteristic of these short tales ... is the manner of their relation, quiet and yet vigorous, combining humour and pathos, and artlessly avoiding the temptation to exaggerate. ('Novels of the Week' 462)

Wood's exaggerated analysis of dress and its frequent appearances seem to have gone unnoticed, or were perhaps even appreciated by, her readership who revelled in the 'fidelity to truth, to the smallest domestic detail' (Sergeant 187). To the middle-class audience of Wood's 'family literary magazine' (Phegley, 'Domestic' 180), didactic purpose ceded to entertainment, and any propensities towards sartorial indulgence could be excused, since Wood's 'faults [were] those of the class for which she wrote' (Sergeant 191). The success of *The Argosy* and the *Johnny Ludlow* stories was aided by 'Wood's public image as a private, domestic woman [which] allowed her to restore propriety to the magazine' (Phegley, ARGOSY 23).[12] As a self-sufficient widow editing her own successful periodical, Wood possessed impressive business acumen and escaped the merciless interference which typified relationships between editors and authors in the mid-Victorian period (Hoppen 384). Her decision to adopt a pseudonym was not based on the usual desire to obtain publication via male-dominated publications, but was a deliberate obscuring of gender for her own personal reasons. Charles Wood comments on the enjoyment that this obscurity rendered to his mother as 'gifts denied to Mrs Henry Wood were found in *Johnny Ludlow*; and points for which Mrs Wood had been blamed—such as the occasional introduction of an element of superstition into her stories—Johnny Ludlow was especially commended for' (248). Despite Wood's 'rare knowledge of boy-nature' (Wood, *Memorials* 292) there is no clear explanation for her choice of male narrator save that it provided the maximum possible distance from her own identity. In terms of authorship in the 1870s, Wood's extensive collection of *Johnny Ludlow* stories deserves further critical attention as testament to her own and her readers' commitment and devotion to the character.

Notes

1. The first Johnny Ludlow story 'Shaving the Ponies' Tails' was published in January 1868 and the final part of the last story, 'Featherston's Story: At the Maison Rogue,' was published posthumously in June 1889. Wood died in February 1887. See Michael Flowers, 'A Chronological Listing of the *Johnny Ludlow* Stories' (2001–2006) for a full chronological list of the stories.
2. There are twenty-six stories in this first series: nine stories in each of volumes 1 and 2 and eight stories in Volume 3. Twelve of the stories were originally published post-1870.
3. Ellen Wood is listed as the seventh most prolific serial author in Troy J Bassett's *At the Circulating Library* Database of Victorian Fiction.
4. In *Memorials of Mrs Henry Wood* (1894) Charles Wood claims that these characters were often based on real-life acquaintances of his mother's.
5. The first *Johnny Ludlow* story 'Shaving the Ponies' Tails' was omitted from the collected edition.
6. Johnny is not biologically related to any member of the family. His father William dies soon after marrying his second wife, Johnny's stepmother, Mrs Ludlow. She subsequently marries the Squire thus Johnny and Tod share a stepmother. The Squire effectively 'inherits' Johnny by marriage.
7. Great symbolism was attached to flowers throughout the Victorian period, and a language of flowers known as floriography spawned large numbers of guides and dictionaries. See, for example, *The Language of Flowers; Or, Floral Emblems of Thoughts, Feelings and Sentiments* (1869) by Robert Tyas.
8. Old Bailey records indicate there were more than forty prosecutions for the theft of items of clothing in 1868 alone.
9. In the follow-up story 'Finding Both of Them' Johnny, Tod, and the Squire make amends to the 'gypsy' family they suspected of Lena's abduc-

tion, providing food and medical assistance to the father of the family who, despite their best efforts, subsequently dies. The woman convicted of stealing Lena's clothing, who also claims to be motivated by starvation, is convicted and sentenced to six months imprisonment with hard labour, a sentence deemed insufficient by the Todhetleys. Extreme poverty is thus never seen as an excuse for immorality.
10. Mr Brandon first appears in 'Major Parrifer' (September 1868) as the owner of a cottage whose tenant fears eviction. Brandon's manner is cold towards Mr Clement-Pell whom he views with distrust: 'whenever he spoke of the Pells his voice was thinner than ever, and most decidedly took a mocking sound' ('Bursting-Up' 3:178).
11. Hoppen notes the prevalence of freely available commercial paper patterns which allowed families to make their own clothes in the mid-Victorian period. Free patterns were given away with some periodicals (348–49).
12. *The Argosy* had been mired in accusations of immorality following the publication of Charles Reade's sexually frank bigamy novel *Griffith Gaunt* in 1866 under Alexander Strahan's editorship, a reputation which Wood needed to reverse if she was to make *The Argosy* a success.

WORKS CITED

Aindow, Rosy. *Dress and Identity in British Literary Culture, 1870–1914*. Farnham: Ashgate, 2010.
Bassett, Troy J. *At the Circulating Library: A Database of Victorian Fiction, 1837–1901*. Victorian Research Web. http://www.victorianresearch.org/atcl/statistics.php. Accessed 27 May 2018.
Brake, Laurel, and Marysa Demoor, eds. *Dictionary of Nineteenth-Century Journalism in Great Britain and Ireland*. Ghent, Belgium: Academia Press, 2009.
Breward, Christopher. *The Culture of Fashion*. Manchester: Manchester University Press, 1995.
Cunnington, C. Willett. *English Women's Clothing in the Nineteenth Century*. 1937. New York: Dover Publications, 1990.
———. *Fashion and Women's Attitudes in the Nineteenth Century*. 1936. Mineola, New York: Dover Publications, 2003.
Flowers, Michael, 'A Chronological Listing of the *Johnny Ludlow* Stories,' 2001–2006, http://www.mrshenrywood.co.uk/chron2.html. Accessed 27 May 2018.
Goyet, Florence. *The Classic Short Story, 1870–1925: Theory of a Genre*. Cambridge: Open Book Publishers, 2014.
Haweis, [Mary Eliza] Mrs H. R *The Art of Beauty*. 1878. London: Chatto & Windus, 1883.

Hollander, Anne. *Seeing Through Clothes*. Berkeley and Los Angeles, CA: University of California Press, 1993.
Hoppen, Theodore K. *The Mid-Victorian Generation 1846–1886*. Oxford: Clarendon Press, 1998.
'Johnny Ludlow.' *The Pall Mall Gazette* 2882 (May 13, 1874a): 11.
'Johnny Ludlow.' *Saturday Review of Politics, Literature, Science and Art* 37.967 (May 9, 1874b): 602–4.
'Johnny Ludlow.' *Saturday Review of Politics, Literature, Science and Art* 50.1307 (1880): 618–19.
Mitchell, Sally. 'Wood [née Price], Ellen [known as Mrs Henry Wood] (1814–1887), writer and journal editor.' *Oxford Dictionary of National Biography*. Oxford: Oxford University Press, 2004. Online. Accessed 12 April 2018, http://www.oxforddnb.com/view/10.1093/ref:odnb/9780198614128.001.0001/odnb-9780198614128-e-29868.
'Novels of the Week.' *The Athenaeum* 2763 (Oct 9 1880): 462–3.
'Our Fun-done Letter.' *Fun* (28 November 1868): 116.
Palmer, Beth. Women's Authorship and Editorship in Victorian Culture: Sensational Strategies. Oxford: Oxford University Press, 2011.
Phegley, Jennifer Jean. 'ARGOSY (1865–1901)'. *Dictionary of Nineteenth-Century Journalism in Great Britain and Ireland*. Ed. Laurel Brake and Marysa Demoor. Ghent, Belgium: Academia Press, 2009. 23.
Phegley, Jennifer. 'Domesticating the Sensation Novelist: Ellen Price Wood as Author and Editor of the "Argosy Magazine."' *Victorian Periodicals Review* 38.2 (2005): 180–98.
Sergeant, Adeline. 'Mrs Henry Wood.' *Women Novelists of Queen Victoria's Reign: A Book of Appreciations*. Ed. Margaret Oliphant. London: Hurst & Blackett, 1897. 174–92.
Tyas, Robert. *The Language of Flowers; Or, Floral Emblems of Thoughts, Feelings and Sentiments*. London: George Routledge, 1869. Internet Archive. Accessed 29 May 2018. https://archive.org/details/languageflowers00tyasgoog.
Wood, Charles W. Memorials of Mrs Henry Wood. London: R. Bentley & Son, 1894.
Wood, Ellen. *East Lynne*. 1862. Ed. Elisabeth Jay. Oxford World's Classics. Oxford: Oxford University Press, 2008.
[———]. *Johnny Ludlow*. 3 vols. London: Richard Bentley and Son, 1874. HathiTrust. Accessed 28 May 2018. https://catalog.hathitrust.org/Record/008720767.

CHAPTER 14

'Sinecures which could be held by girls': Margaret Oliphant and Women's Labour

Danielle Charette

As a frequent reviewer for *Blackwood's Edinburgh Magazine* and one of the most prolific writers of the nineteenth century, Margaret Oliphant knew her trade well. She published an astonishing 96 novels, alongside hundreds of articles on topics ranging from parliamentary history to Italian art. In the 1860s and 1870s, the appearance of Oliphant's six-novel *Carlingford* series (1863–1876) buoyed her popularity, but these were also decades of tremendous personal anguish. After the deaths of her eight-month-old daughter Marjorie and day-old son Stephen in 1854, Oliphant's husband Francis died of tuberculosis in 1859. She was left pregnant, in debt, and the single parent of two small children. In 1864 Oliphant's beloved daughter Maggie died, and by 1868, she was also looking after the financial affairs and children of her bankrupted brother Frank Wilson. These responsibilities were compounded when he, too,

---

D. Charette (✉)
University of Chicago, Chicago, IL, USA
e-mail: dcharette@uchicago.edu

© The Author(s) 2020
A. E. Gavin, C. W. de la L. Oulton (eds.), *British Women's Writing from Brontë to Bloomsbury, Volume 2*, British Women's Writing from Brontë to Bloomsbury, 1840–1940,
https://doi.org/10.1007/978-3-030-38528-6_14

died in 1875. All the while, Oliphant continued to write at an unrivalled rate. As a mother, novelist, editorialist, and primary breadwinner, Oliphant disputed John Stuart Mill's notion that Victorian women were hopelessly subjected. Instead, Oliphant's church novels—above all, *Phoebe Junior: A Last Chronicle of Carlingford* (1876)—articulate an alternative feminism, based upon religious dissent, social pluck, and home economics.

In *Phoebe Junior*, Oliphant dramatizes the moneyed interests surrounding a church sinecure, which comes to stand in for a variety of unjust and inefficient ways of old. The success of Anthony Trollope's six *Barsetshire* novels (1855–1867) had shown Oliphant that mid-Victorians were more than willing to read about the foibles of their clergymen, or what Trollope called 'Christian cant' (Trollope, *Autobiography* 143). Oliphant explicitly names Trollope as a church novelist in *Phoebe Junior* (233), and her own *Carlingford* series features churchmen negotiating sinecures, forged cheques, the Oxford Movement, and the public religious squabbles which readers would recollect from Trollope's novels *The Warden* (1855) and *The Last Chronicle of Barset* (1867). Yet it would be unfair to say Oliphant uncritically recycles the story of Trollope's Septimus Harding, the kind rural warden who unwittingly becomes the centre of a London newspaper war when he accepts an Anglican sinecure. In the place of Trollope's hand-wringing over the role of the modern British 'gentlemen,' Oliphant treats class conflict and Carlingford's corrupt college sinecure with a markedly feminist twist. Not only does she demonstrate that a woman can judiciously comment on ecclesiastical controversy, she also holds the very definition of a sinecure up to gendered scrutiny. By focusing on the definition of a 'sinecure,' Oliphant dramatizes the effect of England's credit economy on the traditional church order.

The town of Carlingford is more widely middle-class than Trollope's Barsetshire, which means it is home to a greater population of religious 'Dissenters' for whom an Anglican sinecure is especially scandalous. Importantly, in Oliphant's setting, power diffuses away from the pulpit, in favour of the sort of 'social politics' that play to Victorian women's strengths. Phoebe Tozer and Lucilla Marjoribanks, the respective heroines of *Phoebe Junior* and *Miss Marjoribanks* (1866), need not be particularly religious to recognize that the reformist emphasis on evangelism and charity made 'political economy' into a possible female asset, especially for young social-strivers (*Miss Marjoribanks* 93).

Etymologically, 'sinecure' stems from the Latin *sine cūrā* for 'without care'—in this case, referring to church endowments without the direct care of souls (OED). The derivation is clearer in the French (sinécure)—which Oliphant knew well from long stays on the continent—since 'curé' also refers to a vicar or cleric, that is, 'without cleric.' A clergyman who accepted his income from such an endowment was gaining a stipend without performing his ordained duty. 'Sinecure' thus became an effective pejorative for accusing Anglican ministers of idleness at best and government embezzlement at worst. However, when Phoebe's cousin Ursula May learns her brother Reginald has secured a church sinecure, she is more impressed than scandalized. Ursula is the industrious but poor eldest daughter of an Anglican perpetual curate and struggles to keep house for her numerous siblings and preoccupied father. She, for one, does not hear a negative connotation in the word sinecure. Humorously, but poignantly, Oliphant writes: 'to get a good income for doing nothing, or next to nothing, seemed to her an ideal sort of way of getting one's livelihood … She wished with a sigh that there were sinecures which could be held by girls' (117). Ursula's fantasy is suggestive of Oliphant's own frustration with her financial situation, which necessitated writing late into the night and accepting payments she perceived to be below her novels' market value. In a quiet moment Ursula consults the dictionary, but if she does read the official meaning of 'sinecure,' Oliphant's narrator avoids informing us. Instead, Ursula defines 'sinecure' for herself, based not on any textual or ecclesiastical authority but, rather, on the social cues of Carlingford.

Ursula's keenness for 'sinecures which would be held by girls' represents more than comedy or female naiveté. By bringing this public controversy into the domestic realm of a young woman's daydreams, Oliphant portrays the all-consuming power of English financial debates and, moreover, insists that these debates are appropriate topics for young women to contemplate. What would it mean for a sinecure to exist for girls? By hypothetically feminizing the institution of a sinecure, Oliphant explicitly associates the inherent unfairness of unearned state income with gender inequality. In a sense, the public controversy over church compensation prompts Oliphant's young women to discover they have been toiling under an inverted sinecure: whereas relatively privileged, well-educated churchmen like Trollope's Reverend Harding collected generous sinecures for little to no work, Ursula and her sister Janey work to manage their father's entire household without pay.

Admittedly, by the publication of *Phoebe Junior* in 1876, the real world politics of state sinecures were almost entirely moot. In the late 1830s, the

Ecclesiastical Commission had mostly curtailed large rural stipends in favour of more regulated, more efficient, and more urban ministries. Thanks to the Commission's findings, the Dean and Chapter Act of 1840 suppressed all 68 known sinecure rectories in Britain (Chadwick 137). In 1869, John Stuart Mill noted, 'With the bulk of the nation the indefeasibility of endowments is a chimera of the past' ('Endowments' 5:616). If Trollope had been somewhat antiquarian in 1855 when he rehashed the sinecure question in *The Warden*, Oliphant was that much more out-of-date by the conclusion of her *Carlingford* series. Nevertheless, it seems plausible that Oliphant revived the notion of a church sinecure in the 1870s not because it was still socially salient but, rather, because the subject of the sinecure opens up a conceptual space for theorizing about women and work. In so doing, Oliphant concentrates on the seemingly abstract, public, male-dominated debate over a state sinecure to comment on the local, feminine, domestic sphere of household management.

By the 1870s, the complicated class antagonisms between increasingly prosperous Nonconformist tradespeople and their Anglican Oxbridge rivals had superseded true theological soul-searching. Not a single character in *Phoebe Junior* is ever found reading the Bible. Low Church or High, everyone is principally concerned with capitalizing a share of the market. The crass railroad tycoon Mr Copperhead voices what Oliphant's characters all seem to be thinking: '"Christianity's been a capital thing for the world,"' yet has been '"carried too far"' (333). Although Oliphant remains aggressively neutral on the details of doctrine, the novel clearly presents a position when it comes to the gender question. In fact, the injustices women face become easier to identify and articulate for characters less invested in doctrinal differences.

The sinecure itself may or may not represent a corruption of church and state, but the inverted sinecure of women's labour is a true abuse. Oliphant garners her readers' sympathy when Reverend May dismisses his daughters as 'useless impedimenta' who must hold their tongues (157). Likewise, readers are encouraged to feel outraged when Phoebe's grandfather, Mr Tozer, rages that she is no more than a 'chit' who cannot possibly have anything to do with business (365). These verbal inequities against Oliphant's female characters embolden readers to conclude the opposite of May and Tozer: women *are* useful, and women can indeed be an asset to business. Sympathetic reactions on behalf of Ursula and Phoebe, however, may themselves be problematic, in that they might imply that women are worthwhile only because they are workers. This risks reinforcing the perception that Oliphant was the 'general utility woman' for *Blackwood's* and thus, something of a conservative pawn of the publishing industry (Oliphant, *Annals* 2:475). Or, as a mostly favourable review in *The Spectator* put it, Oliphant was the 'shrewd' creator of 'the able *bourgeois*' feminine character, even if characters like Phoebe were 'too coarsely worldly' to be realistic ('Phoebe Junior' 769). Likewise, twentieth-century feminists such as Patricia Stubbs struggled with the sense that Oliphant's preoccupation with household economy was simply too bourgeois for the women's movement (39–45).

It is true that when Oliphant defends her female characters' worth—that is to say, when she asserts what it might mean for girls to hold a sinecure—she does so in utilitarian terms. For instance, Janey May encourages her brother Reginald to accept the unnecessarily large parsonage included in his sinecure on the grounds that she can serve as his housekeeper. 'I'm a girl,' says Janey, 'which is a great deal more useful' than the servant Reginald considers taking on at the college. (189). Similarly, even when Ursula romanticizes the notion of a sinecure for girls, she immediately translates it back into the language of labour: 'If *I* had a chance of two hundred and fifty pounds a year!' She fantasizes, '[T]here is nothing I would not do for it. I would scrub floors ... I would do anything, the dirtiest work' (160). 'You will be independent,' she tells her brother, 'able to do what you please, and never to ask papa for anything' (160). Strikingly, Ursula's vision of independence from her father and her domestic duties is associated with manual scrubbing and the 'dirtiest' of work. Reginald hesitates to take the sinecure not only because it is dishonest, but also because it is 'no work' at all (156). Yet, for Ursula, being compensated for pure idleness is impossible to imagine. Instead, she helps persuade Reginald to accept his 'independent position' by reconceptualizing the sinecure's lack of designated work as, in fact, an impetus for her brother to demonstrate his versatility and perform any work that comes his way. As she describes it, taking the wardenship would render Reginald 'always ready to do anything that was wanted in Carlingford. Don't you see that was their meaning? They pay you for that which is not work, but will find you plenty of work they don't pay for' (161). Here Ursula recasts the sinecure in the best possible light: by construing it as women's work. Like a Victorian homemaker, Reginald's tasks will be unspecified but numerous, and he must practice the utmost accommodation effectively to earn his sinecure.

Of course, the Victorian homemaker is never financially compensated—work or no. Monica Cohen highlights the parallel syntax of Ursula's claim that, essentially, the sinecure is pay for no work, but work for no pay, as typical of Oliphant's style and cagey politics:

> The syntax implies that there is an epistemological problem inherent in the relationship between work and pay: because pay makes work culturally legible, pay is often taken as a metonymic representation of work, when, in truth, pay is only a condition that makes work recognizable, not evidence of its being. (102)

Oliphant revisits the public sinecure controversy to spotlight injustice towards women, but, unfortunately, her hedging syntax conveys a muddled argument. Oliphant's advocacy for the equal worth of women becomes material rather than intrinsic. Women, she suggests, ought to be taken seriously because their utility is as great as their male counterparts. When Reverend May complains that his daughters rob him in 'dresses and ribbons, and a hundred fooleries' and 'will never give me back a farthing' (157), his misogyny is objectionable not because he has failed to love his daughters on their own terms but, rather, because he is mistaken that they never earn him a farthing. Oliphant goes out of her way to emphasize that May's daughters do their best to curtail his spendthrift habits and attempt to cook impressive dinner entrées without any extra budget allowance. Oliphant, to be sure, is right to point out women's often overlooked economic contributions in the home, yet she sometimes appears too quick to cede to the utilitarian spirit of the times. She asserts the value of femininity, but it too easily becomes a value measurable only in the marketplace.

In fairness to Oliphant, she does emphasize the vulgar extremes of Victorian tycoons like Copperhead, who view women as 'a waste of raw material' (323). However, Oliphant can never quite bring herself to refute Copperhead's crassly utilitarian worldview. Instead, the novel ends with Phoebe besting the Copperheads at their own capitalist game. She agrees to marry the wealthy but charmless Clarence Copperhead because she reckons he represents 'a big capital—a Career' (300). Phoebe will maximize the Copperheads' railway bounty to 'thrust' Clarence forward in parliament and public affairs: 'He would be as good as a profession, a position, a great work to Phoebe' (300). In other words, Phoebe plans to use Clarence as the 'raw material' towards her own feminine career. This version of utilitarian feminism put forth in *Phoebe Junior* may tempt a return to the common critical narrative that Oliphant was a compulsive writer who churned-out nearly one hundred novels to keep her family's finances afloat, but the story is more complicated.

Notably, *Phoebe Junior*, released a full decade after *Miss Marjoribanks*, was the only *Carlingford* novel not published by *Blackwood's*. Oliphant's switch to the publishing firm Hurst and Blackett was no doubt financially motivated, but may also have been political. It definitely was not a decision Oliphant made lightly. In 1865, she promised William Blackwood: 'I would never for an instant dream of giving a story by the author of the Carlingford Series to any periodical whatever on any terms, unless indeed you were first to throw me overboard' (23 June 1865, *Autobiography and Letters*, 203). However, the compensation she received for *Miss Marjoribanks* left her feeling under-appreciated. It was significantly less than the 'prodigal extravagance' of £1500 she had commanded for *The Perpetual Curate* (1863) and what she termed the rumoured 'prices of my contemporaries' (*Autobiography of Margaret Oliphant* 148, 135). In the spring of 1866, Oliphant expressed her sense of 'the downfall' to Blackwood: 'I know you have no desire to place me at a disadvantage, but at the same time I think you must feel that if I, like others of my craft, had insisted upon a bargain at the time Miss M. commenced, it would have been concluded upon more liberal terms' (qtd in Colby 64). For a more lucrative conclusion to *Carlingford*, Oliphant apparently needed to take the series elsewhere.

Although *Miss Marjoribanks* is a bulky, inconsistent novel, Blackwood's objection to the work may have had to do with its proto-feminist tone. Lucilla Marjoribanks rules as 'sovereign' over Carlingford's social scene, even as she repeats that her one ambition in life is 'to be a comfort to dear papa"' (15). If she were to marry, Lucilla insists, she would be guilty of '"swindling' her father (171). The irony is obvious: despite all his daughter's talk of 'care' and 'comfort,' the doctor dies unexpectedly young and leaves Lucilla a paltry inheritance. By now middle-aged and well-practised in exercising her 'legislative cares' in public and private (204), Lucilla opts to marry her cousin Tom Marjoribanks. With 'no sympathetic soul to fall back upon' (333), Lucilla embraces 'the second period of her career' and, eventually, 'the natural culmination of her career' (331, 495). For Lucilla, this means wedding a man freshly returned from India and stretching her small income across a gentrifying effort to settle the 'Marchbanks' farmland on the edge of the county. Lucilla's triumph in the marriage market is satirical, but Oliphant suspected Blackwood was not in on the joke:

> Most unreasonable and exacting of editors, what would you have? Was it not only the other day that you were abusing me for Lucilla's want of heart, and now, when the poor soul finds herself guilty of caring for someone, you

think she has too much! It is the sad fate of gifted women never to be appreciated. (To William Blackwood, May/June 1866, *Autobiography and Letters* 210)

Oliphant stayed a close colleague of Blackwood after he slighted *Miss Marjoribanks*, but the *Chronicles of Carlingford* remained a contentious subject. In an 1873 letter to her long-time publisher, she recalled: 'The Carlingford books were begun in the year '60 or '61, when I was very low in spirit and hope, and after you had snubbed me very much, as you have been doing lately' (To Blackwood, 13 May, *Autobiography and Letters* 241).

Between *Miss Marjoribanks* and *Phoebe Junior*, Oliphant had written a response to John Stuart Mill's *The Subjection of Women* (1869) and a review of George Otto Trevelyan's *The Life and Letters of Lord Macaulay* (1876). Neither Oliphant nor Blackwood endorsed women's enfranchisement, yet Oliphant worried that the conservative Blackwood would probably find her piece on 'the mad notion of the franchise of women' still 'too respectful to Mill' (To Blackwood, 16 August 1869, *Autobiography and Letters* 211). As for the Macaulay review, she cautioned Blackwood, 'I hope we shall not come to blows over it, though it is ticklish ground' (15 April 1876, *Autobiography and Letters* 257). Oliphant submitted the review unfinished and told Blackwood, 'I do not mind if you throw in a bit of Toryism on your account' (15 April 1876, *Autobiography and Letters* 257). This suggests that Oliphant may have given Blackwood fairly free rein in some of her more traditionalist journalism. It helps explain why Oliphant's *Blackwood's* writings appeared under an anonymous male persona. Oliphant's review of Mill's *Subjection of Women* (1869) deemed the whole book 'an insult not only to men, but to women as we love and admire and desire to keep them' ('Mr Mill' 310). Clearly channelling a male voice, her review claims that Mill's 'mercantile' approach to marriage must mean he 'believes that old women have it in them to manage our finance' ('Mr Mill' 310). Surely Oliphant was aware of the irony of denouncing Mill's 'patronage of old women' at the same time that she was singlehandedly sponsoring her children and extended family ('Mr Mill' 310). As Elisabeth Jay puts it, despite 'the literary transvestism that *Maga* [*Blackwood's Edinburgh Magazine*] had afforded her,' Oliphant was 'constrained by the expectations of publishers and the reading public' (Jay 79). This 'transvestism' came with the expectation that she would answer Mill's feminism as a *Maga* man.

The possibility that Oliphant's political voice was not always her own accords with the view of Oliphant's first biographers, Robert and Vineta Colby, who noted Oliphant's 'equivocating' form of commercialism in the face of 'the triple tyranny of middle-class reader, publisher, and circulating library' (Colby and Colby xiv). According to the Colbys, Oliphant approached literature as a 'commodity' out of necessity: cutthroat publishing demands had 'transformed the genteel profession of letters into a bustling literary market place' (3). Still, the shift in tone—in addition to the shift in publisher—between *Miss Marjoribanks* and *Phoebe Junior* should make us wary of endorsing Virginia Woolf's infamous lament that Oliphant 'sold her brain' so that she might send her sons to Eton and Oxford (Woolf 172). The cares of Phoebe Tozer and Ursula May are more mature and poignant than those of the satirical Lucilla Marjoribanks. Yes, there are brains for sale in *Phoebe Junior*, but they are principally male minds. Treating intellectual acuity as if it were some sort of liquid currency, Copperhead proclaims, 'Money is money, but brains is brains ... and when you want to make a figure in the world, Sir, buy a few brains if they fall in your way' (413). And lest we assume this attitude is limited to a crude businessman like Copperhead, Oliphant also indicts the Anglican Reverend May for falsifying a cheque in the name of saving his family and for attempting to wager his son's intellectual liberty for a public sinecure.

Indeed, a sinecure is the ultimate example of putting one's mind up for sale. Entitled Anglican curates assumed they deserved compensation for their Oxbridge educations, regardless of any active care of Christian souls. To underscore the point, Oliphant depicts Reverend May going half 'mad' over his financial stress. Evidently, May's own soul has gone uncared for, and the sinecure, thus, comes full circle. A clergyman who promoted economic gain at the expense of his parishioners' souls finds his own soul to be thoroughly uncultivated and corrupted. Recognizing this, the Nonconformist Phoebe steps in to perform a modern, feminist version of soul-care. Phoebe does May the financial favour of persuading her grandfather Tozer not to press charges. Moreover, as May's nurse, she brings him the spiritual comfort which has been missing from the May household without the 'medium of the mother' (112). In spite of their doctrinal differences, Phoebe sits by the minister's sickbed and fathoms herself to be May's 'sole guardian' (372). Hence, Phoebe intervenes in May's business in a manner that is nurturing, competent, and progressive.

Whereas a traditional sinecure represents a rigid contract with the past, Phoebe's liberal approach—the closest the novel gets to a sinecure for girls—is flexible and sympathetic. For Trollope, the contractual confusions of the Hiram's Hospital sinecure impede progress, as citizens squabble over the fine print of a fifteenth-century will. In contrast, Phoebe's feminine labour is so flexible that she intuits that contracts may sometimes be broken if breaking them is in the moral interests of the community. In this case, Phoebe decides it is morally acceptable to destroy evidence of May's forged cheque and urges her grandfather to overlook May's wrongs. To ward off the legal inquiry into May's forgery, Phoebe tries to give the bank representative a meaningful glance—a visual 'entreaty'—which Oliphant's narrator says the banker 'would have understood had he been a woman' (363). Phoebe, in this way, inserts a certain feminine compassion into the business proceeding. The whole difficulty of the forged cheque, Oliphant implies, might have been cleared up faster had there been more women playing a '*role*' in the commercial sphere (379). Here Phoebe intercedes in exactly the kind of financial transaction Oliphant's review of Mill's *Subjection of Women* had mocked (1869). But, importantly, Phoebe's intervention is fairly commonplace. What bothered Oliphant most about Mill is that his activism centred on 'exceptional women,' while claiming to speak for the middle classes. She chides him for acting as the self-appointed 'advocate' to 'discern what [woman] is capable of, and to indicate her real work in the world' (309). In this light, Mill comes across a bit like an absentee vicar: privileged, talkative, and out of touch.

Phoebe's open-mindedness accords with that of Carlingford's Dissenting minister, Horace Northcote, who zealously objects to sinecures because they 'contract the mind' (166). The double-meaning of 'contract' is important here. A traditional sinecure narrows men's imaginations while also legally binding them to what Northcote calls the 'gilded fetters of the State' (175). A sinecure, Northcote stresses, takes active '"means of doing good"' and 'lock[s] [them] up in uselessness' (177). In the place of Anglican churchmen who have shackled their minds to a sinecure, Oliphant puts forth flexible, sympathetic characters like Phoebe and Ursula. It becomes a woman's task to watch after communities' souls in ways that are financially savvy but also nurturing and future-oriented.

In this regard, Oliphant actually aligns herself with the progressive utilitarianism of John Stuart Mill. Probably inspired by her own journalism projects, Oliphant clarifies that Phoebe 'was very well got up on the subject of education for women' and 'patronized Mr Ruskin's theory' of the separate spheres (54). At the same time, Phoebe was also busy reading Mill's *Dissertations* (76). Despite never formally retracting her opposition to women's enfranchisement, Oliphant's position evolved, vis-à-vis her essays on Mill, which span the years 1856 to 1880. Whereas her 1850s pieces in *Blackwood's Edinburgh Magazine*, 'The Laws Concerning Women' (1856) and 'The Condition of Women' (1858), argue that traditional separate spheres spring from natural law, her 1866 article 'The Great Unrepresented' genuinely praises Mill as a great public philosopher, even if she finds his statistical worries about political representation too heady and abstracted from household concerns (368–9). Crucially, in this *Blackwood's* article Oliphant drops her male persona and speaks as 'We, the Female Householders of England' ('The Great Unrepresented' 370). In 1869, Oliphant retreated back to a vaguely male voice, but her argument reads as a frustration with an overly intellectualized feminism: The 'vigorous female intellects' who line up behind Mill have admitted 'a need of masculine support' ('Mr Mill' 313). Beyond the 'gifted women' in his philosophic circles, she writes, Mill's 'knowledge of the condition of women ... might seem to be derived solely from police reports and other law columns in the *Times*' (310, 313). In other words, Mill and his supporters fail to account for the diverse middle-class English experience typified by Carlingford's women.

Since her initial essays on the 'woman question' in 1856 and 1858, Oliphant had endured the deaths of two more children, her husband, and her brother. She had once marked 1876—not incidentally, the year *Phoebe Junior* was published—as the time when her sons' and nephew's burdensome education expenses would be mostly behind her. For Oliphant, 1876 was to represent a turning point not only in her family fortunes but also in the quality of her writing. In May 1875 she pleaded with Blackwood: 'Please don't let anyone upbraid me with writing too much until the year 1876, if we live to see it, by which time I hope the bulk of the schooling will be over, and I will not mind it' (241). Unfortunately, the boys did not earn the Oxford scholarships she hoped they would, their professional employments remained spotty, and her sons Cyril and Cecco suffered early deaths in 1889 and 1894.

These unrelenting tragedies only compounded the demands placed on Oliphant as mother and primary breadwinner, and it might therefore be assumed she would be precisely the sort of Victorian to whom the 1870 Married Women's Property Act and burgeoning suffragist movement would have appealed. The general theme underlying Oliphant's political writing, however, is that the economic and spiritual burdens placed on women are so acute that any electoral solutions are bound to be foolhardy.

In the days of the first Reform Bill of 1832, Oliphant, her mother, and her husband Frank 'were all tremendously political and Radical' (*The Autobiography of Margaret Oliphant* 55). Oliphant confessed she knew what it was like to feel a certain 'giddiness in my brain' (*Autobiography* 55). At her most heady, Oliphant's 'giddiness' of brain gave her 'a vague realization of the soft swaying of the world in space!' (*Autobiography* 55). Retrospectively, Oliphant associated such imaginative possibilities with an era of happier family life, yet by 1880, Oliphant's knowledge of personal suffering trumped any idealism she may have once held for public suffrage.

Her most heartfelt response to Mill, 'The Grievances of Women' (1880)—which appeared in *Fraser's Magazine* rather than *Blackwood's*—unequivocally attacks the injustice that 'the poor woman who works so hard is considered as a passive object to her husband's bounty, indebted to him for her living' (702). Oliphant's example of the woman whose work is 'never done' is particularly striking:

> The poor clergymen's wife (I know one such with such hands of toil, scarred and honorable! Hands that have washed and scrubbed; and cooked and sewed, till all their lady softness is gone) is his *curate* as well. ('Grievances of Women' 703; emphasis added)

Once again, Oliphant draws upon the dynamics of church families to illustrate the economic and emotional realities of women. In addition to her backbreaking domestic labours, the clergyman's wife is also responsible for tending to her husband's mental state. As the parsonage's unofficial curate, her duties are always more demanding, yet both her menial and her mental work go unpaid.

Even if Oliphant was never a thorough-going Millian, the balance that *Phoebe Junior* attempts between economic pragmatism, the value of labour, and the expansion of the female mind does reveal Oliphant's thoughtful engagement with Mill. His reflections on the effects the first Reform Bill had on the English consciousness are illustrative. Mill writes: '[it] brought home for the first time to the existing generation a practical consciousness of living in a world of change ... It was to politics what the Reformation was to religion' ('The Claims of Labour' 4:369). Specifically, Mill is discussing enfranchisement, but his language could just as easily apply to church reform. Once the social evil was brought 'before *minds* thus prepared' and 'the conditions of the working classes [were] brought before the *mind* of the nation in the most emphatic manner,' it became 'the *care* of the classes themselves' (4:370; emphasis added).[1] Here Mill underscores national conscious-raising and care as the active achievement of the dissenting classes. Whereas a sinecure is tied down in ancient contracts and denies the soul from receiving paternal religious care, a modern sinecure—perhaps 'a sinecure which could be held by girls'—is focused on cultivating sympathetic minds. Precisely because they are not bound to the 'guided fetters' of state sinecures, the women of *Phoebe Junior* are freer to imagine—if not actually enact—a version of freedom that is mindful and maternal in the face of economic realities.

Of course, this is an optimistic interpretation, which runs counter to Oliphant's own wariness on the 'woman question' and her stoic attempts to balance family life and debt. Still, in *Phoebe Junior* Oliphant gives us an ideal. While railway men like Copperhead chase after 'public works' projects for money, Ursula and Phoebe daydream about having a financial cushion that would enable their independent work—not necessarily on grand national projects, but in quiet rooms and communities like Carlingford. In this way, Oliphant's young women resist unfettered utilitarianism and seem to favour work for its own sake rather than for any material gain. As Oliphant lamented in her *Autobiography* (1899), 'I don't think I have ever had two hours undisturbed ... during my whole literary life' (67). Never having her own work room, she did most of her writing at night in the family drawing room, with the doors always open. Despite Woolf's criticisms, Oliphant's interest in the sinecure may, interestingly enough, anticipate a sort of *Room of One's Own* (1929) formula, whereby a sinecure for girls could enable an independence of work and mind.

Like the female characters of *Phoebe Junior*, Oliphant was restricted by social circumstances and finances, but her consistent emphasis on communal care and work represents a feminist rejoinder to the historic Anglican sinecure. Oliphant was no radical, but her novel acknowledges that change is most often mindful and local. Reginald and Northcote detest each other over the public politics of the sinecure, but Phoebe's feminine 'labour' intercedes and successfully urges the two clergymen to shake hands on the town streets. Phoebe explains, '"It would be better for you both. That is what I call enlarging the mind"' (242). Oliphant's notion of a sinecure for everyday Victorian girls of Carlingford is a quiet call for expanded sympathy, maternal soul-care, and an openness to new possibilities for women's compensation.

Note

1. For Mill's explicit writing on church sinecures, see 'Corporation and Church Property' (1833) 4: 193–222.

Words Cited

Chadwick, Owen. *The Victorian Church*. Vol. I. New York: Oxford University Press, 1966.

Colby, Vineta, and Robert A. Colby. *The Equivocal Virtue: Margaret Oliphant and the Victorian Literary Market Place*. Hamden, CT: Archon Books, 1996.

Cohen, Monica. 'Maximizing Oliphant: Begging the Question and the Politics of Satire.' *Victorian Women Writers and the Woman Question*. ed. Nicola Diane Thompson. Cambridge: Cambridge University Press, 1999: 99–115.

Jay, Elisabeth. *Mrs. Oliphant: 'A Fiction to Herself': A Literary Life*. Oxford: Clarendon Press, 1993.

Mill, John Stuart. *The Collected Works of John Stuart Mill*. 33 vols. Ed. John M. Robson. Toronto: University of Toronto Press; London: Routledge and Kegan Paul, 1963–1991.

[———]. 'Corporation and Church Property' *The Jurist* (Feb. 1833) *Collected Works*. 4: 193–222.

[———]. 'Endowments.' *Fortnightly Review* (Apr. 1869): 377–90. *Collected Works*. 5: 613–29.

[———]. 'The Claims of Labour.' *Edinburgh Review* (Apr. 1845): 498–525. *Collected Works* 4: 364–89.

Oliphant, Margaret. *Annals of a Publishing House: William Blackwood and His Sons Their Magazine and Friends*. 3 vol. Edinburgh and London: William Blackwood and Sons, 1897.

———. *The Autobiography and Letters of Mrs Margaret Oliphant*. 1899. Ed. Mrs. Harry Coghill and Q. D. Leavis. Leicester University Press, 1974.

———. *The Autobiography of Margaret Oliphant*. Ed. Elisabeth Jay. Peterborough, ON: Broadview, 2002.

[———]. 'The Condition of Women.' *Blackwood's Edinburgh Magazine* (Feb. 1858): 139–54.

[———]. 'The Great Unrepresented.' *Blackwood's Edinburgh Magazine* (Sept. 1866): 367–79.

[———]. 'The Grievances of Women.' *Fraser's Magazine* (May 1880): 698–710.

[———]. 'The Laws Concerning Women.' *Blackwood's Edinburgh Magazine* (April 1856): 379–87.

[———]. 'Macaulay.' *Blackwood's Edinburgh Magazine* (May 1876): 614–637.

———. *Miss Marjoribanks*. 1866. Ed. Elisabeth Jay. London: Penguin, 1998.

[———]. 'Mr Mill on the Subjection of Women.' *Blackwood's Edinburgh Magazine* (Oct. 1869): 309–21.

———. *Phoebe Junior: A Last Chronicle of Carlingford*. 1876. Ed. Elizabeth Langland. Peterborough, ON: Broadview, 2002.

'Phoebe Junior.' *The Spectator* (17 June 1876): 769.

'Sinecure.' OED Online. Oxford University Press. Accessed 17 March 2018.

Stubbs, Patricia. *Women and Fiction: Feminism and the Novel, 1880–1920*. Brighton: The Harvester Press, 1979, 39–45.

Trollope, Anthony. *An Autobiography*. 1883. Ed. Michael Sadleir and Frederick Page, Oxford: Oxford University Press, 2008.

———. *The Warden*. 1855. Ed. David Skilton. Oxford: Oxford University Press, 1980.

Woolf, Virginia. *A Room of One's Own and Three Guineas*. 1929; 1938. Ed. Anna Snaith. Oxford: Oxford University Press, 2015.

CHAPTER 15

'More like a woman stuck into boy's clothes': Transcendent Femininity in Florence Marryat's *Her Father's Name*

Catherine Pope

In *Sexual Inversion*, his pioneering study of 1897, Havelock Ellis concluded that 'homosexuality is by no means less common in women than in men' (118). Yet the lesbian figure is largely absent from both fictional and historical writing of the nineteenth century. Lillian Faderman and others have acknowledged the existence of romantic female friendships in the Victorian period, but hesitate to define those relationships as sexual. Such reticence prompted some critics to conclude that lesbianism simply did not exist, leading to what Terry Castle calls the '"no-lesbians-before-1900" myth' (Castle 30): the absence of the term signifying the absence of the behaviour. This reluctance is also present in criticism on Florence Marryat (1833–1899), a prolific author whose writing repeatedly challenges prevailing ideas of nineteenth-century women's identity. For example, in a study of forty Marryat novels, Jean Gano Neisius concedes that her work

C. Pope (✉)
Independent Scholar, Brighton, UK
e-mail: me@catherinepope.com

'suggests lesbianism,' but adds that this notion 'probably would have horrified the *Victorian* Florence Marryat' (Neisius 169; emphasis added). Meanwhile, Greta Depledge detects 'lesbian undertones' in Marryat's *Her Father's Name* (1876), but concludes that they were 'not envisaged by Marryat' (Depledge xviii). This chapter uses *Her Father's Name* to challenge the implication that Victorian lesbians are accidental and anachronistic. As will be shown, Marryat employs traditional sensational tropes disguise, murder, and forgery—as a vehicle for exploring radical ideas around female sexuality. Whereas much of Marryat's fiction in the 1870s was rooted in political debates around marriage reform, *Her Father's Name* embodies a timeless, pantomimic quality. Yet, as here discussed, its provocative themes emerge from events in Marryat's own life as a recently separated woman who was interested in exploring gender boundaries. This novel, therefore, looks back to the sensation heyday of the 1860s, while also anticipating the more progressive ideas of New Woman fiction.

In *Passions Between Women* (1993), Emma Donoghue explains that lesbian activity existed well before its definition by lexicologists and sexologists, refuting the idea that women needed an appropriate vocabulary defined by men before they could express sexual desire for each other (Donoghue 2). Such female desire is not absent from Victorian fiction, but it needs to be sought in more nuanced ways. As Martha Vicinus argues, 'instead of looking for ghostly lesbians lost in a heterosexual text, we need to read the text itself for its own revelations of homoerotic desires' ('History' 577). *Her Father's Name* is replete with 'homoerotic desires.' Heroine Leona Lacoste dresses as a man, inspiring lust in both sexes, and also finds herself attracted to other women. As this chapter discusses, Marryat wrote the novel at a time when she was exploring her own sexuality, in a period when lesbian characters became more conspicuous in fiction. For Marryat, lesbian desire was a form of transcendent femininity—it allowed women to overcome the limits of their gender. As such, it was an empowering act, rather than one that ought to be ignored or suppressed. While the lesbian revelations in *Her Father's Name* are not overt, they nevertheless exist. Marryat also drew on lesbian themes in a number of her other novels and depicted male homosexuality in *Open! Sesame!* (1875).

Although the term 'lesbian' was not widely used before the twentieth century—writers preferred ambiguous terms such as 'lustful elves' (Donoghue 6)—it is used here to denote specifically sexual behaviour, providing what Vicinus calls 'boundaries to a subject that at times seems in danger of disappearing into such overbroad categories as "queer" or "nonnormative"' ('History' 567). Queer and non-normative readings abound in Marryat's novel, offering what Lillian Craton proposes as 'alternative models of femininity' (39), but the following discussion focuses on sexuality, rather than gender. Many Victorian texts invite queer readings, but Marryat's novel is distinctive in presenting a deliberate and sympathetic portrayal of lesbian desire.

This analysis begins by considering how women's sexuality was regulated in the nineteenth century, exploring in particular the diagnosis of hysteria that was used to identify and punish deviant sexuality. Using Elaine Showalter's argument that hysteria was an 'unconscious form of feminist protest' (*The Female Malady* 5), it then engages in a close reading of *Her Father's Name*, demonstrating that through the character of a male doctor the plot evinces Victorian anxieties surrounding female sexuality. The final section compares Leona Lacoste with other nineteenth-century lesbian characters in order to argue that Leona's distinctive character makes Marryat's novel a provocative and subversive text that champions transcendent femininity.

The Wandering Womb: Women's Sexuality in the Nineteenth Century

For centuries, the diagnosis of 'hysteria' was conveniently applied to any woman who exhibited transgressive behaviour, whether through sexual promiscuity or simply by expressing strong opinions. Little progress had been made from Hippocratic medicine, which believed the womb wandered around in search of moisture, thereby causing its owner to behave erratically. For a growing nineteenth-century medical profession keen to assert its authority, hysteria—a disease with no distinguishing symptoms— became a useful diagnosis both to limit women and to pathologize their sexuality. While physician Edward Tilt insisted that gynaecology was the 'accurate study of diseases of women' (Tilt vii), some practitioners were propelled by an imperfect understanding of women's bodies that was based more on ideology than on scientific progress.

American physician Nicholas Cooke is representative of many in his profession who feared that women's sexual and political emancipation posed a threat to society:

> if carried out in actual practice, this matter of 'Woman's Rights' will speedily eventuate in the most prolific sources of her wrongs. She will become rap-

idly unsexed, and degraded from her present exalted position to the level of man, without his advantages; she will cease to be the gentle mother, and become the Amazonian brawler. (Cooke 86)

When Cooke writes 'unsexed,' he is referring specifically to a woman's elimination (or liberation) from the gender binary, and not to sexlessness. Indeed, it was the sexual licentiousness of the unmarried woman that preoccupied him in *Satan in Society* (1870), a bombastic book in which he luxuriates in descriptions of female debauchery. Cooke devotes an entire chapter to female masturbation, beginning 'ALAS, that such a term is possible! O, that it were as infrequent as it is monstrous' (Cooke 100). As Diane Mason observes,

> The 'evil habit' of masturbation not only allowed women a non-reproductive outlet for their sexual impulses but could also lead to a loss of desire for 'normal' heterosexual intercourse and, possibly, to 'another aberration of love', the cultivation of 'Sapphic tastes.' (Mason 61)

A decline in marital fertility in the 1870s had prompted a debate around women's sexuality. (Mason 35), and suddenly it became a matter of national importance. Lesbianism and masturbation excluded men and were also divorced from reproduction. Worse still, women might be enjoying themselves. As Bram Dijkstra observes:

> the nineteenth-century middle-class male's *rediscovery* of feminine sexuality, as well as his discovery of the apparently fearful fact that women could actually 'awaken' sexual feelings in each other, was, to a large extent, a metaphoric expression of the late nineteenth-century male's unstated awareness that only by dividing women, by keeping them from working together, they could be kept in a state of economic and social submission. (Dijkstra 68; emphasis added)

Dijkstra's use of the word *re*discovery is significant, suggesting that feminine sexuality was well known, feared, and subject to suppression. The recognition that its expression posed a palpable threat to society provoked a conscious agenda to contain women's power. The mutable nature of hysteria meant it 'could be modified in order to diagnose all the behaviours which did not fit the prescribed model of Victorian womanhood' (Wood 12), that is, behaviours that acted against the perceived interests of the family institution. With the professionalization of doctors in the middle of the nineteenth century, female sexuality became an area of increased regulation, and this is evident throughout *Her Father's Name*. Through the character of Lucilla Evans, Marryat's novel exposes how hysteria was clearly linked with masturbation and lesbianism to pathologize sexual deviance in women. As explained below, Marryat uses the character of the family doctor to uncover the ways in which the medical profession operated to restore female patients to supposedly 'normative' sexuality. Marryat uses 'deviant' behaviours to assert women's power and to challenge the idea that their role was purely reproductive and subordinate.

AMAZONIAN BRAWLERS AND MASTURBATING HYSTERICS IN *HER FATHER'S NAME*

Her Father's Name opens in Brazil, with heroine Leona Lacoste dressed as Joan of Arc. Flanked by a toucan and a goat, she nonchalantly rolls a cigarette, pausing briefly to deflect a sex pest with her pistol. The reader is immediately alerted to the fact that Leona is no ordinary Victorian woman. In this opening scene, Marryat identifies her with both one of the most famous cross-dressers in history and herself: the author appeared dressed as the Maid of Orleans on her *carte de visite* in the 1870s. As Showalter observes, Joan of Arc was a 'border case—a figure who defied gender categories, who both transcended and represented femininity' (*Sexual Anarchy* 29). Marryat's allusion to this controversial figure is fleeting, yet it sets the keynote for the rest of the novel. Joan of Arc, also identifiable as Cooke's Amazonian Brawler, becomes an aspirational figure, rather than a terrible warning.

After her dead father is wrongly accused of murder, Leona embarks upon an international quest to clear his name. On arrival in London, she sneaks into her uncle's house, posing as a merchant by the name of Don Valera. His adopted daughter Lucilla, a hysteric who on medical advice has been confined to her couch since the onset of puberty, is overcome with lust. She is transfixed by Leona and ignores the handsome doctor her parents want her to marry. Lucilla's ailment is non-specific: 'She had no organic disease, but she had suffered from a weak spine for many years past, and it prevented her taking any active part in life. And the restraint made her fractious' (*Her Father's Name* 131). At first glance, Lucilla is a conventional Victorian invalid, but in the context of contemporary medical debates she becomes more problematic.

Isaac Baker Brown in his famous work *On the Curability of Certain Forms of Insanity, Epilepsy, Catalepsy, and Hysteria in Females* (1866) claims that patients like Lucilla display classic signs of hysteria and masturbation: 'The patient becomes restless and excited, or melancholy and retiring, listless, and indifferent to the social influences of domestic life' (14). By which he means, of course, indifferent to the social influences of men. His supposedly 'distinguishing' symptoms would also apply to all women at least some of the time. The cause was specifically sexual in nature, Brown believed: 'peripheral excitement of the branches of the pudic nerve'—or masturbation—causing a disease with eight stages, progressing from hysteria, through to mania, and ultimately death (Brown vi). Notoriously, Brown's proposed 'cure' was a clitoridectomy, performed with scissors. His model of illness explains Lucilla's subsequent erratic behaviour.

Lucilla's parents are particularly keen for her to marry Dr Tom Hastings—a 'bluff, manly fellow' (*Her Father's Name* 284)—believing that only he is capable of managing her delicate health. To them, his behaviour towards their daughter seems solicitous; for Lucilla, it is overbearing. She is repulsed by him and resists his repeated attempts to control her:

> It was strange ... that [she] should have taken a distaste (it was scarcely to be called a dislike) to the man who had really benefited her health, and was so constantly attentive to her—strange, that is to say, to anyone who did not know the secret of her heart and his. For the cause lay in the fact that Dr. Hastings was too attentive, and that his attentions bore a deeper meaning than mere interest in her as a patient. He was fond of [her], and she felt the influence without acknowledging it; and not being prepared to return his affection, it worried instead of pleasing her. (137–38)

The narrator explains that Lucilla's aversion is not specific to him: 'she would be as happy in the future with [him] as she would have been with anybody else' (323). The reason for her antipathy is revealed when the disguised Leona makes her entrance: 'Lucilla Evans raised her eyes to the stranger's countenance and withdrew them instantly, blushing deeply. There was something in the face of the newcomer that attracted her at once' (142).

Other female characters are aroused by Leona, too. Lizzie Vereker, who is described as 'a fine handsome girl of two or three and twenty, a perfect specimen of the fast young lady of the nineteenth century' (131) (or what Eliza Lynn Linton had recently termed the 'Girl of the Period' [1868]) is instantly drawn to Leona and flirts outrageously with her. When they find themselves performing together in amateur theatricals, the attraction becomes plain:

> [Lizzie] lifted up a very bright face so close to Leona's that it only seemed natural to my heroine to kiss it. The minute she had done it though, she saw by the blush that dyed her companion's cheek, how imprudent she had been, but it was impossible to explain the action away again. She must let Miss Vereker [and the reader] think what she chose. (172)

The narrator continues, 'But what was Leona bringing on herself? She feared she would have to snub Lizzie Vereker for the future' (173). Leona is frightened by her own sexuality, fearing the consequences:

> Leona had no idea she intended going so far as she did that night. Even for two women personating lovers, the action was very strong, but under the supposed circumstances of sex, it almost passed the limits of decorum. (182)

When one of the men questions their behaviour, Lizzie pertly responds: '"Oh! not half what I did when we were alone. You should have seen us together in the close carriage"' (280). Marryat cleverly leaves this scene to the reader's imagination, but it is more than suggestive while neatly avoiding censure. A reviewer for *The Athenaeum* concluded that there was 'a trifle too much promiscuous kissing ... [o]therwise, we have no fault to find with [the novel] on the score of morality' ('Novels of the Week' 760). So, homoerotic readings are clearly possible, but were easily dismissed by Victorian reviewers. Lucilla, who is in the audience for the amateur theatricals, is overcome by jealousy and has to be carried shrieking to bed, her reaction indicative of the fits Brown associated with the masturbating hysteric.

The disruption caused by the disguised Leona is noticed by Dr Hastings, who makes frequent disparaging comments about 'his' appearance, such as '"He looks more like a woman stuck into boy's clothes to me. I should like to try my biceps against his, though I believe he's taller than I am, and broader into the bargain"' (145). Hastings is apparently threatened by this person who exerts such a powerful influence over women and especially over the woman he wants for his wife. His repeated references to Leona's womanly shape make it apparent that he sees through her disguise. Realizing what is happening, he admonishes his patient:

> 'Now, Lucilla,' he said, sternly, 'I cannot have any more of this nonsense, or I shall speak to your father about it ... I know far more than you have any idea of. But I have been watching you closely for some time past, and the absurd fancies you have got into your head are no secret to me.' (183–84)

Here the man of science establishes himself as a moral arbiter, regulating gender and exposing deviance. These 'absurd fancies' are, to him, abnormal desires and must be denounced. Like Brown's hypothetical patient, Lucilla has become 'indifferent to the social influences of domestic life' and must be carefully managed.

Many characters comment on Leona's womanliness, yet all—except Dr Hastings—are prepared to collude in her artifice. They accept both her transvestism and her often reciprocated attraction to women. When Dr Hastings asks Lucilla's father to send his daughter to the country, beyond harm's reach, he refuses. Acknowledging that only the disguised Leona makes his daughter happy and calm, he encourages them to spend time together, even telling Leona that a marriage proposal would be welcome. There is no suggestion that Lucilla's parents are convinced by the unfeasibly handsome youth who suddenly appears in their lives, yet they are prepared for him to 'marry' their daughter. The narrator says of Lucilla:

> [She], who in her weakness and timidity shrunk from the generality of the sterner sex, as something too rough and loud-spoken to give her any pleasure, considered Leona Lacoste, in her male attire, to be the very perfection of all she had ever dreamed of as amiable, and gentle, and winning in a man. (189)

When Lucilla tells a servant about Leona's '"pretty little hands and feet,"' she responds: '"Dear me, miss! that seems more like the description of a young lady than a gentleman to me"' (269). Furthermore, when admonished for '"smirking at the men"' (157), that is, at Leona, another servant retorts that there are no men to smirk at: she can see through the subterfuge. Perhaps Lucilla, at least unconsciously, perceives that Leona is really a woman. Either way, her classically hysterical behaviour is explicitly linked with lesbian desire, or what Dr Hastings diagnoses as 'absurd fancies.' The implication is that Leona makes an utterly unconvincing, if extremely attractive, man. Furthermore, Marryat's 'cure' for Lucilla's hysteria is the realization of her non-normative sexual desires, not Mr Brown's scissors.

Conscious of the influence she holds over Lucilla, Leona encourages her to respond to Hastings's advances. She is frightened of the events that are unfolding and believes their marriage to be the safest outcome. Lucilla consents, desperate to agree to whatever Leona suggests. Initially relieved, Leona then has second thoughts, as Marryat writes: '[o]nly as she passed the drawing-room door on her way downstairs the smile faded from her features, and gave place to a wild look of longing that was much more like pain' (285). This solitary and easily overlooked sentence is the only hint of Leona's true feelings. Her 'wild look of longing' confirms that Lucilla's attraction is reciprocated, but Leona is either unconvinced that her artifice can be sustained or perhaps unsure what the consequences of success might be. Nevertheless, this scene shows that Leona's male persona goes beyond transvestism and expedience to encompass lesbian desire.

Any opportunity for their union is neatly avoided by a plot twist in which Lucilla is revealed to be Leona's half-sister. As Leona divests herself of the male disguise, Lucilla realizes her ideal man was a chimera and accepts her fate as the doctor's wife. Meanwhile, Leona reluctantly agrees to marry her long-suffering childhood friend, Christobal, whose identity she stole. While some might argue that this is a highly conservative plot resolution, it is important not to ignore what Lyn Pykett calls the 'complex middle' of a narrative by concentrating too much on its ending (Pykett 50). Marryat presents a *disruptive* middle, one in which she foregrounds a thinly veiled lesbian relationship and subverts, even if only temporarily, the traditional courtship plot.

'By No Means Uncommon': The Victorian Lesbian

Her Father's Name is even more disruptive when examined in the context of Victorian lesbian experience. Dismissing the novel's 'lesbian undertones,' Depledge concludes that 'Leona is simply using male dress ... to escape the restrictive role assigned to her as a woman,' characterizing the romantic trysts as 'mere interludes' (Depledge xx). The scenes between Leona and Lizzie Vereker and Lucilla's obvious sexual attraction to Leona are, however, highly significant. Although the lesbianism of these relationships is not overt, its subtextual presence would have been discernible to an enlightened reader, while remaining suitably opaque to those not expecting its presence in the pages (such as the *Athenaeum* reviewer cited above). As Donoghue writes, 'anyone wanting to know how to interpret passion between women could have had access to stories about it, even if many other readers averted their gaze' (Donoghue 15–16). Marryat effectively hides a lesbian courtship in plain sight.

Sharon Marcus, in her brilliant book *Between Women* (2007), writes that 'nineteenth-century authors openly represented relationships between women that involved friendship, desire, and marriage. It is only twentieth-century critics who made those bonds unspeakable, either by ignoring what Victorian texts transparently represented, or by projecting contemporary sexual structures onto the past' (75). Indeed, the female marriage that is almost realized in the plot of *Her Father's Name* had many precedents in mid-Victorian life and fiction. Celebrity lesbians such as Frances Power Cobbe, Emily Faithfull, and Rosa Bonheur lived openly in same-sex relationships that were largely accepted by the circles in which they moved. Writing to her sister in 1852, Elizabeth Barrett Browning relates a meeting with the actress Charlotte Cushman and the author Matilda Hays, whom she describes as living together in a female marriage. Although Browning was surprised by this unconventional relationship, her urbane friend Mrs Cochrane assured her that such unions were '"by no means uncommon"' (qtd. in Marcus 202). As Marcus points out, in the 1860s and 1870s, before the rise of the sexologists and the idea of inversion, the female couple was often accepted as a variation on legal marriage, and not necessarily a threat to its stability (Marcus 203). Even supposed beacons of moral conservatism, such as William Gladstone, Samuel Smiles, and Anthony Trollope, counted lesbians among their friends (Marcus 51). In *Her Father's Name*, this permissiveness is represented by Lucilla's parents urging Leona to propose marriage, along with the tacit acceptance of the women's relationship by other characters. Dr Hastings's lone attempt to enforce normative behaviour is textually resisted.

Marryat's positive portrayal of lesbianism is a marked departure from earlier eighteenth- and nineteenth-literary representations, which were usually dominated by the giant phallic clitorises of pornography, or the fairy-tale monsters of didactic fiction. In Maria Edgeworth's short story 'Angelina; or, L'Amie Inconnue' (1801), for example, sixteen-year-old Anne Warwick elopes from her guardian's home to live in the Welsh cottage of Araminta Hodges, an author with whom she has conducted a passionate epistolary romance. When they finally meet, Anne discovers that the woman of her dreams is a masculine creature who reeks of brandy. In *Belinda*, her novel of the same year, Edgeworth presents Harriot Freke, an eccentric character who enjoys capering about in men's clothing and who is tormented by unrequited love for another woman. Edgeworth's lack of subtlety is emphasized when- Harriot startles Lady Delacour (the object of her affections) by springing into her carriage under the cover of darkness and crying '"Who am I? only a Freke!"' (*Belinda* 43). Lady Delacour's fear of sexual assault contrasts with the carriage encounter between Leona and Lizzie Vereker—one that, according to the latter, is both consensual and consummated.

The salutary figure of the freakish lesbian persists throughout the nineteenth century, increasing in popularity as the lesbian became a more visible figure. Deborah T. Meem has argued cogently that Eliza Lynn Linton in particular chronicled the 'growing lesbian presence in England during the last third of the nineteenth century' ('Eliza Lynn Linton' 538), most definitively in *Sowing the Wind* (1867), *The Rebel of the Family* (1880), and *The New Woman in Haste and at Leisure* (1895). As Meem observes, there is a clear distinction between Jane Osborn—a male-identified, yet sympathetically drawn hero(ine)—in Linton's 1867 novel, and the threatening figures of Bell Blount and Phoebe Barrington, in the 1880s and 1890s texts respectively (Meem 544). Linton expresses sympathy for the woman who experiences what would now be termed gender dysphoria, but only censure for female characters who are attracted to their own sex without also craving exclusively masculine identities.

Donoghue asks: '[i]f a woman wanted a woman, was she no longer a woman herself? Did her desire turn her into a man, stem from or cause the growth of a phallic member, require a phallic dildo or lead to cross-dressing?' (Donoghue 25). For Linton, the answer was 'yes.' In her novel *The Autobiography of Christopher Kirkland* (1885), a work described by Meem and Kate Holterhoff as an 'autobiography in drag' (7), Linton recalls her relationships with other women, but under the identity of a male alter ego. In the same text, she writes of celebrity lesbian Charlotte Cushman that 'things cling about her name which it is well not to disturb' (*Autobiography* 142). Although Cushman was initially a member of Linton's inner circle, she was shunned once she became notorious for her sexuality and willingness to play male roles such as Romeo on the stage (Merrill 154).

Linton accepts women who fully embrace masculinity, but condemns those who merely appropriate *elements* of it. Conversely, Marryat suggests that gender is fluid, and women can choose to be male or female—a more provocative idea than Linton's. For Linton, a person had to be one or other gender; Marryat understood how to be both. Whereas in Linton's novels masculine women such as Bell Blount are feared and derided as vectors of lesbian contagion, Marryat's Leona is portrayed as an entirely sympathetic—even aspirational—character. The authorial voice, always dominant in Marryat's novels, is never censorious of Leona's actions. Through her, Marryat allows women a greater range of sexual expression, presenting lesbianism as an alternative, rather than a threat, to heterosexual marriage. For her, it is not an ugly subversion of the feminine ideal: Leona is intelligent, resourceful, and irresistible.

As Donoghue argues, the agenda behind authors presenting lesbians as hermaphrodites (or, at least, not entirely female) was to 'frighten women into heterosexual passivity. By cutting off lesbians from their own femaleness, writers could reduce them to exceptional (and therefore harmless) freaks of nature' (Donoghue 28). These negative portrayals dissuade the female reader from identifying with them, instead pathologizing deviance and reinforcing ideas of normative sexuality. For Linton, figures like Cushman were a terrible warning; for Marryat they suggested exciting possibilities.

As Lisa Merrill explains, '[Cushman's] male personifications pointed out to her audiences how provisional any performance of gender could be and how it was possible to uncouple gender and biological sex, masculinity and male bodies' (Merrill 263). Both Cushman and Leona transcend femininity to create their own selves. Cushman died in January 1876 and *Her Father's Name* began serialization two months later. Given that Cushman toured extensively in the years leading up to her death, it is certainly plausible that Marryat saw her on the stage, and that this novel is a homage to the unconventional, yet widely accepted, Cushman. Indeed, Marryat's father (the novelist and mariner Captain Marryat) met Cushman in 1837 and wrote approvingly of her '"determination to remain single and not to be the slave of one when she could reign despotic over thousands"' (qtd. in Merrill 38). Along with Joan of Arc, Cushman could have been a figure who for Florence Marryat symbolized transcendent femininity. Like Cushman, Leona ultimately enjoys a successful career playing male leads on the New York stage; even a cursory perusal of Cushman's biography suggests they were similarly attractive to women.

Marryat herself could be described as sexually adventurous, too. Some of her spiritualist writings reveal that she used the séance room as a means of exploring sexuality. In one account, a spirit guide encourages her to explore the naked form of the female medium; in another, she shares a bed with a woman whose hands are tied and finds herself menaced by a phantom hand (Marryat, *There Is No Death* 68–69). Marryat was writing *Her Father's Name* in the 1870s when she first started attending séances, and the impact of her experiences is clear—not least in the name of a spirit who visits her: Charlotte Cushman. (Marryat, *There Is No Death* 241)

Conclusion

Seen in the context of known nineteenth-century lesbians such as Charlotte Cushman, Leona Lacoste's behaviour is unmistakably homoerotic. Vicinus rightly cautions against researchers who 'ransack the past to find women who fulfil current expectations' (Vicinus, 'Sexuality and Power' 147), but Marryat actually exceeds these expectations, which is exactly why Leona proves slippery. Marryat's heroine does not fit the nineteenth-century lesbian stereotype, and if she is sought on those terms, she will not be found. She resists the specifically lesbian identity of either century. Marryat emphasizes Leona's femaleness throughout. She is emphatically neither an 'invert' (the late-nineteenth-century term for one attracted to their own sex) nor a mannish woman, nor an ingénue—the three most prominent lesbian stereotypes in nineteenth-century fiction. Leona is simply a woman who is attractive to and *attracted* by other women. She is not limited by a particular identity, nor is she defined by her behaviour. Leona is whatever she chooses to be at the time—a very modern idea, even now. For this reason, she escaped detection by many Victorian readers and has eluded some twentieth- and twenty-first-century scholars, too.

As Vicinus urges, 'we need to be sensitive to nuance, masks, secrecy, and the unspoken' ('They Wonder to Which Sex I Belong' 469–70). There is never going to be incontrovertible evidence of lesbian sex. Outside such sources as the pornographic publications of Holywell Street, we are unlikely to find scenes of clitoral stimulation in a Victorian novel, so other ways of interpreting lesbian desire are needed. Leona's protean nature allows Marryat to explore radical ideas in what is—at least on the surface—a pantomimic text. It is, however, a text that yields deeply subversive readings.

In Leona, Marryat presents a heroine who comprehensively challenges dominant notions of Victorian women's sexuality. Marryat both exposes the regulatory agenda of the medical profession and confronts the idea that a woman's role was purely reproductive. What society denounces as deviant and hysterical, Marryat celebrates as transcendent femininity.

Although Marryat conforms to convention by marrying her heroine to a man at the novel's conclusion, their marriage will be anything but conventional. Indeed, it is very obvious who will be wearing the trousers.

WORKS CITED

Brown, [Isaac] Baker. *On the Curability of Certain Forms of Insanity, Epilepsy, Catalepsy, and Hysteria in Females*. London: Robert Hardwicke, 1866.
Castle, Terry. *The Apparitional Lesbian: Female Homosexuality and Modern Culture*. New York: Columbia University Press, 1995.
Cooke, Nicholas Francis. *Satan in Society*. 1870. Chicago: C. F. Vent, 1890.
Depledge, Greta. Introduction. *Her Father's Name*. 1876. By Florence Marryat. Ed. Greta Depledge. Brighton: Victorian Secrets, 2009. i–xxvii.
Dijkstra, Bram. *Idols of Perversity: Fantasies of Feminine Evil in Fin-De-Siècle Culture*. New York: Oxford University Press, 1986.
Donoghue, Emma. *Passions Between Women: British Lesbian Culture, 1668–1801*. London: Scarlet Press, 1993.
Edgeworth, Maria. 'Angelina; or, L'Amie Inconnue.' *Moral Tales for Young People*. London: J. Johnson, 1801.
———. *Belinda*. 1801. New York: Macmillan & Co., 1896.
Ellis, Havelock. *Sexual Inversion*. 1897. 2nd ed. Studies in the Psychology of Sex. Vol. 2. Philadelphia: F. A. Davis, 1908.
Faderman, Lillian. *Surpassing the Love of Men: Romantic Friendship and Love between Women from the Renaissance to the Present*. 1981. London: The Women's Press, 1985.
Hartley, Lucy, ed. 'Introduction: the "Business" of Writing Women.' *The History of British Women's Writing, 1830–1880*. Volume 6. Basingstoke: Palgrave, 2018. 1–20.
Linton, Eliza Lynn. *The Autobiography of Christopher Kirkland*. 1885. Ed. Deborah T. Meem and Kate Holterhoff. Brighton: Victorian Secrets, 2011.
Marcus, Sharon. *Between Women: Friendship, Desire, and Marriage in Victorian England*. Princeton: Princeton University Press, 2007.
Marryat, Florence. *Her Father's Name*. 1876. Ed. Greta Depledge. Brighton: Victorian Secrets, 2009.
———. *There Is No Death*. New York: National Book Company, 1891.
Mason, Diane Elizabeth. *The Secret Vice: Masturbation in Victorian Fiction and Medical Culture*. Manchester: Manchester University Press, 2008.
Meem, Deborah T. 'Eliza Lynn Linton and the Rise of Lesbian Consciousness.' *Journal of the History of Sexuality* 7.4 (1997): 537–560.

Meem, Deborah T., and Kate Holterhoff. Introduction. *The Autobiography of Christopher Kirkland*. 1885. By Eliza Lynn Linton. Ed. Deborah T. Meem and Kate Holterhoff. Brighton: Victorian Secrets, 2011.5–17.
Merrill, Lisa. *When Romeo Was a Woman: Charlotte Cushman and Her Circle of Female Spectators*. Ann Arbor: University of Michigan Press, 1999.
Neisius, Jean Gano. 'Acting the Role of Romance: Text and Subtext in the Work of Florence Marryat.' PhD dissertation. Texas Christian University, 1992.
'Novels of the Week'. *The Athenaeum* (9 Dec. 1876): 759–80.
Pykett, Lyn. *The 'Improper' Feminine: The Women's Sensation Novel and the New Woman Writing*. London: Routledge, 1992.
Showalter, Elaine. *Sexual Anarchy: Gender and Culture at the Fin de Siècle*. London: Virago Press, 1992.
———. *The Female Malady: Women, Madness and English Culture 1830–1980*. London: Virago, 1987.
Tilt, Edward John. *The Change of Life in Health and Disease: A Practical Treatise on the Nervous and Other Affections Incidental to Women at the Decline of Life*. Philadelphia: Lindsay & Blakiston, 1882.
Vicinus, Martha. 'Sexuality and Power: A Review of Current Work in the History of Sexuality.' *Feminist Studies* 8.1 (1982): 133–56.
———. 'The History of Lesbian History.' *Feminist Studies* 38.3 (2012): 566–96.
———. '"They Wonder to Which Sex I Belong": The Historical Roots of the Modern Lesbian Identity.' *Feminist Studies* 18.3 (1992): 467–97.
Wood, Jane. *Passion and Pathology in Victorian Fiction*. Oxford: Oxford University Press, 2001.

CHAPTER 16

'I am writing the life of a horse': Anna Sewell's *Black Beauty* in the 1870s

Adrienne E. Gavin

Unlike most novels by Victorian women writers, *Black Beauty* has endured since publication largely unbuffeted by the winds of literary and critical fashion. London booksellers inauspiciously bought only 100 copies of Sewell's novel when it was published by Jarrold and Sons near the end of 1877, but within its first year *Black Beauty* sold over 12,000 copies (Lansbury 64), by 1888 it was in its 23rd edition, and 90,000 copies had been sold in Britain by 1890. In the same year, it was pirated in America for humane purposes, and with the tag line 'The "Uncle Tom's Cabin" of the Horse,' by animal-welfare activist George Thorndike Angell whose organization, the American Humane Education Society, alone distributed between 2 and 3 million free copies of the book between 1890 and 1910 (Dent 546). In 1923 critic Vincent Starrett claimed, 'since the invention of printing, than *Black Beauty* only the Bible has found a wider distribution' (205). Jarrolds in 1924 termed it the 'sixth best seller of any books

---

A. E. Gavin (✉)
Department of English and Language Studies, Canterbury Christ Church University, Canterbury, UK

The University of Auckland, Auckland, New Zealand
e-mail: adrienne.gavin@cantab.net

© The Author(s) 2020
A. E. Gavin, C. W. de la L. Oulton (eds.), *British Women's Writing from Brontë to Bloomsbury, Volume 2*, British Women's Writing from Brontë to Bloomsbury, 1840–1940,
https://doi.org/10.1007/978-3-030-38528-6_16

in the world' (*The House of Jarrolds* 25), and by 1927 when the copyright expired had themselves published it in over 150 editions. In 1935 worldwide sales were calculated to be 20 million (Margaret Sewell 1), rising in 1995 to an estimated 40 million compared to 50 million for Charles Dickens's entire works (Dalby 14). Some of these statistics are hard to verify, but what is indubitable is that *Black Beauty* is both a bestseller and an acknowledged classic, a novel which endures because of the extraordinary, empathy-induced emotional link it has always had with readers.

This chapter, however, is concerned not with *Black Beauty*'s enduring nature but with its creation and publication in the specific context of the 1870s. By the early 1870s there was a social and cultural sense that Britain had (or should have) a clear handle on what it meant to be Victorian, but also that the twentieth century was glinting up ahead; not close enough to create anxiety or excite extremes, but near enough to stimulate a subtle awareness that it would, within envisagable time, be judging its predecessors. A generation or so equidistant from the beginning and (what would be) the end of the Victorian period, the 1870s were marked by an underrunning sense that, instead of simply following current paths, it was also time to take stock of the moral and ethical here and now of being, both nationally and individually. Certainly such reflection, or urging of reflection, is evident in women's writing of the decade, perhaps most notably in *Black Beauty* (1877), a novel which in its seeming simplicity—the life story of a black horse told in simple language and short chapters—offered an emotionally powerful, affective and effective, challenge to its readers.

Black Beauty's autobiography recounts his pleasant foalhood, his breaking in, and the adventures and hardships of his working life from his position as a beautiful and valuable gentleman's carriage horse to his collapse from overloading as a cab horse. Repeatedly changing owners as he falls lower and lower down the equine social scale, he is sold for less and less and does increasingly hard work, experiencing varieties of neglect and misuse until, unlike many horses of the 1870s, he finds a final happy home. He also reveals the lives of other horses including his companions: tragic chestnut mare Ginger who has been badly treated since youth, plucky grey pony Merrylegs, and war horse Captain who served at the Charge of the Light Brigade.

In writing her only novel Sewell expressed the experiences and beliefs of her life, but as the following discussion argues, she also broke literary gender barriers, wrote with acute topicality on equine concerns, and, perhaps surprisingly, drew on the sensual techniques of the sensation fiction that prevailed in the previous decade—to starkly realist and didactic ends—in creating the powerful empathetic bond readers have with her equine protagonist. '"I am writing the life of a horse,"' Sewell recorded on 6 November 1871 (qtd. in Bayly 271), but what she produced was more than the life of a horse in the sense of equine autobiography. She also powerfully reminded readers that horses *had* lives and were not machines; they were living beings worthy of kindness and care. That Black Beauty's account of his life is so powerfully moving makes readers not only see but also feel what the life of a Victorian working horse must have been like.

Possibly partially motivated by knowing that she was terminally ill, and at around the same time having to give away her own pony, Sewell started writing *Black Beauty* in 1871. On 1 March that year, just weeks before her fifty-first birthday, she wrote in her journal '"I have not been well. Dr. R. thinks it is a troublesome case"' (qtd. in Bayly 228-29). She was probably suffering from tuberculosis and 'Chronic Hepatitis,' which would be listed as her official cause of death, combined with exacerbation of her longstanding lameness and Systemic Lupus Erythematosus (SLE), a severe form of lupus, which it has been suggested had caused her invalidism since her teens (Gavin, *Dark Horse* 72). Given eighteen months to live, she survived for seven years, but was housebound and largely confined to her sofa or bed. *Black Beauty* took six of the central years of the 1870s to complete, including lengthy interruptions due to illness. Sewell began her story in 1871 by dictating portions of the novel to her mother, the poet Mary Sewell. A temporary rally in her health in the winter of 1876-1877 allowed her to complete the novel by writing sections of it in pencil on pieces of paper, which her mother then transcribed. '"I have for six years been confined to the house and to my sofa,"' she recorded, '"and have from time to time, as I was able, been writing what I think will turn out a little book, its special aim being to induce kindness, sympathy, and an understanding treatment of horses"' (qtd. in Bayly 272).

Completed in 1877, the novel was published in time for Christmas that year as *Black Beauty: His Grooms and Companions. The Autobiography of a Horse.* 'Translated from the Original Equine, by Anna Sewell.' *Black Beauty* was the culmination of Sewell's life's work, and she died on 25 April 1878, just five months after its publication. A highly religious, middle-class woman, she had spent her life, as her health allowed, working closely with her mother in a range of charitable projects to improve working-class lives ranging from training girls as servants in their own home, teaching children in Sunday and day schools, setting up and teaching at an evening institute for working men, and establishing mothers' meetings, a library, and temperance groups. Raised in a strong Quaker tradition Sewell in adulthood dabbled in, without joining, a range of Protestant denominations. Her views, however, remained fundamentally Quaker in their emphasis on equality, plainness in all things (dress, word, and deed), the importance of active charity, and in actively preventing and interceding in the face of any type of cruelty, whether to humans or animals. The words of a 'real gentleman' in *Black Beauty* express one of her fundamental beliefs: "'[m]y doctrine is this, that if we see cruelty or wrong that we have the power to stop, and do nothing, we make ourselves sharers in the guilt'" (127). Sewell acted on her principles without hesitation, as her niece recalled:

> The sight of cruelty to animals or to the helpless, or even thoughtlessness and indifference to suffering, roused her indignation almost to fury, and wherever she was, or whoever she had to face, she would stop and scathe the culprit with burning words. (Margaret Sewell 3)

Black Beauty is similarly 'unflinching fiction,' which is 'unafraid to reveal pain, brutality, suffering, and death in making its protests against cruelty' in clear and unqualified terms (Gavin, "'I saw'" 114).

The novel's first readers praised both its denunciation of cruelty and its call to action. "'You have so filled my mind with the thought of what these poor animals suffer from the bearing-rein,'" an early female reader told Sewell in December 1877, "'that I feel quite breathless as I look at some of them, and only my sex, and fear of the police, prevent my cutting the leathers and setting them free'" (Unknown to Anna Sewell, 24 December 1877, qtd. in Bayly 275). This recitation of gender as a restriction on what a woman might do in relation to horses, direct action, or in public reflects 1870s views on feminine behaviour, but *Black Beauty* countermanded these assumptions by breaching gender, class, and readership assumptions about equine writing. Taking as its subject the ostensibly male, public environment of working horses and equine-reliant transport systems, *Black Beauty* broke expectations about the subjects on which women should write. Female authors had, of course, previously written against animal cruelty, especially in literature for children. Animal autobiographies, too, were not new, having been popular in the late eighteenth and early nineteenth centuries. Sewell's detailed and accurate focus on the working life of horses was, however, novel in women's authorship of the time.

Indeed, in the 1870s literary works devoted to horses were rare, aside from hunting reminiscences, and generally in the nineteenth century equine books were written by *male* authors for *male* readers of the horse-owning classes (Grimshaw xix–xx). By contrast, *Black Beauty* was written by a female author for those who worked directly with horses—coachmen, grooms, cab drivers, ostlers, and stable hands—and was read by men, women, and children of all classes. *Black Beauty* not only had a wide audience but also in readily accessible book form provided a range of practical knowledge about horse care, something which was very useful in the 1870s when workers' knowledge of horses was largely acquired through hands-on practice or passed down orally (Grimshaw 40). *Black Beauty* was for this reason widely taken up by humane charity groups who gave copies of it away to cab drivers and other equine workers. In class terms, too, the novel protested against that stalwart of Victorian equine writing: hunting, and focused instead on 'lesser' equine roles like cab-work, coal-heaving, and carting, and foregrounded horses' suffering, which standard 1870s horse writing marginalized.

As Anne Grimshaw states, in the Victorian period, the 'female writer on horses was [a] rarity,' and it was not until the post-World War I period, that 'women more widely became readers and writers of horse books' (Grimshaw xix, xxi). Sewell's trenchant inroad into the male world of equine writing opened new subject areas to women writers, and her breach of gender expectations was commented upon by contemporary reviewers who admired the novel but judged Sewell's detailed equine knowledge 'unfeminine.' 'The author displays no small amount of knowledge of equine nature,' a reviewer commented, 'and she has evidently given more attention to the subject than ladies usually bestow' (Review, *Eastern Daily Press* 3). One of her cousins told Sewell that *Black Beauty* was '"so unladylike that but for 'Anna Sewell' on the title-page, and a certain gentle kindliness all through the story, no one, I think, would believe it to be written by a lady. Where you have obtained your stable-mindedness I can't imagine, but that you fully understand your business is a *fact*"' (Unnamed cousin to Anna Sewell, c. December 1877, qtd. in Bayly 274). Another correspondent commented '"I cannot think how you could ever write such an Equestrian story. One would think you had been a horse-dealer, or a groom, or a jockey all your life"' (Unnamed to Anna Sewell, 24 December 1877, qtd. in Bayly 275). '"It is written by a veterinary surgeon ... by a coachman, by a groom"' anti-bearing-rein campaigner Edward Fordham Flower exclaimed, '"there is not a mistake in the whole of it. ... How could a lady know so much about horses!'" (Mrs Toynbee to Mary Sewell, 29 January 1878, qtd. in Bayly 276–77). Although many Victorian women rode horses and it was regarded as healthy exercise, too great a knowledge of, or passion for, horses was seen as 'masculine' and might also have scandalous connotations. The perceived impropriety of being a 'horsey woman' had been heightened in the 1860s by popular fascination with Catherine Walters, also known as 'Skittles,' a courtesan, fashion setter, and skilled horsewoman who people regularly flocked to see ride in Hyde Park. Journalists had also linked Walters with Edwin Landseer's 1861 painting 'The Taming of the Shrew,' which depicts a dark-haired woman reclining against a beautiful black horse, dubbing the painting 'The Pretty Horsebreaker,' a term which swiftly became a euphemism for prostitution. The horsiness of the eponymous heroine of Mary Braddon's *Aurora Floyd* (1862–1863) was similarly seen as risqué and 'fast,' and publication of several popular fictional biographies of Skittles in the 1860s heightened moral concerns over horsey women. Indeed, Margaret Oliphant in her 1867 review 'Novels' stated plainly that *'horsey'* was 'akin to immoral' (272). With *Black Beauty*, however, Sewell was writing *as* a horse rather than about female characters in relation to horses so although her equine expertise in itself was seen as unusually masculine there is no evidence that it was judged immoral, especially as hers was such an overtly moral book.

Sewell certainly had extensive equine knowledge. Very dependent on horse transport due to her lameness, she was an excellent rider and driver of horses. Horses had also offered her freedom and companionship in a life which was restricted by her health, her unmarried state, and having to move with her parents every few years as her father's jobs dictated. On one level in writing *Black Beauty* she surely aimed to improve the lives of horses in gratitude for the ways in which they had improved hers.

Sewell claimed horse writing for women *authors*, but her novel also has particular resonance for female *readers*. One of its earliest readers told Sewell "'It has made me cry more than twice or thrice. Poor Ginger! Then the fall on Ludgate Hill!"' (Unnamed to Anna Sewell, 18 January 1878, qtd. in Bayly, 275), and women's reactions to the novel have often been of deep and ineffable sadness.[1] As Kathryn Miele observes in her examination of non-fictional Victorian accounts of working horses, '[i]t was not necessarily easy to see (or to touch, or to feel) the sufferings of the working horse in Victorian London. ... The experience of the horse was both persistently visible and invisible (especially as pain is invisible): seen and felt, and yet ultimately inaccessible' (138). *Black Beauty* attempts to make that experience accessible and, as scholarship on the novel has argued, Black Beauty's narrative can also be read as expressing other unheard and disempowered voices of the period: those of children, slaves, the working class, servants and, especially, women. Although early reviewers saw the novel's subject matter as masculine, and despite Black Beauty being the male narrator of an ostensibly male equine *Bildungsroman*, the novel can be read as voicing female experience and protest. Indeed Ruth Padel terms it 'almost ... one of the great feminist texts' (48). Much of what it condemns are behaviours and beliefs valorized within the male public sphere: war, hunting, drinking, party politics, and capitalism that seeks profit without regard to the wellbeing of the means of production—in this case horses. Apart from the Lady of Earlshall Park insisting that the fashionable but cruel bearing reins be tightened on Black Beauty and Ginger, cruelty to horses in the novel tends to come from boys and men.

More particularly, the novel's equine characters can be read as echoing the position of middle-class Victorian women like Sewell. Nineteenth-century conduct manuals for women and training manuals for horses, for example, promoted the same qualities as ideal: ready obedience to a master, good temperament, compliant nature, and sound character free from vice or displays of passion (Gavin, Introduction xxii). As Padel and Coral Lansbury discuss, Victorian pornography, too, often used horse breaking and training imagery in its depictions of women. Lacking the legal rights to full self-integrity, both bodily and economically, horses and women were potential victims of legal brutality, subject effectively to forced breeding, and being judged by physical appearance. Black Beauty's value in the horse market declines rapidly when his broken knees damage his appearance, just as a woman's prospects in the Victorian marriage market reduced when she aged or lost her looks. Bits, bridles, and bearing reins like women's dress and corsetry restricted movement and caused pain and physical damage in the interests of fashion—the following of which the novel condemns. The powerlessness Black Beauty experiences, the silencing, the restraints and checks upon his behaviour, his lack of freedom, and the fact that, as he says, 'I could not complain, nor make known my wants' (97), reflect, too, the cultural infantilization to which Victorian women were subject, particularly unmarried, economically dependent, and disabled women like Sewell.

Although some feminist theorists reject the link between women and animals, it is clear that connections and parallels can be drawn. Examining animals in women's fiction Marian Scholtmeijer notes:

> [i]n their work on animals ... women writers perform that most antiandrocentric of acts: thinking themselves into the being of the wholly "other," the animal. It turns out that this is not an act of self-sacrifice but of empowerment. ... Women writers use fiction to concretize, affirm, and empower the state of being "other," which dominant ideology objectifies as a site of weakness, but which finds living expression in nonhuman animals. (233)

Writing autobiographically as horse, Sewell pushes that identification even further. She translates from Equine, a language not understood by the implied reader but understood by the implied author. Her translation reveals a hidden voice, simultaneously Black Beauty's and her own. Safely distanced as *translator* of a *male, horse's*, narrative, she translates her own life into fiction, the more acutely as she knew she was dying. She might be read as an amalgam of Black Beauty: the obedient, dutiful, narrator who suffers hardship without complaint, and Ginger: the brutally treated mare who when provoked too far, bites and snaps and kicks out against injustice.

Sewell broke gender expectations in writing so intensively about horses, but her topic was also timely. The 1870s was the period of New Imperialism, the world map was increasingly marked by pink, and Victoria was proclaimed Empress of India on 1 January 1877. Transport systems and consumer culture were rapidly expanding. It was a decade, too, of industrial innovations. Thomas Edison in America invented the phonograph in 1877 and the light bulb in 1879, and Alexander Graham Bell in Britain invented the telephone in 1876. Communications were expanding, and, as in technology, in women's writing it was a good time to make your voice heard as the decade was growth orientated and receptive to some kinds of change. The year 1870 saw the passing of the first Married Woman's Property Act and the Elementary Education Act which made education available for all children aged between five and thirteen. The 1880 Elementary Education Act would make it compulsory for children up to ten. The Education Acts meant that *Black Beauty* was well positioned to be taken up as a school reader, and school editions of it were published within months of its initial appearance.

Sewell wrote *Black Beauty* primarily for those who worked with horses whose literacy skills might not be advanced, and the novel's clear language and short-chaptered episodic structure meant that it immediately attracted dual adult-child readerships. *Black Beauty* shares concerns, too, with children's literature of the period, in its *explicit* attention to ill-treated working animals and its *implicit* concern with disability. Working and talking horses feature in more minor ways in both Jean Ingelow's *Mopsa the Fairy* (1869) and George MacDonald's *At the Back of the North Wind* (1868–1870), and in 1872 Ouida (Marie Louise de la Ramée) published her novel about a boy and a maltreated dog *A Dog of Flanders* (1872). Charlotte Elizabeth [Tonna]'s *Kindness to Animals* was also reprinted in 1877.

While *Black Beauty* is not overtly about disability, it is striking how often legs come into the novel as a site for damage or comment, echoing Sewell's own disability. Like Martineau's *Autobiography* (posthumously published in 1877 although written in 1855), *Black Beauty* was written by a woman whose disability began in adolescence and a connection between disability and adolescence, particularly female adolescence, is also evident in the decade's literature for or about children including American Susan Coolidge's *What Katy Did* (1872), Charlotte Yonge's *Pillars of the House* (1873), and Dinah Maria Mulock Craik's, *The Little Lame Prince* (1875). Comparisons in other ways can also be made with another enduring children's classic produced in this period, the American Louisa May Alcott's *Little Women* (1868, 1869), centrally in the tragic deaths of Beth in *Little Women* and Ginger in *Black Beauty*.

Wider cultural interest in re-considering animals was also evident in Charles Darwin's *The Expression of the Emotions in Man and Animals* (1872) and Eadweard Muybridge's innovative use of stop-motion photography to capture horse locomotion in 1877, the images published as *The Horse in Motion* in 1878. Following the first dog show in 1859 the popularity of dog shows, too, had risen across the 1860s, and in 1873 The Kennel Club, the first kennel club in the world, was founded in London. Notably, Sewell in *Black Beauty* protests against the docking of dogs' tails and the cropping of their ears.

Centrally of course *Black Beauty* is about horses. Whether ridden, driven, owned, or hired, horses were an essential part of the aural, visual, and olfactory daily life of Victorian cities and countryside. They were central to Britain's industrialization and wealth. Railway expansion in the 1840s had ended the coaching age, but unexpectedly the need for, and numbers of, horses increased rather than decreased over ensuing decades. In London alone there were over 70,000 horses in the mid-1860s (Turvey 57). As Ulrich Raulff notes, the 'nineteenth century ratcheted up the use and consumption of horses to a historically unprecedented level' (Raulff 41). Horses were central to commerce, industry, agriculture, and employment and as well as providing transport, also serviced other transport systems including rail, canal, and shipping. Central to personal and national income generation, horses were used in carriage, carting, omnibus, and cab transport, and for coal-heaving, shop and mail deliveries, state occasions, 'dust' removal, emergency services, the military, weddings, and funerals.

Horses were particularly topical in the 1870s when Sewell was writing *Black Beauty* as Britain's demand for horsepower was at its height. Samuel Sidney in *The Book of the Horse* (1874) states that the price of horses doubled between 1863 and 1873 (Sidney 189–90), and prices rose 'to 160 per cent of [their] 1870 level by 1876' (Turvey 55). As Ralph Turvey notes, '[e]ven dead horses rose in price during the 1870s' (Turvey 54). A House of Lords Select Committee on Horses in 1873 found that there were 'no fewer' horses than previously, but there was a scarcity because mares were being exported, there was heightened demand from increased population and wealth, farmers preferred profits from breeding sheep and cattle rather than horses, and there were more minor causes such as export of horses for the Franco-Prussian war (1870–1871), and smallholdings being consolidated into large farms (Turvey 55). In the 1870s there was also stronger demand for horses for omnibuses, trams, and rail carrying and as a result of the strong growth in building construction (Turvey 56).

Increased equine purchase and hire prices led to more pervasive infliction, or overlooking, of cruelty to horses by those wanting or needing to get their money's worth and the cruelties described in *Black Beauty* were commonly seen: flogging, whipping, underfeeding, overloading, poor stabling, exhaustive riding, damaging driving, working injured horses, excessive hours, the 'using up' of horses literally on their last legs, and injured or exhausted horses collapsing on the street. 'At the same time, there was dramatic growth in steam power for work formerly done by horses, not only railway haulage but agricultural machinery, leading to increased risks to horses from people grown accustomed to steam-engine outputs' (Gavin, '"I saw"' 104). Black Beauty himself experiences the 'steam-engine style of driving' which he states 'wears us up faster than any other kind' by 'drivers [who] ... generally travelled by rail,' and 'think that a horse was something like a steam-engine, only smaller' (92). The ubiquity of horses in the 1870s obscured their real situation, something Sewell sought to change. Like much antivivisectionist agitation of the 1870s, which led to the passing of the Cruelty to Animals Act, 1876—which related to experimentation on animals—*Black Beauty* repeatedly emphasizes horses' sentience. It also reminds readers that horses are not machines. 'Like machines, however, they were valuable commodities, depreciating assets with a time-linked value and income-generating capacity, worth more the younger, fitter, and more aesthetically pleasing they were' (Gavin, '"I saw"' 104). And like Black Beauty horses commonly fell down the ranks from carriage horse, to cab horse, to job horse, to cart horse, to collapse from overwork, to being flayed and butchered at the knackers' yards which in London operated twenty-four hours a day.

For Black Beauty, as for many Victorian horses, working as a London cab horse inflicts the most harm. Two of the novel's most dramatic scenes also occur when Black Beauty is a London cab horse: his own collapse from overloading on Ludgate hill, and the death of Ginger. Soon after Black Beauty by chance in London re-meets the once glorious, feisty Ginger, who is now a starved, exhausted, suffering animal who is being 'used up' in jobbing cab work and longs to die, he sees what he thinks is her body being carted away:

> The head hung out of the cart-tail, the lifeless tongue was slowly dropping with blood; and the sunken eyes! but I can't speak of them, the sight was too dreadful. It was a chestnut horse with a long, thin neck. I saw a white streak down the forehead. I believe it was Ginger; I hoped it was, for then her troubles would be over. Oh! if men were more merciful, they would shoot us before we came to such misery. (132)

Black Beauty believes it is Ginger's body, but this is never confirmed. 'The anonymity of the dead chestnut points to the unindividuated status of the horses who were, on London streets, to borrow Charles Dickens's rhetorical phrase on the death of street child Jo in *Bleak House*, "dying thus around us every day"' (Gavin, Introduction, xxiii–xxiv).

Cities like London halved horses' lives (Gordon 13), and cab horses' conditions were so hard that they lasted on average only two years (Mitchell 375). 'I saw a great deal of trouble amongst the horses in London,' Black Beauty states, 'and much of it that might have been prevented by a little common sense' (133). Sewell accurately renders the financial, temporal, and physical pressures of cab life on both cab horses and their drivers. In 1864 it had been estimated 'that probably fifty thousand people were directly dependent on the cab for their livelihood' (May vi), and there were over 10,000 licensed cab drivers in London in the 1870s (May 97). Unlike omnibus, railway, and delivery companies which frequently owned stables of horses,[2] cab drivers often hired from job masters who rented horses by the season, week, day, or hour. Sewell's depictions of the wide variety of horse-drawn vehicles in the capital also reflected 1870s concerns about traffic congestion and corroborate Gustave Doré's illustrations in *London: A Pilgrimage* (1872). Black Beauty, for example, is trapped in a traffic jam at 'the bottom of Cheapside' (115), which in 1879 was described as 'the busiest thoroughfare in the world, with the sole exception perhaps of London Bridge' (Dickens), which Black Beauty also often crosses, once reporting that he has 'for a wonder had a good clear time on London Bridge' (115).

The novel also topically protests against the use of the bearing rein which had become fashionable in the 1870s (Huggett 26) and was the object of other protest works such as Flower's *Bits and Bearing Reins* (1875).[3] Used in driving, the bearing-rein was an extra fixed rein attached to the bit and hooked to the saddle pad on a horse's back to keep its head pulled up high. Wearing the bearing-rein made it impossible for horses to lower their necks to pull uphill, to correct a stumble when going downhill, or to rest comfortably when standing. Straining the back, legs, neck, and mouth, it caused pain and breathing difficulties, and shortened horses' lives. Sewell condemns both its cruelty and the blind following of fashion which gave rise to its use. It was therefore a very dark irony that when Sewell died, the horses drawing the hearse that came to take her for burial arrived wearing bearing reins, forcing her mother to rush out to have them removed (Bayly 279).

As Raulff observes, the nineteenth century 'brought moral innovations. The most important was undoubtedly compassion,' which the century gave 'a new fundamental value' 'as the basis of humane moral feeling and behaviour' (297). This 'new way of feeling,' he argues, needed figures 'who were personifications of a calamity, which witnesses found so awful, so unbearable' around whom it could 'crystallize—that is, become visible and intelligible' (297). Four of the key 'suffering individuals from which the societies of the nineteenth century formed their experiences, and which permanently changed their moral system' (297), he identifies are 'the working child, the wounded soldier, and the orphan,' and the figure Sewell focused on in *Black Beauty*: 'the whipped horse, the tortured animal' (297).

In *Black Beauty* Sewell expresses her strong humane beliefs and captured the topicality and particular significance of cruelty to horses in the decade in which she wrote. She also drew in subtle ways on the techniques of the sensation fiction which had been so popular in the 1860s, traces of which influenced many strands of 1870s writing. Sewell was clearly not writing a sensation novel per se, nor is she herself likely to have read many, or any, or rated them highly. Her Quaker-influenced religious faith and devotion to active charity meant that fiction for Sewell, like any activity she undertook, should have a clear moral purpose. Her skills in transmitting clear literary messages had been honed by her role in the late 1850s and 1860s as the unofficial and uncompromising editor of her mother's works of didactic poetry, fiction, and non-fiction which were written to teach and improve the lives and faith of children and the working classes. The effectiveness of *Black Beauty*'s own moral message, however, owes something to sensation which the novel uses to didactic ends in order to provoke a powerful reader response. In other words, in creating the powerful empathetic bond readers have with her equine protagonist, Sewell drew in starkly realist ways on the sensual techniques of sensation fiction. Just as a sensation novel provided a fast-paced, comparatively easy read, full of extreme and exciting events which stimulated readers' physical sensations and stirred their emotions, so, too, did *Black Beauty*.

The speed with which *Black Beauty* can be read (and understood) reflects the paciness of sensation writing. In Sewell's case, ease of reading is increased, and barriers between reader and meaning are reduced, by short chapters, episodic structure, and plain, clear language. By Victorian terms the novel is also comparatively short—around 60,000 words—in part no doubt because of Sewell's illness but also perfectly judged for its voice, content, and readability. Like sensation fiction, too, it contains a string of dramatic and violent events which Black Beauty experiences or relates: a hunt and consequent accident that ends in bloody death for a hare, a horse being shot due to a broken leg, and a young huntsman dying from a broken neck; Black Beauty much later discovering that the horse destroyed was his unknown brother; Ginger's brutal breaking-in which has been likened to a gang rape (Padel; Lansbury); a wild stormy night during which an uprooted oak tree crashes in front of Black Beauty and he saves his passengers by refusing to cross a broken bridge over a swollen river; a deadly fire (a common trope of sensation fiction) in which horses perish; a frantic gallop through the night for the doctor and saving of the mistress's life; Black Beauty himself falling dangerously ill; a dramatic race to stop a bolting horse; Black Beauty falling and having his future ruined by the furious riding of a drunken rider who himself dies in the fall; an account of the charge of the Light Brigade; the excitements and maltreatments of London and its traffic; terrible accidents; the heart-wrenching death of Ginger; Black Beauty's terrible collapse on Ludgate Hill; and scene after scene of violence to horses—lashing, whipping, beating, and subjection to all kinds of cruelty, neglect, and ignorance. These are not the rippling difficulties of domestic fiction but the stormy extremities of sensation writing. Their power in *Black Beauty* comes from the fact that, as readers realize, this is *not* a novel of sensation, and these are—in large part—the norms of Victorian horses' lives. The real villains here are humans: characters, but also implicitly readers themselves. This melding of sensational incident and readability with didactic message is recognized in the comments of one of the novel's earliest readers who told Sewell: "'You will be shocked to hear that a work intended to benefit mankind has been the cause of my neglecting all my duties—I *could not* leave Black Beauty till I left him safe in Joe's care [at novel's end]'" (Unnamed to Anna Sewell, 24 December 1877, qtd. in Bayly 275).

If we accept the imaginative leap into equine interiority, *Black Beauty* is a realist novel, and in the 1870s fiction generally became more realist in its shift away from sensation modes towards more serious concerns. At the same time, a work such as *Black Beauty* could make use of sensation's affective qualities in order to protest about or reflect topical issues. As Tara MacDonald argues in this volume, empathy, feeling what others feel, was central to the work of Ellen Wood and other female sensation writers of the 1860s. Sensation fiction, among other things, used affect to create physical sensation in the bodies of readers, something for which many contemporary reviewers condemned it; but as MacDonald shows, in works like *East Lynne* (1861) 'empathy can itself be an ethical response' (MacDonald). In *Black Beauty* empathy is wrought to even greater heights by Black Beauty's testimony and physical descriptions of his own life, and the 'novel's affective qualities, which are created through an identificatory, intersubjective, yet partially masked sense of equine interiority, are central to its power' (Gavin, '"[F]eeling"' 54). As has been elsewhere discussed, however:

> despite the cruelties he recounts, Black Beauty's voice is comparatively calm and measured. He expresses sorrow for others but rarely for himself. His own negative emotions are, as it were, reined-in, thereby deflecting affective response onto readers who feel on his behalf. Readers' emotions—rage at injustice, anguish over cruelty, grief upon tragedy—fill the affective gap in the text created by Black Beauty's under-expression of emotion. (Gavin, '"[F]eeling"' 52)

Like sensation fiction, *Black Beauty* also articulates the previously unexpressed physical. Just as female sensation writers of the 1860s and 1870s like Florence Marryat and Rhoda Broughton (as discussed by Tamara Heller, Melissa Purdue, and Catherine Pope in this volume) were portraying female desire in boundary-breaking ways, *Black Beauty* reveals the little-depicted sensual responses of equine beings. Black Beauty repeatedly reports physical responses to pleasure and, more frequently, to pain. He describes pats and strokes—'he patted me kindly' (17)—and lashes, cuts with whips and other injuries, such as Ginger recounting 'the flies swarmed round me, and settled on my bleeding flanks where the spurs had dug in, … The skin was so broken at the corners of my mouth that I could not eat the hay' (26–27). He tells of the stench and eye-stinging vapours of a foul stable and notes the tones of human voices—'her voice was sweet' (35); 'his voice was as harsh as the grinding of cart wheels over gravel stones' (154)—and the sounds of other horses: 'there was a dreadful sound … the shrieks of those poor horses that were left burning to death in the stable—it was very terrible' (57). He recalls the pleasures of good food when he has it: 'Oh! what a good supper he gave me that night, a good bran mash and some crushed beans with my oats, and such a thick bed of straw, and I was glad of it, for I was tired' (45). He also describes the physical sensations of being broken in, the bit 'a great piece of cold hard steel as thick as a man's finger … pushed into one's mouth, between one's teeth and over one's tongue, with the ends coming out at the corner of your mouth, and held fast there by straps over your head, under your throat, round your nose, and under your chin; so that no way in the world can you get rid of the nasty hard thing; it is very bad' (14–15) and the pain of being negligently ridden over sharp stones: 'with one shoe gone, I was forced to gallop at my utmost speed, my rider meanwhile cutting into me with his whip, and with wild curses urging me to go still faster. Of course my shoeless foot suffered dreadfully; the hoof was broken and split down to the very quick, and the inside was terribly cut by the sharpness of the stones' (83).

'I have heard men say, that seeing is believing; but I should say that *feeling* is believing' (154), Black Beauty states, and 'the novel insists that readers both *see* and *feel*—viscerally, sensually, and emotionally—the brief pleasures and pervasive pains of Victorian equine existence' (Gavin, Introduction xviii). That the novel is Black Beauty's autobiography, 'straight from the horse's mouth,' enhances the emotional impact of the story, and his incomprehension at human behaviour aids the sense that he is both innocent and *an* innocent, deserving of human protection and kindness. When he first sees a hunt, for example, and hears the 'one shriek' that is the end of the terrified hare, and sees the dogs that would 'soon have torn her to pieces' but for one of the huntsman holding her up 'by the leg torn and bleeding ... all the gentlemen seem[ing] well pleased,' he is 'so astonished' (12).

The power of Sewell's work, her precise knowledge of horses, and the affective strength of her vision also astonished her 1870s readers. She broke gender barriers as a woman writing about horses and revealed to her readership the plight of horses and the acute cruelties they suffered which, like their numbers, were at their height in the 1870s. Her work drew innovatively on strands of sensation writing in its readability, paciness, use of dramatic incident, and stimulation of physical and emotional response in her readers to transmit her anti-cruelty message. Sewell began by 'writing the life of a horse' and completed it against almost insuperable odds as the 1870s moved forwards. The life she revealed in *Black Beauty* was the summation of her life's work and the expression of her beliefs, knowledge, and creativity. It was also an evocative, provocative, call to action to 1870s Britain to pay attention to, and actively prevent, the daily cruelties so visible within it. Significantly, Sewell offered a new voice and a new vision to women's writing by combining activism with fiction and realism with sensation. Above all, it was a work that succeeded in its aim to 'induce kindness, sympathy, and an understanding treatment of horses'; then as now, few who read *Black Beauty* ever again look at horses in quite the same way.

Notes

1. Probably because of the authenticity of its narrative voice *Black Beauty* has continued to speak to women readers on an inexplicable level. Many women remember it from childhood as both beloved and almost unbearably sad. 'In many ways,' Coral Lansbury observes, '*Black Beauty* has always been a woman's book, and ... its effect upon adolescent girls has always been one of unbearable anguish. Generally read at the perilously emotional time when a child crosses the threshold to adult life, *Black Beauty* is a work of inconsolable grief. It is read obsessively, as though it contained lessons which must be learned, no matter how painful' (97). *Black Beauty* 'remains in the mind like a buried landscape' (Lansbury 64). Pony novelist Josephine Pullein-Thompson similarly recalls: 'As soon as I could read,' 'I had devoured *Black Beauty* eight times, sobbing over Ginger and the hardness of human life' (79), while author Jane Smiley writes:

    > When I first read *Black Beauty* at age ten. ... What I got was what every reader of *Black Beauty* gets: an experience of almost uncanny empathy that went so deep into my memory that even now, after fifty years, I almost cannot read Anna Sewell's novel or think of it without tearing up ... the power of this book remains with me. (x–xi)

2. In 1875 major horse owners in London included the London General Omnibus Company (8000 horses), Pickford & Company carriers and railway agents (900), Thomas Tilling (Jobmaster, carrier, omnibuses 750), Great Northern Railway (720), Great Eastern Railway (500), livery stables, brewers, jobmasters, carriers, and cab proprietors (cited in Turvey 39).
3. Flower, to whom Sewell sent a copy of her book, greatly admired *Black Beauty*, and two illustrations from Flower's *Bits and Bearing Reins* showing the horse's pain 'with the bearing rein' and greater comfort 'without the bearing rein' were added to many British editions of *Black Beauty* from the 1880s till the end of the nineteenth century.

Works Cited

Bayly, Mrs [Mary]. *The Life and Letters of Mrs Sewell*. London: James Nisbet and Co, 1889.

Dalby, Richard. 'Anna Sewell's "Black Beauty."' *Book and Magazine Collector* 132 (March 1995): 14–25.

Dent, A. A. 'Miss Sewell of Norfolk.' *East Anglian Magazine* 15:10 (August 1956): 542–47.

Dickens, Charles, Jr. *Dickens's Dictionary of London* 1879. victorianlondon.org; http://www.victorianlondon.org/dickens/dickens-chr.htm. Accessed 17 Feb 2019.

Doré, Gustave and Blanchard Jerrold. *London: A Pilgrimage*. 1872. New York: Dover, 1970.

Gavin, Adrienne E. *Dark Horse: A Life of Anna Sewell*. Stroud: Sutton, 2004.

———. '"[F]eeling is believing": Anna Sewell's *Black Beauty* and the Power of Emotion.' In *Affect, Emotion, and Children's Literature*. Ed. Kristine Moruzi, Michelle J. Smith, and Elizabeth Bullen. London: Routledge, 2018. 52–65.

———. Introduction. *Black Beauty* by Anna Sewell. Oxford World's Classics. Oxford: Oxford University Press, 2012. ix–xxvii.

———. '"I saw a great deal of trouble amongst the horses in London": Anna Sewell's *Black Beauty* and the Victorian Cab Horse.' In *Transport in British Fiction: Technologies of Movement, 1840–1940*. Ed. Adrienne E. Gavin and Andrew F. Humphries. Basingstoke: Palgrave Macmillan, 2015. 101–19.

Gordon, W. J. *The Horse World of London*. London: The Religious Tract Society, 1893.

Grimshaw, Anne. *The Horse: A Bibliography of British Books 1851–1976*. London: The Library Association, 1982.

The House of Jarrolds 1823–1923: A Brief History of One Hundred Years. Norwich: Jarrolds, 1924.

Huggett, Frank E. *Carriages at Eight: Horse-drawn Society in Victorian and Edwardian Times*. Guildford: Lutterworth Press, 1979.

Lansbury, Coral. *The Old Brown Dog: Women, Workers, and Vivisection in Edwardian England*. Madison, WI: University of Wisconsin Press, 1985.

May, Trevor. *Gondolas and Growlers: The History of the London Horse Cab*. Stroud: Alan Sutton, 1995.

Miele, Kathryn. 'Horse-Sense: Understanding the Working Horse in Victorian London.' *Victorian Literature and Culture* 37 (2009): 129–40.

Mitchell, Sally, ed. *Victorian Britain: An Encyclopedia*. Chicago and London: St James Press, 1988.

[Oliphant, Margaret]. 'Novels.' *Blackwood's* 102 (Sept 1867): 257–80.

Josephine, Diana, and Christine Pullein-Thompson. *Fair Girls and Grey Horses: Memories of a Country Childhood*. 1996. London: Allison and Busby, 1998.

Padel, Ruth. 'Saddled with Ginger: Women, Men and Horses.' *Encounter* 55.5 (November 1980): 47–54.

Raulff, Ulrich. *Farewell to the Horse: The Final Century of Our Relationship*. 2015. Trans. Ruth Ahmedzai Kemp. Harmondsworth: Penguin, 2017.

Review of *Black Beauty*. *Eastern Daily Press* (22 December 1877): 3.

Scholtmeijer, Marian. 'The Power of Otherness: Animals in Women's Fiction.' *Animals and Women: Feminist Theoretical Explorations*. Ed. Carol J. Adams and Josephine Donovan. Durham: Duke University, 1995, 231–62.

Sewell, Anna. *Black Beauty.* 1877. Ed. Adrienne E. Gavin. Oxford, Oxford University Press, 2012.
Sewell, Margaret. 'Recollections of Anna Sewell.' *Black Beauty.* 1877. London, Harrap, 1935, 1–6.
Sidney, Samuel. *The Book of the Horse.* 1874. Classic Edition. New York: Bonanza Books, 1985.
Smiley, Jane. Foreword. *Black Beauty* by Anna Sewell. New York: Penguin, 2011, ix–xiii.
Starrett, Vincent. '"Black Beauty" and Its Author.' *Buried Caesars: Essays in Literary Appreciation.* Chicago: Covici-McGee, 1923, 205–23.
Turvey, Ralph. 'Horse Traction in Victorian London.' *Journal of Transport History* 26.2 (2005): 38–59.

CHAPTER 17

Forging a New Path: Fraud and White-Collar Crime in Mary Elizabeth Braddon's 1870s Fiction

Janine Hatter

> Whether deservedly or not, the present age has been stigmatised as the age of counterfeits and adulterations; an age of outward show, of gloss, and of inward rottenness. (Duthie, 'Gold and Glitter' 461)

This statement, made in the February 1870 issue of *Belgravia*, a monthly periodical conducted by Mary Elizabeth Braddon, set the tone for the change of criminal activities depicted within her fiction in the ensuing decade. The 1870s saw Braddon attempting to break free from her reputation as 'the author of *Lady Audley's Secret*'—that is, as a writer of bigamy, incarceration, and murder—despite still publishing using this signature to attract her loyal readership. She expanded her literary criminal repertoire to focus on 'counterfeits and adulterations': financial frauds that drew on the emerging popular appetite for reading about such crimes.

J. Hatter (✉)
University of Hull, Hull, UK
e-mail: j.hatter@hull.ac.uk

As Heather Worthington notes, 'by the mid-century, fear of fraud had apparently overtaken fear of murder or robbery' (98). As crime became more sophisticated, so did Braddon's engagement with people's fears as her 1870s criminal narratives expanded to include counterfeit money ('Mr. and Mrs. de Fontenoy' [1870]); identity fraud and embezzlement (*Taken at the Flood* [1874]); forged wills ('Dr. Carrick' [1878]); and postnuptial fraud (*The Cloven Foot* [1879]). In the 1870s Braddon not only continued focusing on her protagonists' fraudulent double lives, but also her new northern publishing syndicate (discussed below), expanded the circulation of her narratives of fraud, securing her a wider reputation as an author striving for respectability, while simultaneously playing on her 'sensational' fame.

To examine fraud and white-collar crime, the specific context and terminology need to be understood. The 'fight against fraud' began in Britain in the 1850s as a direct result of 'the railway boom and the aftermath of the collapse of the railway share market and the 1840s commercial crisis' (Wilson 146). 'Fraud' is a generic term for a type of offence of which the actions usually comprise 'the dishonest non-violent obtaining of some economic advantage or causing some economic loss' (Kirk and Woodcock 1). Typical types of fraud include forged signatures, counterfeit money, and food adulteration. Fraud aims to fulfil personal greed either through quick gratification or through an activity over a prolonged period of time. Notably, it has the dual effect of personal gain or self-advancement for the perpetrator and loss or prevention of gain for the victim. Usually nonviolent, fraud has a different *modus operandi* from crimes such as robbery, arson, or murder; fraud is distant, tactical, and passive. Fraud can be committed by people of any class or gender; however, the 'criminal classes' were socially and fictionally constructed over the nineteenth century as coming from the lower echelons of society. The emergence of white-collar crime changed this perspective.

'White-collar' crime is a specific type of fraud, but one that was not considered a separate crime in the nineteenth century. White-collar crime was only defined in 1939, by Edwin Sutherland, as an offence that is 'committed by a person of respectability and high social status in the course of his occupation' (9). This definition can be applied to white-collar workers of the nineteenth century, such as company directors, bankers, lawyers, businessmen, and politicians, and by extension their office workers. White-collar crime by such professionals demonstrated that instead of the respectable middle classes simply needing the law's protection from the supposed criminal lower class, they also needed shielding from those among their own class who were using criminal means to rise up the social ranks. Generally, 'fraud' was the term 'used to articulate "alleged misconduct in business" during the nineteenth century' (Wilson 152), as it covers dealings by both professionals and the people they are doing business with, be they other professionals or clients. Throughout this chapter, 'fraud' will be used as a generic term for economic crimes within the narrative, while 'white-collar crime' specifically relates to business-related economic crimes committed by supposedly respectable professionals in the course of their work. Overall, fraud and white-collar crime cross economic, geographic, social, and gender boundaries within Victorian Britain and so are adaptable crimes for a sensation author such as Braddon to utilize.

The rise of fraud and white-collar crime in the mid-nineteenth century coincided with one of the most significant pieces of legislation to be enacted in that period. The year 1870 saw the passing of the first Married Women's Property Act, as one result of ongoing agitation for women's rights. While the Act gave married women more financial freedom, it also increased the potential for women, as well as men, to be victims of fraud, and of white-collar crime specifically. Not only as a woman directly affected by the Act (Braddon married her publisher and long-time romantic partner John Maxwell in 1874 on the death of his first wife), but as a writer who was most famous for her active female protagonists, this naturally had an impact upon Braddon's work. If women were now more responsible for their own financial freedom, then they, too, were at much greater risk from financial fraud. This discussion argues, therefore, that the passing of this Act changed the course of Braddon's fiction; Braddon began writing sensation fiction in which women were not only the victims, but also the perpetrators, of financial fraud.

EXPLOITING THE PROFESSIONS: *TAKEN AT THE FLOOD* AND 'DR. CARRICK'

In an anonymous article, the *Saturday Review* states that Braddon's 1874 novel, *Taken at the Flood*, 'is of course a story of crime and mystery' that goes back to her 'old hunting-grounds' ('Taken at the Flood' 666, 665). This is a fair comment when considering the novel's main focus is the Lady-Audley-type anti-heroine, Sylvia Carew. After dissolving an engagement to Edmund Standon because his mother will disinherit him if he marries her, Sylvia marries Sir Aubrey Perriam in order to live a luxurious lifestyle. Describing Sylvia as a 'mercenary heroine' because she marries for financial security, rather than love, Emma Liggins links Braddon's 1870s mercenary marriages to the ongoing agitation for better educational and working opportunities for women (74). However, Liggins misses the link to women's changing legal position. Commenting upon the newly enacted Married Women's Property Act, Sir Aubrey states, "'I do not understand or approve the modern system of making a wife independent of her husband. Dependency is one of woman's sweetest attributes ... I should not like my wife ... to possess an independent income during my lifetime"' (*Taken at the Flood* 156). Sylvia's restricted lifestyle—she is allowed no money of her own, is told to dress simply, and rarely leaves the confines of Perriam Place—leads her to commit identity fraud. Sylvia commits Aubrey to an insane asylum under the guise of being his brother, Mordred. Just like Lady Audley, Sylvia emulates the Angel of the House in order to increase her social standing through marriage. Ironically, it is precisely Sir Aubrey's desire for Sylvia's dependency that makes it necessary for her to commit identity fraud in order to have an autonomous existence. Braddon therefore uses Sylvia to comment upon different perceptions of the Married Women's Property Act. Far from being detrimental to a happy union, as critics such as Sir Aubrey suggest, increasing female autonomy is, Braddon intimates, essential to a happy marriage, and stifling female independence means that even financially supported women remain in precarious circumstances.

Increased female autonomy in the home is a positive development for Braddon, which she contrasts to the problematic increase in male power within the banking industry. Fraudulent practices by bankers were widely enough known by the 1870s for Edmund's second fiancée, Esther Rochdale, to fear that his working in a bank is related to his falling from his mother's grace: '[h]orrible visions of possible calamity flashed across her mind. Edmund had been forging, or embezzling, or something dreadful of that kind. People in banks so often end by forging. It seems almost a necessary consequence of a confidential position' (304). While Edmund had not been embezzling—his disgrace was caused by eloping with his first fiancée, Sylvia—the fact that such crimes are assumed echoes Sylvia's father's white-collar crimes enacted before the novel opens.

Sylvia's father, the schoolmaster, James Carew (alias Carford), like Edmund, used to work in a bank. In order to maintain himself and his wife in the manner to which they were accustomed, James had '"falsified the accounts of the house"' by both signing his employer's name on bills (forgery) and keeping back money that should have been deposited (theft) (86). White-collar crime was topical in the 1850s when this section of the narrative is set as this is when the first banking fraud cases were tried. Historian Sarah Wilson traces the growth of the banking industry and how it was matched by the first criminal fraud trials, such as those of Walter Watts for fraud against the Globe Assurance Office in 1850, of W. J. Robson against the Crystal Palace Company in 1856, and of the directors of the Royal British and City of Glasgow banks in 1858 and 1878–1879 respectively (152). Such cases provided not only a backdrop of financial scandal, but heightened the public awareness of such possibilities taking place. The increasing public awareness of such crimes fostered a growing paranoia in the public imagination that, in turn, made them inherently exploitable by skilled sensation authors. This is particularly notable in the last example, as the fraud undertaken in 1858 was repeated 20 years later, demonstrating that high-level financial fraud had not been counteracted by the emerging contemporaneous system of policing, and so was still topical in the 1870s when Braddon was writing. Thus, while Charles Dickens in *Bleak House* (1852) compared an individual's financial struggle with the gigantic and inhuman legal system that no-one could manoeuvre, Braddon changes tactics later in the century to demonstrate how an individual can manipulate the banking system for personal gain.

James's white-collar crime is contrasted with his wife's desertion of him and their daughter, Sylvia, for her husband's employer at the bank, Mr. Mowbray. Mrs. Carford argues: '"My crime served as a set-off against yours, James … But for that you might have stood in the felon's dock"' (86). Embezzlement and adultery are crimes 'set off' against each other, but hers is seen as morally more corrupt due to the nineteenth-century's sexual double standard and her child-abandonment. While James speculated on the financial market and gambled to try and save his reputation and position, putting countless people's livelihoods at risk in the process, Mrs. Carford speculated on the marriage market and lost her position as a respectable wife and mother. This betrayal she lays at her husband's door: '"Do you think I would have been reckless if you had told me the truth [of our financial ruin]?"' (86). Through Mrs. Carford, as with Sylvia, Braddon advocates for woman's equality within marriage on emotional and financial grounds.

An evaluation of the penalties inflicted on the two Carford spouses is emphasized when James uses financial terminology to plead his dishonoured situation: '"Mr. Mowbray could not *afford* to prosecute the husband of the woman he seduced"' (86, emphasis added). 'Afford' here has several meanings: Mr. Mowbray cannot financially, morally, or reputationally afford to prosecute James as he has seduced James's wife, indicating that his moral crime cancels out James's financial one. James stresses the '"*price* of [his] dishonour"' by noting what his fraudulent activity cost him (87, emphasis added): '"the house would spare me the disgrace of a prosecution on condition that I withdrew myself from the commercial world, and refrained from any future attempt to obtain credit or employment in the city of London"' (87). He takes their daughter, Sylvia, and becomes a schoolmaster, continuing to earn money in a respectable, though lower-class, situation. James suffers no public punishment nor does he have to make any legal reparations.

Mrs. Carford, on the other hand, eventually leaves Mr. Mowbray and becomes a starving, homeless beggar, who returns to her husband to plead for forgiveness, food, and shelter (which he provides), but she still dies at the novel's end. Mrs. Carford's 'fallen-woman ending' invites a contrast to her husband's comparatively comfortable position as a schoolteacher. Despite barrister Luke Owen Pike asserting in 1876 that '[f]orgery is now considered an offence of the greatest magnitude' (541), Braddon's novel, published just two years before this statement, refutes this message, as James's punishment is significantly more lenient than his wife's. Her 'crime' of deviating from the Angel in the House was still considered the greater 'offence.' As Elizabeth Gaskell's own forger, Richard Bradshaw, in *Ruth* (1853) remarks, '"many things are right for men which are not for girls"' (117), meaning that dominant men are sheltered by both their gender and professional standing, while women who express sexually deviant behaviour have dramatic and tragic ends.

A similar situation in which a trusted professional abuses his position for his own financial advantage is found in Braddon's short story 'Dr. Carrick,' which was published in *All the Year Round* in 1878. As his medical practice fails to grow, Carrick gets desperate, and so when he finally gains one profitable patient, Eustace Tregonnell, he turns to fraud. Carrick mesmerizes Eustace, getting him to forge a will that presumably leaves Carrick his fortune. Carrick's fraud is discovered by his own suspicious cousin and housekeeper, Hester Rushton, because Eustace is not usually 'very business-like in his habits' ('Dr. Carrick' 9). It is business etiquette specifically that raises the alarm as Eustace is usually 'so indifferent to money' (9). Being 'indifferent to money' is the prerogative of the wealthy, as it is precisely Carrick's financially insecure position that tempts him, like Sylvia, towards fraudulent activities. While he is not destitute, Carrick believes himself to be worth more than his current social standing. When Eustace signs his will, Hester uses the language of business to note an anomaly: 'It seemed to her as if Mr. Tregonnell, though to all appearance a *free agent*, had been acting under the influence of the doctor' (9, emphasis added). In keeping with the general definition of fraud as a non-violent crime, Carrick does not use any violence when ensuring the fraudulent signing of the will—the mesmerism does not hurt Eustace; however, Carrick does then progress to attempted murder in order to fulfil the will's provisions by covering Eustace's face with a chloroform-laced pillowcase, but is foiled by Hester hiding in a cupboard. As the conclusion of the tale summarizes: '[Carrick] had tried honesty; he had tried fraud and crime. Both had failed' (16). Eventually, Eustace marries Hester and Carrick is imprisoned. Braddon thereby combines the sensation fiction trope of mesmerism with the more topical, and less supernaturally inflected, theme of financial fraud. This is what makes Carrick such a dangerous villain: it is the supposedly sane, socially acceptable, trusted professional who deviates from society's rules that poses the most threat.

Desire for personal fulfilment and social advancement through any means necessary is not specifically gendered in Braddon's work, as the pressure to conform to society's norms is applied equally, if in different ways, to both sexes. 'Dr. Carrick' and *Taken at the Flood*, however, take the desire for self-advancement one step further than *Lady Audley's Secret* (1862). In these 1870s texts, Braddon examines what happens when it is our legal protectors or other professionals who have confidential knowledge about us, and who are therefore under a higher duty to protect us, who become the oppressors; the basis of Victorian society's marital, medical, and legal systems breaks down and it is up to the individual to restore order.

Fakery, Forgery, and the Lower Classes: *The Cloven Foot* and 'Mr. and Mrs. de Fontenoy'

Braddon's 1879 novel, *The Cloven Foot*, relies on her 1860s trope of bigamy as a sensational hook for her readership, but gives it an 1870s twist. As an anonymous review in *The Observer* noted, the novel is replete with 'love and crime and mutual deception' ('The Cloven Foot' 3), including a double bigamy plot, several financial frauds, and characters with multiple identities. The male protagonist, John Treverton (alias married man Mr. Chicot), commits bigamy because of a complication in the will of his deceased cousin: he can only inherit his cousin's estate if he marries his cousin's ward, Laura Malcom. John marries Laura in order to enact a postnuptial agreement that signs over the estate to Laura, but his bigamy undermines its legitimacy. John's 'audacious fraud' inflicts wider harm upon the community (*The Cloven Foot* 217), because if John and Laura do not marry the estate is to be sold to establish a charitable hospital. This stipulation compounds John's fraudulent actions because it widens his financial crimes to affect a greater geographical, social, and economic area. Such fraudulent behaviour does not merely prey upon the wealthy and the intricacies and eccentricities of their wills, but also has implications that can affect all echelons of society.

In true 'sensational' style, however, the complications of the sensation plot are actually used to prevent John being criminalized. It transpires that John's first marriage to La Chicot is invalid (due to La Chicot herself already being married), and so he is innocent of bigamy and postnuptial fraud as his marriage to Laura is legal. While *The Observer* notes double bigamy may be 'rather stale' as a plotting device (3), it technically means that '[a]lthough guilty in intention, he had been innocent in fact' (*The Cloven Foot* 278), complicating John's position within the fraud narrative. Just as James Carew's banking firm did not press charges, thereby on some level condoning his actions, John's lawyer, Mr. Sampson, advises John not to give himself up to the police as '[h]is interests as well as his client's were at stake' (252). In each case the larger organizational systems work to protect the individual who originally threatened their authority and security. This is only true for James and John, however, because they show great criminal ingenuity and commit strategic ('higher-class'), rather than violent ('lower-class'), crimes. While James and John confirm that the middle classes themselves can be criminal—as opposed to the Newgate Novels' 1830s lower-class criminals, and Braddon's 1860s Lady Audley who fraudulently married her way up the social scale and violently protected her position against any threats—the companies eschew their prescribed morality and cover up James and John's fraudulent behaviour. This may be in part because proving white-collar crime in court was difficult (Odden 142; Wagner 123), but it also meant that the companies avoided unnecessary scandal and so protected their own reputations.

Intertwined in *The Cloven Foot*'s double bigamy plot is a narrative regarding the murder of La Chicot, and the theft of her diamond necklace, by her friend, Desrolles. A financially hard up '"swindler, and an adventurer"' (194), Desrolles tries to sell the stolen necklace to a diamond merchant, only to be told it is a worthless fake—all 'outward show.' Through their violent nature, the murder and theft are specifically related to the lower-class characters, inviting a direct comparison with John's legal fraud to emphasize how all classes of society equally are made up of, in Duthie's term, 'inward rottenness.'

As a fake object, *The Cloven Foot*'s diamond necklace links to the counterfeit money present in Braddon's earlier short story 'Mr. and Mrs. de Fontenoy,' published in *Belgravia* in 1870. In this tale, the eponymous characters are coiners—people who forge counterfeit money. Not white-collar criminals because they are not from the professional classes, they are lower-class criminals who commit fraud. Mr. and Mrs. de Fontenoy have a particular pattern of victimization: they pretend to be aristocrats and rent large and expensive houses in remote seaside towns in order to have enough space for their enterprise. Specifically, they target houses that have failed to let in off-peak periods, when their owners rush into 'wild expenses in the way of advertising' ('Mr. and Mrs. de Fontenoy' 449), and they rely on the owner being desperate regarding the lack of rent. The influence of personal advertisements on sensation fiction has been examined by Matthew Rubery, who argues that 'unlike other sections of the newspaper, the advertising columns brought readers into potential contact with a variety of criminals' (58). Criminals there advertised their fraudulent schemes, and also answered advertisements with deceitful replies as it allowed them to 'refashion themselves into legitimate members of society' (Rubery 62). Falling into the latter category, Mr. and Mrs. de Fontenoy's arrival is a welcome relief to a deserted town, although as the epigraph to this chapter asserts, the 1870s were 'an age of outward show, of gloss, and of inward rottenness' (449), and Braddon's tale stresses Mr. and Mrs. de Fontenoy's aristocratic 'appearance,' which hides their inner fraudulent selves. It is specifically their looks, manners, and attitudes that allow them to defraud the seaside town, St. Dunstans-by-the-sea: like La Chicot's diamond necklace, they are 'all outward show.'

Fraudulent coining has several detrimental effects on society: it reduces the value of real money; it increases inflation due to more money being circulated in the economy; and it causes losses to business owners as banks may not reimburse them for detected counterfeit coins. Thus, the de

Fontenoys' supposed aristocratic heritage potentially allows them to destroy the livelihoods of multiple shop owners—and by extension an entire seaside town—by buying goods, and belatedly paying for them with counterfeit money. The issue of fraudulent gold was topical in 1870, and concern enough to Braddon's *Belgravia* readers for the periodical to include, immediately after 'Mr. and Mrs. de Fontenoy,' Duthie's article 'Gold and Glitter,' which examines the goldsmith and jewellery trade. While not directly related to coining, the article discusses different standards of gold. Duthie argues that while Continental gold standards are lower (18- and 16-carat gold) than traditional British standards (22 and 18 carats), the introduction into Britain of 9-carat gold would not, as some feared, diminish the 'strong, massive [and] durable' quality of British gold (Duthie 464). The discussion is evocative of similar debates surrounding sensation fiction, with the middle-class reviewer William Fraser Rae's outrage at the genre 'making the literature of the Kitchen the favourite reading of the Drawing Room' because it blurred strict social structures (204). In terms of gold, Duthie advocates for the inferior carat so that the lower classes can have jewellery that is 'well worth the money, and will answer every purpose of use and ornament' (465), but is strictly *not* the real thing: the social boundaries remain firm, with the higher classes having the best quality gold and the lower classes having gold for 'outward show.' This need by the lower classes to own gold, even if it is merely plated, reflects their desire to emulate the higher classes (hence La Chicot's fake diamond necklace), while also referencing the warning that 'all that glitters is not gold.' Mr. and Mrs. de Fontenoy need the glitter of the counterfeit gold and the aristocratic lifestyle to dazzle the seaside resort against detecting their fraudulent selves. Overall, the coining by these lower-class career criminals is on the same level as the embezzlement undertaken by James Carew; both exploit a perceived higher-class respectability, but ultimately have a devastating impact upon the local economies.

One key difference, however, is that while the middle-class fraudsters James and John are not legally punished for their actions, the de Fontenoys are, and in this tale, unlike in the other three here discussed, the police are consulted. Mr. Migson, the owner of the house the de Fontenoys' are renting, contacts Scotland Yard via a retired detective when he sees a newspaper item detailing the death of Mr. de Fontenoy in Scotland. Mr. Migson's description of Mr. de Fontenoy matches that of 'Slippery Joseph, one of the most daring coiners that ever lived' (459). Having escaped early from the seaside town, Joseph/de Fontenoy, his wife and their coining crew are captured undertaking their next scam and are 'sentenced to penal servitude' (460). The lower classes in Braddon's narratives are brought to justice by the law, while her middle-class fraudsters are not, suggesting Braddon capitulates to her middle-class *Belgravia* readers' expectations.

The different types of fraud used in Braddon's 1870s fiction depend on the class of the fraudster. The lower-class forgers Mr. and Mrs. de Fontenoy use the ancient method of coining; they use the actual object, counterfeit money, because that is what they have access to. They do not have reputations upon which they can borrow or obtain credit, financial, or otherwise. By contrast, the middle-class fraudsters James and John use and abuse the banking system via their birthright, education, and connections. The contemporaneous technological banking system therefore enables this new type of white-collar crime where the fraudsters need to blend into the background in order to hide their activities rather than dazzle using false personas; James and John are dangerous *because* they look and act like everyone else, and also partially because of that they avoid prosecution by the criminal justice system. As with *The Cloven Foot*'s lawyer, Mr. Sampson, Mr. and Mrs. de Fontenoy have an 'ardent love of money-making' (24), which is the downfall of most fraudsters from any social strata. Nevertheless, in Braddon's 1870s fiction it is the lower-class career criminals who are locked up, or transported, for the good of society. Middle-class criminals who succumb to greed are morally, and socially, redeemed.

Dispersing Fraud: Braddon's Northern Publication Syndicate

As the sections above demonstrate, Braddon combined the historical background of high-profile fraud cases of the previous decades, with the ongoing agitation for women's rights and sensation writing conventions to create tales that spoke directly to her 1870s readership. Her clever use of these themes coincided with a change in her publication style. From 1873, Braddon began syndication with William Tillotson of Bolton in a deal that was 'original in the sense that it created the first syndicate of British provincial newspapers systematically covering most of the country for new work by an author with a reputation already established in the metropolitan book market' (Law 43). The newspapers Braddon published in at this point of her career were the *Bolton Weekly Journal and Guardian* (which published *Taken at the Flood*), *Manchester Weekly Times, Leigh*

Journal and Times, Sheffield Weekly Telegraph, and *Newcastle Weekly Chronicle* (which published *The Cloven Foot*). Thus, over the 1870s Braddon's novel publications became geographically widespread, pushing beyond London-based journals, such as her own edited periodical *Belgravia* which was sold in 1876 to Chatto and Windus. Braddon's short stories, however, continued to be published in London-based periodicals, such as *Belgravia, The Illustrated Newspaper, All the Year Round* and her 1879 newly formed Christmas annual *The Mistletoe Bough,* which maintained her influential standing in London literary circles and reviews.

The impact of this northern publishing syndicate on her literary reputation is significant. While such an alteration might initially suggest Braddon suffered a decline in popularity and author prestige in this period because the popular London periodicals were no longer publishing her fiction in the vast quantities in which she was producing it, there were in fact many benefits to this new mode of publication. Braddon's fiction was now being dispersed across the entire country, gaining her a wider readership—socially, economically, and geographically—that increased her literary impact (Carnell and Law 140). The positive connotations of this publishing manoeuvre are compounded by the fact that these newspapers were based in some of the major industrial cities of the north. This wider readership also had a significant impact on her criminal narratives in particular. While Braddon's fictions continued to be read alongside real-life crimes that were reported in newspapers, the fact that her fraud and white-collar crime narratives were set outside London—for instance, Devonshire in *The Cloven Foot,* Cornwall in 'Dr. Carrick,' Hedingham in *Taken at the Flood,* and Brighton in 'Mr. and Mrs. de Fontenoy'—meant that they were consistently warning all strata of society against fraudulent activities, as they were not restricted to one area of Britain. Portraying fraud in fiction also emphasized the effects of such actions on both men and women; financial fraud was often perceived to be a 'victimless crime,' but the sensational and tragic results for both victims and perpetrators depicted in Braddon's novels showed a dimension news reports often lacked.

* * *

While the *Saturday Review* asserted in 1864 that Braddon's early sensation novels 'are simply stories of exciting incident, without any sort of relation to the social system' ('The Perils of Sensation' 559), ultimately, through combining her brand of sensationalism with the changing context of criminal behaviour and the continuing agitation for women's rights, Braddon was able to 'forge a new path' in the 1870s that delved specifically into professional and criminal systems that threatened society at large. Through her innovative newspaper syndication, Braddon continued to establish herself as a reputable author, adapting and exploiting her changing publication strategies. The fact that Braddon turned her attention towards more sophisticated crime echoed the increasing complexity of her own literary productions. Braddon's already twist-laden sensation fiction narratives encompassed more modern modes of criminal enterprise in the 1870s, updating the sensation genre alongside it. Her 1870s criminal characters have greater emphasis within the narrative itself, instead of their crimes simply being the means of creating overwrought or emotional impacts in their victims. Coupled with the inclusion of less violent crimes, is greater emphasis on strategic crime and thus criminal ingenuity. The villains of these pieces are not the violent lower-class Newgate criminals or the ambitious, social-climbing Lady Audley; instead, they are formidable and complex middle-class characters straining to maintain their status through financial schemes. Such changes in fictional crimes and criminals were significant steps forward in modernizing sensation writing into the crime writing of the twentieth century and beyond.

WORKS CITED

Braddon, Mary Elizabeth. 'Dr. Carrick.' *All the Year Round: The Extra Summer Number* 20.500 (1878): 1–16.
———. 'Mr. and Mrs. de Fontenoy.' *Belgravia* 10 (1870): 447–60.
———. *Taken at the Flood*. 1874. London: Maxwell, 1891.
———. *The Cloven Foot*. 1879. London: Maxwell, 1895.
'The Cloven Foot.' *The Observer* 4615 (1879): 3.
Carnell, Jennifer and Graham Law. '"Our author": Braddon in the Provincial Weeklies.' *Beyond Sensation: Mary Elizabeth Braddon in Context*. Ed. Marlene Trompe, Pamela K. Gilbert, and Aeron Haynie. New York: State University of New York Press, n.d. 127–64.
Duthie, William. 'Gold and Glitter.' *Belgravia* 10 (1870): 461–66.
Gaskell, Elizabeth. *Ruth*. 1853. Ed. Angus Easson. London: Penguin, 2004.
Kirk, David and Anthony Woodcock. *Serious Fraud: Investigation and Trial*. London: Butterworth, 1996.
Law, Graham. *Serializing Fiction in the Victorian Press*. Basingstoke: Palgrave, 2000.
Liggins, Emma. 'Her Mercenary Spirit: Women, Money and Marriage in Mary Elizabeth Braddon's 1870s Fiction.' *Women's Writing*, 11.1 (2004): 73–88.

Odden, Karen, 'Puffed Papers and Broken Promises: White-Collar Crime and Literary Justice in *The Way We Live Now.*' *Victorian Crime, Madness and Sensation*. Ed. Andrew Maunder and Grace Moore. Aldershot: Ashgate, 2004. 135–46.

'The Perils of Sensation.' *Saturday Review of Politics, Literature, Science and Art* 18.471 (1864): 558–59.

Pike, Luke Owen. *History of Crime in England*. 2 vols. London: Smith, Elder, & Co., 1876.

Rae, William Fraser. 'Sensation Novelists: Miss Braddon.' *North British Review* XLIII (1865): 180–204.

Rubery, Matthew. *The Novelty of Newspapers: Victorian Fiction After the Invention of the News*. Oxford: Oxford University Press, 2009.

Sutherland, Edwin. *White Collar Crime*. 1939. New York: Holt, Rinehart & Winston, 1949.

'Taken at the Flood.' *Saturday Review of Politics, Literature, Science and Art* 37.969 (1874): 665–66.

Wagner, Tamara S. 'Detecting Business Fraud at Home: White-Collar Crime and the Sensational Clergyman in Victorian Domestic Fiction.' *Victorian Secrecy: Economies of Knowledge and Concealment*. Ed. Albert D. Poinke and Denise Tischler Millstein. Surrey: Ashgate, 2010. 115–33.

Wilson, Sarah. 'Fraud and White-Collar Crime: 1850 to the Present.' *Histories of Crime: Britain 1600–2000*. Ed. Anne-Marie Kilday and David Nash. New York: Palgrave, 2010. 141–59.

Worthington, Heather. *The Rise of the Detective in Early Nineteenth-Century Popular Fiction*. Basingstoke: Palgrave, 2005.

Index[1]

A

Adam Bede, see Eliot, George
'Address to Working Men, by Felix Holt,' see Eliot, George
Adoption, 30, 107
Adultery, 32, 154, 156, 183, 193n5, 269
Albert, Prince, 2, 5
Alcott, Louisa May, 13, 16, 253
    Little Men, 13
    Little Women, 253
    Work, A Story of Experience, 16
All the Year Round, see Dickens, Charles
American Humane Education Society, the, 245
'Angelina; or, L'Amie Inconnue,' see Edgeworth, Maria
'Angel in the House, The,' see Patmore, Coventry
Angell, George Thorndike, 245

Anglicanism, 76, 77, 214–216, 221, 222, 225
Anglo-French Reminiscences, see Betham-Edwards, Matilda
Animal cruelty, see Cruelty, animal
Antifeminism, 105
Argosy, The, 12, 20, 195–198, 208, 210n12
Art of Beauty, The, see Haweis, Mary Eliza
Athenaeum, The, 119, 154, 169, 208, 235, 237
At His Gates, see Oliphant, Margaret
At the Back of the North Wind, see MacDonald, George
Aunt Judy's Magazine, 91
Aurora Floyd, see Braddon, Mary Elizabeth
Austin Friars, see Riddell, Charlotte
Autobiography, see Martineau, Harriet

---

[1] Note: Page numbers followed by 'n' refer to notes.

An Autobiography, see
  Trollope, Anthony
*Autobiography of Christopher Kirkland,
  The*, see Linton, Eliza Lynn

B
Bain, Alexander, 44, 174
  The Emotions and the Will, 44
Bankruptcy, 14, 15, 18, 22, 153,
  157–160, 162n10, 162n11
Bankruptcy Act, the, 15, 19, 157, 158
Barnaby Rudge, see Dickens, Charles
Bearing reins, 248, 251, 256, 261n3
Beeton, Isabella, 5
  Book of Household Management, 5
Belgravia, see Maxwell, John
Belinda, see Edgeworth, Maria
Bell, Alexander Graham, 18, 252
Bentley, Richard, 17, 120, 121, 126,
  192n1, 196
Besant, Annie, 18
  The Law of Population, 18
Betham-Edwards, Matilda,
  11, 135–147
  Anglo-French Reminiscences, 139
  *The Flower of Doom: or, The
    Conspirator and Other
    Stories*, 140
  'The Golden Bee,' 139
  Kitty, 140
  The Lord of the Harvest, 146
  Mid-Victorian Memories, 139
  'Mrs Punch's Letters to Her
    Daughter,' 11, 137, 142
  The Sylvestres, 140
  Through Spain to the Sahara, 138
  The White House by the Sea, 139
  A Winter with Swallows, 138
Bigamy, 2, 7, 15, 22, 32, 70, 83,
  115, 154, 210n12,
  265, 271–273

*Biographical Dictionary of Celebrated
  Women of Every Age and Country,
  A*, see Lamb, Charles and Mary
Bird, Isabella L., 18
  *A Lady's Life in the Rocky
    Mountains*, 18
Black Beauty, see Sewell, Anna
Blackstone, William, 162n11
  *Commentaries on the Laws of
    England*, 162n11
Blackwell, Antoinette Brown, 17
  The Sexes Throughout Nature, 17
Blackwell, Elizabeth, 139
Blackwood's Edinburgh Magazine, 38,
  174, 181n1, 213, 223
Blanc, Louis, 140
Blandford Edwards, Amelia,
  139, 147n2
  A Thousand Miles up the Nile, 139
Bleak House, see Dickens, Charles
Bodichon, Barbara, 139, 140, 145
*Bolton Weekly Journal and Guardian,
  the*, 275
Bonheur, Rosa, 238
Book of Household Management, see
  Beeton, Isabella
Book of the Horse, The, see
  Sidney, Samuel
Braddon, Mary Elizabeth, xiv, xvi, 4,
  6, 7, 9, 12, 15, 21, 22, 32, 45,
  57–73, 105, 108, 115, 120, 140,
  184, 250, 265–277
  Aurora Floyd, 57, 250
  The Cloven Foot, 21, 266, 271–276
  The Doctor's Wife, 60
  'Dr Carrick,' 22, 266, 276
  Lady Audley's Secret, 9, 22, 32,
    58, 59, 65
  'Mr and Mrs de Fontenoy,' 22,
    266, 271–276
  Taken at the Flood, 21, 266–271,
    275, 276

Three Times Dead (The Trail of the Serpent), 6, 32
The Trail of the Serpent; or, the Secret of the Heath, 32
Brenda, *see* Smith, Georgina Castle
Brock, Frances Carey, 10, 90, 93, 98–100
  Charity Helstone, 90
Brontë, Charlotte, xi–xvi, 5, 6, 13, 90, 99, 125, 130, 132n4
  Jane Eyre, 130
Brontës, the, 2, 5, 31
'Brother Jacob,' *see* Eliot, George
Broughton, Rhoda, 6, 10–12, 17, 19, 20, 45, 119–131, 131n2, 132n5, 132n6, 140, 142, 183–192, 192n1, 259
  Cometh Up as a Flower, 10, 119–126, 128, 183
  Good-bye, Sweetheart, 131
  'The Man with the Nose,' 17, 19, 183–192
  Not Wisely, But Too Well, 6, 10, 119–126, 128–130
  Red as a Rose Is She, 10, 119–121, 126–131, 132n9
  Twilight Stories, 19, 184, 187, 192n1
  'Under the Cloak,' 192
Brown, Isaac Baker, 234–237
  On the Curability of Certain Forms of Insanity, Epilepsy, Catalepsy, and Hysteria in Females, 234
Browning, Elizabeth Barrett, 238
Burckhardt, Jakob, 36
  The Civilization of the Renaissance in Italy, 36
Burnett, Frances Hodgson, 12
Butler, Josephine, 7, 16, 91, 102

C
Capitalism, 28, 152, 160, 161, 251
Cartomania, 4
Censorship, 120
Charity Helstone, *see* Brock, Frances Carey
Charity work, 89, 93, 95
Charles VIII, King, 36
City and Suburb, *see* Riddell, Charlotte
City of Glasgow bank, 269
City of London, 15, 16, 152, 154, 155, 270
'City Women,' *see* Riddell, Charlotte
Civilization of the Renaissance in Italy, The, *see* Burckhardt, Jakob
Class
  lower-class, 22, 200, 201, 270, 272–275, 277
  middle-class, 3, 14, 20, 22, 49, 52, 54, 89, 91, 92, 97, 141, 143, 145, 159, 195–209, 214, 221, 223, 232, 247, 251, 274, 275, 277
  ruling-class, 39
  upper-class, 52, 102, 107, 141
  upper-middle-class, 70
  working-class, 8, 9, 13, 14, 46, 50–55, 91, 247
Clive, Caroline, xiv, xxii, 10, 107
  Paul Ferroll, xxii, 10, 107
Cloven Foot, The, *see* Braddon, Mary Elizabeth
Coates, James, 188
  Human Magnetism or How to Hypnotise, 188
Cobbe, Frances Power, 92, 139, 238
Colby, Robert and Vineta, xxi, 219, 221
Coleridge Samuel Taylor, 128, 139
  'The Rime of the Ancient Mariner,' 128
Collins, Wilkie, 45, 105, 107, 108, 111, 115
  The Woman in White, 45, 107, 108

Cometh Up as a Flower, see
  Broughton, Rhoda
Comin' Thro' the Rye, see
  Mather, Helen
Commentaries on the Laws of England,
  see Blackstone, William
Confession
  criminal, 66
  dying, 81, 82
  public, 86, 87
Contagious Diseases Acts, 5, 7,
  16, 17, 102
Cooke, Nicholas, 231–233
  Satan in Society, 232
Coolidge, Susan, 13, 253
  What Katy Did, 13, 253
Corinne, see de Staël, Germaine
Cornhill Magazine, The, 33, 36,
  83, 181n1
Counterfeiting, 15, 22
Cousin Phillis, see Gaskell, Elizabeth
Craik, Dinah Maria Mulock,
  xxi, 13, 253
  *The Little Lame Prince and his
  Travelling Cloak*, 13
Crime fiction, xxiv, 12
Criminal confession, see Confession,
  criminal
Cruelty
  animal, 21, 22, 248
  human, 21, 248
Crystal Palace, 124
Crystal Palace Company,
  the, 269
Cushman, Charlotte, 238–241

D

*Daisy Chain, The; or, Aspirations: A
  Family Chronicle*, see Yonge,
  Charlotte
Daniel Deronda, see Eliot, George

Dark Night's Work, A, see Gaskell,
  Elizabeth
Darwin, Charles, 2, 4, 17, 44, 253
  *The Descent of Man, and Selection in
  Relation to Sex*, 17
  *The Expression of the Emotions in
  Man and Animals*, 253
  On the Origin of Species, 2, 4
Davenport-Hill, Rosamund, 139
David Copperfield, see Dickens, Charles
Davies, Emily, 91
de' Medici, Lorenzo, 36
de Staël, Germaine, 131
  Corinne, 131
Dean and Chapter Act of 1840, 216
Dickens, Charles, 29, 50, 77, 83, 90,
  109, 139, 140, 159, 162n10,
  246, 255, 256, 269, 270, 276
  All the Year Round, 77, 83, 139,
  140, 270, 276
  Barnaby Rudge, 50
  Bleak House, 90, 255, 269
  David Copperfield, 109
  Dombey and Son, 162n10
  Household Words, 83
  A Tale of Two Cities, 77
Didactic fiction, 238
Dissenters, 214
Doctor's Wife, The, see Braddon, Mary
  Elizabeth
Dog of Flanders, A, see Ramé,
  Maria Louise
Dombey and Son, see Dickens, Charles
Domestic realism, 20, 32, 112
Doré, Gustave, 256
  London: A Pilgrimage, 256
'Dr Carrick,' see Braddon, Mary
  Elizabeth
Dublin University Magazine, The, 29,
  120, 126
Dying confession, see
  Confession, dying

INDEX 283

E
East Lynne, see Wood, Ellen
Edgeworth, Maria, 29, 142, 238, 239
  'Angelina; or, L'Amie
    Inconnue,' 238
  Belinda, 238, 239
Edison, Thomas, 18, 252
Elementary Education Act,
  the, 16, 252
Eliot, George, 2, 3, 7, 8, 12, 13, 19,
  27–40, 55, 79, 80, 86, 131, 140,
  159, 162n10, 165–180, 181n1
  Adam Bede, 27–30, 79, 80, 86
  'Address to Working Men, by Felix
    Holt,' 38
  'Brother Jacob,' 32–35, 38
  Daniel Deronda, 19, 131, 165,
    167–171, 175,
    177–179, 181n1
  Felix Holt, the Radical, 27,
    38–40, 170
  Impressions of Theophrastus Such, 13,
    19, 171, 174, 179
  'The Lifted Veil,' 174, 180
  Middlemarch, 12, 19, 27, 28, 37,
    38, 86, 131, 165, 167–173,
    175–180, 181n1
  The Mill on the Floss, 28–34, 36, 38,
    162n10, 170, 176
  'The Natural History of German
    Life,' 31
  Romola, 27, 30, 32, 33,
    35–38, 181n1
  Scenes of Clerical Life, 27, 28,
    36, 181n1
  Silas Marner, 34–35, 176
  'Silly Novels by Lady Novelists,' 31
  The Spanish Gypsy, 27, 40
Ellis, Havelock, 229
  Sexual Inversion, 229
Embezzlement, 15, 22, 215, 266,
  269, 274

Emotions and the Will, The, see Bain,
  Alexander
Enfranchisement, see Suffrage
Evans, Marian, see Eliot, George
Ewing, Juliana Horatia, 13, 84, 91
  A Flat Iron for a Farthing, 13
  Six to Sixteen: A Story for Girls, 13
Examiner, the, 158, 168
Expression of the Emotions in Man and
  Animals, The, see Darwin, Charles

F
Faithfull, Emily, 4, 238
Felix Holt, the Radical, see
  Eliot, George
Femininity, 5, 21, 47, 89, 91, 93,
  96–100, 125, 153, 185,
  218, 229–242
Flat Iron for a Farthing, A, see Ewing,
  Juliana Horatia
Flaubert, Gustave, 204
  Madame Bovary, 204
Flower of Doom, The: or, The
  Conspirator and Other Stories, see
  Betham-Edwards, Matilda
Forgery, 21, 222, 230,
  269, 271–275
Fortnightly Review, 38
Framley Parsonage, see
  Trollope, Anthony
Franchise, see Suffrage
Fraser's Magazine, 83, 86, 224
Fraud, 14, 15, 21, 22,
  102, 265–277
'French Life,' see Gaskell, Elizabeth
Frith, William Powell, 70
Froggy's Little Brother, see Smith,
  Georgina Castle
Fruits of Philosophy, see
  Knowlton, Charles
Fun, 144, 196

284 INDEX

G
Gaskell, Elizabeth, xv, 2, 3, 6, 9, 10, 31, 75–87, 101, 204, 270
  Cousin Phillis, 78
  A Dark Night's Work, 3, 9, 75–87
  'French Life,' 86
  'The Heart of John Middleton,' 78
  The Life of Charlotte Brontë, 79
  'Lois the Witch,' 76, 77
  Mary Barton, 204
  Ruth, 78, 101, 270
  Sylvia's Lovers, 3, 9
  Wives and Daughters, 75, 78
Gaskell, Marianne, 77, 78
Gaskell, William, 77
Gatty, Margaret, 91
Gendered identity, 47
Gender politics, 5, 37
George Geith of Fen Court, see Riddell, Charlotte
'Girl of the Period, The,' see Linton, Eliza Lynn
Gissing, George, 161
Gladstone, William, 157, 238
Globe Assurance Office, the, 269
'Golden Bee, The,' see Betham-Edwards, Matilda
Good-bye, Sweetheart, see Broughton, Rhoda
Good Words, 140
Gordon Riots, the, 50
Gothic literature, 32, 33, 174
Grand, Sarah, xiv, 139, 145
Green, Anna Katharine, 12
  The Leavenworth Case, 12
Griffith Gaunt, see Reade, Charles

H
Haweis, Mary Eliza, 204
  The Art of Beauty, 204
Hays, Matilda, 238

'Heart of John Middleton, The,' see Gaskell, Elizabeth
Heir of Redclyffe, The, see Yonge, Charlotte
Her Father's Name, see Marryat, Florence
Hidden Depths, see Skene, Felicia
Homicide, 2, 3, 7, 15, 21, 22, 39, 47, 53, 70, 83–86, 106, 113–115, 129, 184, 230, 233, 265, 266, 271, 273
Homoerotic, 230, 235, 241
Horse in Motion, The, see Muybridge, Eadweard
Household Words, see Dickens, Charles
How I Managed my Children from Infancy to Marriage, see Warren, Eliza
How I Managed My Household on £200 a Year, see Warren, Eliza
Human Magnetism or How to Hypnotise, see Coates, James
Hurst and Blackett, 219
Hypnotism, see Mesmerism
Hysteria, 45, 185, 231–234, 237

I
Identity fraud, 22, 266, 268
Illegitimacy, 7, 106
Illustrated Newspaper, The, 276
Impressions of Theophrastus Such, see Eliot, George
Industrialisation, 92
Industrial novel, 39
Infanticide, 114
Ingelow, Jean, 253
  Mopsa the Fairy, 253
Insanity, 60, 63, 71, 72, 106, 107, 113, 114, 116
Insolvency, see Bankruptcy

J

Jane Eyre, see Brontë, Charlotte
Jerrold, Douglas, 136–138
  'Mr Punch's Letters to his Son,' 136
  'Mrs Caudle's Curtain Lectures,' 137
Jessica's First Prayer, see Stretton, Hesba
Jewsbury, Geraldine, 17, 121, 126
Joan of Arc, 114, 233, 240
John Halifax, Gentleman, see Mulock, Dinah
Johnny Ludlow, see Wood, Ellen

K

Kendall, Kay, 136, 141
Kindness to Animals, see Tonna, Charlotte Elizabeth
Kitty, see Betham-Edwards, Matilda
Knowlton, Charles, 18
  Fruits of Philosophy, 18
Künstlerroman, A Struggle for Fame, see Riddell, Charlotte

L

Labour activism, 16
Lady Audley's Secret, see Braddon, Mary Elizabeth
Lady's Life in the Rocky Mountains, A, see Bird, Isabella L.
Lamb, Charles and Mary, 139
  A Biographical Dictionary of Celebrated Women of Every Age and Country, 139
Landseer, Edwin, 250
Last Chronicle of Barset, The, see Trollope, Anthony
Law of Population, The, see Besant, Annie
Le Fanu, J. S., 120–121
Leavenworth Case, The, see Green, Anna Katharine
Leigh Journal and Times, the, 275
Leighton, Frederic, 36, 37
Lemon, Mark, 135–137, 140, 142, 146
Lesbianism, 229, 230, 232, 233, 237, 238, 240
Lever, C. J., 73
  Tales of the Trains, 73
Lewes, George Henry, 30–33, 36, 38, 140, 166, 168, 172, 174, 180, 181n1
  Physiology of Common Life, 166
  Problems of Life and Mind, 166
Life and Letters of Lord Macaulay, The, see Trevelyan, George Otto
Life of Charlotte Brontë, The, see Gaskell, Elizabeth
Life's Assize, A, see Riddell, Charlotte
'Lifted Veil, The,' see Eliot, George
Linton, Eliza Lynn, 5, 7, 10, 12, 31, 105, 106, 108, 109, 111, 113, 116, 123, 124, 128, 132n7, 132n8, 136, 137, 142–146, 235, 239, 240
  The Autobiography of Christopher Kirkland, 239
  'The Girl of the Period,' 5, 105, 123, 124, 128, 136, 142–146
  The New Woman in Haste and At Leisure, 239
  Patricia Kemball, 12
  The Rebel of the Family, 132n8, 239
  Sowing the Wind, 7, 10, 105–116, 239
  The True History of Joshua Davidson, 12
Little Lame Prince and his Travelling Cloak, The, see Craik, Dinah Maria Mulock
Little Men, see Alcott, Louisa May

Little Women, see Alcott, Louisa May
Lives of the Queens of England, see Strickland, Elizabeth and Agnes
'Lois the Witch,' see Gaskell, Elizabeth
London: A Pilgrimage, see Doré, Gustave
London Society, 189
Lord of the Harvest, The, see Betham-Edwards, Matilda
Lower-class, see Class, lower-class
Ludlow, Johnny, see Wood, Ellen

M

MacDonald, George, 53, 253, 258
   At the Back of the North Wind, 253
Macmillan's Magazine, 188
Madame Bovary, see Flaubert, Gustave
Madness, see Insanity
Maiden of Our Own Day, A, see Wilford, Florence
Manchester Weekly Times, the, 275
'Man with the Nose, The,' see Broughton, Rhoda
Married Women's Property Act 1870, 15, 18, 19, 22
Marryat, Florence, 12, 17, 21, 140, 229–242
   Her Father's Name, 17, 21, 229–242
   Open! Sesame!, 230
Martineau, Harriet, 12, 21, 31, 92, 219, 224, 225, 239, 246, 247, 253, 260
   Autobiography, 12, 253
Marx, Karl, 5, 139
Mary Barton, see Gaskell, Elizabeth
Masculinity, 9, 47, 62, 113, 115, 239, 240
Masturbation, 232–234
Mather, Helen, 13
   Comin' Thro' the Rye, 13

Matrimonial Causes Act of 1857, 106
Maxwell, John, 12, 140, 184, 265, 267, 273–276
   Belgravia, 140
Medical Act of 1876, 16
Memorials of Mrs Henry Wood, see Wood, Charles
Mesmer, Franz Anton, 188
Mesmerism, 19, 183–192, 271
Middle-class, see Class, middle-class
Middlemarch, see Eliot, George
Mildred Arkell, see Wood, Ellen
Mid-Victorian Memories, see Betham-Edwards, Matilda
Mill, John Stuart, 4, 140, 155, 214, 216, 220, 222–225
   On the Subjection of Women, 4
Mill on the Floss, The, see Eliot, George
Misogyny, 60, 218
Miss Marjoribanks, see Oliphant, Margaret
Miss Mulock, see Craik, Dinah Maria Mulock
Mistletoe Bough, The, 276
Mitre Court, see Riddell, Charlotte
Monomania, 9, 57–73
Mopsa the Fairy, see Ingelow, Jean
Moral literature, 3
Morning Chronicle, the, 109
Mortomley's Estate, see Riddell, Charlotte
'Mr and Mrs de Fontenoy,' see Braddon, Mary Elizabeth
'Mr Punch's Letters to his Son,' see Jerrold, Douglas
'Mrs Caudle's Curtain Lectures,' see Jerrold, Douglas
'Mrs Punch's Letters to Her Daughter,' see Betham-Edwards, Matilda
Mudie's circulating library, 4, 7

Mulock, Dinah, 13, 29, 253
  John Halifax, Gentleman, 29
Murder, *see* Homicide
Muybridge, Eadweard, 253
  The Horse in Motion, 253

N

'Natural History of German Life,' *see* Eliot, George
Newcastle Weekly Chronicle, the, 276
Newcomes, The, *see* Thackeray, William
Newgate Novels, the, 272
New Woman fiction, xiv, 21, 32, 230
New Woman in Haste and At Leisure, The, *see* Linton, Eliza Lynn
Nigel Bartram's Ideal, *see* Wilford, Florence
Nobly Born, *see* Worboise, Emma
Nothing to Nobody, *see* Smith, Georgina Castle
Not Wisely, But Too Well, *see* Broughton, Rhoda
'Novels,' *see* Oliphant, Margaret

O

Observer, The, 271, 272
Oliphant, Margaret, 12, 14, 15, 17, 20, 21, 31, 45, 46, 120, 123, 125, 126, 213–225, 250
  At His Gates, 14
  Miss Marjoribanks, 214, 219
  'Novels,' 14, 20, 45, 120, 213, 214, 250
  The Perpetual Curate, 219
  Phoebe Junior: A Last Chronicle of Carlingford, 15, 214
  On the Curability of Certain Forms of Insanity, Epilepsy, Catalepsy, and Hysteria in Females, *see* Brown, Isaac Baker

On the Origin of Species, *see* Darwin, Charles
On the Subjection of Women, *see* Mill, John Stuart
Open! Sesame!, *see* Marryat, Florence
Ouida, *see* Ramé, Maria Louise
Oxford Movement, the, 214

P

Pall Mall Gazette, The, 38, 197
Papers for Thoughtful Girls, *see* Tytler, Sarah
Parkes, Bessie Rayner, 91
Patience Hart's First Experience in Service, *see* Sewell, Mary
Patmore, Coventry, 5
  'The Angel in the House,' 5, 72
Patricia Kemball, *see* Linton, Eliza Lynn
Paul Ferroll, *see* Clive, Caroline
Perpetual Curate, The, *see* Oliphant, Margaret
Philanthropy, *see* Charity work
Phoebe Junior: A Last Chronicle of Carlingford, *see* Oliphant, Margaret
Physiology of Common Life, *see* Lewes, George Henry
Pillars of the House, *see* Yonge, Charlotte
Poe, Edgar Allan, 189
Private confession, *see* Confession, private
Problems of Life and Mind, *see* Lewes, George Henry
Prostitution, 99, 100, 102, 126, 128, 201, 250
Public confession, *see* Confession, public
Punch, 8, 11, 135–147

Q

Quaker, 248, 257
Quarterly Review, the, 57

R

Race for Wealth, The, see Riddell, Charlotte
Railway mania, 59, 60, 64, 72
Ramé, Maria Louise, xv, 12, 13, 145, 189, 253
  A Dog of Flanders, 13, 253
  Under Two Flags, 189
Reade, Charles, 210n12
  Griffith Gaunt, 210n12
Realist fiction, 7, 83, 174, 183, 198
Rebel of the Family, The, see Linton, Eliza Lynn
Red as a Rose Is She, see Broughton, Rhoda
Reform Bill of 1832, 224
Reform Bill of 1867, 4, 38
Regency satire, 137
Riddell, Charlotte, 12–15, 18, 19, 151–161, 161n1, 161n2, 162n9
  Austin Friars, 13, 18, 153–157, 160, 162n9
  City and Suburb, 152
  'City Women,' 18, 151–161
  George Geith of Fen Court, 151, 152, 161n1
  Künstlerroman, A Struggle for Fame, 161
  A Life's Assize, 151
  Mitre Court, 161
  Mortomley's Estate, 19, 153, 157–161
  The Race for Wealth, 152
  The Senior Partner, 161
  Too Much Alone, 152
'Rime of the Ancient Mariner, The,' see Coleridge Samuel Taylor

Ritchie, Anne Thackeray, 12–13
Romantic, 7, 10, 79, 93, 98, 103, 121, 123–125, 127, 128, 131, 136, 169, 172, 217, 229, 237, 267
Romola, see Eliot, George
Room of One's Own, A, see Woolf, Virginia
Royal British bank, 269
Ruling-class, see Class, ruling-class
Russell, Dora, 12, 13
Ruth, see Gaskell, Elizabeth

S

St. James's Magazine, 151
St. Martin's Eve, see Wood, Ellen
Satan in Society, see Cooke, Nicholas
Saturday Review, the, 5, 29, 106, 142, 144, 145, 154, 156, 158, 202, 208, 267, 276
Savonarola, Fra Girolamo, 33, 36, 37
Scenes of Clerical Life, see Eliot, George
Scotland Yard, 274
Scott, Sir Walter, xxi, 35, 79, 142
  Waverley, 79
Second Reform Act, 4
Senior Partner, The, see Riddell, Charlotte
Sensation and Intuition: Studies in Psychology and Aesthetics, see Sully, James
Sensation novel, 3, 8, 9, 11, 19, 32, 43, 45, 46, 57–60, 64, 65, 106, 108, 112, 114, 116, 120, 121, 184, 196, 201, 204, 257, 276
Sergeant, Adeline, 195, 207, 208
  Women Novelists of Queen Victoria's Reign, 195
Sewell, Anna, xiv, xxii, 3, 12, 13, 15, 21, 245–260

Black Beauty, xxii, 3, 12, 13, 15, 21, 245–260
Sewell, Mary, 13, 247, 250
Patience Hart's First Experience in Service, 13
Sexes Throughout Nature, The, see Blackwell, Antoinette Brown
Sexual Inversion, see Ellis, Havelock
Sheffield Weekly Telegraph, the, 276
Sidney, Samuel, 254
The Book of the Horse, 254
Silas Marner, see Eliot, George
'Silly Novels by Lady Novelists,' see Eliot, George
Sinecure, 15, 20, 21, 213–225
Six to Sixteen: A Story for Girls, see Ewing, Juliana Horatia
Skene, Felicia, 10, 90, 93, 99–103, 103n2
Hidden Depths, 10, 90, 93, 99–103, 103n2
'Skittles,' see Walters, Catherine
Smiles, Samuel, 238
Smith, George, 33, 36, 38, 181n1
Smith, Georgina Castle, 13
Froggy's Little Brother, 13
Nothing to Nobody, 13
Smith, Sarah, see Stretton, Hesba
Social mobility, 39, 58, 59, 63, 70, 203
Society for the Propagation of Christian Knowledge (SPCK), 7
Southey, Robert, 13, 139
Sowing the Wind, see Linton, Eliza Lynn
Spanish Gypsy, The, see Eliot, George
Spectator, The, 34, 122, 217
Spielmann, M. H., 135, 138, 141, 142
Spinoza, Baruch, 174
Spiritualism, 8, 9, 29, 36, 83, 92, 221, 223, 240
Steele, Richard, 34

'Stray Letters from the East,' see Wood, Ellen
Stretton, Hesba, 13
Jessica's First Prayer, 13
Strickland, Elizabeth and Agnes, 35
The Lives of the Queens of England, 35
Suffrage, xii, 4, 28, 139, 140, 220, 223, 224
Suicide, 115
Sully, James, 174
Sensation and Intuition: Studies in Psychology and Aesthetics, 174
Supernaturalism, 19, 20, 183, 184, 188, 192, 271
Sylvestres, The, see Betham-Edwards, Matilda
Sylvia's Lovers, see Gaskell, Elizabeth

T
Taken at the Flood, see Braddon, Mary Elizabeth
Tale of Two Cities, A, see Dickens, Charles
Tales of the Trains, see Lever, C. J.
Temple Bar, 120, 140, 184, 187, 192, 192n1
Thackeray, William, 29, 159, 162n10
The Newcomes, 162n10
Thousand Miles Up the Nile, A, see Blandford Edwards, Amelia
Three Times Dead (The Trail of the Serpent), see Braddon, Mary Elizabeth
Through Spain to the Sahara, see Betham-Edwards, Matilda
Tillotson, William, 275
Tilt, Edward, 231
Tomahawk, 144
Tonna, Charlotte Elizabeth, 253
Kindness to Animals, 253

Too Much Alone, see Riddell, Charlotte
Trail of the Serpent; or, the Secret of the Heath, The, see Braddon, Mary Elizabeth
Transvestism, 220, 236, 237
Trevelyan, George Otto, 220
  The Life and Letters of Lord Macaulay, 220
Trinitarianism, 77
Trollope, Anthony, xxi, 20, 36–38, 162n10, 214–216, 222, 238
  An Autobiography, 214
  Framley Parsonage, 36
  The Last Chronicle of Barset, 214
  The Warden, 214, 216
  The Way We Live Now, 162n10
True History of Joshua Davidson, The, see Linton, Eliza Lynn
Twilight Stories, see Broughton, Rhoda
Tytler, Sarah, 90–92, 103n1
  Papers for Thoughtful Girls, 90

U

'Under the Cloak,' see Broughton, Rhoda
Under Two Flags, see Ramé, Maria Louise
Unitarian, 9, 77, 78
Upper-class, *see* Class, upper-class
Upper-middle class, *see* Class, Upper-middle
Utilitarianism, 39, 222, 225

V

Victoria, Queen, xvi, 2, 16, 18, 252

W

Walters, Catherine, 250
Warden, The, see Trollope, Anthony
Warren, Eliza, 5
  How I Managed my Children from Infancy to Marriage, 5
  How I Managed My Household on £200 a Year, 5
Waverley, see Scott, Sir Walter
Way We Live Now, The, see Trollope, Anthony
Westminster Review, the, 31
What Katy Did, see Coolidge, Susan
White-collar crime, 14, 21, 265–277
White House by the Sea, The, see Betham-Edwards, Matilda
Wiertz, Antoine, 185, 188, 189, 193n3
Wilford, Florence, 6, 10, 90, 93, 94
  A Maiden of Our Own Day, 10, 90, 93
  Nigel Bartram's Ideal, 6
Winter with Swallows, A, see Betham-Edwards, Matilda
Wives and Daughters, see Gaskell, Elizabeth
Woman in White, The, see Collins, Wilkie
Womankind, see Yonge, Charlotte
Women Novelists of Queen Victoria's Reign, see Sergeant, Adeline
Wood, Charles, 208, 209, 209n4
  Memorials of Mrs Henry Wood, 208, 209n4
Wood, Ellen, 3, 6, 8, 12, 15, 20, 32, 43–55, 195–209, 258
  East Lynne, 3, 8, 43–55, 196, 204, 258
  Mildred Arkell, 53
  Johnny Ludlow, 15, 20, 195–209
  St. Martin's Eve, 53
  'Stray Letters from the East,' 197

Woodhull, Victoria Claflin, 16, 18
Woolf, Virginia, xiii, 12, 14,
    221, 225
  A Room of One's Own, 225
Worboise, Emma, xiv, 7
  Nobly Born, 7
Work, A Story of Experience, *see* Alcott,
    Louisa May
Working-class, *see* Class, Working-class

Y
Yellowback' editions, 59
Yonge, Charlotte, 12, 14, 81,
    82, 90, 253
  *The Daisy Chain; or, Aspirations. A
    Family Chronicle*, 90
  The Heir of Redclyffe, 81, 82
  Pillars of the House, 253
  Womankind, 14

CPI Antony Rowe
Eastbourne, UK
January 13, 2021